Help us Rate this book...
Put your initials on the
Left side and your rating
on the right side.
1 = Didn't care for
2 = It was O.K.
3 = It was <u>great</u>

DATE DUE

NOV 07 2018			

_____ 1 2 3
_____ 1 2 3
_____ 1 2 3
_____ 1 2 3
_____ 1 2 3
_____ 1 2 3
_____ 1 2 3
_____ 1 2 3
_____ 1 2 3
_____ 1 2 3
_____ 1 2 3
_____ 1 2 3
_____ 1 2 3
_____ 1 2 3

PRINTED IN U.S.A.

THIEF OF
CORINTH

Center Point
Large Print

Also by Tessa Afshar and available from
Center Point Large Print:

Bread of Angels

**This Large Print Book carries the
Seal of Approval of N.A.V.H.**

THIEF OF CORINTH

TESSA AFSHAR

CENTER POINT LARGE PRINT
THORNDIKE, MAINE

This Center Point Large Print edition
is published in the year 2018 by arrangement with
Tyndale House Publishers, Inc.

Thief of Corinth is a work of fiction. Where real people, events, establishments, organizations, or locales appear, they are used fictitiously. All other elements of the novel are drawn from the author's imagination.

The text of this Large Print edition is unabridged.
In other aspects, this book may vary
from the original edition.
Printed in the United States of America
on permanent paper.
Set in 16-point Times New Roman type.

ISBN: 978-1-68324-917-7

Library of Congress Cataloging-in-Publication Data

Names: Afshar, Tessa, author.
Title: Thief of corinth / Tessa Afshar.
Description: Center Point Large Print edition. Large Print edition. |
    Thorndike, Maine : Center Point Large Print, 2018.
Identifiers: LCCN 2018026178 | ISBN 9781683249177
    (hardcover : alk. paper)
Subjects: LCSH: Large type books. | GSAFD: Christian fiction.
Classification: LCC PS3601.F47 T48 2018b | DDC 813/.6—dc23
LC record available at https://lccn.loc.gov/2018026178

To the Hakims, my second family in faith, friendship, and love: Faegh, Noureen, Ramin, Linda, Christian, Alexandra, and in loving memory of our precious Farshid and Alana

And for John, who believes in me and pays the price

THIEF OF
CORINTH

PROLOGUE

—ɯ—

YOU ASKED ME ONCE how a woman like me could become a thief. How could I, having everything—a father's love, a lavish home, an athlete's accolades—turn to lawlessness and crime?

Were I in a flippant mood, I could blame it on sleeplessness. That fateful night, when I abandoned my bed in search of a warm tincture of valerian root to help me rest, and found instead my father slithering out the side door into the dark alley beyond.

He was a man of secrets, my father, and that night I resolved to discover the mystery that surrounded him. A mystery so cumbersome, its weight had shattered my parents' marriage.

Snagging an old cloak in the courtyard, I wrapped myself in its thick folds and followed him along a circuitous path that soon had me confused. The moon sat stifled under a cover of clouds that night, shielding my presence as I pursued him.

Finally, Father came to a stop. The clouds were dispersing and there was now enough light to make out the outline of the buildings around me. We had arrived at an affluent neighborhood.

During the day, we Corinthians left our doors open as a sign of hospitality. At night, we shut and latched them, both for safety and to indicate that the time for visitation had passed and the occupants were in bed. As one would expect, the door of this villa had long since been barred.

I hunkered down behind a bush, wondering what Father meant to do. Rouse the household with his knocking? He fumbled with something in his belt and proceeded to cover his face with a mask.

I gasped. Was he playing a jest on the owner of the house? Did he have a forbidden assignation with a lady within? He was an unmarried man, still handsome for his age. I had never considered his private life and felt a twinge of distaste thinking of him with a woman. Now was perhaps a good time for me to beat a hasty retreat. But something kept me rooted to the spot.

My father approached the south wall of the villa and nimbly climbed a willow tree that grew near. I had to admire his agility when he jumped from the tree to the wall. Deftly, he grabbed hold of the branches of another tree growing within the garden and swung himself into its foliage. I lost sight of him then.

I sat and considered the evidence before me. Father's stealthy movements in the middle of the night. The mask. The furtive entry into the villa. The answer stared me in the face. But I refused to believe it.

As I waited, I found it hard to gauge the time. How long since he had scrambled into the villa? An hour? Less? No alarm had been raised . . . yet. I began to fret. What was he doing in there? What if someone caught him? I left my hiding place and, slinking my way toward the villa, made a quick exploration of the area. The place seemed deserted. Tucking my tunic and cloak out of the way, I climbed the same willow my father had and nestled in its branches. Still I could discern nothing.

I laid my forehead against a thick branch. What should I do? Wait? Go in search of him? Then I heard a noise. Feet running through bushes. More than one pair of feet.

A man cried, "Halt! You there! Stop at once!" My hold on the branch slipped. I thought a guard had seen me, and I prepared to leap back into the street. What I saw next made my blood turn to ice.

Father was running toward me with a large man in close pursuit, his hand clutching a drawn sword. The man bearing the weapon was quickly gaining on my father. I estimated Father's distance from the wall, the time he would need to climb up the tree on one side, and then back down the other. He would never make it in time.

He was about to be caught. Killed, as I watched helplessly from my perch of branches.

Well. You know the rest of that story.

I suppose I could accuse my father of leading me astray that night, of setting the example that ruined my best intentions, for had he not tried to rob that house, I would not have turned to thieving myself.

But the choices that lead us into broken paths often have their beginnings in more convoluted places.

Places like the thousand words spoken mercilessly by my grandfather when I lived in his house—barbed and ruthless words; or a thousand phrases never spoken by my mother, soft and nurturing expressions that would have healed my wounded soul. I could blame the years in Athens, when I became invisible to my family, a girl child in a world meant for men.

Yet the final blame, as you and I know, dear Paul, rests with me.

It was I who chose as I did. I could have taken the wounds of my early life and turned them to healing. Instead, they became my excuse to do as I wished.

Until you taught me love.

I write you this letter while I sit waiting by a funeral pyre, memories assailing me. The fires blaze and burn the bones of one I failed to love. The smell of ashes fills my nostrils as I remember your words: *"Love never fails."* And even in the shadow of this conflagration that swallows up its human burden with such hunger, I am comforted to know that there is a love that shall never fail us. A love that covers the many gaps I have left in my wake.

Part 1

THE DISCOVERY

—∞—

And if one asks him, "What are these wounds
on your back?" he will say, "The wounds
I received in the house of my friends."

ZECHARIAH 13:6, ESV

CHAPTER 1

—∞—

THE FIRST TIME I climbed through a window and crept about secretly through a house, the moon sat high in the sky and I was running away from home. *Home* is perhaps an exaggeration. Unlike my brother Dionysius, I never thought of my grandfather's villa in Athens as home. For eight miserable years that upright bastion of Greek tradition had been my prison, a trap I could not escape, a madhouse where too much philosophy and ancient principles had rotted its residents' brains. But it was never my home.

Home was my father's villa in Corinth.

I was determined, on that moon-bright evening, to convey myself there no matter what impediments I faced. A girl of sixteen, clambering from a second story window in the belly of night without enough sense to entertain a single fear. Before me lay Corinth and my father and freedom. As always, waiting for me faithfully in uncomplaining silence, was Theodotus, my foster brother. Regardless of how harebrained and dangerous my schemes might be, Theo never left my side.

He stood in the courtyard, keeping watch, as I made my way down the slippery balustrade outside my room, my feet dangling for a moment into the nothingness of shadows and air. I slithered one finger at a time to the side, until my feet found the branches of the laurel tree, and ignoring the scratches on my skin, I let go and took a leap into the aromatic leaves. I had often climbed the smooth limbs, unusually tall for a laurel. But that had been in the light of day and from the bottom up. Now I jumped into the tree from the top, hoping it would catch me, or that I could cling to some part of it before I fell to the ground and crushed my bones against Grandfather's ancient marble tiles.

My fingers seemed fashioned for this perilous capering, and by an instinct of their own, they found a sturdy branch and clung, breaking the momentum of my fall. I felt my way down and made short work of the tree. My mother would have been horrified. The thought made me smile.

"You could have broken your neck," Theo whispered, his jaw clenched. He was my age but seemed a decade older. I boiled like water, easily riled into anger. He remained immovable like stone, my steady rock through the capricious shifts of fortune.

The tight knots in my shoulders relaxed at the

sight of him, and I grinned. "I didn't." Reaching for the bundle he had packed for me, I grabbed it. "The gate?"

He shook his head. "Agis seemed determined to stay sober tonight." We both looked over to the figure of the slave, huddled on his pallet across the front door, his loud snores competing with the sound of the cicadas.

"I am afraid there's more climbing in your future if you really intend to go to Corinth," Theo said, his voice hushed. He took a step closer so that I could see the vague outline of his long face. "Nothing will be the same, you know, if you do this thing, Ariadne. Whether you fail or succeed. It's not too late to change your mind."

In answer, I turned and made my way to the high wall that surrounded the house like an uncompromising sentinel. Grandfather had made it impossible for me to remain. I should have escaped this place long ago.

I studied the daunting height of the wall and realized I would need a boost to climb it. By the fountain in the middle of the courtyard, the slaves had left a massive stone mortar that stood as high as my waist. It would do for a stepping-stone. The mortar proved heavier than we expected. Since dragging it would have made too great a clamor, we had to lift it completely off the ground. The muscles in my arms shook with the effort of carrying my burden. Halfway to our destination,

I lost my hold on the slippery stone. With a loud clatter, it fell on the marble pavement.

Agis stirred, then sat up. Theo and I dropped to the ground, hiding in the shadow of the mortar. "Who goes there?" Agis mumbled.

He rose from his pallet and looked about, then took a few steps in our direction. His foot came within a hand's breadth of my shoulder. One more step and he would discover me. Blood hammered in my ears. My lungs grew paralyzed, forgetting how to pulse air out of my chest.

This was my only chance to break away. If Agis raised the alarm and I were apprehended, my grandfather would see to it that I remained locked up in the women's quarters under guard until I capitulated to his demands. He held the perfect weapon against me. Should I refuse to marry that madman, Draco, my grandfather would hurt Theo. I knew this was no empty threat. Grandfather had a brilliant mind, sharp as steel's edge, and a heart to match. It would not trouble his conscience in the least to torment an innocent in order to get his own way. He would beat Theo and blame every lash on me for refusing to obey his command.

The fates sent me an unlikely liberator. Herodotus the cat came to my rescue. Though feral, it hung about Grandfather's property because Theo and I had secretly adopted it and fed the poor beast when we could. My mother had forbidden this act of mercy, but since the cat had an appetite for mice and other vermin, the slaves turned a blind eye to our disobedience.

Just when Agis was about to take another step leading to my discovery, Herodotus ran across his foot.

"Agh," he cried and jumped back. "Stupid animal! Next time you wake me, I will gut you and feed you to the crows." Grumbling, the slave went back to bed. Theo and I remained immobile and silent until we heard his snores split the peaceful night again.

This time, we carried our burden with even more attentive care and managed to place it next to the wall without mishap.

I threw my bundle over the wall and stepped cautiously into the center of the mortar, then balanced my feet on the opposite edges of the bowl. We held our breath as the stone groaned and wobbled. Agis, to my relief, continued to snore.

The brick lining the top of the wall scraped my palm as I held tight and pulled. I made my way up, arms burning, back straining, my toes finding holds in the rough, aged brick. One last scramble and I was sitting on the edge.

Theo climbed into the mortar next, his leather-shod feet silent on the stone. I leaned down and offered my hand to him. Without hesitation, he grasped my wrist and allowed me to help him climb until he, too, straddled the wall. We sat grinning as we faced each other, basking in the small victory before looking down into the street.

"Too far to jump," he observed.

On the street, next to the main entrance of the house, sat a squat pillar bearing a dainty statue of Athena, Grandfather's nod to his precious city and its divine patron. At the base of the marble figurine the slaves had left a small lamp, which burned through the night. I crawled on the narrow, uneven border of bricks twelve feet above ground until I sat directly above the pillar.

As I dangled down the outer wall, I took care not to knock Athena over, partly because I knew the noise would rouse Agis, and partly because I was scared of the goddess's wrath. Dionysius no longer believed in the gods, not as true beings who meddled in the fate of mortals. He said they were mere symbols, useful for teaching us how to live worthy lives. I wasn't so sure. In any case, I preferred not to take any chances. Should there really be an Athena, I would rather not draw her displeasure down on me right before starting the greatest adventure of my life. She was, after all, the patron of heroic endeavor.

"Excuse me, goddess. I intend no disrespect," I whispered as I placed my feet carefully on either side of her, balancing my weight before jumping cleanly on the street.

Being considerably taller, Theo managed the

pillar better. His foot caught on the goddess's head at the last moment, though, and smashed it into the wall. I dove fast enough to save her from an ignoble tumble onto the ground. But her crash into the plaster-covered bricks had extracted a price. Poor Athena had lost an arm.

"Now you've done it," I said.

Theo retrieved the severed arm from the dust and placed it next to the statue on the pillar. "Forgive me, goddess," he said and gave an awkward pat to the marble. "You're still pretty."

I caught his eye and we started to laugh, half mad with the relief of our escape, and half terrified that the goddess would materialize in person and punish us for our disrespect.

"What are you doing?" a voice asked from the darkness, sharp like the crack of a whip.

I jumped, almost knocking Athena over again. "Who is there?" I said, trembling like a cornered fawn.

The speaker stepped forward until the diminutive lamp at Athena's feet revealed his face.

My back melted against the wall as I made out Dionysius's familiar face. "You scared the heart out of me," I accused.

"What are you doing?" he asked again, his gaze taking in our bundles and my unusual garments— his own cloak wrapped loosely about my figure, hiding my gender.

I swallowed hard, struck mute. I was running

away from my mother and grandfather. But in escaping, I was leaving behind a beloved brother. Dionysius was Grandfather's pet, the son he had never had. I think the old man truly loved him. He certainly treated him with a tenderness he had never once demonstrated toward Theo or me. Grandfather would not stand for Dionysius leaving. He would follow us like a hound into the bowels of Hades to get him back.

My escape could only work if my brother remained behind.

I told myself Dionysius loved Athens. He fit perfectly into the mold of the old city with its rigorous intellectual pursuits and appreciation for philosophy. Athens suited Dionysius much better than the wildness of Corinth. I was like a scribe who added one and one and tallied three. I lied to myself, twisting the truth into something I could bear.

Dionysius had a more brilliant mind even than my grandfather, a mind that prospered in the academic atmosphere of Athens. But he had inherited our father's soft heart. The abrupt separation from Father had wounded him. To lose Theo and me as well would cut him in ways I could not bear to think about. Not all the glories of Athens or Grandfather's affection could make up for such a void.

I had not told him of my plan to run away, convincing myself that Dionysius might cave and betray us to the old man. In truth, I was too much of a coward to bear the look on his face once I confessed I meant to leave him behind. The look he was giving me now.

Theo stepped forward. "She has to leave, Dionysius. You know that. Or the old wolf will force her to marry Draco."

My brother shifted from one foot to the other. "He is angry. He will cool."

I ground my teeth. Where Grandfather was concerned, Dionysius was blind. He could not see the evil that coiled through the old man. "He threatened to have Theo flogged if I refuse to marry the weasel. One stripe for every hour I refuse."

"What?" Theo and Dionysius said together. I had not even told Theo, worried that he might think I was running away for his sake more than my own, and refuse to help me.

"He has no scruples when it comes to Theo. Or me."

"Mother—"

"Will take his side as she always does. When has she ever defended me?"

I rubbed the side of my face, where the imprint of her hand had left a faint bruise, and winced as I remembered her iron-hard expression as she hit me.

Two days ago, Draco and his father, Evandos, had come to visit Grandfather. After drinking buckets of strong wine, the men had crawled to bed. The wind had pelted the city hard that evening, screaming through the trees, making the house groan in protest. The rains came then, sudden and violent.

I had risen from my pallet and slid softly into the courtyard. I loved storms, the unfettered deluge that washed the world clean. Within moments, I stood soaked through and grinning with exultation, enjoying the rare moment of freedom.

An odd sound caught my attention. At first I dismissed it as the noise of the wind. It came again, making me go still. The hair on my arms rose when it came a third time, a tortured wail, broken and sharp. No storm made that sound. My heart pounded as I followed that unearthly wail to a narrow shed on the other side of the courtyard. I slammed the door open.

He had brought a lamp with him, and it burned in the confines of the shed, casting its yellowish light into every corner. My eyes were drawn to the whimpering form on the dirt floor, lying spread-eagle. In the lamplight, blood glimmered, slick like oil, staining her thighs, her face, her stomach.

"Alcmena?" I gasped, barely recognizing the slave girl.

"Mistress!" She coughed. "Help me. Help me, I beg!"

I turned to the man standing over the slave, his face devoid of expression. "You did this?"

He smiled as if I had paid him a compliment. "A foretaste for you, beautiful Ariadne. I look forward to teaching you many lessons when you are my wife."

"Your *wife?* Get out of here, you madman!"

"Your grandfather promised me your hand in marriage. We drank on it earlier this evening." He stepped toward me. His gait was long and the space narrow. In a moment, Draco towered over me. He twined his fingers into my loose hair and pulled me toward him. The smell of the blood covering his knuckles made me gag. Without thinking, I fisted my hand and shoved it into his face. To my satisfaction, he staggered and screeched like a delicate woman. "My nose!"

"I beg your pardon, Draco. I was aiming for your mouth."

He rushed at me, hands clenched. I screamed as I stepped to the side, missing his bulk with ease. I had good lungs, and my voice carried with eerie clarity above the howling gale.

He faltered. "Shut your mouth."

I screamed louder.

The muscles in his neck corded as he hesitated for a moment. Then he lunged again, and I braced myself for a shattering assault. It never came.

Dionysius and Theo burst through the door, causing Draco to skid to a stop. My brothers seemed frozen with shock as they surveyed the state of Alcmena. Relief washed through me at the sight of them, and I sank to my knees next to the slave.

"What have you done?" my brother rasped, staring at the broken girl who could not even sit up in spite of my arm behind her back. "You brutal maggot. You've almost killed her."

Theo placed a warm hand on my shoulder. "Are you all right?"

I nodded, crossing my arms and trying to hide how badly my fingers shook.

Grandfather sauntered in, my mother in tow. "What is all this yelling? Can't a man sleep in peace?" He wiped his bristly jaw.

"Draco hurt Alcmena," I said.

My mother had the grace to gasp when she saw the slave girl, though she said nothing.

"He asked my permission to take the girl, and I gave it." Grandfather tightened his mouth when Alcmena doubled over and retched painfully. "You must have drunk too much, boy. Go back to your father."

Draco bowed his head and left without offering an explanation.

"He is crazed," I said. "He claims he will marry me. That you made an agreement with him earlier this evening."

"What of it?" Grandfather said, his voice hardening.

I expelled a wheezing breath. "You can't be serious! Look at what he did to the girl."

"The boy is a little hotheaded. Too much wine. Things got out of hand. Nothing to do with you. I have made the arrangement with my friend Evandos. It is done."

"Grandfather!" Dionysius cleared his throat. "I think we should ask Draco to leave the house."

"We shall do no such thing. If an honored guest wants to abuse your furniture, you must allow him," Grandfather said. "She is my slave, and the damage is to my property. I say it is of no consequence."

"She's hardly a woman. Younger than I am," I cried. "What do you think Draco will do to me if he gets his hands on me? You should be ashamed of yourself for even entertaining the notion of my marriage to such a man."

Calmly, my mother raised her arm and slapped me with the flat of her hand, putting the strength of her shoulder into that strike. I tottered backward and would have fallen if Theo had not caught me.

"Don't be rude to your grandfather. Now go to bed."

Furniture. That's what the poor girl amounted to in the old man's estimation. And I was not far above her in his classification of the world. In the morning, Grandfather insisted that my betrothal to Draco would stand. He expected me to honor his precious word by marrying Evandos's brutal son. My mother watched this tirade, eyes flat, as her father bullied me. She expected me to obey without demur as any good Athenian girl would.

With effort, I pushed away the memories and returned my attention to my brother. "Mother informed me yesterday afternoon that she had started to work on my wedding garments."

Dionysius blinked. In the flickering light of the lamp his eyes began to shimmer as they welled with tears. I knew, then, that he would not hinder us. Knew he would cover our departure for as long as he could, regardless of the pain it caused him.

I encircled my arms around him. Grief shivered out of us as we tried to make the moment last, make it count for endless days when we wouldn't have each other to hold. I stepped away, mindful of time slipping, mindful that we were far from safe. Theo and Dionysius bid a hurried farewell, locking forearms and slamming chests in manly embraces that could not hide their trembling lips.

Grabbing my bundle, I threw one last agonized glance over my shoulder at my brother. He stood alone, blanketed by shadows save for a luminous halo of lamplight that brought his face into high relief. I swallowed something that tasted bitter and salty and entirely too large for my throat, and stumbled forward.

Theo and I started to run downhill through the

winding streets of Athens, our initial excitement dampened by the grief of leaving Dionysius behind. Before the sun began to rise over the hilltops, Theo came to an abrupt halt. "You should cut your hair now, Ariadne, while it's still dark."

We had decided that a young girl traveling with a boy, even a boy as large as Theo, would attract too much attention. Instead, we had concluded that we would travel as two boys. Dressed in Dionysius's bulkiest tunic and cloak, with my chest bound tightly beneath its loose folds, I looked enough a boy to pass casual inspection. Except that my hair remained long and uncut, a fat braid hanging to my hip.

I pulled out a knife from my bundle and handed it to Theo. "You do it," I said, trying to sound indifferent. I was vain about my hair, which was thick and soft, like a river of chestnuts.

Theo took a step back. "Do it yourself. Your father would skin me alive."

I threw him a disgruntled look but had to concede his point. Theodotus was courting untold trouble for agreeing to accompany me on this desperate escapade. Grandfather's outrageous threats aside, my mother would have him whipped for encouraging me, if she could get her hands on him. My father, I hoped, knew me better. If ever Theo and I were embroiled in trouble together, he would realize who had led that charge.

I held out my braid with my left hand and started hacking at it with the knife, wincing with pain as the strokes pulled on my scalp, until the long rope of my hair sat in my palm like a dead pet. With a grunt, I threw my feminine treasure into a ditch and we resumed our journey toward the Dipylon Gate, Athens' double gate on the west. I remembered to make my steps wide and swaggering, imitating Theo's athletic gait.

There were two ways of getting to Piraeus, the seaport for the city of Athens. One was through an ancient, walled corridor, which led from the Pnyx hill straight into the seaport, and the other, by means of an open road, which led southwest. We chose the open road, reasoning that if our absence were discovered earlier than expected and Grandfather sent men to find us, we would be able to hide better in the surrounding fields than the confines of a walled avenue.

To our relief, no one followed us. Save for a few inebriated men weaving through the winding streets, Athens seemed deserted, and we made our way into Piraeus unmolested.

The Aegean Sea greeted us with deceptive decorum, its aquamarine beauty muted in the predawn light. The air tasted of salt and fish. My mouth turned dry. The outlandish plan that I had hatched in the wake of the furious exchange with my grandfather never accounted for all of the obstacles we were bound to encounter in Piraeus.

How could we find an honest captain who would not try to cheat us or, worse, conscript us into forced labor? We had no sealed letter from a recognized official to lend us legitimacy and were too young to travel abroad on our own.

I looked about, trying to find my bearings in the large seaport. There were three different harbors built into the port, two of them strictly for military use, and the third for commercial business. That is where we headed. The sprawling harbor was dense with ship sheds, where vessels could take shelter from bad weather. We found the port stirring with activity in spite of the early hour. Ships were getting ready to sail, bustling with sun-browned sailors stocking their ships and getting their cargo ready for transport.

"Let me do the talking," I said.

"How would that be different from any other day?"

I asked a sleepy man in respectable clothing which ships were sailing to Corinth that day. He named three and pointed them out in the harbor.

"What do you think, Theo?" We studied the ships in silence for some time. One was a narrow Roman trireme, sleek and fast, transporting soldiers. The second, a massive Greek merchant ship, bulged with amphorae of imported wine and vast earthenware vessels of grain. Hired mercenaries as well as passengers crawled all over its deck. Our eyes lingered on the third ship, which stood out in the harbor for her dark-colored wood and an elegant design that contrasted with her huge, odd-shaped sails. Her sailors had skin the color of a moonless night and laughed good-naturedly as they worked.

"That one." Theo pointed his chin at the odd ship. "They are small enough to be happy for a bit of extra income. No soldiers or passengers to ask awkward questions, either."

I nodded and surreptitiously wiped my damp palms on my clothing. We approached the captain. "We want to buy passage on your ship, Captain," I said, my voice an octave lower than its normal pitch.

"Do you, now?" He looked me up and down, his hand playing with the hilt of the dagger that hung from his waist. "What brings two fine fellows into the sea so early in the day?" His accent lilted like music.

"We are looking to make our fortune," Theo said.

The captain laughed. The sound came from deep in his belly and flowed out like a drumbeat. He loosened his hold on the dagger's hilt. "Fortunes cost money. How much do you have?"

For my sixteenth birthday, my father had sent me a gold ring domed with a red carnelian, along with a modest purse of silver. If he had sent them in the usual way, my mother would have apprehended both ring and silver before I ever caught sight of them. But he had dispatched his gifts by means of a friend who had delivered them to my brother in person.

I wore the ring hung on a strip of leather under my tunic. The purse would pay for our passage.

I haggled until the captain and I settled on the price of our passage, which left us with a few pieces of silver for food and emergencies should we run into trouble before finding my father in Corinth.

"How long does the passage take?" I asked.

"Five hours if the wind blows right."

"Is it blowing right today?"

The captain lifted his face and sniffed the air. "Right enough." He told us to sit in the bow of the ship while the crew readied for departure, out of the way of the sails. We sat quietly, hoping the sailors would forget our existence. Hoping the captain wouldn't change his mind.

We discovered that the Kushites called their ship *Whirring Wings*. They told us that the ships in their land were all called by that name.

We found out why when we set sail an hour later. As those tall sails, so awkward-looking at rest, unfurled fully, they looked like wings, stretching out from our hull. For a moment, I wondered if we would take off into the air like an osprey. Once we left the shelter of the harbor and found our way into the Saronic Gulf, the other part of the ship's name began to make sense.

Something about the fabric of the sails caused them to flutter and shiver in the wind, sounding like a thousand birds in flight. The noise was deafening, making our attempts at conversation futile.

The vibrations wormed their way into your ears, into your head, into your heart, and it became impossible to hear anything but their noise. I found the experience strangely familiar. In a way, this was how life had felt at Grandfather's house for the past eight years. The whirring wings of everyone's demands, the noise of their expectations swallowing my voice, drowning out life and desire and dreams, so that only they could be heard. Once in Corinth, there would be blessed silence and I would live again.

We had sailed for two hours when dark clouds whipped across the sun with sudden ferociousness. A fierce squall shook the hull of our ship. Lulled into sleepy stupor by the calm of our passage, I snapped awake as a huge wave rolled over us, followed by another. Wind gusts snapped at the sails viciously, and before the sailors could pull them down, the largest tore in half.

Another wave broke over us, raising the ship as high as a two-story building, and flinging it back down into the restless sea with such force that Theo, who was sitting near the stern, flew bodily into the air, and to my horror, was thrown overboard.

I lunged after him, and at the last moment was able to grab at his ankle. By then, half of my own body had sailed overboard and I dangled into the stormy sea, salty water spurting into my eyes and nose. Both my hands held on to Theo's ankle with a strength I did not know I possessed. To let go of him meant losing him to the storm. But with my hands thus occupied, I had no way of securing myself. The force of Theo's weight pulled on me, and I slipped over the edge.

There is a thin line between courage and stupidity, and I crossed it with a frequency that pointed to a lack of wit rather than a surfeit of bravery. I did not know how to swim, not even in calm waters. I certainly would not survive a dunking in this tempest. I tried to anchor my feet into the edge of the ship's railing and found it a losing battle. One deep breath, and my head sank into the waves.

CHAPTER 2

—ⱳ—

FINGERS SANK INTO THE MUSCLES of my calf and pulled hard, followed by a hand that tangled in the fabric twisted at my waist. Coming out of the water, I bashed my jaw against the hull and saw a burst of shimmering stars. Still I held on to Theo's ankle. Together, we were pulled out of what might have been our grave.

Panting and retching water, we collapsed on the deck. I looked up at the sailor who had saved us, a man the size of a city gate with a complexion the warm hue of cinnamon bark.

"Thank you," I shouted over the noise of the wind. "You saved our lives."

He flashed a smile. "Don't thank me yet. You could still die." He waved at the squall whipping about us, then vanished to help the other sailors who were busy with ropes and sails, trying to keep the ship from sinking.

Theo coughed next to me, spewing water. When he had breath to spare, he said, "You have no sense. You almost drowned."

"You're welcome," I said, grinning.

He pointed at my jaw. "You look like you were in a fight."

I pointed at his eye, which was swelling and red. "You look like you lost."

Reaching for his hand, I squeezed it, resisting the urge to throw a toddler-size emotional tirade. He had come too close to dying.

The storm passed as quickly as it had come, like a nightmare vanishing in moments. The sun shone again, drying our soaking clothes and restoring hope that we would see land again.

Theo motioned to the large sailor who had saved our lives, and the man joined us. Opening his bundle, Theo pulled out a piece of fresh cheese and bread fragrant with the scent of cloves and offered it to the man.

The sailor politely took only a small piece and returned the rest to Theo. "Smells good," he said. He stretched the words and added to them a strange music, so they lengthened by an extra syllable. "Almost as good as our Kushite bread," he said after he tasted the morsel.

"Where is that?" I asked.

"Far from here, little man, a kingdom south of Egypt." He drew a pouch out of his belt and extracted a couple of pieces of dried fruit, which he gave to Theo and me. I bit into mine and tasted apricot.

"Goood," I said, mimicking his cadence, and he laughed.

The sailors repaired the torn sail and hoisted it aloft again. Once more, the noise of the whirring wings intruded into our conversation, and Theo and I lapsed back into silence. I studied his battered face, my stomach twisting with guilt. Away from Grandfather's home for barely four hours, and I had already almost caused his death.

I could not regret my decision to leave, however. I needed to be free from that house. I needed to find my father.

That was the sum total of my plan.

I was like a child bitten by a viper. All I could think of was finding a way to remove the fangs sunken into my skin. I had no notion that I still had to contend with the venom pumping through my veins. Thinking myself free of Athens, I wilted with relief, not knowing the poison of that household still lurked inside me.

I had known for years that my father harbored a secret. Even as a young child I could not miss the comings and goings at odd hours, the stealthy meetings, the whispered conversations. It was not until my brother's twelfth birthday that I realized whatever he held so close to his chest had the power to destroy. To unravel marriages and consume families.

That evening, my father had thrown a lavish

feast in Dionysius's honor. The house was crawling with young lads and men, and my mother had kept me out of the way so I would not be a nuisance to Dionysius and his friends.

My father, an athlete in spite of his age, never fully understood his son, who preferred books to the sweat-drenched grunts of a gymnasium. For all that he found Dionysius incomprehensible, his gaze never fell on him without pride or affection. So on his birthday, instead of purchasing him wrestling instructions by a great athlete at the palaestra, Father bought Dionysius an ancient scroll by Plato and earned one of my brother's rare smiles.

As soon as the guests left, Dionysius tucked his new treasure under an arm and disappeared into the eaves of the house to read by lamplight. I saw my chance, after a whole day of separation, to sneak to Father's side for a private chat. My father had a great heart and loved me with the same passion as he did my brother, though I was a mere girl, and by Greek standards, hardly worth his notice.

As I made my way on bare feet through the atrium, I could see him in his library, a tired smile on his lips. He was slouching in a high-backed chair, fingers playing absently with an ornate stylus he kept on his table. Then I spied my mother, and knowing that I would earn her displeasure for being out of bed at this hour, hid myself behind a broad marble column. Mother sailed past without seeing me, her beautiful face shuttered with displeasure. This was not an unusual sight, for she often found reason to be displeased. But on this particular evening, it welled out of her like a flood.

My parents did not have a happy union. My mother's unremitting disappointment was too great a burden for any man to carry without growing weary.

"Celandine!" Father sat up when he saw my mother approach him. "To what do I owe this pleasure?"

"To my departure. I am taking leave of you." I could only see her back, which was as straight as a sword shaft. But her voice was shaking with rage.

"Pardon?" Father sounded confused. He half rose from his chair. Then stopped when my mother threw a roll of papyrus in his face. He took his time reading it. Even from where I stood, I saw his face drain. His features went limp.

"You disgust me," Mother said.

"Celandine, it's not what you imagine."

She ignored his attempts at an explanation. "You have shamed me, shamed the name I was born with, shamed the blood of Athens in my veins."

"Please! Listen to me!"

"I am leaving. And the children are coming with me. I don't want you to ever see them again."

"No! Celandine, you can't take them. I won't allow it."

"I think you will. You have no choice. I will share what I know with the world. You will lose them, in any case. Lose them in honor, or lose them in dishonor. I care not what you do."

"For pity's sake, woman. They need me. They need their father!"

"They will have mine. What can you give them but ruin and disgrace? What do you think they will learn from you? To grow into a man and woman I can be proud of? You will only corrupt them."

"I will *love* them. Celandine, listen. I will stop. It was an aberration. And besides, I never took advantage—"

"Enough. I am leaving in the morning for Athens. And the children are going with me."

I ran into the room then. "I won't go with you to stupid Athens!" I screamed. "I won't."

"Ariadne, be still," Father said. I froze when I saw tears running down those beloved cheeks.

Mother turned her wrath on me. "You will do as you are told."

My temper was ever a nuisance. In the intervening years, I sometimes asked myself if pleading with her, using honeyed words in that

43

moment, might not have softened her heart where my father's supplications had left her cold. But an eight-year-old has no sweet words when gripped by fear. I sensed that I might lose my father and my home. The dread of such a loss overwhelmed me. And with the fear came a fury I could not master. I kicked my mother in the shin as hard as I could.

Her scream echoed in my ears as I ran out of the house and into the night. I did not go far. I was young but not entirely stupid. In the orchard behind the villa one of the old oak trees had died, leaving a hollow at the base of the tree trunk. I was just small enough to fit inside it.

It was Dionysius and Theo who found me two hours later.

"Did you hit Mother?" Dionysius asked, his voice high with shocked accusation.

"I did not. I *kicked* her. And I would do it again. She made Father cry."

"Don't be silly."

"She did, I tell you. And she is going to take us to Athens in the morning. Except I am not going to filthy Athens. I am staying right here."

"What are you talking about?" Theo said.

"Athens isn't filthy. It's beautiful. What's wrong with visiting Grandfather for a week or two?" My brother grasped my arm and tried to pull me out. "Now stop making a goose of your-self and come apologize to Mother."

I dug desperate nails into the side of the tree, my fingers wrapping themselves about the dried wood like vines. "It's not for a visit, Dionysius! It's forever."

His hold on me slackened. "What?"

"She wants to take us away from Father. She told him so."

The boys went quiet and looked at each other. Dionysius shrugged. "They had a fight. In a month it will blow over, and we will come back, and life will be normal."

I stuck my head out of the hole. "Do you really think so?" Next to my father and Theo, there was no one on earth I trusted so much as my big brother. He was never wrong.

"I do."

"Then why was Father crying? He didn't think we were coming back."

Dionysius hesitated. "Maybe he had drunk too much wine."

"Have you ever seen Father cry, even when he is in his cups?"

Dionysius shook his head. "I don't know what's going on, but you can't spend the night here. There are wild dogs and hordes of mosquitoes. You have to come inside."

It showed the measure of my brother's agitation that he did not return straight to his Plato. Instead, he took hold of my hand and went to find our father in his tablinum, Theo trailing behind.

Father was slumped in his chair, head buried in his hands. There was no sign of Mother, thank the gods.

Dionysius cleared his throat, and my father jerked. For a moment he stared at us, and then opened his arms, fell to his knees, and enclosed the three of us in an embrace. This was far from the first time we had found ourselves in the grip of his affection. That night, though, we felt the difference. Felt a sting of desperation, of choking anguish in those tender hands.

"Is it true?" Dionysius said, his voice faint. "Are you sending us away to Athens?"

"*Sending* you? Gods! Never. But you are going. Yes. You are going away from me."

"I don't understand. Surely you will come and fetch us when Mother has cooled?"

There was a rumble in his chest that made his massive torso shake. It took me a moment to realize that the giant of a man I had thought indestructible was weeping like a babe.

And I had my answer. He would not come for us. Mother would not allow him.

I made to fly, to hide again, but he held me fast. "No, child. Don't run. It's no use. She will only grow more agitated with you. You ought not to have kicked her."

I frowned. "I should have kicked her harder."

He laughed through his tears. "Well, save some ammunition for the coming months. You still owe her an apology. She is your mother, and you must respect her."

"I won't go." A donkey had nothing on me. I could be more stubborn than a block of stone.

"You have no choice. You will go, you and Dionysius."

A blanket of frost covered the ice that had become my heart. "What about Theo?" To lose my father and my home was like losing an arm. To lose Theo, too . . . You might as well plunge a dagger into me.

Father wiped a hand over his white face. "He needs to stay here, Ariadne. Life in Athens would be too hard for him."

"No!" I screamed. "You can't send me without Theo! I won't go."

"Be reasonable, child. Your mother barely tolerates Theo. I hate to think how she will treat him without me there to shield him."

"I'll take care of him," I said. "I promise." I was too young to appreciate how impossible it would prove to keep such a promise, too ignorant to know how selfish was my desire to cling to my foster brother. "I can't go without him," I pleaded, wet lashes sticking to each other, blurring my vision.

Father squeezed his eyes shut for a moment. Turning to face Theo, he said, "You have a choice, Son. You can go with Ariadne, or you can stay with me."

"I must choose?" Theo took a staggered step back. "Between you?"

Father caressed his head. "Dionysius will fare well in Athens, I think. He will bond with his grandfather; they are drawn to similar interests. He will have many companions. Be happy.

"Ariadne, on the other hand . . . Well, she could use a faithful friend like you, Theo."

Theo reached out a hand and took hold of mine. The pressure of that small hand steadied my spiraling world.

Father gazed at us, his eyes swimming. "If you choose to go and keep watch over Ariadne, I would owe you my life, Theo. But you must know that in Athens you will not be treated as you are here. They will consider you little better than a slave. I have always treated you as if you were my own flesh. In my father-in-law's house, you will not receive the same consideration.

"Whatever you choose, to stay or to leave, I will love you. The decision is yours. It is unfair to ask a boy of eight to make such a choice. Know this: if a day dawns that you change your mind, you write me, and I will bring you home. I give you my word as a Corinthian."

For a moment Theo looked what he was: a frightened little boy. He pursed his lips and dashed the back of a hand against red eyes. "I will go," he said.

His hair was in disarray, standing in spikes

toward the front, revealing the silver streak he often tried to hide. I sometimes thought that it was a mark from the gods, an acknowledgment of the wisdom they had poured into him. At eight, Theo was more adult than most grown-ups I knew. Once he gave his word, his whole soul braced that commitment. Stolid and dry-eyed, he clung to me while I was dragged wailing and battling every step of the way to my new life in Athens.

To my knowledge, he never wrote my father to ask for help. Though in my grandfather's house his life proved harder than mine, Theo did not complain. Once, after Grandfather beat him for some minor infraction, I demanded that he return to my father. He looked at me as if I had kicked him in the teeth. I never suggested it again.

I could not remember life without Theo. He came to us without warning on the day of my birth, like a lightning strike. I had been born in the middle of the night, too impatient to wait for a convenient time, apparently. When the sun rose, Father went to offer libations to the gods and to thank them for my safe delivery.

On his way to the public square, the outdoor court with its exquisite cream and blue marble, he walked past the *bema*, his mind wrapped up in his newborn daughter. A sound distracted him, a soft mewling that reminded him of a kitten.

Tender from the recent experience of becoming a father to his second child, he turned aside to investigate and to feed the starving feline he imagined he would find.

In a corner of the deserted platform, under the shade of a column, he found a blanket made of high-quality wool, woven to perfection. Something within cried and wriggled, making my father rear back in surprise. Pulling the corner of the blanket aside cautiously, he found a baby, fresh to this world, judging by the size of him.

My people sometimes abandon babies when they are imperfect or damaged in some way. Undesirable children are left to die by exposure— or to be saved by the gods if fortune smiles upon them.

At first, my father thought this poor creature such a child. He pulled the blankets off the baby, seeking whatever disfigurement had precipitated its abandonment.

He found no blemish. Save for a streak of silver hair, the babe was perfect. A healthy boy with a head full of dark hair.

In the folds of the wool sat a gold rattle in the shape of a lion. An expensive, delicately carved piece, and certainly not a toy for a poor child.

Hungry and cold though he must have been, the babe stopped crying the moment he had my father's attention. When Father reached out to cover him again, he grasped the strange man's finger and held on. Held on with fragile confidence and a strange familiarity that disarmed his visitor. My father said his heart was snared as securely as his finger in that one moment.

It never occurred to Father he should inquire my mother's feelings on the subject; the boy was his from that hour. He named the child Theodotus, "given of God," for he saw Theo as fate's gift to our family.

Mother was not moved by the story. "If there weren't something wrong with him, Galenos, they wouldn't have discarded him like garbage. How could you bring that thing into my house?" She had given her husband a perfectly good baby hours before, and saw his decision to bring home a vagabond's child an insult to her performance as wife.

Father would not be shaken from his conviction that the child came as a blessing from the gods rather than a burden. Through the years, neither budged from their position. Theo inhabited our world, slept in our rooms, ate our food, shared our sorrows, and became part of the fabric of our lives as familiar as air and bread. But his life was divided into two halves.

To Father, Theo was like a son. To Mother, he was a thorn and an embarrassment. Not a slave, for Father refused to make him such, nor a legal son by adoption, for Mother had drawn her line in the sand. With the passing of time, my parents' marriage grew more frayed, and Theo occupied the space between them like a bone of contention. To Dionysius and me, he was a treasured brother and friend no matter what transpired between our parents.

What Theo thought of this confusing clash of opinions, he never said. All I knew was that he would never leave me.

CHAPTER 3

—⁓—

WE ARRIVED AT THE HARBOR of Cenchreae seven hours after we had set sail from Piraeus. The storm that had almost drowned us had delayed our arrival by a mere two hours.

I stared, transfixed by the beauty of Cenchreae as we pulled into the harbor, by the stunning, pale hills dotted with rugged pines that stretched over us.

Cenchreae had grown in the years of my absence. The port had expanded almost beyond recognition, the way Corinth liked to do, with a fast pace, and an eye to quick riches. Several blocks of warehouses fronted the wharf, and surrounding the harbor sat a ring of commercial buildings and taverns divided by narrow streets.

The broad-chested sailor who had fished us out of the sea approached us as we stood uncertainly, trying to find our bearings.

"Going into Corinth?" he asked, biting into a fat, juicy apple. I nodded.

"I am headed that way myself. Come. I will

show you the way. I pass through the city often and know it well." He smiled, displaying wide, even teeth. "Are you bound for the temple of Aphrodite, little men?"

Theo's face turned a curious shade of crimson, which made me grin. The temple of Aphrodite sat near the peak of Acrocorinth and was famed for its thousand temple prostitutes, trained slaves who catered to whims both mundane and peculiar. Sailors were known to squander a whole year's wages there in a matter of hours.

"That is not our destination. I take it it's yours?" I widened my eyes at him in mock innocence.

He smiled. "No, little man. Taharqa is too old and well married for such pastimes."

"Then, Taharqa, you are a rare man," I said.

"So young, and already a cynic. Come. I will guide your way." He threw his apple core into the waters lapping at the dock, where it joined the leftover flotsam of numberless ships.

We accepted Taharqa's invitation, for in truth, the road to Corinth was no safe place for two untried boys. I treasured my city, but I could not refute the charge of immorality that the world held against her. Corinth was exciting and full of charm. It also brimmed with danger and corruption.

The city sat at the neck of an isthmus, a narrow strip of land between the Ionian and Aegean Seas. The isthmus saved the Peloponnese from being an island and tied us to the mainland of Graecia like a belt's buckle. Because of it, the riches of the nations poured into Corinth with regularity, for the gods had blessed Corinth with a singular gift. The only way to sail between the Ionian Sea to the west and the Aegean Sea to the east, was to traverse the long way around the Peloponnese in the Mediterranean, where many sailors had found a watery grave in those treacherous waters. Corinth provided an ingenious alternative.

Ships brought their goods into her harbor on one side of the isthmus and off-loaded their merchandise to be transported to the opposite side using carts and wagons. There, they loaded a new ship, so that from east to west and west to east the seas were conquered by way of carts. The whole process took hardly a day, and ships avoided the rough waters south of the Peloponnese as well as a longer journey. And for this security, ship owners were happy to pay a tariff. Wares could also be stored in ventilated warehouses for a price.

In exchange for so much aid and welcome, Corinth received exorbitant wealth. It grew explosively. Any capable man who wished to make a rapid fortune eventually made his way into one of Corinth's harbors.

"And what will you do, my young friends, once you arrive in Corinth? If not to Aphrodite, where are you bound?" Our Kushite companion strolled at a leisurely pace on the limestone blocks of the street and jumped onto the narrow sidewalk when carts threatened to run him over.

"We are going to stay with a relative," I said.

"A relative? What is his name? Perhaps I can help you locate him."

I realized, too late, that Taharqa was determined to protect us from danger. His kindness, which had earlier rescued me from certain death, now irritated me. I had no use for a defender. His meddling merely complicated a delicate situation.

My father had no idea that we were about to descend on him. I had not told Theo, but I feared that as soon as I arrived, Father would try to send me packing on the fastest ship back to Athens. He had already given in to my mother's demands that she have full charge of his children. Why should this time prove any different merely because we were older?

I had come on this long journey not sure of the reception I would receive. I needed time to convince Father that he should keep me with him. Time I might not have if this well-intentioned Kushite stuck his nose into my business. I certainly did not need a large, exotic sailor telling tales about the dangers we might have encountered had we been left to our own devices.

"We know the way already. Thank you," I lied, keeping my voice steady.

"Are you certain? This city holds many

dangers for two unaccompanied young men."

"We can take care of ourselves," I said, drawing a curious glance from Theo.

"No doubt. No doubt." The black eyes slithered sideways from me to Theo. "Yet I ask your indulgence, young master."

I ground my teeth and walked on in silence.

The journey from the harbor into Corinth lasted almost three hours as we made our way along the valley of Hexamili. The city of my birth had been built on a hill, and the way to her was steep and hard on the lungs and legs. The closer we drew to the city, the more congested the roads became. In the distance, the dusky rock of Acrocorinth cast its shadow over the metropolis that sprawled among its foothills. We passed by many new houses and villas, a suburbia that had not existed eight years before. I had forgotten how beautiful the wide, tree-lined avenue was, which brought us straight to the open Cenchreaen Gates.

My eyes grew gritty and hot as we walked through those gates. I was in Corinth. I was home.

"Look." Theo pointed. Before us stood the breathtaking agora, one of the largest in the empire, with its new public buildings and burning bowls of fire ready to receive sacrifices. In neat rows about us were a dizzying array of shops selling fruits I had never seen, spices, fabrics, silver, olive oil, and nameless wares from across the empire. I turned and turned, trying to consume the bright sights with my thirsty eyes.

"Which street?" said the big Kushite.

"This way," I pointed.

Theo lowered his brows. He must have been wondering why I did not simply speak the truth and give the name of my father.

The avenue had grown choked with crowds, so that the three of us could not walk abreast. Taharqa occupied the width of the whole sidewalk with his broad shoulders. I contrived to have Theo and me walk behind him, though he turned often to ensure we remained near.

I prayed that my childhood memories had not deceived me, and what I sought would still be there. A sigh of relief escaped me when I spied the simple sign overhead with its Latin inscription that read, *Lucius the Butcher*. I grabbed Theo's hand and pulled him behind me, shoving past the line of customers toward the back of the narrow store.

"What are you doing?" Theo demanded.

"Wait. We are almost there." At the back I spotted the tapered door with its chipped gray paint. I hoped it had not been sealed in the intervening years, and that I had not trapped us within the confines of the diminutive store without an exit. To my relief, the door gave as I shoved, and Theo and I were disgorged into the alley that ran behind the shop, just as I had remembered.

"Why are you trying to ditch the Kushite?" Theo said, stopping dead. "He seems an honest man. In case you had not noticed, we could use his help. I have no idea how to get to your father's house from here. Have you?"

"How hard can it be? We will ask for directions."

Theo narrowed his eyes. "You don't know if Galenos will send us back."

"I am sure he will be overjoyed to see us," I said, defiant.

Without another word, he began to walk toward the end of the alley. "How did you know about that door in the butcher shop?" he said.

"My mother used to send me shopping with one of the slave girls. She was sweet on the butcher's assistant, and they would slip out the back door for a few moments of stolen chatter. I was supposed to stay in the shop and wait."

"Poor slave. She clearly thought you capable of following directions." The alley had dead-ended into the main avenue. He turned right and halted abruptly.

"That was a sleek trick." Taharqa seemed to appear from nowhere. "I had half a mind to let you go your way. Then I saw a boy with painted lips and blank eyes and my heart took pity on you. Now stop wasting my time and tell me the name of this relative, if he exists, or I will take you to the magistrate."

"His name is Galenos," Theo said. "He lives in a large villa to the north. We would welcome your help."

"Traitor!" My elbow aimed for his ribs. Theo sidestepped neatly and avoided my assault. He did not contradict me often. When he did, I knew neither resistance nor whining would gain me an advantage.

Taharqa delivered us to the door of Father's villa in less than half an hour. I stood before that open door and shook.

A slave I did not recognize led us into the court-yard and went to fetch my father. I wrapped my arms about my stomach, feeling nauseous, feeling elated, fighting a contrary desire to run away.

He did not notice me at first, his attention fixed on the large Kushite stranger standing in his courtyard. His hair had thinned and grayed and there were new lines on his forehead. I tried to swallow the lump in my throat and found my mouth too dry.

"How may I help you?" he asked.

"I have brought you a couple of visitors," the sailor said, sweeping his hand in our direction. "They say they know you."

Father saw Theo first. "Theodotus!" With a leaping step, he enveloped my foster brother in an embrace. "My boy! Has something happened?" He gave me a blank gaze before turning his face back to Theo. Midmotion, he stopped, arrested.

"Ariadne? Dear girl! My child!" He pulled me roughly into his arms, weeping and uttering endearments. Theo joined us in the circle of his arms. We had grown too big to fit well, I noticed. But it didn't matter. I had found safety again. I had come home.

In Grandfather's house, I had learned not to waste my tears. In the shelter of my father's love, tears came freely, until I turned into a human waterfall, moisture pouring from eyes and nose and dribbling on Dionysius's clothing, which I still wore.

"You two rascals. How did you get here?" my father asked when the lightning shock of seeing us passed and he had been assured of Dionysius's safety. "Where did you get these bruises? And what happened to your hair?" he asked me. Without waiting for a response he addressed Taharqa. "Sir, I thank you with my whole heart for bringing my son and daughter to me."

"Daughter?"

"Yes. This is Ariadne."

The Kushite laughed. "It seems I should have asked her to keep *me* safe in Corinth. Until this moment, this sly girl had me convinced she was a boy."

"How odd. Did Celandine not tell you?"

"Who is Celandine?"

My father went still. "Who asked you to bring the children to me?"

"No one. They boarded our ship unattended."

Father whipped his head toward me. "You ran away," he accused.

"Well, I didn't exactly run." I loosened the awkwardly bulky cloak. "I climbed."

CHAPTER 4

—∽—

TO HIS CREDIT, Taharqa said nothing to muddy the waters of my situation. He bowed with dignity. "I will take my leave of you, Master Galenos," he said. "I only wished to ensure these two adventurers came to no harm."

Upon discovering that the sailor had not only delivered us safely into his hands but had also rescued us from drowning, my father insisted that the Kushite stay to supper and sent him to the dining room to partake of a meal worthy of an emperor. Theo and I were given a bowl of tepid water to wash our hands and faces, while a slave hurriedly cleaned our feet, before we were unceremoniously bundled into the tablinum, the room usually reserved for Father's business.

"Explain yourselves. Leave nothing out. If Celandine and Dexios are going to show up at my door, I want to have ample warning of what I am facing." Father paced as he spoke, though he stopped every few moments to stroke my hair or squeeze Theo's shoulder.

"Grandfather wants to marry me off to a monster."

Father came to an abrupt halt. "To whom?"

"Draco, the son of Evandos."

"Evandos the magistrate?" Father curled his lip. "Was it an empty threat?" He looked at Theo as he asked the question.

"Have you known Dexios to make empty threats?" My foster brother hunched his shoulders and leaned forward. "I fear it's my fault we have turned up here. The old wolf threatened to beat me if Ariadne would not obey him."

"He wanted to ensure I was wed by next month."

"Why the haste?" Father crossed his arms and leaned back against the table.

I shrugged, wiping my face of expression. "Ask him."

Father did not move. I squirmed under his scrutiny. "I may have thrown a cup of wine at Mother. It was very watered down. Hardly pink. I doubt it will leave a stain."

Father sat down, looking older than his years.

"May I ask what precipitated this display of appalling discourtesy?"

"She informed me that she had started working on my wedding garments."

"I see. As I recall, Celandine is an able seamstress. I trust it is not the quality of her workmanship to which you objected?"

"No. It's the quality of her mothering. Draco is ruthless. He beat Alcmena, Grandfather's slave. She is only fifteen. Grandfather gave him permission to . . ."

"Bed her," Theo interjected.

"Right. But I doubt even the old man expected Draco to treat the girl so savagely."

"I was there when the physician tended her," Theo said. "She will never fully recover. That boy ought to be whipped."

"Instead of shielding me against Grandfather's demand that I marry such a man, Mother informed me that she was making my wedding garments."

Father looked at Theo. My foster brother lowered his eyes. "In the past eight years, Ariadne has spent more time locked up in the women's quarters than out of them. She has been beaten, starved, insulted, and threatened. The marriage to Draco is the last in a long litany of daily injuries. That boy is not right in the head. I would not allow him to join a cohort of bloodthirsty soldiers, let alone become bridegroom to a young woman. Dexios has convinced himself that Draco's treatment of Alcmena was an aberration due to too much drink. But any fool can see that Ariadne would be safer living with a wild bear."

Father swore under his breath. "You never said, when you wrote me."

"They would only send you the letters that had

no complaints in them. We learned quickly that if we denounced anything about our circumstances, they destroyed our messages, and to chastise us, they withheld the letters you sent to us, as well."

Father seemed confounded by that bit of information. He stared at us, mouth hanging open.

"You can't send me back," I whispered. "Don't you *want* me?" My heart cracked as I said the words out loud.

Father fell to his knees before me. "Of course I want you!"

"Why did you send me away, then? Why did you leave us there? You never even tried to fetch us."

"Your mother would not allow it."

"Because of your secret?"

He blinked. "My secret?"

"The reason she was angry with you that night. On Dionysius's birthday."

"Yes. Because of that."

"You promised me, when I was a little girl, that you would always be there when I needed you. That this would always be my home. Do you remember, Father? You promised."

His eyes flooded. He opened his mouth and closed it again, speechless.

"Keep your promise now." I reached for his hand and grasped it. "I beg you. Find a way. I cannot be a bride to Draco. Nor a prisoner to my mother and grandfather any longer. I feel like I am choking, one day at a time. I can't go back."

He sank into a chair, his movements slow. "I won't send you back." Pulling a fresh piece of parchment to him, he began to write. His fingers trembled as he held the stylus. Curious, I moved behind him and bent my head to read.

The letter was addressed to my grandfather, Dexios. As the sentences accrued, I gasped. "You can't do that." I spread my hand flat on the parchment to prevent him from writing further.

According to a contract made between my parents years before, Dionysius remained legally under Grandfather's guardianship until the age of twenty-one. He was already considered an adult as far as Roman law was concerned. The contract kept him under Grandfather's supervision for another eighteen months. Once the terms of the guardianship were completed, he could choose where he wished to reside. He could return to my father, and no one could do anything about it. My mother and grandfather had no scruples about blackmailing Father. Over Dionysius, however, they had no hold. In eighteen months, they could lose him, if he so chose.

The letter sitting on the ebony table before me changed these terms. In essence, Father was giving up his right to Dionysius in order that he might keep Theo and me.

"You can't do that," I said again, the lump in

my throat choking me. I knew the affection my father held for his son. If he sent this letter, he would not see Dionysius again until my brother turned twenty-five, when he gained full majority. At that age, every form of guardianship would dissolve and he would be free to make his own decisions. By the terms of this letter, Father effectively put four additional years of separation between them.

This was no slight delay. It was an amputation.

He pulled my hand away with a gentle movement. "It's the only way, Ariadne. They will not release you to my care for a lesser incentive. Dionysius is happy with his grandfather. His letters to me are full of enthusiasm for his friends and his studies. Last year, when he managed to visit me for a few days while traveling with Dexios, he assured me of his happiness. He leads a fulfilling life."

"He misses *you!* Grandfather cannot replace you."

He sprang to his feet. For a moment he swayed, and I thought he might topple onto the table. His hands turned into fists, and with visible effort, he regained his wavering balance. "I cannot have you both. You will not survive in that house. Dionysius will."

He sat down again and put the stylus to the parchment. He signed his name, a sprawling stain on the ivory sheet, and without further delay, rolled the missive closed. His seal was in the wax before I could think of an argument that would change his mind.

My dream had come true. I was going to be released from tyranny. I was going to live with my father, free from the torment of my mother's constant harassment. Instead of feeling over-joyed, I tasted ashes.

My freedom came at too great a cost. The expense was laid in its entirety upon my brother and father.

"Dionysius was made for Athens," Theo said later, when he found me huddled on my bed in the dark. "He has his studies and friendships to keep him content. He probably would have made the sacrifice willingly if you had asked him."

"That is the point. He had no choice in the matter. By coming here, I robbed him of his father."

We both knew that although Dionysius did not wear his feelings on his sleeves as I did, he was devoted to our father. This separation would hurt. Worse yet, Father had chosen me over him. Dionysius was a man of logic and reason. But he had a heart. Even if his logic understood the decision, his heart would feel abandoned.

I wrote a letter to my brother, begging his for-giveness. He wrote back, his words civil and gracious. His decorum cut deeper than his anger would have.

Dionysius behaved as if his life had not changed by my hands. He helped by writing frequent letters, regaling us with tales of his success. My brother was a prodigy. In time, Athens fell at his feet in worship. He only had to open his mouth and young men fawned and wished they could be like him, while older men admired his talent and called him the flower of their city.

Father would read his letters out loud to visiting friends, laugh at his jests, acknowledge that most of his quips were over his head and show him off with the pride of familiarity, as if the years had never driven them apart. And if he sometimes wept silently into his chalice of wine, I turned a blind eye and told myself it was the drink and not a broken heart.

CHAPTER 5

—◊—

AFTER THE COPIOUS RESTRICTIONS of Athens, the freedom of Corinth felt strange to me. Years of being locked up in solitude for days at a time had left a mark. Now I found myself uneasy among strangers and fretful in large crowds. One day, when we were attending a feast given by one of his friends, Father discovered me hiding behind the foliage in the courtyard.

He dragged me from behind the shelter of the greenery and introduced me to Diantha, a pretty creature with long, dark lashes and artfully arranged hair. I think he expected us to become instant confidants. My father had a talent for making friends with enviable ease and could not understand the rest of us mortals who stumbled about in the dark, hoping for genuine camaraderie and meeting with rare success.

I cleared my throat. The language of Corinth was Latin. After years of speaking Greek, my Latin, though very correct, felt rusty. Carefully,

I formed the words. "Your shoes are pretty."

She stared at me as if I were a buffoon. She was barefoot.

"I saw them when we came in," I explained.

"They're ancient. I only wore them because my father forced us to walk here. Our house is at the end of the street."

"Glorious afternoon for a walk."

"It is horrible. We should have arrived in a chair like all the other fashionable people instead of traipsing around like peasants."

I scratched my ear. *We* had come on foot.

"What is wrong with your hair?" Diantha pointed at my shockingly short coiffure.

"Er . . . a misadventure." My mother's voice echoed in my ear. *You are an embarrassment.*

Diantha smirked as though she could hear those words as clearly as I. I cast about desperately, looking for reprieve from this awkward conversation, when I spotted Theo standing alone and waved him over. "This is Theo," I said proudly, expecting Diantha to be impressed by his good looks and unimpeachable manners.

"Theo?" Diantha studied my foster brother's face for a moment. "Oh, I remember. You are the foundling."

Blood surged to my face. Theo placed a calming hand on my shoulder. "I am," he said, his manner amiable.

I forgot my intention to make a favorable

impression. "He is my brother," I hissed. "And your toes are crooked."

Grabbing Theo's arm, I walked off in the opposite direction. He shook his head. "Why did you lie?"

"I did not! Her toes are more twisted than the streets of Athens."

"About me being your brother."

"You *are* my brother."

He expelled a short sigh. "You should not have provoked her. She has many friends with important connections."

"I don't care if she's Zeus's cousin. She has the tongue of an adder."

Later, I saw Diantha whispering to a group of fashionable young women. They turned and stared at me, their necks swiveling together like a five-headed beast before bursting into laughter. I answered them with a frosty smile as if being the butt of their jests meant nothing. But something inside me wilted. My mother's daughter hungered for friendship, longed for acceptance. Their public rebuff hurt like an unset broken bone, a throbbing wound that time could not fix.

A few months after our arrival in Corinth, Theo began attending the palaestra, a specialized school for athletic training where young men learned the art of wrestling and practiced boxing and other sports. In the afternoons, when the weather allowed, we made our way to the fallow tract of land that sat between our villa and our neighbor's property.

Theo practiced wrestling with one of Father's servants, a man who had once served in the arena, while I hitched up my skirts and ran barefoot through the grass.

I loved to run.

When I ran, I felt as if I could outstrip my past. All thought left me but this one exulting reality: my body could soar. I ran until my calves throbbed; my muscles quivered and stalled. Then I pressed through the pain and ran until I felt myself almost splitting. When I persisted beyond the physical agony, I found a strange elation.

I could beat both men in a short race, whipping into top speed from the first step. This was not an unusual occurrence. I had been beating boys in footraces since I had turned eleven. When we set a longer course, however, their stamina proved superior and they won every time.

One afternoon, Theo's wrestling partner was busy with an errand and I challenged my foster brother to a race. I took a flying start, winning the short-distance race with ease, and came to a stop, hands on bare knees, trying to take in more air than my lungs seemed able to consume.

"I think you need more serious competition," a voice drawled somewhere above me. I leapt upright, staggering in my haste. I knew that voice, knew its warm timbre. It belonged to Justus, our neighbor.

When we were children, Justus had been my brother's closest companion. I had been too young and female to be worthy of his note then. He had maintained his friendship with Dionysius, visiting him whenever his father's business took him to Athens. But he remained aloof toward me.

Now that I lived in Corinth, our villas separated only by this fallow piece of land, I saw him often, as he was fond of my father and a regular visitor to our home. For some perverse reason known only to himself, Justus still treated me with the tolerance one displayed toward precocious children. Though he was twenty-two to my sixteen, I was considered a woman grown in the eyes of the world. He had no cause to act superior in my presence.

"I suppose you think you can do better?" I challenged.

He smiled. He was not handsome in the classic sense, not like Theo with his straight nose and chiseled mouth, nor like Dionysius with his finely drawn features. Justus had a craggy face, with golden skin and a crooked nose that had been broken in an old wrestling match. When he smiled, his teeth flashed white and his cheeks split into two deep lines. I would have called them dimples, but didn't dare, even in my own head. There was something too hard and masculine about Justus. And somehow, that odd assortment of imperfect features proved irresistible. I was not the only girl who felt it. Justus left a trail of swooning women in his path. I had determined I would not be one of that silly brood.

"Modesty forbids me to boast." He pointed to the tree Theo and I used as a marker. "Shall we?"

I tucked my skirt higher into the ribbons at my waist, too engrossed in the challenge to care how much bare leg I had put on display.

Justus's smile widened. "Theo, would you do us the honor of calling the winner? In case it is a close race."

Theo took his stance at the tree and signaled the start. I felt confident. My feet flew in the air, each step falling in glorious precision. I ran a perfect race. To my utter chagrin, I saw Justus go past me by half a stride, and then a whole stride. It took me a moment to fathom that Justus had unequivocally defeated me.

"Impressive, for a girl your age," he said. "Don't lose heart. I am sure that eventually, with the right training, you will improve."

Heat traveled up my neck until I thought I might breathe fire.

He gestured at my legs. "You might want to let your skirt down now. The mosquitoes are coming out. I am sure *they* will be tempted by the flesh you have put on display." How could it be possible to turn even redder? I had become a lump of vermilion.

To my further vexation, Theo ran up to him. "Will you participate in the chariot race at the next games?" Justus was a three-time champion of the Isthmian Games. He had been catapulted into the kind of fame that is reserved for few in our world. His fierce driving style and seemingly unbeatable record had turned him into a legend in Corinth. Theo, whose greatest ambition was to become a successful charioteer, adored Justus. No one was perfect, but I thought this misplaced affection indicated a dangerous slippage in Theo's moral fiber. I would have to speak to him about it.

"No more races for me. I have retired."

"Surely not! There is no one in Corinth who can replace you." Dismay leaked out of Theo's pores.

Justus patted Theo on the shoulder. "My father's health is declining. He needs help with the business, and I must set aside youthful pastimes. It's your turn now, Theo."

Theo looked crestfallen. "Galenos does not keep racehorses. He says they are a needless expense."

"He is a wise man. I will make you a proposition. Why don't you come over and help me exercise the horses? The ones I use for practice. I will coach you whenever I can."

If someone had handed Theo a dog that turned wood into gold every time it barked, he could not have looked more thrilled. His smile flashed so wide, I could see all the way to the back of his head. I was embarrassed for him.

"Did you hear, Ariadne? Justus will teach me how to race war chariots."

"And gain a free groom in the bargain, no doubt," I said and, turning my back, started to walk home.

I found Father flush with pleasure, poring over a new letter from Dionysius. "He was invited to a private supper at the house of Ephialtes, the man who rules the council of elders in Athens," Father said. "My son is entering into exalted circles."

"So is my brother." I grinned.

Father read in silence for a moment. "He sends regards to you and Theo," he said, reading Dionysius's parting words aloud.

> Remember me to my sister with love, and tell Theo I long to see him. I send you all my deepest affection. How I wish I could be with you, my dearest father.

With care, Father rolled up the scroll and wrapped it with a crimson ribbon. Opening an alabaster box, he laid the scroll atop a mount of similar letters. He had preserved every scrap of correspondence from Dionysius and knew most of them by heart. Theo's and my letters were there also, though having us with him meant he no longer needed to reread our missives to ease the ache of absence.

CHAPTER 6

—w—

ONE EVENING, Father came home with news that made my jaw drop to my toes. "I have decided to formally enter you in the Isthmian Games."

Attempting to stand, I lost my footing, collided with a table, and sprawled back into my chair.

One of the four celebrated Panhellenic festivals, the Isthmian Games were honored by people throughout Graecia. Though they were not as highly esteemed as the famed Olympic Games, the Isthmian Games held a favored place in Corinth. Every other spring, the world gathered to admire the athletic and musical talents of the young.

"The last time I tried to play the harp, the ducks stopped laying eggs," I croaked. "Please, do not humiliate me."

"I do not wish to enter you for the musical competition. I have my heart set on the short sprint race." If I had not been on the chair, I would have landed on the floor.

To the outraged disapproval of conservative

Greek families, women were permitted to participate in some of the athletic games in Corinth. They even raced two-horse war chariots. While I could not handle a horse, I knew how to run.

The short sprint—or *stadion* race—could be run under one minute and was one of the events in which women were allowed to participate.

"You can't mean it!" I gasped, sounding like a frog. The idea of running a race before thousands of people when I could barely carry on a conversation in public seemed ludicrous.

He ruffled my short hair. "This will be good for you."

I slapped a palm against my sweating forehead. "I have a mother who rarely permits me to step outside and a father who has no scruples about my participation in one of the Panhellenic festivals. Couldn't the gods have given me just *one* normal parent?"

"The people of Corinth love their athletes. True, some of the older conservatives will cringe upon seeing a woman enter a race. But the young will applaud your courage." He buffed his nail with a corner of his toga. "Especially if you have reasonable success at the *stadion*. It would be a good opportunity for you to make some friends."

So he had not missed the debacle with Diantha and her friends. I still felt small when I remembered the sound of their cutting laughter. The thought of winning the admiration of Corinth, and of rubbing Diantha's face in my victory, made me reevaluate my intention to refuse Father. If, as he suggested, a modicum of success opened opportunities for me to make a true friend or two, then I had every reason to agree to his plan.

I tamped down the twinges of unease that made my stomach swirl like a restless eddy, and focused on my dream of victory. To run, to race, to show those pale-faced girls what I could do. To win! The possibility breathed new life into me. To my delight, Theo entered the chariot races. We had almost two years to prepare ourselves for the games. They seemed too far away to be real, a distant dream I could push to a recess of my mind and forget.

Later that week, our neighbor Servius, Justus's father, invited us to a formal banquet at his home. Dressed in our best tunics, we traipsed over to Servius's villa on foot, forgoing a carriage for such a short distance. It had rained most of the morning, and though the downpour had ceased, steel-gray clouds continued to cover the sun, and in their shadow, I missed a puddle. My foot sank up to my ankle, smearing mud over my sandals, squishing between my toes. Father handed me a handkerchief. It was like trying to dry a pond with a sponge.

As was customary, I took off my sandals when

we arrived, and a slave tried his best to wash my feet, but the edge of my tunic had become hopelessly stained with mud.

Worse still, I realized as I made my entrance that my best tunic seemed shabby in the company that had gathered at Servius's house. Women adorned with colorful jewels sparkled in their priceless silk robes. Their necks and arms were embellished with gold and silver beads, winking in the lamplight. They floated from one group to another with an ease I could only dream of. This was a gathering of the sophisticated and the beautiful. I felt coarse in comparison.

I gulped as I glimpsed Diantha and one of her friends standing next to Justus in a corner, their heads bent toward him in a pose that suggested intimacy.

Servius welcomed my father with a gracious embrace. "And you have adorned my house by bringing the lovely Ariadne into it," he said, affectionately kissing my cheek. His appearance shocked me. I remembered him as a robust man, tall, muscular, with a sinewy strength that seemed unyielding. Now, he looked hollow, so frail that a strong wind might snap his bones in two. Justus had mentioned that he was unwell, but I had not realized the serious nature of his illness.

His sickness had not robbed him of his business interests, obviously, as he engaged my father in a discussion about an apple orchard he wished to purchase. Within moments, they had walked off. Theo followed them, leaving me to fend for myself.

I stood alone, shifting my weight from one foot to another. My mouth fell open when Diantha's friend approached me. I saw that her eyes were as violet as the tunic that accentuated her spectacular curves. My hope that she had come to welcome me plummeted to a quick death.

"So you are the brazen wench who plans to run the *stadion*," she drawled.

"I am the brazen wench who plans to win it," I said, chin high. I would have swallowed a wriggling mouse rather than reveal how awed I felt by her.

She arched an eyebrow, the violet eyes sparkling like the amethysts at her throat. "Pert, aren't you? For a girl who will bring nothing but disgrace to Corinth by running in a public race."

"I predict she will inspire a new trend," Justus drawled from behind me. "Every little girl will now dream of registering for the short sprint at the Isthmian Games. Ariadne will make such a pretty display."

My head snapped up and I bristled. *Little girl?* I was about to reply with a sharp retort when reason took hold. Justus had praised me in public, extending his considerable influence to defend me.

Caught between appreciation for his support and annoyance at his derisive compliment, I said, "Thank you," though the words almost made me choke.

"*Pretty!* Surely that's an exaggeration," the woman said, readjusting the folds of silk at her chest, drawing attention to her exquisite figure.

"Stop tormenting the child, Claudia." Justus drew her shapely arm through his own and walked away with his smirking guest swaying next to him.

Theo came to stand by me. "I would have come to your rescue, but Justus seemed to have it in hand. He is the best of men."

I reached for a large piece of melon from a nearby tray and shoved it into my mouth.

We found an unoccupied couch, and I was about to recount the full story when a slim girl about my age threw herself next to me. "Isn't she simply vile?"

"Who?" I said, nonplussed, staring. She was short, flat-chested, and wrapped in a tunic even plainer than my own.

"Claudia, that's who. I heard what she said to you. I swear by Hera, she has fangs and talons." She pushed out her chest and fluttered her lashes. " 'Surely that's an exaggeration,' " she mimicked, making Theo and me grin. "Don't listen to a word, Ariadne," she said. "You are ravishing."

My eyes widened. "You know my name?"

"You are famous! The first girl from a good Corinthian family to register for an athletic event in the Isthmian Games. My friends are dying to meet you."

Something in me melted a little. Something hard and corrosive. My shoulders relaxed. "Do you have a name?" I said.

"I am Claudia the Younger. I have four sisters, and all of them are called Claudia, in honor of the great family connection."

The Claudians were a mighty family in Rome, related by blood to such notables as Caesar Augustus and Tiberius. I arched a brow. "Impressive."

"The connection is minor. Enough to foist the name upon the girls in our family. That Claudia, whom you had the ill luck of meeting, is my oldest sister."

"No!"

"It is the tragic truth. Pity me. I share a house with that harridan." She leaned toward me. "By any chance, would you be willing to teach me to run?"

I sized up the thin arms and legs. "I can try."

"That is all I ask! I am trying to discover something at which I am gifted. So far, I have failed learning several musical instruments, including the flute and cithara, I am miserable at weaving and needlework of every variety, and I can't paint or cook." She ticked the subjects off on her fingers. "There must be some endeavor at which I excel."

Not surprisingly, it turned out that Claudia was not gifted at running, either. But I discovered one exquisite talent in the slim girl. She knew how to be a true friend.

When Justus told me that he planned to travel to Athens and visit Dionysius while conducting business there, I sat down to write a letter to my brother. My letters to him were usually carefully phrased, devoid of personal revelations as I suspected they would be inspected before they found their way into his hands. On this occasion, knowing that Justus would give the missive to my brother personally, I wrote more freely.

As the words flowed without restrictions, I felt my heart contract. I missed my brother beyond words: missed his dear face, the serious eyes, the slight shake of his head when I was ridiculous or impish, the tolerant smile when I chose to be stubborn. A part of me had been torn when I left him behind in Athens. A part of me kept tearing each day that I prevented him from coming to Corinth.

I blinked back tears. I aimed to cheer him, not depress the man with maudlin thoughts. I took up the stylus and began to write.

From Ariadne, your devoted sister,
to my beloved Dionysius,

I send you my heart and greetings with this letter. How I give thanks that you are well and prospering, dear brother.

By now, you will have heard of my intention to participate in the upcoming Isthmian Games. Before you lay the blame for such a reckless scheme at my door, you should know it was Father's idea. I neither nagged him nor begged him into compliance. In any case, it is done, and you will not be ashamed, I hope! And Theo has been training with Justus for the chariot races. I only wish you could be here to complete our joy.

Your absence is the one blight in my life, Dionysius. I know I am the cause of it.

With an angry swipe, I wiped the tears that had dampened my cheek. So much for being cheerful.

Theo and Father will write their own letters. I wish you good health and happiness, and hope the years will pass quickly so that I may see you again. Pet Herodotus the cat for me, and do not give my regards to Grandfather. Father says I must send Mother salutations as befits a dutiful daughter. And so I greet her most dutifully, and wish her as far away from Corinth as a tempest.

With all my affection,
Ariadne

CHAPTER 7

—w—

RUNNING SWALLOWED a large part of my focus and time. When he was not with Justus, learning what he could about chariot races, Theo showed me new exercises, which he learned at the palaestra. One day he returned from the gymnasium with a new trick. "I met a man from Crete who taught us how to flip. Watch."

He stood perfectly still for a moment, then jumped backward. His body didn't leap high enough, and he landed on his belly. I laughed so hard, I must have turned blue. Theo ignored me. Dusting himself off, he came to his feet and tried again. And again, until he managed to do it. I was enthralled.

"This man could flip forward and backward, and leap from a whole story down without hurting himself," Theo said. "He seemed boneless. He assured us that with practice, we could learn to do the same."

"Teach me," I said, captivated by the new sport and determined to master it.

Though Theo himself had only grasped the basics of the exercise, he started to teach me what he knew. The rest we made up or learned by experimenting.

Theo and I pushed ourselves to become proficient in flips, cartwheels, and tumbling. We kept this new exercise a secret. While we were experimenting, we were clumsy and often fell. If Father had seen our bruises, he would have put a stop to our activities. Day after day, Theo and I pressed our bodies until we grasped the technique and correct form needed for the sport, gaining confidence and expertise.

As we improved, we grew used to wrapping this part of our lives in secrecy. I suppose we both felt that one day we would share this new talent with the world. We simply were not ready yet.

With practice, the flipping, jumping, twisting in the air, and landing with precision had become second nature. To my delight, the grueling drills we put ourselves through made our bodies more agile, so that my balance improved and I could run faster than ever before.

In the spring, Theo's palaestra held a public competition. Although this was merely a local event, the school, which was famed for its excellence, had drawn a strong showing of influential patrons from Corinth, and the modest arena teemed with an eager crowd. They had invited Justus, their exalted graduate, to host the competitions and hand out the awards this day.

I spotted Claudia the Elder and Diantha among the crowds and suspected it was Justus's presence that had drawn them to a humble athletic contest. They walked by me without acknowledging my presence. This was the first formal wrestling match I had ever attended, and I refused to allow their snub to ruin my enjoyment. I was there to support Theo, who was participating in the competitions.

I saw my fair share of well-oiled, sun-bronzed male bodies that morning, strutting about like roosters, crowing for attention. Most young men competed in the nude, though some, like Theo, opted to wear a small loincloth. I pretended not to ogle, especially when my father would clear his throat loudly and elbow me in the ribs.

Justus opened the ceremonies with a short but moving speech about courage and perseverance. The spectators clapped enthusiastically when he finished. Claudia threw a pink rose at his feet, making the crowds cheer even louder. Inexplicably, I felt a surge of anger at her presumption. Who was Claudia to act so familiar with him? With a smile, Justus picked up the flower. I was relieved when he threw it back into the throng.

Tamping down my temper, I cheered when Theo entered the arena. Months of relentless practice and the resulting bulge in muscle had turned my foster brother into a brutal force of nature. He was a deadly combination of balance and strength. Our secret exercises had toned his body, giving him the agility and speed of a panther.

Wrestlers cast lots to determine their combat partners, and Theo found himself matched against a young man of his own age. They were of even size and weight, so the outcome would depend on skill, perseverance, and boldness. The boys, pumped up with excitement and slippery from the application of too much oil, leapt at each other the moment the match began. Theo had an edge from the start, taking his opponent down with a shoulder hold.

The next round lasted a matter of minutes before Theo grasped the tall boy in a chin lock, making short work of the match. To my stupefaction, he defeated his next opponent as well, besting an older and more experienced wrestler. This placed Theo in the final round for the prize, facing Kylon, the previous year's champion at the palaestra.

Except for Father, Justus, and me, as well as a polite smattering of Father's friends, no one rooted for my foster brother. He was a nobody who was threatening a well-liked champion. The man was bigger than Theo and more experienced. I had barely had time to blink when Kylon flipped Theo onto his back. He scrambled onto Theo's stomach, his broad shoulders flexing as he tried to strangle my foster brother. The crowd roared its approval. Theo tried to roll away but found himself stuck under the massive weight. Within moments, he was choking, his face turning purple.

I thought an official would intercept since a point had already been scored, but no one called a halt. The referee wanted to force Theo to capitulate, ending the match early. He did not know my foster brother. Theo did not give up easily. Father stood rigid by my side, his brow drenched in sweat. I pressed a fist against my mouth.

Somehow Theo managed to grasp Kylon's arm. With lightning speed, he twisted and rolled, throwing Kylon on his back, landing on top of him before the huge man could escape. The point belonged to Theo. An official immediately signaled for the men to rise, giving the wrestlers a few moments to recover. They were now even, having each earned a point.

At a sign from the referee, the two men came together again. This time, Theo took Kylon down so swiftly that I could not even discern how he had done it. He slammed his body on top of the other man and followed through with a powerful choke hold that forced a chalk-faced Kylon to concede defeat. The spectators were silent with shock for a moment. Then Father and I screamed with delight. I could not help grinning when Justus joined his voice to ours, pumping his fist in the air and shouting my foster brother's name.

Theo was declared victor and awarded a wreath of laurel leaves by Justus, though the crowd's applause was muted at best.

After putting on a short tunic, Theo joined us, glowing with exhilaration and oil, looking like one of the immortals. A sculptor trailed him, pestering him to model for one of his statues. "With all that muscle, you would make a perfect Ares, young man. Who better to pose as the god of war?" he was saying.

Theo blushed, making us laugh. "Perhaps another time," he said. Asking Theo to stand still for any length of time was like asking a bee to pirouette to the music of a flute. He simply was incapable.

Diantha ambled past us just at that moment. She lingered for a moment and gazed at Theo. "The foundling wins," she said, her tone disparaging. "Corinth's standards are slipping."

I lunged, planning to wrestle her to the ground, when Theo grabbed one arm and my father the other, pulling me back. "Let her be," my level-headed foster brother whispered. I could tell from his pallor and gritted teeth that Diantha's words had cut deep.

He had fought valiantly and won every match

with grace. Yet instead of holding him in high esteem, Corinth had spared him a stingy applause and barely given him his victor's due. All because he came from dubious parentage. I wanted to weep at the unfairness of it.

Theo reminded me of the butterfly bush I had once planted in our garden. With great care, I had been tending the scraggly plant, nurturing it with special feed and plentiful water. For my reward, it produced clusters of purple flowers that drew butterflies of breathtaking beauty. It was my pride and joy, that plant. I was astonished when Father told me that on the isle of Britannia, butterfly bushes were considered a weed, and the inhabitants pulled them out by the root and discarded them.

All that beauty, a weed! I could not conceive it.

Now, as Diantha and the rest of Corinth called my brother a foundling instead of a champion, I felt the same incomprehension. How could they be so blind? How could they not see the treasure he was?

Diantha and Claudia made their way to Justus, who stood surrounded by a knot of admirers. To my surprise, he pushed past the tangle of fans, leaving Diantha mid-speech, and walked to us.

"Brilliant match, Theo," he said, clapping my foster brother on the back.

Theo grinned, his eyes shining at the compliment. "When you were my age, you won your first chariot race at the Isthmian Games. *That* is what I call brilliant."

"One accomplishment does not diminish the other. Do not sell yourself short. I could never wrestle so well as you."

I noticed his attention wavering, and when I followed the direction of his gaze, I saw a man dressed in a Greek tunic shrieking at a young girl.

"That is my steward," Justus said with a frown.

The man bellowed at the girl again, looking enraged. Without a word, Justus took off toward the pair. Before he could reach them, the steward grabbed the girl's arm roughly and twisted it, bringing her to her knees. She was pleading with him. Her words came to an abrupt halt when he backhanded her across the face, his ring leaving a faint trail of blood. I cringed, nauseated by his violence.

Justus slithered through the crowd like an eel and skidded to a halt next to the girl. The man had his arm raised, about to deliver another strike to her already-bruised cheek. Justus grabbed a fistful of fabric at the man's chest and pushed him back. Losing his balance, the steward sprawled on the ground. I gave Theo a silent look and began to run in their direction, Theo in my wake. I wanted to be close at hand should Justus need help.

"How dare you hit the child? She is half your size!" Justus was saying when we arrived. A vein pulsed at the base of his neck.

His steward sat frozen to the ground. "Master! She disobeyed me."

"You know I forbid the beating of slaves. Especially the women."

"That was not what I would consider a beating." The steward gave a weak smile and made to rise. "I barely grazed her. They need a little discipline or they run wild."

Justus grew very quiet. His eyes narrowed. "Do you *graze* my slaves often?"

The man sat down again abruptly. "No, master."

The girl dropped her gaze. A tear coursed down her cheek, followed by another. Justus dropped to one knee in front of her. "Niobe, has he done this to you before?"

The girl peeked quickly at the steward and shook her head no.

"He has no power to hurt you. Not ever again. I give you my promise. Now tell me the truth. Has he hit you before?"

The girl gave a quick nod.

"She lies!" the steward howled.

Justus sprang to his feet. "Speak one more word without permission and I will make you regret it." He turned his attention to the girl. "Have you seen him hit others?"

She lifted large brown eyes, liquid with tears and dread, and stared at him mutely.

"Be brave. Be truthful, and you shall have nothing to fear from him. I will protect you." Justus's voice was soft, brimming with fatherly comfort. I felt my chest squeeze tight as I watched his gentleness with the girl.

"He only hits us with his hands, master. Never with a whip."

"You see? I told you I did not beat them." The steward straightened his twisted tunic.

Justus ground his teeth, his jawbone protruding. Without moving a single muscle, he exuded threat. The steward recoiled.

"Consider yourself unemployed. If I were you, I would leave Corinth. You will find it hard to find work in this city. I will see to that."

My father, who had been speaking with friends, joined our circle. "Wasn't that your steward who just raced out of here, Justus?"

"Not any longer." Justus pulled a hand through his hair and blew out a long breath. He patted the girl on the head. "Shall we go home, Niobe?"

We joined them on their walk home, and Justus recounted to my father how he had caught the steward striking Niobe. "I do not put up with the mistreatment of my slaves," he said. "No one will raise a hand against a helpless woman in my house."

It took me a moment to realize that I was

crying. I dashed the tears from my face and tried to crush the rush of emotion that was choking me. Justus had protected her. He had considered her worthy of a fight and made sure of her safety. He had done for a slave what my own mother had refused to do for me.

CHAPTER 8

—⁓—

CLAUDIA THE YOUNGER lived in the smallest house located at the farthest edge of a fashionable neighborhood near the agora. Five boisterous sisters made the place too cramped for comfort. I tried to avoid visiting there as often as I could, which suited my friend. We fell into a habit of spending several days a week at my house.

In spite of the time we spent in each other's company, it was by sheer accident that I discovered Claudia's secret shame. I had just received a package from my brother, and it was with no small amount of pride that I showed Claudia the scroll Dionysius had sent me. Stretched across my bed, she sat up and looked at it askance. "What is it?"

"Book one of Ovid's *Metamorphoses*. I love the first line. 'I intend to speak of forms changed into new entities.' " I waved a hand to stress the words. " 'Changed into new entities.' Doesn't that give you hope for this life? Hope that we can be changed, transformed into something new, something better? Do you want to read it with me?"

She hung her head. "I can't."

"Why not?"

"I can barely read. Ovid is beyond me."

I studied her red face in surprise. I had heard Claudia the Elder read a sophisticated though rude poem at a party. She read with passable facility. "I thought you and your sisters were literate."

"Father forked out enough silver to pay for the education of my two eldest sisters. After that, his funds ran out. He was too busy to teach us himself, and my mother too overworked to pay the matter any heed." She set the scroll aside.

"The Stoic philosopher Musonius Rufus argues eloquently for the education of women."

Claudia held up her palms in surrender. "I have no quarrel with you or Musonius Rufus. I wish I could read. I have simply never had the opportunity to learn." She hesitated. "My sister calls me ignorant, and that is what I am, though it shames me to admit it."

"Then I shall teach you," I said.

That was when we discovered Claudia's second talent. Her mind proved nimble for grammar and languages. She consumed everything I taught her with ravenous hunger.

An almost incandescent satisfaction consumed me as I taught my friend. I loved the knowledge that, day by day, I was helping to change her life. My new endeavor could not have come at a better time.

Without consulting me, Theo had made a momentous decision. He had accepted an invitation to work for Justus and his father, leaving him little time for me. When he could, he still trained with me for the Isthmian Games, though he had grown obsessed with Justus's horses and spent a great deal of his spare hours in the stables, learning what he could about chariot races.

My time with Claudia helped to fill the hole Theo's absence had left in my life. It was not a fair exchange. Theo had become a part of me, the one foundation that did not crumble. I had never known life without his constancy and affection. Claudia's companionship helped to dull the ache.

A new routine established itself in our lives. In the mornings I taught Claudia. In the afternoons I trained for the *stadion*. I had not given up on the dream of proving my worth to Diantha and Claudia the Elder, as well as all of Corinth, along with my mother and grandfather. And, well, everyone.

Diantha and Claudia the Elder and the rest of their friends continued to make their disdain of me palpable whenever we met in public. I found that the sting of their cruelty did not grow dull with time, especially since their opinion held great sway, and influenced others of my generation to follow suit.

The Dianthas and Claudias of this world ruled my heart with too much ease. The hurt of my old life lingered so that I felt the cut of every rejection with a greater resounding sharpness than it deserved. Claudia the Younger became my one haven.

One morning, she arrived at our house, two other girls in tow. "This is Claudia the Fourth." She introduced me to a girl with violet eyes and Claudia the Younger's dainty physique. "As you may have guessed, she is my fourth sister. And this—" she indicated the girl with curly blonde hair and dimpled cheeks—"is my cousin Junia."

"Welcome," I said, at a loss. Claudia was the only female friend I had. I was not accustomed to visits from strangers.

Claudia the Fourth straightened the skirt of her faded tunic. "Claudia the Younger says you would be willing to teach us to read and to study philosophy."

I gave my friend a wide-eyed look. She grinned and shrugged. Junia dimpled at me, showing a row of admirably straight teeth. "Please, Ariadne. Would you teach us?"

"Do you really want to learn?"

Three heads began bobbing at the same time. I bit my nail. "Fine," I said. "But I am calling you Fourth." I pointed at Claudia's older sister. "By the time I say the whole thing, I will be too old to teach anyone."

And that was how I began my own school for women.

Taharqa the Kushite, the sailor who had saved us on the *Whirring Wings* and delivered us to Father's door when we first arrived from Athens, had fallen into the habit of visiting us whenever his travels brought him to Corinth. He had become a favorite with the whole household. That afternoon, he showed up unannounced.

"Taharqa!" I cried in welcome when I spied him.

"You look like a proper lady," he said, pointing to my hair, which had grown out and now fell partway down my back. "That is goood."

"I will be eighteen in a month."

"Truly? I thought that since you run so fast, time might not be able to catch you. I see it has ensnared you the way it does the rest of us."

Drawn to the sound of our voices, Father came to the vestibule. "Taharqa! I rejoice to see your ugly face."

The Kushite, who had an undeniably handsome visage, grinned and placed an affectionate hand on Father's shoulder. "Galenos, my friend. You are as old and withered as ever." His grin wavered and he looked at his feet. "I fear I bring you poor news."

"My son?"

My heart sank. Taharqa sometimes carried messages between Father and Dionysius, and had come to know my brother well.

Taharqa shook his head. "He is well."

"Then it is nothing that cannot be undone," Father said, leading us into his tablinum. He served Taharqa and himself a cup of his best Spanish wine once we had settled down. "Now tell me. What is this ill news you bear?"

"Did you not tell me that you had purchased a share in the ship *Paralus*?"

"I have."

"A large share?"

"Most of the ship and its cargo belong to me. A new venture."

"I fear it has gone down."

Father took a sharp breath. "Are you certain?"

"There is no doubt, Galenos. I spoke with one of the sailors who survived the wreck. He said the ship hit an unexpected squall and was driven against rocks. It was smashed to bits. Most of the men and the cargo it carried sank within moments. Only a handful of sailors survived, and that was by a miracle."

"A complete loss, then." Father's hands shook as he placed his cup back on the table.

"I fear so. A monstrous casualty in life and goods. Will you . . . be all right?"

I sat up straighter at Taharqa's tone. His question carried an edge that hinted at more than a casual inquiry regarding my father's well-being.

Father tented his hands and looked out the window. "It was foolish of me to risk such a sum. Sea trade is hazardous business."

"It could have happened to anyone," Taharqa said. "It could have happened to me."

"But you are not the one who spent your savings on a perilous venture."

I gulped. Father loathed speaking of money. He avoided every reference to expenses and accounts. The situation must be dire indeed for him to sink into such a discussion.

When Theo arrived home that evening, I told him the account of the ship's loss. He sagged onto a couch, knuckles pressing into his knees. "That is grave news. Galenos told me how much he had put into the purchase of the *Paralus*. I don't know how he will recover, or even meet expenses for the rest of the year."

"Is it that bad?"

Theo nodded. "Your father will be frantic." He dragged his hand through his hair. "I have saved a bit of money. He can have all of it. But it won't be near enough to save him, I fear."

A week melted into two. Father did not bring up the *Paralus* again, and when Theo and I tried to broach the subject, he swept our questions aside. I worried silently, wondering how to address our financial difficulties. One night, as I lay sleepless in my bed, a faint and subtle sound in the courtyard drew me to the window. A host of innocent things might have caused it: the rustling of a curtain, a prowling cat, wind moving through a tree. But something about it felt out of place.

My lamp had burned out, and I had not bothered to relight it. Used to the darkness, my eyes quickly spanned the distance as I looked into the courtyard through the narrow window of my chamber. I thought I detected movement. There! A man dressed in a dark, short tunic and cropped military trousers was moving furtively across our atrium.

A thief! Something about the way he moved seemed familiar. I realized he was not coming in, but had left the house through a side door. Had he already robbed us? He must have been stealthy indeed to do so, undetected. Without thinking, I crawled onto the parapet, tucked my tunic into my belt, and began to climb down the fluted column abutting my chamber. The man turned when I jumped to the ground. I shifted into the shadows with a quick move. He could not see me, but I saw him for a fraction of a moment. That was enough. I recognized him at once.

It was my father.

Why would he sneak out of his own house when there was a perfectly good front door available? I told myself it was no affair of mine. If the man had private assignations, who was I to object?

Father slithered out through the courtyard gate, closing it softly behind him. I paused. Then I thought of the quarrel with my mother and how our family had splintered because of some secret Father kept. I resolved with sudden determination to discover what it was. Rising out of my hiding place, I rushed to the gate and opened it, but my father had long since disappeared.

The next day I forgot all about Father's strange departure from our house when something even more confounding consumed my attention. Dionysius showed up at our doorstep, unannounced.

It was our custom to eat supper fashionably early, and by the time the first course was on the table, Dionysius appeared in our midst, a big grin splitting his face. I screamed with delight and bolted toward him. Theo, who by rare coincidence had stayed home for dinner that evening, joined me in squeezing my brother until he yelped. My father sat frozen on the couch, his eyes all but swallowing my brother.

Dionysius disentangled himself from Theo and me and sprinted to him. The two melded in an embrace I shall never forget. It was as if the gods had turned back the clock and Dionysius were a little boy again, burrowing inside Father's arms, finding safety and belonging there.

"I missed you," Dionysius said. "I could not bear to stay away one more day."

"My son." Normally loquacious, Father seemed to have lost all his words save those two. He repeated them over and over. I waited until Dionysius turned his face to me and then ran to join them. In the midst of our joy, I sensed something missing and realized that Theo was not with us. He was rooted to the spot where I had left him. His face had a crumpled look to it, as if he wanted to cry.

I motioned him over, and Dionysius, realizing his absence, called for him. Theo came, but he sat apart from us, on the couch that faced ours.

"How did you convince Dexios to allow you to visit?" Father asked, too caught up in the shock of seeing Dionysius to notice Theo's remoteness.

My brother pulled on an earlobe. "I did not."

Silence fell. "I see," Father said.

"I will return tomorrow, before Grandfather explodes. I simply needed to see you, if only for a few hours."

Father grinned. "I'm glad you came. We shall deal with Dexios's anger when it comes. It will be worth having you here."

"You are the best of fathers," my brother said. I gulped when I looked at Theo. He had turned the color of bones.

Early the next day, before my mother and

grandfather could turn the combined force of their considerable hostility toward my father, Dionysius returned to Athens. He promised to smooth Grandfather's ruffled feathers. His visit had breathed new life into my father. But afterward, I noticed Theo spent even less time with us.

Two weeks later, our fortunes took an unexpected turn. Father received a sizable profit from a modest investment he had made the previous year. I was too young to understand how so significant a sum of money could be gained from so trifling an investment. But in truth, I did not care. What mattered to me was that the cloying air of defeat that had clung to Father since the sinking of the *Paralus* was lifted.

Our salvation from impending poverty coincided with an exciting event that had the city abuzz for months. Theo brought us the news. "Have you heard that the new *praefectus*, Gaius Orestes, was robbed recently?"

We were sitting in the courtyard and eating with desultory appetites. Summer had come with a heavy hand that year and the heat carried with it the stench of garbage and an oppressive humidity that made breathing hard.

I fanned myself between bites of fruit. "Orestes? Isn't he the official who became unpopular within three months of arriving here?"

Father popped an olive in his mouth. "Matters are dire indeed when the auditor needs an auditor. Orestes treats the state treasury like his personal inheritance. Worse yet, he makes the lives of his subordinates a waking nightmare."

"They have their revenge now." Theo grabbed his chalice and gulped down spring water in large mouthfuls. "Someone robbed him last night. Apparently the thief did not even leave him a pin to hold his toga in place."

I grinned. "That is a tragedy."

Togas were an awkward garment to manage. If not for the social statement they made, no man would ever willingly wear one. Only a Roman citizen like my father had the privilege of arraying himself in its bulky lengths. My father's dresser pressed the folds of his toga for hours, using delicate wooden squares to make the pleats look neat before pinning them on his shoulder. A man was not supposed to use a pin on his toga, but the mass of fabric on the left arm grew cumbersome, and most men used them for convenience.

"Here is where the story turns into a comedy," Theo said. "Orestes's wife, who had been bathing, came in just as the thief was about to leave her chamber. In her surprise, she dropped her towel."

I put down the fig I had dangled in front of my mouth. "What happened?"

"The thief turned his back respectfully, and restored the towel to the lady with his eyes averted."

I giggled. "She must have been disappointed."

"Ariadne!" Father said, sounding shocked.

The women of Corinth had an unfortunate reputation, one most of us had not earned justly. The world used the term "Corinthian girl" to refer to women of a certain profession. This inference came from the many cult prostitutes who served in the temples, especially the ones belonging to Aphrodite. In truth, the average Corinthian girl was as chaste as any other. If my father was an example to go by, Corinthian parents were as vigilant of their daughters' virtue as the rest of Graecia or Italia.

"Your pardon. What did the lady do then, Theo?"

"Apparently, she was so impressed by her nocturnal visitor's manners that she complimented him. 'You are courteous for a thief,' she told him. 'I am a thief of things, my lady; I do not rob virtue,' he said."

I roared with laughter. "Did she not try to stop him? Scream the house down?"

"By the time she raised the alarm, the culprit had flown too far afield to be captured."

"What did he look like, this thief?"

"No one knows. He wore a mask. According to the lady, he had the cultured accents of a man familiar with Homer. The city has already dubbed him the Honorable Thief."

"He won't have an honorable end when they capture him."

Father picked up a fan of swan feathers. "*If* they capture him. Corinth seems to have more love for this Honorable Thief than it does for Gaius Orestes. There is not much motivation to find him."

CHAPTER 9

JUSTUS AND SERVIUS were entrusting Theo with heavier responsibilities. He was traveling more, sometimes with Justus, and sometimes with one of Servius's managers in order to learn their business better. One rare morning Theo surprised me by dropping in on my class of young women. I found their response to his presence amusing. Lips plumped, backs straightened, hair flicked over shoulders.

"Who are you studying?" he asked, unrolling one of the scrolls.

"Ovid and Seneca," I said.

"Well, they are," Fourth confessed. "I am still just trying to read."

Theo nodded with compassion. "Latin can be a challenge."

Claudia asked, "Who is your philosophy teacher?"

"Abantes," Theo said.

Claudia groaned. "Not that old buffoon. My cousin once told him he should teach the lyre instead."

"He doesn't know how to play the lyre," Theo said.

"He doesn't know how to teach philosophy either. That does not stop him."

Theo grinned. I wondered if he knew the effect that breezy smile had on Claudia. I sensed that she had lost her heart to my foster brother. Theo did not seem to reciprocate her feelings. I noticed the subtle distance he maintained from her. I knew Theo would not intentionally hurt her. He would not play with her feelings to make himself appear more a man. But he could not protect her from a broken heart either.

My father's great-great-great-grandmother Agathe was born to one of the noble families of Corinth. She had been married off to an Athenian man, a merging of politics rather than hearts. Father still had some of her letters to a long-dead friend, which spoke of Corinth with longing. She had not been a willing bride, apparently. But she had been a fortunate one.

Two weeks after Agathe set sail for Athens, the Roman army attacked the Greek military forces gathered outside Corinth. Rome won an easy victory. In a matter of days, the Roman general Mummius smashed his way into the city.

He came not merely to vanquish, but to demolish. Corinth had had the audacity to rebel against

Rome. Mummius intended to teach Corinth an unforgettable lesson.

He marched in, followed by ranks of soldiers the likes of which the world had never known. They executed the entire male population of Corinth. Every woman and child who was not put to the sword became a slave. Mummius looted the city, stripped it of its treasures, and torched the rest, leaving nothing but ashes.

When Mummius finished with Corinth, there were a handful of peasants left behind to mourn its destruction. Corinth and its people had all but vanished.

Agathe was one of the few true Corinthians who survived that massacre. Some of her history trickled its way into our lineage. Thus I was one of a smattering of people in the city who could legitimately claim to have the blood of ancient Corinth.

The new Corinth, the one my father had grown up in, owed its existence to another Roman. Caesar himself had commanded the rebuilding of Corinth a hundred years after its destruction. He was no fool. He knew the potential of the city, knew its priceless worth for trade. So he resurrected Corinth from the bitter ashes of its annihilation like the phoenix. Rome tore the city down and Rome salvaged it from the grave. Hail Rome.

This Corinth looked more Roman than Greek

in its architecture. Its population contained an amalgam of people: freedmen and Greeks and Romans mixed together. We were Greek and Roman without being truly either. Bold and confident, rich and religious, bawdy and brash. We held on to old traditions with tenacious defiance, and made new ones of our own with an easy disregard for the past.

Julius Caesar's city was a new entity entirely. Its topography remained the same. Beyond that, a fresh world emerged. The roads, houses, engineering, architecture, all became Roman. The residents spoke Latin and came from different parts of the empire with a hunger for riches. The new Corinth was a city to dream in. We were everything Athens was not and we were proud of that reality. Corinth had become a center of commerce and trade, unparalleled in the Roman world.

Time and Rome divided Corinth into two parts: the Greek city that existed before General Mummius laid it to waste, and the Roman city that was built on the ashes of that destruction.

I had much in common with the city of my birth. Like Corinth, my history had a before and an after. Divorce divided my life into two parts. What we had before, and what we salvaged after. When I ran away from Athens, I thought I had solved the problems that had plagued me in Grandfather's house. I thought I had slain the monsters that chased me. But the monsters had exacted their price. And they were still exacting a price.

Divorce left nothing the same. It pumped its poison with pinprick precision so that we barely noticed its lingering effects.

On the surface, life moved on as always. Theo and I celebrated our birthdays quietly. The changes came slowly, so inconspicuous that I did not notice as they carved their mark into our lives with the patience of water careening over rock. It was as if with each passing day, Theo slid further away from me.

He always had a good excuse for his absence. But I could feel his heart withdrawing from me as surely as his presence. I felt as if I were losing him bit by bit. He was detaching himself from Father and me, guarding his heart against us. I did not realize then that this distance had ancient roots. Roots that sank into the rotting soil of my parents' divorce.

Each morning I would tell myself that I was imagining this disconnection. I would promise myself to mend it, breach it. Reach the man who could have been my brother. At night, when I slipped into my bed, I would pretend that I had not failed.

One afternoon, Theo arrived home followed by an older woman. I dropped my watering can when he announced that he had squandered his hard-earned savings to purchase her from the slave block. She had seen at least forty summers, though by some trick of nature, her skin had not turned leathery and creased. Delia had been a hairdresser to the wealthy until her debts forced her into slavery. She had a filthy mouth and swore constantly. My father would later put her on bread and water rations for a week to try to curb her crude language. We did not notice a great improvement, though she did stop discussing my father's bathroom habits after that.

I asked Theo, when he brought her home, why he had bankrupted himself buying a slave for whom he had no use.

He shrugged a wide shoulder. "She had massive bruises everywhere. Did you see? The slave master who owned her is known for his cruelty. You can imagine how she would have provoked such a man with that mouth of hers. She must have endured indescribable cruelty."

"That's why you bought her? The bruises? Gods, Theo. The slaves will love you. They bear stripes and wounds by the hundreds. Not everyone is as gracious to their servants as we are."

He rubbed the bridge of his nose. "Not the bruises. The eyes. I noticed as I passed by that they brimmed with outrage at whatever she had suffered. In spite of all her fury, I knew she had no hope of relief." He angled back against a silk cushion and crossed his arms. His face had turned pale. "I'd like to think that if I have a mother living in a far-flung corner of this world, someone would take pity on her if she were in anguish."

My mouth fell open. This was the first time Theo had ever made reference to his mother. I had assumed he never thought about his real parents.

His detached tone did not deceive me. It was obvious that Theo cared passionately about his origins. For eighteen years I had looked upon him as my true brother. And yet, for eighteen years he had wondered who his mother and father really were.

I wished to pester him with questions. Did he want to search for his family? And if he should find them, what then? What did he hope to accomplish?

Were *we* not enough? Did we not lavish him with sufficient love? One look at his expression and I knew not to venture further. He had opened the door for a glimpse and slammed it shut. I swallowed my questions and spent a sleepless night thinking of my Theo longing for his mother.

I was exercising in the plot next door when to my delight Theo joined me, a bag of grapes under one arm and a jar of water under the other.

121

Gratefully, I gulped down a few swigs of the water he offered and challenged him to a race. The years fell away as we stood side by side in our old clothes, knees bent, arms at the ready. We were children again, without the entanglements of adulthood, without the complications of our bruised hearts.

"To the old tree and back," Theo said, and we took off.

I beat him, but by a small margin. Whatever he had been doing to prepare for the chariot race had increased his speed.

"You have improved. I used to leave you in the dust." I grabbed a bunch of grapes from the bag and stuffed a handful in my mouth. "Do you want to climb?"

He flashed a smile. "Only if you pull me up."

Climbing the sycamore tree did not present a challenge for me. I found a few good handholds, and pushing my toes into hollows and over protruding knobs, I lifted myself into the leafy canopy within moments. Tucking a sturdy but slim branch into the bend of my knees, I hung upside down toward the ground, my hands free.

Theo grasped my wrists and I pulled. I was no delicate flower; constant exercise had turned my body into a hard mass of muscles. But Theo weighed a lot more than I did, and lifting him all the way up was no easy task. My arms and belly quivered by the time he sat next to me.

"What have you been eating?" I sniffed. "Stones?"

Theo punched his chest with a fist. "Hard as rock." To prove it, he did a handstand on the branch, jumped, twisted in the air, and landed back on the branch. Delia would have fainted if she had seen him.

For good measure, Theo somersaulted and sat on the branch, legs hanging casually. I scuttled until I stood over him, balanced my frame for a breath, and then leapt off. I turned in the air and grasped his thighs to prevent from falling, swinging from his legs for a moment, then jumping safely to the ground.

Barely had I landed before I flipped again, flying as high as I could, and grasping Theo's dangling ankles, I hung from him until he pulled his feet up, his legs stretched out, straight as a board. I let go, twisted one rotation, and landed safely. A moment later, Theo stood next to me.

I grinned with exhilaration. "We should do this more often."

He shrugged. "We are not children anymore." He had not kicked me when we were dangling and somersaulting in the air. He did now, with his words.

Junia arrived late to our class the next morning, panting from exertion. "My uncle stopped by our house with delicious news. The Honorable Thief struck again last night. I stayed to hear the details and then ran all the way here." She collapsed on a couch.

"I had not heard," Claudia cried. "Was he caught?"

Every few months, reports of the Honorable Thief's latest heist became the talk of all Corinth. Except for his victims, the population seemed to adore him. This was partly due to the people he chose to rob. He seemed to have a singular taste for the wealth of corrupt and unscrupulous men. There were even rumors that after each robbery, some poor family in Corinth found itself the recipient of an anonymous gift.

I believed there was more legend than truth to most of these rumors. But I enjoyed hearing the stories as much as everyone else.

"He got away as always, leaving behind his usual note," Junia said, pulling wisps of blonde hair from her face.

Since the incident with the naked lady, the bandit had begun writing short letters about his victims, signed by the appellation *the Honorable Thief*. The letters shared a delicious satirical edge and had become a popular source of amusement.

Written in Latin and often quoting literary giants, the letters found their way onto some public pillar in the dead of night. Come morning, the gleeful hordes would read the contents before an official got around to removing the scroll.

The victims were thereby robbed twice. Once of their goods, and again of their dignity. No wonder the man had gained the status of a hero in Corinth. But those he had harmed were men of influence, with power and resources enough to ensure a death sentence should his identity ever be discovered.

"What did he say?" Claudia asked.

"Whom did he rob?" I added.

"He robbed Gaius Orestes, the man whose wife gave him the title of Honorable Thief."

I gasped. "Again?"

Junia grinned, displaying winsome dimples. "He explains that. His letter began with a quote from Heraclitus:

> "No man ever steps in the same river twice, for it is not the same river and he's not the same man." So you need not accuse me of robbing you twice. The first time, I took from you what you had stolen from many. This time, I rob what you have taken from one: your own good wife.

"His *wife?*"

"He has fallen in love with another lady, it seems, and insisted on divorcing his wife. She had no choice in the matter. The court stood with him. Worse yet, he refused to pay her the full amount of her dowry, which is her right. He said she had grown too old, and therefore the dowry should be reduced."

"No!" Claudia and I cried in unison. "That is against the law," I pointed out.

"The law is flexible, it seems. In any case, the lady received a fraction of what was due her."

"Then he deserved to be robbed twice," I said. "I have grown fond of this thief. I think we should dedicate a plaque in his honor and mount it in the agora for the world to enjoy."

The Isthmian Games were almost upon us. The thought of competing in front of thousands had started to weigh on me. One evening, sleepless with anxiety, I decided to prepare a tincture of valerian root to help me rest. Little did I know as I padded on bare feet into the atrium that such a simple quest could change my life. Halfway down the staircase that led from the upper story into the courtyard, I saw my father creeping in the darkness, slithering out the side door.

This time, I was determined to follow him. Without hesitation, I snagged an old cloak of Theo's that lay crumpled on a bench where he had abandoned it. I wrapped myself in its dark folds and pulled the edge over my head to cover my long hair. I had moved fast enough to keep up with my father, and I caught the outline of his body as he turned rapidly into a narrow lane.

I tried to maintain a safe distance. Yet in spite of my noiseless steps, he must have sensed a presence behind him. Twice he turned and stared into the shadows. Unable to detect me, he moved on, and I allowed the distance between us to increase.

His path proved convoluted. He favored alleys and dirt tracks over paved roads, and we encountered no one in our circuitous journey. The confident manner with which he navigated the lanes told me that he was familiar with his route, though I myself had lost any sense of our location.

When Father came to a stop, I realized that we had arrived at an affluent neighborhood. I hid behind a bush. To my shock, he covered his face with a mask and nimbly climbed a willow tree that grew on the street. The villa was attached to a large garden, and with a deft movement, he jumped onto the wall that surrounded the garden and, grabbing hold of the branches of another tree growing within, swung himself into its foliage.

I sat down hard, wondering if the world had turned mad. What was my father doing scaling walls in the middle of the night? The longer he delayed, the more apprehensive I grew. Finally, I left my hiding place and snuck toward the villa. Tucking my tunic and cloak out of the way, I climbed the same willow my father had and nestled in its branches.

Laying my forehead against a branch, I wondered what to do. Wait? Go in search of him? As I dangled from the branches, trying to decide on a course of action that would not prove deadly, I heard feet running through bushes.

A man cried, "Halt! You there! Stop at once!" My heart froze.

Father was running toward me, a large man in close pursuit, his hand clutching a drawn sword. The man bearing the weapon was quickly gaining on my father. I estimated Father's distance from the wall, the time he would need to climb up the tree on one side, and then back down the other. He would never make it in time.

CHAPTER 10

—ᴍ—

SERVANTS HAD STARTED TO GATHER in the atrium of the house, seeking the source of the commotion. Some, recognizing the presence of an intruder, ran toward the door. They would leave that way and wait for Father in the street.

I had to act quickly. Years of training came to my aid, and my body took over. I balanced on the branches of the willow and stood, my knees loose, my body surging with fear. Then I sprang onto the edge of the wall and, without stopping, plunged into a tree within the garden. I grunted when I slammed into its trunk with brutal force. My hands, thighs, and calves clung tight to the coarse bark, even though dozens of splinters pierced my skin.

Readjusting my stance, I balanced again, knees bent, arms loose, aiming for a sturdy oak six paces ahead of me. I leapt. It was farther than I was used to jumping on the ground. This high up, if I fell, I would be certain to break bones. No help to my father then. My wrist wrenched as I clutched a branch. I gasped with the pain. Abruptly, my hand slipped and I dangled with one hand. Wrapping my legs around the trunk, I braced myself until I was secure. Time was running out.

With a lightning push and pull, I hung by my knees from a slim branch, leaving both arms free as I dangled upside down. I had made it without a moment to spare.

Father had just reached my tree. I hissed, "Grab my hand."

He froze for an infinitesimal breath, then looked up. "Hurry!" I urged. He grabbed my hands and I heaved with all my strength. He was beside me in a moment. Beneath us, the large pursuer stood confused, his sword wavering. He turned a full circle, trying to divine how his quarry had disappeared.

Meanwhile, I began the torturous route back through the tops of trees, flying in the air with nothing but desperation giving me wings. Whenever I gained purchase, I would hold out my arm, grabbing and steadying Father as he followed.

We vaulted over the wall into the last willow, slid down its trunk, and began to run like the wind.

"Cover your hair," he whispered.

I pulled the corner of my cloak over my head once more, hiding my long braid. From behind, I looked like a man, barefoot and garbed in a worn cloak.

I was faster than Father, but he knew the way better. Stripping the dark mask from his face, he pointed north. We began traveling in a different direction than the one we had come, pursued by half a dozen men. The longer we ran, the greater our distance from them grew, for they did not know their way and became confused by the labyrinthine paths we chose. We were saved by one thing: in their haste, our pursuers had not thought to bring torches. Or dogs.

We left the dirt track we had been traveling on and veered into an olive grove. I could hear the sound of our pursuers in the lane beyond. Father pointed to a copse where I could see the vague outline of a well.

"Down," he ordered when we came upon it.

"Down?" I said.

"Now, Ariadne!"

I threw my hands up in the air. It had been an unreasonable night, to say the least. I had followed my father like a prowler through deserted streets. I had seen him sneak into a house as if he were a common criminal. I had climbed trees and jumped from one branch to another like an African monkey. We had been chased by men brandishing swords and clubs.

And now, I was supposed to descend into a murky well that led who knew where.

"Trust me," Father whispered softly.

What else could I do? With a gulp I lowered my body into the tight circle of stones, grabbed the rope that lay on the edge, and descended within. I felt the walls enclose around me, suffocating me. The space was so small, I could not breathe. I would have scrambled back up if Father were not lowering himself on top of me. I had no choice but down.

To my profound relief, the bottom was not so deep as I had feared. The well shaft was as tall as the height of two men and ended in a dry foundation that gave me room to stand without hitting my head. If there had ever been any water down here, it had long since evaporated. Father landed beside me.

"What . . . ?" I began.

He put a finger to his lips. "We need to be silent until they give up searching. We can talk when we return home."

With the urgency of pursuit gone, I felt my knees weaken. Sinking to the ground, I pulled my thighs to my chest and tried to stop shivering. I ignored the sting of a hundred scratches in my hands and legs, ignored my parched throat, ignored the myriad of questions that crowded my mind.

Gingerly, Father perched next to me. I could not see his features in the dark. Searching until I found his fingers, I took his hand in my own. I had saved him. Whatever he had done, I did not care. He was safe.

The hours dragged as we sat side by side, holding hands, our breaths mingling like mist in the cold, predawn air. When we could see the pale light of the rising sun above us, Father climbed the rope. After ensuring that no one waited for us in the grove, he motioned for me to follow.

We brushed the dust from our clothing. I undid my braid, allowing my hair to hang down my back, and folded Theo's cloak over one arm. Father reversed his dark cloak, and to my astonishment, I saw that although one side was black, the other was a bright blue. By the time we finished, we looked a far cry from last night's adventurers. Instead of two brigands, we were now a gentleman and a lady, though somewhat rumpled and weary.

I thought I would die of curiosity before I reached home. Questions swirled in my mind with each step.

"So tell me," I said when we arrived at our villa. He lowered himself gingerly onto his bed. His legs were a mass of contusions. I poured wine into a goblet and passed it to him.

"Food first, I think," he said. "And fresh water to wash."

I curbed my raging curiosity once more until his slave brought us warm water and food. Father's wounds were superficial, though they needed to be cleaned. He winced every time I pressed a damp towel against his broken skin. Briskly, I cleaned the lacerations on my own arms and legs. The splinters would have to wait. I shuttered the window, barred the door, and sat down, no longer willing to be put off.

"Explain," I said.

He took a deep swallow of his cup of warm spiced wine. "What made you follow me?"

I ground my teeth. "This is no time for me to give you an accounting of *my* actions."

He grimaced. "No." Fumbling with his belt, he pulled out a roll of parchment and handed it to me.

The parchment had become crumpled during our escape. It took me a few moments to smooth it out with impatient hands. The missive contained five lines. I yelped when I read them. "Zeus's eyeballs! You are the Honorable Thief."

Father winced as if someone had poked him with the tip of a nasty dagger. "I never liked that title, though I was forced into using it."

"Well, it's the only one you've got." The world had become unhinged and he was prattling on about titles? My father was a thief!

"How . . . ? What . . . ? This is why Mother divorced you?" I managed. I had opened Pandora's jar, and I did not know which plague to address first.

He twirled the gold ring that sat on his little finger, first one way, then another. It had belonged to his grandfather, that ring. At least that was the story he had told me. "Is that really yours?" I said, pointing to it. "Or something you plundered?"

"Of course it is mine, Ariadne. And my grandfather's before me."

"I don't know what to believe anymore." I abandoned the stool, turned in a circle trying to find a thread of reason somewhere in that demented chamber. Finding none, I sat down again, facing him. "Promise you won't lie."

"I promise. I never have."

"You have merely hidden the truth."

"There is that. Yes."

"How did you start this . . . this . . . career?"

"I fell into it by accident."

"What, you tripped over your feet and when you got up, you had someone else's jewels in your pouch?"

"Do you want to hear the truth or do you want to spend the day shooting clever barbs?"

"A little of both, I think. It's not every day one discovers one is related to a renowned criminal."

Father sighed. "You are right. I beg your pardon, Daughter." He gulped a mouthful of wine.

"I started when you were six years old. My dearest friend at that time was a man by the name

135

of Periander. A Greek of good family, but not a Roman citizen. At the time, Corinth had been cursed by a brutal and dishonest consul who cheated Periander out of a fortune. Because of it, he lost his home. Denied justice in a corrupt court, my friend took his own life in despair, leaving behind a grieving widow and three defenseless girls.

"I watched helplessly as my friend's life unraveled. The law was no help, being less merciful to those like Periander who are not citizens of Rome.

"I wanted to help his family but did not have the means. The idea came one night, when the consul invited us to his home as guests. I attended, even though I hated the man, hoping to find an opportunity to sway his heart—convince him to bestow a trifling sum upon Periander's widow. While there, I glimpsed a treasure box in one of the rooms and knew I could take it."

Father took a deep breath. "Later that week, I made my way back and robbed him. That first crime was not on my own behalf. I gave the proceeds to Periander's wife and daughters. It bought a roof over their heads. The girls are happily married now, you know. Their mother managed to make the money stretch with a few good investments and set aside a respectable dowry for them. She had no idea it was stolen, of course."

I nodded slowly. "I can understand what drove you to rob the consul. You wished to protect your friend's family. To avenge his death. Why did you continue?"

"A year after that first robbery, I found myself in financial difficulty. We own land, Ariadne, and that is where our income has always been tied: olives and grapes and barley. The farmers who lease our land depend on the weather. If there is drought, if the rain falls at the wrong time, if pestilence strikes the crops, we do not have income for a year. When you stretch that year into two or three . . ." He shrugged. "I sold slaves and a parcel of land. But it was not enough. Then I remembered how easy it had been to divest the consul of some of his ill-gotten gains. So I chose another man, just as dishonest, and struck again."

I put my head in my hands. My problem was that I could fathom his reasoning. His actions made a spiraling kind of sense. My father was a thief, and instead of feeling shocked, I felt sympathy. The world had gone awry, or I had. I could not discern anymore. "Go on," I said.

Father shrugged. "I found I had a talent for it. I could devise ways to get around barred doors and barking dogs and vigilant guards. I always gave part of what I took to the poor. And I only targeted the dishonest. Corrupt men who made the lives of others unbearable.

"My success was short-lived. I could outwit

my victims, but I could not deceive your mother. After the fourth robbery, she caught me."

"How?"

"She had her spies in our household. I knew that, of course, and found ways around them. But she was too clever for me. She bribed the servant I trusted most. Bribed and threatened. I had written a letter to a man who took the stolen jewels, reset them, and found new buyers for them. Your mother intercepted the letter. The rest, you know."

"She divorced you because of it?"

"She could not bear the dishonor. I cannot blame her. Ariadne, you need to know that I gave up that life when you and Theo returned to me. Gave it up for good, I thought. When I lost you children, I did not care about anything. But with your return, I felt I had been given a new chance. I stopped stealing.

"That was the reason I took a chance on the *Paralus*, hoping it would provide for our future. I risked too much. Every coin I had saved through the years went down with that ship. Not only that, I had borrowed heavily, hoping the profits of the venture would set us free from financial burdens forever. Instead, it devastated us. We were about to lose the house. The land."

"So there was no modest investment that paid off."

"There was. I never lied to you. But that investment would not have paid off my debts, let alone cover our expenses. So I had to return to thieving." His fingers twisted into each other. "The sum I owed was substantial. A few jewels and gold coins cannot erase it. I am sorry, Ariadne. You must be ashamed of me. I am ashamed of myself."

Was I ashamed of him? He brought about a strange justice with his crimes. The poor benefited more from his dishonesty than they did from the honesty of most wealthy men. There was logic to his actions. An odd rightness. I was having difficulty condemning Father's choices. I felt neither ashamed nor horrified by his actions. Shocked, yes. But not offended.

Perhaps I had allowed Corinth's admiration for the Honorable Thief to influence my thinking. I had learned how to paint his robberies with a virtuous brush. Then I thought of a new puzzle.

"Why did you write those letters?"

He curved his back against the wall, his arms wrapped about his belly. "Will you leave me no dignity, girl? You want truth? Well, the truth is that my pride demanded it. My vanity. I wanted people to know why I chose my victims. I liked being lauded as a hero rather than derided as a criminal. It helped me salve my conscience."

Heavy silence filled the room. "You are honest for a thief," I said, finally. He remained mute. What more could he say?

I picked at a particularly large splinter lodged in my shin. "Pride or no, it was a sly move. Because of those letters, the public has no interest in your arrest. Other than those you robbed, no one is thirsty for your blood or pressuring the city magistrates to find you."

Father raised an eyebrow. "You seem to be taking this well."

It was true. I had not stormed away in outrage. "Does Theo know?" I asked.

"No. And I thank you not to tell him."

I nodded, my mouth a grim line. I had no notion how Theo would react to this new turn of events.

"You saved me last night," Father said. "If not for your intervention, I would have been caught. Perhaps even killed. The man chasing me had an overzealous air about him."

Unaccountably, I giggled. "He certainly had a big sword and fast feet."

"How did you manage those jumps from tree to tree? I was too pressed at the time to pay sufficient attention to your performance. Now, with a clear head, it seems astonishing to me."

"Theo and I used to practice flips and twists and cartwheels." I told him about the man from Crete who had demonstrated the art at Theo's school. "It improved our balance and strength. I can climb a straight column a whole story tall, flip over from the top, and land on my feet."

"You never said."

"No. It seems keeping secrets runs in our blood."

He looked at me thoughtfully. "You should have Delia take out those splinters."

I ignored the suggestion. "What did you take this time?"

"Nothing. They had hired extra guards, and one discovered me. The best I could do was to get away with my anonymity intact."

"So you still need silver," I said, pronouncing the words carefully. "How many more thefts before we are out of debt?"

He shook his head. "I am giving up, Ariadne. If nothing else, last night taught me this is no game. My earlier successes spoilt me. This life poses too much danger. If I am caught, you and Theo would be ruined. Your mother had the right of it."

Instead of making me feel relief, his words came as a disappointment. I picked up his cup of spiced wine and gulped down a mouthful. It had grown cold, the spices settling on the bottom. They tickled my throat as I swallowed cinnamon powder and crushed cardamom seeds, making me cough.

Setting the cup down, I wiped my mouth with his napkin. "We shall speak later. I need time to think."

Father nodded. "Of course. But you should know we have enough money for a year, at least.

Perhaps more if we economize. After that—" he shrugged—"we shall think of something."

I stood, preparing to leave. The room swayed for a moment. I realized for the first time how much the last twelve hours had cost me. The confusing pursuit, the sight of my father almost being gored by a sword, the sleepless hours in the well, wondering if we would be discovered. And the confessions of the past hour. This was not a day I would soon forget.

"Ariadne," Father called when I had reached the door. I turned to face him. "I thank you. For saving my life and my reputation."

Something melted in me as I looked upon that beloved face. I smiled and pulled the door shut behind me.

Part 2
THE UNKNOWN GOD

—⚏—

For you are a slave to whatever controls you.

2 Peter 2:19, NLT

CHAPTER 11

—ᴍ—

I WAITED UNTIL THE AFTERNOON before asking Delia to help me with the splinters that had lodged deeply under my skin. If she had found me in this state early in the morning, I would have had no explanations to offer, not without divulging that I had gone wandering from my bed in the middle of the night.

I'd snuck out of the house following the noonday meal and cooled my heels for an hour in the plot of land next door. When I returned, I concocted a story about an unfortunate attempt at climbing a tree there. She had seen me spend endless hours in that place. Over the months, she had witnessed enough superficial injuries on my flesh not to grow unduly curious.

I bathed first, softening my skin in preparation for her ministrations. The bath was hot and fragrant, soothing my taut nerves.

Father's face swam before me, scared and vulnerable as he slumped against the wall, looking at me with desperate eyes. He had survived so much loss. First when Mother had divorced him and taken his children away, and again when he was forced to be apart from Dionysius. Was he now to lose home, property, and respect before the world as well?

I thought of my mother's censorious nature, which had ripped our lives asunder. That woman was more judge than wife. Her frigid heart knew no mercy. If she had given Father a second chance, a hint of grace, how different our family could have been.

Try as I might, I could not denounce him. Running through my heart was an undeniable admiration for the way he gave corrupt men a taste of their own poison. His letters publicly indicted men who would otherwise remain beyond punishment. If he profited a little by his stealth and wit, who could blame him? It was a just reward for the service he performed.

I thought of his assurance that we had another year of financial stability, and felt grateful for the respite. But I knew I was not finished with the Honorable Thief.

The following day Justus dispatched a servant to our home, informing us of the passing of his father. Though I had known of Servius's ill health, the news shook me. I suppose none of us can truly prepare for death.

According to common custom among Romans,

Servius's body was laid out at his house for three days, where close friends and family could visit. We went, of course, to show our respect to Father's old friend and to lend Justus what support we could.

Servius was covered in his toga, a fragrant wreath on his head, and a coin placed in his mouth to pay the fare demanded by Charon, the ferryman of the underworld. I shivered despite the heat as I looked upon the face of death. *This could have been my father,* I thought.

On the third day, Servius's body was carried on its bier to the family tomb. Justus, wearing a thick black tunic, his hair cut short in mourning, led the procession. He looked ashen, his eyes hollow and sunken. I wanted, with a desperation that shocked me, to hold him in my arms and bring comfort to those bruised eyes.

It was my first real experience of death—of its finality. I found no help in the words of the priests or the stories of our people. Did the world have no more consolation to offer than vapid platitudes in the face of so great a loss?

The weather had been dry for months, withholding rain from the earth. Even the evergreens seemed to have lost their color, and the world was shrouded in gray. When we returned home, I collapsed on a couch in the dining room across from Father while Theo paced like a caged panther. I felt exhausted and in need of sleep.

An image of Justus flashed before my eyes, enveloped in the black of his mourning garb, his shoulders slumped with grief. I wanted to burst into tears.

As if reading my thoughts, Father said, "Justus bears a heavy burden besides the grief of losing a beloved father. He is alone now. No other family in Corinth."

"I know his mother was a freed slave. But where is Servius's family?" I asked.

"Servius was born in Rome. He enjoyed considerable wealth and imperial connections until he fell in love with Parmys, a Persian slave without family or connections of her own. She was a far cry from what his family considered desirable."

"But the Romans marry freed slaves all the time."

"Rarely when they are patricians. In any case, Servius's father found the liaison objectionable and threatened to disown him. That did not dissuade Servius. He adored Parmys. After the wedding, Servius's father made good his threat and cut him off. He had three other sons. I suppose he felt he could afford to lose one."

"He sounds like a fool," Theo said, his tone bitter. "What kind of man would treat his son like garbage, to be disposed of when convenient?"

Father gave Theo a lingering look. "Yes, I believe Servius might have agreed with you. If he nurtured any hopes of a reunion with his family, it never came to pass. After he came to Corinth, they refused to reach out to him."

"Why did he settle in Corinth?" I asked.

"His grandmother had land here. And a soft spot for him in her heart that his marriage did not change. She gave him property and a hefty bag of gold with which to start his new life. He multiplied that inheritance many times over. His grandmother was the only one with whom he continued to communicate. When she died years ago, he severed all personal ties with Rome."

"Has Justus never tried to contact his family?"

"He wants nothing to do with them. They rejected his mother and cast out his father. None of his uncles tried to right that wrong. As far as he is concerned, he has no family."

"He must have cousins," Theo pointed out. "They were not involved in what happened long ago. Perhaps he will reach out to them."

Father shrugged. "I think Justus will have his hands full for some years, administering his inheritance. He is young to bear so considerable a responsibility and will feel the full weight of it. I doubt reestablishing lost ties will be a priority."

"What happened to Justus's mother?" I said, curious. "The Persian slave?"

"Childbirth fever, I think. What a terrible tragedy that was. Servius never quite recovered from her loss."

"What was she like?"

"Parmys? She had the kind of beauty that makes people stare. If you were sick, she would put on her old tunic, cook broth with her own hands, and bring it over herself instead of dispatching a servant. Her kindness was as legendary as her beauty. I found the combination striking."

Father's tone was wistful as he talked about the beautiful slave. I wondered with sudden insight if he might have loved her from afar. His own marriage had proven an emotional pit, a far cry from Servius's love match. Father's marital alliance had been more like warfare than companionship, a reality that had affected all our lives. While Justus had grown up in a home filled with affection, my brothers and I had lived in a temporary truce at best, and at worst, in a siege. Father, too, had felt the burden of that ice-cold union, so different from Parmys's natural warmth.

The Isthmian Games took place in mid-spring when the weather normally obliged us with warm, sunny days. That year, however, the games coincided with unusually heavy rains. By the time the festival began with a trumpet blast, the deluge had stopped, but the field had turned into a slippery mud bath.

The roiling crowds fell quiet as the dedication ceremony to Poseidon, the official patron of the games, proceeded. Iuventius Proclus, the president of this year's games, stepped into view. Wrapped in a dazzling white toga, he raised his arms to draw every eye to himself. With a careful motion, Proclus pulled the corner of the toga over his balding head. This was a sign. Roman men never veiled their heads in public proceedings except when they were about to perform some religious act. By covering his head with his toga, a man demonstrated that despite his high standing among other men, before the gods, he was humble. And Proclus wanted everyone present to know that he was an important man, the one charged with offering an augury for the games. He stretched the sacrifice and prayers so long that I almost collapsed from exhaustion before the ceremonies came to an end.

A dense horde of people surrounded the outdoor arena. Some of the wealthier citizens sat on folding leather chairs and enjoyed the protection of umbrellas, which their slaves had installed before the rising of the sun. The majority of the spectators simply stood around the arena, jostling for a good view.

After our city's defeat two hundred years before, the Isthmian Games had been moved to Sicyon. Ten years ago, Corinth had finally reclaimed the games, and their popularity had grown in leaps since. They were a point of pride, a declaration of honor regained. And every one of us who participated in the competitions carried a small part of that honor as we tried to best contestants from other city-states in Graecia.

I would not compete on the first day, which was dedicated to the chariot races, the most prestigious and popular of the games. But Theo would. He had entered the race driving Justus's horses and chariot.

I studied the state of the arena with a worried gaze and hoped they would postpone the event until the following day, allowing the track to dry. Chariot races were dangerous at the best of times. But the treacherous condition of the course now made it a death trap.

Unfortunately, pushing the race back by one day meant all the competitions would have to be delayed. Many athletes and spectators had to travel long distances and could not afford to linger an extra day in our city. In the end, the president decided to hold the games according to the usual schedule, and competitors began to enter the arena for the famed four-horse chariot race.

Father and I took our places at the edge of the track, mute with apprehension as we observed the depth of the mud. Justus joined us after helping Theo harness and hitch the horses. The teams lined up at their assigned places.

"Did Theo spend the night at your house?" I

asked Justus. I had seen him slip out in the afternoon. He had never returned home.

A muscle jerked in Justus's cheek. "One of the horses had colic. He sat with it through the night."

I gasped. "He is racing through this muck with a sick horse?"

Justus gave me a heavy-lidded look. "I trust his judgment. So should you."

At the very first turn, one chariot toppled over, crushing the driver under its heavy body. We had never seen so many accidents at a race. Lame horses, broken axles, drivers thrown from their perch into the air, tumbling into the gasping crowds. Turn after turn, the race exacted a bloody price. Theo held a steady pace, avoiding wounded horses and overturned chariots with the agility of a dolphin.

By the seventh turn, he began to move ahead. With deceptive ease, he overtook one chariot after another, jostling, surging, slithering, and ducking through impossibly narrow openings. Father shouted himself hoarse when an Athenian charioteer, bent on preventing Theo from passing, veered into his path, his deadly spiked wheels aiming for the white chariot made famous by Justus. With a deft swerve, Theo evaded the Athenian's trap and pressed forward. A team from Delphi moved like an eel, slipping past Theo, settling in second place behind a Spartan driver.

We were now entering the tenth lap. The tension in the crowd grew explosive.

With a combination of intuitive skill and sheer reckless courage, Theo drove his team forward, overtaking the team from Delphi.

He seemed stuck in second place, unable to overtake the Spartan. I bit my knuckles, nerves stretched beyond bearing.

Theo shouted something to the horses and suddenly they shot forward. It became evident that he had held them back until that moment, controlled the wildness of their speed for the final lap. The beasts took off as one, their hooves stamping into the ground, spraying mud on those spectators in the first row. No one cared. We knew we were watching history being made.

Theo came neck and neck with the Spartan. The driver turned his head and gave Theo a long look. With an unexpected swerve, he drove his team into Theo, forcing him from the track.

The crowd held its breath.

Theo's white chariot lurched, one of its wheels popping off the track, tilting to the left. For a moment, he hung in the air. My father and Justus swore together. I was beyond words.

With any other driver, that chariot would have flipped over with crushing force. But Theo twisted his body, throwing his weight against the right side, the whole time remaining in control of the spooked horses. His weight righted the tottering vehicle, and he carried on with hardly a ripple. What Theo did in those moments became the stuff of legend in Corinth, creating an intoxicating spectacle no one would forget for a generation.

With a speed that defied logic, he pressed forward until, just before reaching the finishing posts, he drew even with the Spartan once again. It was his turn to give the other driver a lingering look. And then, stretching on tiptoes, he leaned forward and adjusted the reins. The horses responded to that delicate touch and shot forward one last time, and overtaking the Spartan, they passed the finish marker first.

The crowd let out an adoring roar. No one thought of Theo as the foundling anymore. He had become Theodotus the champion.

With defiant courage, he had brought Corinth to its knees. I turned to find my father weeping. Justus clutched his short hair as if he could not believe what his eyes had just witnessed. I became aware of the taste of blood in my mouth. I had been so terrified my foster brother would come to grievous harm during the race that I had bitten the inside of my lips raw.

We pushed and pressed our way to Theo. It took us an age to get through the multitudes who wanted to be near him. By the time we arrived, several men had lifted him onto their shoulders and were singing a bawdy anthem as they jostled him about. I thought this might well prove more dangerous than the chariot race and grinned.

Finally, the hordes calmed enough to allow him to be formally honored. By then, some measure of order had been established, so that Father and I could stand near him. His crown of pine sat crooked on his brow, and his eyes sparkled in a way I had not seen in months.

From the corner of my eye I saw Diantha and her five-headed beast heading his way and winced. If that woman tried to sour his victory, she would have a taste of my knuckles.

She stood in front of Theo, so close they almost touched, and reached out to straighten his crown. "That was well done, Theodotus. You ran a daring race."

For a moment, I doubted my ears.

Theo gave her an odd, lopsided smile. It was the first time I had ever seen that smile on his lips. It would not be the last.

"My father is hosting a feast this evening. Why don't you come?" Diantha said.

Theo said nothing for a moment. Then his arm reached out and he pulled me forward. "She comes too."

Diantha hesitated. "Of course."

"She comes as *my* guest." He bent his head a fraction, his eyes boring into Diantha. "Understand?"

Diantha blinked. Her head nodded graciously. "Yes, Theodotus."

"Why did you do that?" I griped when she had left. "I don't want to go to that woman's house."

"You are coming," Theo said, not bothering to explain further.

That night, Diantha and her friends left me alone. No barbs. No jibes. They even attempted a polite conversation. I understood. For Theo's sake, they had declared an end to their war. Theo had made it clear that if they wanted him, they had to treat me with dignity. And they definitely wanted him.

I watched my foster brother drink too much and give that lopsided smile all night. Diantha floated about him like a brilliant butterfly. She had competition. Now that he had won Corinth's heart, women found him irresistible. Theo did not seem impressed. It was as if the victory and flattery belonged to someone else. A part of him found it amusing. But another part, an older and wiser piece of him that still remembered being called a foundling, held back.

As I watched him, surrounded by a throng of devotees who never left his side, I had a piercing realization. Theo was lonely. Achingly, utterly lonely. And I could do nothing to remedy his pain. I knew he cared for me still, but he had relegated me to the outer fringes of his world. I no longer had access to his thoughts. The knowledge was like a punch in my gut. I almost doubled over with the pain of it.

The morning of the footraces, I awoke with an aching throat and a pounding in my head that foretold the coming of worse pain. My father burst into my room, Theo in tow.

"Are you ready for your debut into the annals of Corinthian history?" he asked with the booming voice of an actor. I tried to cover my discomfort with a wan smile. "Come now. Make haste. You do not wish to miss all the fun."

"How are you?" Theo asked me when Father left the chamber.

I shrugged. My confidence had ebbed with the rising of the sun. Why had I ever thought this public humiliation a good idea? I pictured Diantha's face witnessing my defeat, saw her and her charming companions snickering as I came in last, straggling behind everyone. Blanching, I swallowed bile. "I hope I don't disgrace you and Father," I said, my voice reedy.

Theo squeezed my hand. "You will find few who can keep up with you. I have seen you run."

I washed and dressed carefully in my new chiton, the special linen tunic Father had ordered for the occasion. The style was inspired by the costume of the athletes who competed in the Heraean Games, the only sanctioned women's athletic competition in our land. The loose hemline ended just above my knees. Unlike the true Heraean tunics, the sky-blue linen covered my chest and shoulders modestly. The original tunics hung from one shoulder and bared a lot more flesh.

Though the other women would be dressed in similar garb, it felt quite daring to show so much skin in public. Of course, I would not walk about in my costume throughout the day. Over the chiton, I wore a longer tunic whose thick folds covered me with ample decency.

My race was not until the afternoon, and we watched a few wrestling matches until lunchtime. Proclus had purchased free food and drinks for the crowds, a common practice for the president of any festival. As the athletic activities stopped for the noonday meal, the throng of commoners started chanting Proclus's name. Instead of the usual rough bread and boiled chickpeas, Proclus had arranged for food vendors to serve free hot pastries, fruit, and fragrant breads. For a few additional coins, the wealthy could purchase roast meats and a variety of sweets.

I tasted little of the feast before me. The ache in my throat had deepened to a burning throb.

I did not mention feeling ill for fear that Father would ban me from running. I could not imagine a greater catastrophe. My name had already been announced as a contender. Withdrawing now would make me look a coward.

I was determined to make Diantha sorry for humiliating me. Somehow, this race had become my answer to every disparaging remark others had made against me. It was my way of vindicating myself against my grandfather's vitriol, the remedy to every wound he and Mother had inflicted on me.

I would run and I would win. I would press their haughty noses into my victory. I would prove them all wrong.

CHAPTER 12

—m—

LONG AGO, my race against Justus had taught me one essential truth: I could lose. The fact that I had won every short footrace for years merely meant that I had not faced expert opponents. Justus taught me not to be brash and overconfident. I thanked him for that lesson. Arrogance would not fuel my steps today. I would run with resolve. Determination drove me that afternoon.

A total of nineteen contestants had registered for the *stadion*. Two other women were scheduled to participate in the race besides me. They both hailed from Sparta, the only city-state in Graecia that actively encouraged their women to train in sports. Since they believed strong women bred strong sons, they taught their girls a range of athletic exploits, including wrestling, running, and jumping. The Spartan girls showed up wearing nothing but diminutive bands of cloth over chest and groin. Compared to them, I appeared a goddess of modesty.

Tentatively, I removed my outer tunic and started to stretch in my blue chiton. A man garbed in a sleeveless Greek tunic shook his head. "Disgraceful wench."

A younger man grinned. "Lovely nymph, only smile upon me, and I will devote myself to your altar forever."

Father, noting the unwanted attention, moved near to discourage further comments from both admirers and critics. I gave him a grateful smile and continued to stretch my back and legs. The other athletes were engaged in similar exercises. I became aware of each muscle-bound form, sinewy from hard practice, and powerful enough to best me. Some of these men competed at every festival held in the land, including the Olympics, and were paid for their pains.

With a lurch I began to doubt my sanity. What had I done? Forget winning; I only hoped I would not lose so poorly as to make myself the target of every joke for decades to come.

When I had been a girl in Athens, my favorite shrine had not belonged to one of the famous gods, housed in grand temples and visited by thousands of ardent worshipers. My favorite shrine had been made of plain white marble with a simple inscription in Greek: "To an Unknown God."

I had always felt that the Unknown God would be better disposed toward me than the others would. I, too, had been unknown, a stranger among my own relatives. Even though I had long since stopped believing in the gods, this divinity could still sometimes stir my soul. If the heavens contained such a thing as a God, surely he was unknown. Now, facing defeat and shame, it was to him that I prayed, asking for strength beyond my own.

I took my place at the starting line. The world shrank around me. I forgot the pain in my head; forgot the fire in my throat; forgot the shortness of my hemline. I forgot the strength of my competitors. Bending my knees, I arranged my body in a straight line, fingertips resting on the ground, and stretched my strongest leg, the left one, forward. The start signal rang out. My left arm came up, driving me forward as I took off with an explosion of movement.

I had never raced against so many runners at once. I ignored their jostling bodies, the dust of their feet, and pressed on, lengthening my steps. The *stadion* required speed from start to finish. I pushed myself beyond the boundaries of my body, beyond pain and breath, until I started to pass other runners. Male, female, I flashed by them and pressed farther, holding on to the momentum I had gained at the start. Setting my gaze on the finish line, my arms swung hard, pumping me forward, my steps wide and fluid. I lost awareness of whether I was ahead or behind.

My world narrowed to that one post, the slender painted column that indicated the end of the race.

Only after I had passed it and come to a slow stop did I become aware of the world around me again, of the crowds cheering, of a dignified man shoving a wreath of pine on my head, and my father embracing me and shouting incoherent words. Theo seemed no better. His voice had grown hoarse from shrieking with excitement.

Tears mingled with sweat and the fragrance of pine as it sank into my benumbed mind that I had won. I had truly won the *stadion* at the Isthmian Games. To this day, the scent of pine arouses a vague sense of weepy happiness in me.

As my heart stopped pounding, I became mindful of the state of my body once more. My throat felt parched and burned with fresh agony. I felt light-headed with the pain in my skull. A wave of paralyzing nausea rolled over me without warning.

"I don't feel well," I gasped. "Can we go home?"

"Home? You just won the short race! There is a sea of people who want to congratulate you." Father clapped me on the back.

"Something is wrong with her," Theo said.

"I feel sick," I moaned. "Please, Father! Take me home before I shame myself."

My father looked about. "It is a good distance to where we left the litter. Can you walk?"

I bit my lip. I must have used the last of my strength at the race. Now I felt wobbly and uncertain on my feet. My stomach heaved. The thought of a long walk through the crowds overwhelmed me. I had run faster than the best athletes in Graecia, but I doubted I would be able to walk the length of the stadium. The irony made me want to weep.

"I could carry you," Theo offered.

"No!" I cried. Everyone would say this was why women should not be permitted to participate in the games. They would blame the delicacy of my sex, claiming that the race had proven too much.

"May I help?"

"Justus!" Father sagged in relief. "We need to get Ariadne away from here. She feels unwell. My litter is too far away. I don't want to carry her in front of the rabble."

Justus looked at me. His eyes were dark green, like my victory wreath, and filled with uncharacteristic kindness. "I have my chariot near. If you can lean on me, we will ride away together, and it will seem like we are making a triumphant parade. Two Corinthian winners, making a circuit. What do you think?"

"It will be better than jostling through the crowd."

"Best praise I have received this day," Justus said, his tone dry. I was too sick to appreciate that any of the thousands of men and women

165

present at the stadium that day would consider it an unforgettable honor to ride in a champion's chariot.

He sent his groom and gave instructions for the chariot to be driven as close to our location as possible. He had driven the white chariot to the arena, the one in which Theo had won this year's race. That vehicle had obtained supernatural acclaim, having now won four Isthmian Games. People made way for it as for a holy object.

Justus stood near us like a sentinel. It dawned on me that his presence kept others at bay. Justus's demeanor indicated that he wanted privacy. One victor to another. By remaining with me, he also added to the glory of my modest achievement. The *stadion*, being the shortest and easiest of the races, did not carry the weight of other competitions. Having Theo to one side and Justus to the other made up for that.

By now, I was leaning heavily on my father, trying to keep the contents of my stomach in their rightful place, rather than on someone's sandals. "Here comes the chariot," he said. "You go home with Justus. Theo and I will follow as fast as we are able."

I pulled the last of my strength about me like a cloak and stood tall. "Shall we go?" I said, holding my head up like a queen.

Justus laughed softly. "That's the girl I know. Dionysius would be proud of you."

I climbed into the chariot, leaning on Justus's arm. The spectators thought the ride a prearranged show, celebrating the athletic prowess of Corinth. They cheered us as we pulled forward, chanting Justus's name.

The horses pulled in smooth unison, keeping the chariot steady. Even the slight movement of wheels rolling on grass made my belly heave. I clasped the smooth wooden rim, my fingers bloodless from the force of my grip.

"Was it something you ate?" Justus asked, turning to look at me.

"No. I woke up with a sore throat and head-ache."

"You ran that race while you were ill?"

"It seemed like a good idea at the time. Look," I said, sensing a lecture coming, "could we forgo the conversation? I fear something other than words might spew from my lips. And the people would scourge me for fouling your precious chariot."

Justus's eyes widened. "I will try to evade any large puddles in the road."

In a blur of motion and misery, we made our way home, and by some mercy, I avoided disgracing myself in front of Corinth's favored son. When I was tucked into my bed that night, my stomach more settled, my throat eased by a physician's potion, I cradled my pine wreath to my chest and tried to think of the race I had miraculously won. Instead, it was Justus's face that swam before my eyes. The feel of his arms wrapped about my back and thighs as he carried me to my room haunted me as I fell asleep.

My victory did not lift me into the annals of glory. I was a woman, and my gender prevented me from being catapulted into popularity. There had been polite applause when I won, a few congratulations over the following weeks, and then I returned to my ordinary life. I did not even enjoy the benefits of a monetary reward. The Isthmian Games, unlike other athletic events in Graecia, offered no silver or gold to its champions. Those of us who participated did so to win honor.

Something within me wilted with the knowledge that all my hard work had not won me my heart's desire. I had been a victor at the Isthmian Games and proved nothing. I used my pine wreath as a room freshener and said a permanent farewell to competitive training, though I would never give up running. That was a true part of me. I ran not to win glory now, but simply to experience the joy of the sport.

With a restless heart, I returned to my reading and philosophy lessons with Claudia, Junia, and Fourth.

One late evening Father and I lounged together in the atrium to watch the moon, which sat full and white, like a self-satisfied bride in the midnight sky.

"I met a sea captain at a feast last week," I said. Thanks to Theo, I now received a smattering of invitations and had something akin to a social life. "He claimed to have survived three shipwrecks. I told him I was surprised anyone hired him with that kind of track record."

"The fact that he survived to tell the tale speaks highly of his skill," Father said.

"That is what he said. What ships are the safest, do you think? War ships or merchant ships?" I tipped my head back to see the moon better through the opening in the atrium roof.

"The ones docked in a warehouse," he said, making me laugh. He would never forget the anguish of his lost ship.

We heard a distant crash at the front door. The hour had grown so late that the slaves had closed and barred the door even though Theo had not yet returned home. Then came the sound of the door opening, and another crash. I tensed.

Theo stumbled into the courtyard and came to an abrupt stop when he saw Father and me.

"Is this a party?" His voice echoed loudly, the words pronounced with exaggerated care.

"It is now that you are here." Father patted the cushion next to him. "Come join us."

Theo hesitated for a moment. His eyes were bloodshot and swollen. He looked exhausted. I thought he would refuse the invitation and go to bed. But he stayed, though he chose a seat across from Father instead of sitting next to him.

A flagon of wine sat on the table, and he reached out for it. His hands were not quite steady and he knocked cup and flagon to the floor. The silver crashed on the tiles with a loud clatter. Theo swore.

"Don't you think you have had enough, Son?" Father said, retrieving the dented cup.

"I am not your son," Theo said through gritted teeth.

If an archer had loosed his arrow into my belly, I would not have been more stunned.

Theo's stark pronouncement exploded in our midst like a thunderbolt. All three of us froze. The words stung. Bruised. Broke.

Theo shot to his feet. His hands were balled into fists and a red flush crept up his face. "Or am I?"

Father answered, his voice level. "Have I not always treated you like the son of my own flesh?"

"Is that what I am? A son of your own flesh? Am I a by-blow of some slave you were too ashamed to acknowledge? Is that why Celandine hated me so much? Because when she looked at me, she knew you had cheated?" In his gray eyes, usually so warm and kind, I saw roiling resentment.

Father let out a deep breath. "Is that what you

have believed all these years? No, Theo. I found you as I said I did, the day Ariadne was born. You were not conceived from my seed."

Theo stared at Father defiantly, and then reading the truth in his expression, he sagged back onto the couch.

Father reached out a hand. "Theo, even though you are not a child of my flesh, you are in every other way my son."

"I am not, though. Am I?"

It was my father's turn to flush. He could not hold Theo's gaze. With shaking fingers, he rubbed his eyes. I felt like the ground under me had cracked open between my feet. With each passing moment, I was being torn further apart.

Theo sat up, his back rigid. "I used to dream about it when I was a child, you know. Dream that you would adopt me. That one day, you would pull me into your arms and say, 'It is done! It is real! Now the whole world will know that you are my son and I am your father.' But it never happened. I told myself it was because of Celandine. Because she would not allow you to take such a public step.

"Then you divorced and I thought, *Now he will do it. With Celandine gone, Galenos will claim me. No one will dare call me a foundling anymore. I will finally be a real son.* Instead, you sent me to Athens." He held up his hand, clarifying his point. "I chose to go. I went

171

willingly, knowing Celandine would never accept me if you adopted me. Going meant that yet again my dreams would be crushed under her foot. So I made a vow. If I could not be your son in the eyes of the world, I would be the son of your heart."

"And you were! You are."

Theo slashed a hand violently in the air, negating Father's words. "I lived like a son, faithful to your concerns and your needs. I thought this would be enough.

"When Ariadne and I ran away, I dared hope again. *Finally! Finally he will acknowledge me,* I thought. There were no more barriers to your adopting me. No Celandine. No Athens. Finally I would belong." He took a shivering breath. Tears sprang to his eyes. Tears he would not release.

I bounded over and tried to wrap my arms around him. He pushed me away. I was weeping for the pain he had borne these endless years. The pain of not being truly one of us. And the shame of being a castaway.

Father rose on shaky legs. "Theo, I could not do it. Do you not understand? I had already chosen Ariadne over Dionysius. It was the only way to save her. I knew Dionysius felt the sting of that rejection. If I then went on to adopt you, he would have been devastated. Put yourself in his place. He would have believed I had completely replaced him."

The world crashed. This. This was my fault? Theo's broken heart, his loneliness, his lack of proper family, all down to me. Because Father had chosen me over Dionysius, he could not also adopt Theo. Gods. I had shattered both my brothers' lives. I had stolen their father.

I bit my lip and swallowed both my blood and my words. It was the only gift I could give Theo. Silence. By quashing the devastating guilt that overwhelmed me, I could give Theo room to confront his own grief. To allow it to run its course. This night, this sorrow, this mourning, this bitterness was Theo's due. I would not ask him to suppress his own emotions in order to comfort me.

Theo shot back to his feet. "In the battle between you and Celandine, there was always a price to pay, and you chose me as the payment. Celandine's anger had to be assuaged. So I paid that price. Ariadne had to be kept safe. So I paid that price. Dionysius had to feel loved. So I paid that price.

"I am no son to you. I am your sacrificial lamb. Every time someone has to shed blood at the altar of this family, you drag me out and slit my throat.

"You fed me and clothed me and paid for my education. But you also made sure that the world never forgot that I was nothing but an unwanted orphan."

The boil had burst and its infected purulence

poured out, putrid, pungent, robbing us of breath. We stood, the three of us, in a haze of disbelief, covered in the suppuration of years, covered in guilt and bitterness, hurt and shame.

Father staggered toward Theo. "I am . . . I am sorry, Theo! Forgive me. I have wronged you. You need to believe me, now. In spite of everything, I love you. You are my son in every way but the pronouncement of law."

We had been cut with the sharp edge of too many hurts to find healing that night. Father's words, though sincere, did not yet have the power to calm Theo. You cannot cauterize a pus-filled wound without permitting the poison to ooze out first. It had taken wine and years of cumulated disappointment, but Theo had finally allowed his acrid accusations to flow freely.

Winter gripped Corinth hard that year. When you breathed, your breath came out in white, thin wisps, like little bits of your soul that left you forever. We stepped on eggshells around each other. We lived as those who have lain under a surgeon's knife, recuperating slowly. Theo acted like a polite acquaintance rather than my best friend. But I sensed a release in him, as if a boiling pot had blown its lid and now could rest. He stopped drinking to excess, and when he accepted an invitation, he seemed less on edge among strangers.

I did not expect to see Dionysius again for two more years, when he would turn twenty-five. To my astonishment, one morning, before the midday bell had rung, a young man stepped into the courtyard. It took me a moment to recognize the tall, gangly man with the shock of dark, unruly hair and grim expression.

"Dionysius!" I shouted and sprang wings to go to him. He accepted my embrace but did not return it.

"Where is Father?" he said. No greeting. No expression of joy at seeing me.

"Dionysius . . ."

"Where. Is. Father?" His tone held no trace of affection. I felt like he had stabbed me with an icicle. Before I had a chance to respond, he shoved me aside and walked toward Father's tablinum.

I pursued him like a confused puppy and tried to follow him into Father's tablinum when he stepped inside. Dionysius pushed me back. "Not you." He shut the door in my face.

I stood, immobile, my mouth agape. Never had I seen my brother behave with such severity. I wondered if he had turned into my grandfather. Had the old man managed to leave his stamp on Dionysius's soul? Had he twisted his affections into scorn?

I sank to the floor, unable to take another step. Through the door, I could hear the murmur of voices, Father's quiet statements interrupted by Dionysius's staccato monotone.

"Is it true?" he shouted once. Whatever Father said, I did not hear. He spoke for some time.

"How could you do it? How?"

"Dionysius," Father said, his voice soothing. "I never meant to hurt you."

"Hurt me? You will be the ruin of me. This is your fault. The divorce. Our being torn apart from each other. For so many years, I blamed Mother. But it was you!" Dionysius howled. Even through the door I could hear the grief clogging his voice.

It dawned on me that they were speaking of the Honorable Thief. Somehow, Dionysius had discovered Father's secret. And unlike me, he could not bear the burden of it. I blamed my mother for Dionysius's defection. Blamed her and Grandfather for filling him with their venom and their harsh judgments.

"I never want to see you again," Dionysius cried. "You are not my father. I am not your son."

I felt my world splinter. Our family had lived far away from each other for years. But Dionysius and the rest of us had been welded together by love. We were bonded so tightly that years and distance could not tear us apart. Whatever was happening inside Father's tablinum meant the rupture of that love. Of that unity.

The door slammed open and I bounded to my

feet. At the threshold, Dionysius turned to face our father. His skin had turned the color of ivory. In his eyes hatred burned like a fever.

"I will tear your name from my heart," he said coldly. "I will burn your letters. Do not send more."

As he stepped over the threshold and turned to go, I clung to him, trying to hold him back. "Dionysius, please!"

He shook me loose. "Leave me be."

"Will you listen to what I have to say?"

He stopped for a moment and studied me. "To think, I used to be jealous of you for having him. Well, you are welcome to him. Enjoy him to your heart's content." As he stormed away, not sparing me a backward glance, I knew that I had lost my brother forever.

Father looked like an old man, withered in the course of an hour. I drew him back into his tablinum and shut the door, lest someone overhear us.

"Dionysius knows . . . who you are?"

Father stared at me slack-jawed, his face thunderstruck. He took a gulping breath. "Celandine heard rumors of the Honorable Thief's antics. She guessed they were my doing. What other criminal could write cultured Latin and quote our poets? Given what she knew, she connected the two. Until then, she had not divulged my secret to anyone save Dexios. Not because she wished to protect me, but out of concern for a possible scandal that might reflect on her.

"When my . . . activities took such a public turn, she told Dionysius what I had done years before and showed him the letter she had intercepted as proof. I suppose it was her revenge because not only had I resumed stealing, now the public was justifying my actions. I had been bestowed a kind of virtue. No doubt that infuriated her.

"Dionysius did not believe her accusations. So the boy came straight here. I could not deny his allegations, of course." He went silent. I saw in his eyes the cost of that interview with my brother. Saw the humiliation of a man who had lost his son's esteem. His throat convulsed. "Having put me on a pedestal, he could not bear the depths to which I had tumbled. Nor do I blame him, Ariadne. A man deserves better of his father."

He cradled his head in his hands. "Go," he said. "I need time alone." The one person who had always known how to comfort me, how to answer my cry for help, shook helplessly and sobbed while I stared, unable to help.

I felt like I had been through a siege, a mutilating war, and I was on the losing side. My family had shattered, and I did not know how to restore it. I felt it in my bones. This schism could not be repaired.

Years ago, I had seen a field devastated by

locusts. The swarming locusts had eaten the crop, followed by the hopping locusts that had attacked and swallowed the leftovers. I felt like that field, stripped bare of everything good, stripped to the knobby core, and stripped again until nothing was left. Everything I wanted had been taken from me.

First Theo and now Dionysius. Our money was about to run out. Soon, we would lose our land and home into the bargain.

CHAPTER 13

—ɯ—

CLAUDIA, JUNIA, FOURTH, AND I were poring over the story of Midas, the king who had been blessed by the gods to turn everything into gold with one touch. That ability, it turned out, proved more a curse than a blessing, for even his food congealed into the precious metal when he touched it. Delia came to sit in one corner, listening to the story.

"Are you well, Delia?" I asked.

With Theo gone so often, Delia had become like a pale ghost, floating through our house with shadowed eyes. The blinding headaches that plagued her—a condition we believed was the result of the cruel beatings she had endured at the hands of her former master—seemed to come with more frequency.

She doted on Theo. It had not escaped her notice that my foster brother had little personal wealth. His purchase of her had come at a considerable sacrifice for a young man who could have found a hundred better ways to squander his silver. He was to her a savior, son, and master all in one. He had become her reason for living.

She nodded her head and pointed at my hair, which had grown long and hung in an untidy braid to my waist. "What do you call that?"

"A braid."

She sniffed. "A disgrace, that's what. What a waste of perfectly beautiful hair." She walked over to tuck a strand into place with surprisingly gentle fingers. "I could make you look a goddess instead of a scarecrow. All of you." She pointed at the four of us and nodded. "I can make you look lovely." Given her manner, one quickly forgot that Delia was a slave. I believe she herself forgot that fact with admirable regularity.

"Delia is a hairdresser," I explained to my friends.

"Truly?" Fourth looked like I had just introduced her to the empress of Rome. "Please, Ariadne. Will you let your slave style our hair?"

"She is not my slave." I shrugged. "I don't suppose Theo would mind."

With childlike glee, Delia sent the other girls home to fetch what pomades, combs, pins, and curling irons they could. She knew there were few such things to be found in our house. After my mother's suffocating efforts to turn me into a replica of herself, I had given up on feminine frippery. She had always managed to make me feel like a failure as a woman.

181

But I had to admit—to myself if to no one else—that I longed to be beautiful. To fit in with the likes of Claudia the Elder and Diantha. And to turn Justus's head a little. Perhaps more than a little. If Delia was able to transform me into the kind of woman who could win his admiration, I was willing to give her cosmetics and combs a try.

The rest of that morning and well into the afternoon, Delia worked on the four of us. We were willing victims as she massaged, plucked, painted, braided, looped, and scraped us until we shone and glittered like Aphrodite rising from the foam of the sea. Junia's wispy hair turned into golden loops and whorls, much of it still hanging loose down her back to indicate her unmarried status. Fourth had short curls at the front of her face that accentuated her striking eyes, and Claudia's delicate features came into ravishing focus when Delia wove a ribbon over the crown of her head, pulling her hair away from her face. She applied a subtle layer of cosmetics that made our eyes larger and our lips fuller, and our skin smoother.

My mouth fell open when I saw myself in a mirror. Delia had transformed me into a new creature. It was like Ovid's *Metamorphoses*. I hardly recognized myself. As I perched on the sofa next to my friends, it occurred to me that we made as beautiful a sight as Diantha and her five-headed monster ever did.

"Delia, can you do this again, next week?"

"With my eyes closed."

For the first time, the pall that had cast its weight upon me since Dionysius's visit lifted. Here was something I could look forward to. Justus, having settled his business affairs, was finally rising out of mourning. He had invited the hordes to his home for a banquet. And my friends and I were invited. Only, we were not going to attend as ourselves. We were going to arrive as whatever it was Delia had transformed us into.

Claudia, Junia, Fourth, and I wasted a whole day getting ready for the banquet at Justus's house. We bathed in hot and cold water. We sat in steam and let Delia exfoliate our skin before rubbing it down with aromatic oils. We washed our hair and drenched ourselves in perfume. Delia shaped and crimped and curled our tresses.

For me, she chose a linen tunic the color of the Aegean Sea. It had no adornments save for a narrow band of gold embroidery at the hem. I asked her if it seemed too plain for such a grand occasion.

"A woman with your figure does not need a hundred embellishments. If you were Venus, I would say go naked. But since you are merely human, a simple tunic will be your best ornamentation." Using green ribbons, she cinched the soft linen below my bosom and crisscrossed them lower down so that the curves of my figure were displayed with some exaggeration. The linen clung and flowed in all the right places.

Claudia and Fourth had to make do with old hand-me-downs, though Delia did her best to freshen the old wool with colorful bands of ribbon. When Delia finished with us that evening, we looked like four fashionable young women ready to conquer the world.

Father and Theo were drinking watered wine in the dining room when we joined them. Father set down his cup slowly. "Ravishing!" he pronounced, beaming.

Theo's response was a little harder to read. He choked on his wine and stared at me for a long moment.

"Well?" I said, prompting him to speak.

"I'm going to sell that slave," he said with a scowl.

"Good. I will buy her from you," I said, hurt.

My friends and I made a minor sensation at the banquet upon our arrival. We were astonished to find ourselves surrounded by a boisterous group of young men. They paid us more compliments that one night than we had received the rest of our lives put together.

One of Justus's friends, a man with broad shoulders and thinning black hair, fell on his knees before Junia. "Love me, sweet nymph, and I will be your devoted servant."

" 'If you want to be loved, be lovable,' " she said, quoting Ovid.

The man rose slowly. "This one has thorns."

She gave him her dimpled smile. " 'The sharp thorn often produces delicate roses.' " Ovid again. I could see the youth was charmed, though whether by her intellect or dimples, I could not say.

A Roman with an angular jaw, garbed in a toga and expensive purple tunic, approached me. "You won the *stadion* at the Isthmian Games, I believe. Am I right?" I nodded. He kissed my hand and hailed me a daughter of Artemis. Why this old news should raise such fresh excitement was beyond me. That night, men called me incomparable and worthy of worship. I liked the sound of that.

Justus kept his distance once he had discharged his duty as a host and welcomed me to his home. Tired of waiting for him, I cornered him as he ate pastries and talked about horses with a friend.

"Greetings, Justus," I said, making my voice sweet like honey. Arching my back, I pushed out my chest the way I had seen Claudia the Elder do with laudable success.

Justus studied me with an air of amusement. "Ariadne."

"Do you like my attire? I am told it makes me look like Artemis."

He took a bite of his pastry. "Never met that

particular deity." He took another bite. "These are excellent. Just the right combination of almonds and figs. I am thinking of buying a grove of almonds. They taste so good in everything."

"They give me hives," I said.

"Perhaps you will outgrow them when you are more mature."

I imagined shoving the pastry into his face. My efforts were clearly wasted on him. I gathered the frayed edges of my dignity and walked away. My only consolation was that Justus assiduously avoided Claudia the Elder all night. At least he had deigned to talk to me. She had not fared so well.

The physical transformation I had worked so hard to achieve catapulted me into the heights of a popularity I had once dreamed of. I was declared a rare beauty, the jewel of Corinth, the offspring of Aphrodite. Overnight, I became a sensation. Justus might not want me. Other men did.

But this new acclaim came at a cost. I lost our school for women. Junia and Fourth had found serious admirers at Justus's banquet. It was not long before they celebrated their betrothals. With weddings to plan, our daily meetings came to a halt.

With the school gone, I became like a rudder-less ship anchored to nothing. So many of the sure foundations of my life had been cracked.

I had lost Theo. I had lost Dionysius. Without friends and family, the glamour of my newfound acclaim derailed me.

Popularity can dull the senses like a drug. It can numb the heart. It robs one of truth. I flitted through life, moving from one circle of friends to another, from one thrilling event to the next. I ate up praise like a starved man. Accolades gave me a few moments of satisfaction. Then I found I was hungry for more. I careened from joy to wretchedness with astounding speed.

I had dozens of acquaintances and no true friends in this new world I had chosen to inhabit. I knew no one and no one knew me, not truly. We spoke of superficial things, laughed about mundane matters, and coasted through our days in a meaningless succession of banquets, festivals, and drinking parties. I led a fruitless life.

Women were permitted to mingle with men in Corinth as they did in Rome. Feasts with exquisite music, supple dancers, and wondrous performers from all over the empire became ordinary to me. I saw leopards on golden chains, bears dancing to the flute, men swallowing flames. I drank wine without water, learned to flirt without blushing, and grew accustomed to the bold gaze of men.

When the dizzying pace of my life allowed me a rare moment of reflection, loneliness pierced me. I lived in an enigma, always accompanied and yet utterly solitary. Flattery and adulation had become my daily bread. My belly was full and it ached and twisted, still unsatisfied, growing sick.

Before my parents divorced, I thought my mother cool, but not unloving. The separation changed her. Without Father's softening influence, my mother began to approach motherhood as Caesar approached Rome, with a dictator's imperiousness. I had to conduct myself by her standards or face punishment, usually in the form of imprisonment in the women's quarters at the back of Grandfather's house, where the lack of windows and fresh air was worse than her beatings. I knew that place as well as my own face, for I had spent many miserable hours there.

Nothing about me seemed to please my mother. My taste in clothes was abominable; my skin turned too dark in the sun; my love of athletics was deemed unbecoming in a woman. My manners irked her; my boisterous speech shamed her. The fact that I ran faster and jumped higher than boys my age seemed a sacrilege to her. She turned sour at the mere mention of my name.

In the early years of my life in Grandfather's house, I was determined to win my mother's approval. I thought if I tried hard enough, managed to be good enough, I could convince her to cherish me. Make her realize I was worthy of her love.

Once, I spilled a jar of oil. The punishment, nine lashes of my mother's whip—one for every year of my life—had seemed inequitable when I had not meant to be unruly, and I objected to the injustice of her discipline. This was my mistake, of course. She could not bear to be challenged. So she gave me another nine lashes and said it would teach me to be graceful if I knew that gawky manners would have consequences.

In retaliation, I refused to speak to her for a whole week. One afternoon, as I sat alone weaving wool with unwilling fingers, I remembered a night, years before, when my mother had nursed me during a bout of childhood sickness. She had sat next to my bed and sung Greek songs and wiped my face with a cool towel. I remembered the smell of her, like lilies, sweet and clean in the stale sickroom. Tenderness welled up in me. I missed her. For all her hardness and intractable temper, she was the only mother I had. The only parent I was allowed. I determined to seek her out and apologize. To tell her that I loved her.

I found her in the olive grove conversing with one of her attendants. I could not wait to demonstrate my love, to pour the balm of forgiveness and healing that overflowed from my memories.

"Hello, Mother," I said, my heart in my eyes,

my tongue tumbling over the words I wanted to say.

She gave me a cold gaze. "How many times have I told you never to interrupt me? Nine more lashes for you."

Day after day, lash by lash, my mother taught me an unforgettable lesson. She wove a paradox in me, that woman. I grew desperate to win approval. When I won it, it tasted like ashes. Meaningless and futile, because in my heart, I would always be the girl who could not gain the love of the one person who knew me best. No approval in the world could wash away the sting of that wound.

CHAPTER 14

A NUMBER OF MEN began to pursue me with relentless determination. Their attentions meant nothing. Then an alarming truth dawned on me. They could never mean anything because I cared for another. I loved Justus. He thought me juvenile, while I . . . I had thrown my heart at his feet. Despair licked at me like a flame when I thought of him. He did not want me. It was enough to drive me deeper into my reckless habits.

The feasts blurred one into another, growing indistinguishable in my mind, wearing me down. One night, a supple dancing girl held all the men mesmerized with her sinuous movements. I had drunk too much honeyed wine out of boredom and a desperate desire to fit in. I pushed myself into the center of the crowd and began to imitate her gyrations. Catcalls and applause urged me on.

An arm clamped about my waist and I felt myself lifted off my feet, propelled out of the crowd. I heard the complaints of a dozen voices behind me as I struggled to get myself free. In the shimmering lamplight, I saw Justus, tight-lipped and pale, towering over me.

"Let go of me," I hissed, trying to pull myself free from his hold.

"No." His hand tightened around me, and he pulled me closer into his arms. "You can come with me willingly, or you can come yelling like a fishmonger's wife. Either way, we have an audience. What would you prefer?"

I became aware of eyes following my every move. Pasting a smile on my face, I stopped squirming. "I do not wish to leave," I said through my teeth, my voice quiet so that we could not be overheard.

He stared at me wordlessly, his chest rising and falling as if he had run the long race in the Isthmian Games.

I thought of how he had found me, dancing in a way that would have shamed my father, and blushed. Giving in, I allowed him to pull me out the door. We were in his chariot in a flash.

"What are you doing?" I squeaked as he shoved me in front of him in the chariot, flattening me against the front wall with his body while taking the reins.

"You have drunk too much. Once I start moving, you will lose your balance. I can't risk having you tumble out and get crushed under the wheels. You will stay here, where I can keep an eye on you."

I felt heat from my neck down to my ankles, wherever our bodies came into contact. I tried to object, but all that emerged from my lips was a faint peep.

He held the reins, his fingers playing with the leather, but made no move to start. Bending his head, he whispered in my ear. "You disappoint me, Ariadne. I thought you had enough sense to withstand their empty adulation. You have lost yourself."

"It's no business of yours," I said. Heat gave way to a chill as his words sank in. I was picturing myself the way he had found me. Dancing with sensuous abandon, my tunic slipping over one shoulder, hair tumbling out of Delia's careful arrangement. Drunk on sweet wine. For the first time in months, I saw with brutal clarity what I had become, and blanched.

"Don't worry. I won't tell your father." His voice was quiet. Even in my intoxicated state, I could feel pity edging out the anger that had driven him.

I swallowed a rush of tears. "Thank you."

He flicked the reins and we started to move. The fresh air settled on me like a blanket on a sleepy child. I felt altogether weary. My eyes closed. I leaned back imperceptibly. Behind me, Justus took in a sharp breath. An arm wrapped around my middle, tightening for a moment. He bent his head. I could feel the warmth of his face against my neck.

With a speed that caused me to stumble, he stepped back, withdrawing his hand, leaving enough space between us to make me feel cold. I had to grab the wall of the chariot to steady myself. The chariot picked up speed, as if he could not wait to deposit me at my doorstep. He escorted me to our door without a word and handed me to Delia when she unbarred the front gate. Before I could thank him, he walked away.

"What made him so cantankerous?" Delia asked.

"He does not like sharing his chariot," I said and kicked a pot of basil on the way to my chamber.

It had taken a whole year and an embarrassing encounter with Justus for me to realize that I did not like the life I had created. I felt empty, useless, without a worthy end. All the praise I had won had not touched the wounds left by my mother and grandfather.

Justus stayed away from me after delivering me home half-tottering with drink. After three weeks, he finally condescended to visit us. His manner toward me had a frigidity that made me wince. Time and loneliness had tamed my temper. I would rather have his friendship than my pride.

Father left us alone in the atrium when he went to fetch the letters he had written for Dionysius. I said, "Forgive me, Justus."

He gave me a considering look. "You owe me no apology."

"Of course I do. An apology as well as gratitude. Thank you for taking me away from that place before I disgraced myself beyond repair. I want you to know I heard your words that night. I haven't gone back to that life."

Justus plucked a basil leaf from a pot and twirled it in his hand. Its fragrance filled my nostrils. "I was young when I won my first chariot race. Too young," he said. "For a few months, I lost my way too."

I gave a pained smile. "You were seventeen. You had conquered champions. Grown men. Of course it went to your head. I have no excuse."

"Perhaps it is not so much the years we live as the experiences we have in them. You were not prepared for that wave of spurious worship." He dropped the basil leaf back into the clay pot and fingered the long crack on the side. "What happened to this?"

I colored. "I may have kicked it."

He grinned. "You weren't picturing my face at the time you did it, were you?"

"Of course not. I was picturing your kneecaps."

Father came in, carrying a bundle of presents and letters to give to Justus. In spite of my brother's injunction that we not write him, Father continued to send him letters. It would be Dionysius's birthday soon, and Justus was traveling to Athens. He had purchased his first ship and was taking it on its maiden voyage. I thought of the *Paralus* broken into shards, lying somewhere at the bottom of the Mediterranean, the corpses of its passengers floating in the waves, becoming fish food. I shuddered.

"Take care of yourself, Justus. Ships are not always reliable." My eyes must have given away the anxiety I felt at the thought of him sailing on a frail contraption of wood, floating like flotsam at the mercy of Poseidon.

His mouth tipped. "After driving bloody chariot races for years, I look forward to the peaceful waves of the sea."

With little to occupy my time, my thoughts returned to our financial woes. I knew they cast a gray shadow over Father. He was scraping the bottom of his resources. The previous week, he had even sold a piece of land that had been in our family since the rebuilding of Corinth. He seemed determined to retire the Honorable Thief, considering it too dangerous. The more I thought on the matter, the more I concluded he was wrong. He had lost too much already. Were two sons not enough? Must he lose his home and inheritance also?

No, the answer was not that he should stop. The answer came in giving him the aid he needed. Fortune had prepared me for this task. My agile body, explosive speed, and physical strength made me a priceless weapon in Father's hand. With me at his back, he could not be beaten. By day, we would collect secrets freely as we circulated in the best houses of Corinth. By night, we would use that knowledge to our advantage.

I considered the wasted months of my life, the way I had staggered from one worthless pursuit to another, desperate to find meaning. To find purpose. And now I had found it. I would help my father. Unlike him, I was too young, yet, to know my own heart fully. Too young to take note of my hunger for adventure.

"You need my help," I said that afternoon over a quiet supper. I had dismissed the household, packed cheese, apples, olives, herbs, and hot bread, and carried our repast into a deserted corner of the garden. No one would overhear our conversation here. I was mastering the art of furtiveness.

"Need your help for what?" he asked. His voice held an edge of dread.

"To protect the Honorable Thief, of course."

"No, Ariadne. If you are suggesting what I think you are, forget the idea. It is impossible. Put it out of your mind."

"What, then? You will lose the house. The land you inherited from your great-grandfather. Become a laughingstock in Corinth."

"I may become poor, but I will be respectable."

I winced. "You sound like Grandfather Dexios. He has enough respectability for our whole family and three more besides. Father, listen to me. What you do is important. Those men answer to no one. They plunder and pillage as they wish. Rome will not stop them."

"Neither am I stopping them. Robbery is not true justice or a deterrent against future abuse, Ariadne."

"It's more than they would otherwise receive."

He vaulted off the ground and began to pace among the barren clumps of lavender. "Even if I go on, you cannot join me. Don't permit the taste of our adventure to lure you, Ariadne. It takes one minor mistake, one false step, and your life would be destroyed."

"You cannot continue alone. You need my assistance."

"In that case, I will not go at all."

"I will go without you, then. Short of tying me to a post, you have no way of stopping me."

He halted mid-pace. "This is too much! When did you become so defiant?"

I grinned, knowing I had won. "When was I ever not defiant?"

"No. You always had spirit. A bright spark of

fire that lit up our home." He shook his head. "Celandine thought you obstinate. I suppose you were. But I also thought you demonstrated a rare kind of strength and resolve. I tried always to encourage that part of you, Ariadne, though I knew Celandine believed it ought to be extinguished.

"But this—this insistence that you have your own way at any cost is something else."

I threw my napkin on the ground. "Would you prefer it if I walked away from you like Dionysius?"

Father fell silent. We spoke no further that night, both of us wounded. For a week, the matter sat between us, an unresolved snarl. I forced the issue on the eighth day, too impatient to give him more time.

"I have thought of an official who would serve our purpose," I said.

"No doubt you have. But I will choose the man. And the time. Three houses, no more. We can pay off the debt with that. And then we stop."

"Agreed." I grinned, ignoring his pallor. He would learn to appreciate my help, I thought.

Justus returned, bringing our letters and gifts back unopened, the seals unbroken.

"He would not tell me what troubles him," Justus said as he handed us the packages, still as pristine as when we had given them to him

199

several weeks before. "He only said to tell you not to write him again." Justus looked at his feet. "I am sorry, Galenos. I cannot imagine how this pains you."

My father nodded once. His hands shook. I tried to hold him. He gave me a thin smile and stepped out of my arms. He had not allowed me to embrace him since the day Dionysius had come to accuse him. He acted as if he could not bear to receive my comfort.

Shoulders hunched low, he turned on wobbly legs and disappeared into his tablinum, where he spent most of his time these days.

I swallowed. "Would Dionysius not read my letter either?"

Justus shook his head. "What happened between you?"

"Family quarrel."

Justus took my hand in his. "Tell me how to help you."

Tears filled my eyes, and I ground my teeth to try and dispel them. Justus pulled on my hand until I fell against his chest. "You can cry," he said, cupping the back of my head with a gentle hand.

Sometimes tears are a gift. They are the words our tongues cannot speak, the gall our bodies cannot expel. I wept in Justus's arms that day, wept as he held me with a compassion that gave me leave to shed my tears. And though he offered me no solution and dangled no hope before me, I felt better once I was done crying.

When I stepped out of his arms, I sensed a shift. A subtle change in the way he looked at me. I thought that perhaps, for the first time, he saw me as a woman.

"Do you think he will change his mind?" I asked.

"It will require a miracle."

Like Dionysius, I did not believe in miracles. The legends of our people might teach a moral lesson or two, but they had no power to reconcile man to man.

CHAPTER 15

—∿—

WHILE I WAITED for Father to make a decision, I spent the time training, restoring to my body its former agility and strength. Though I had never stopped running, not even through those wild months of wine-soaked feasting, my body had lost its edge. My muscles ached as I pushed them once again into peak condition.

My jaw dropped when Father informed me of the identity of the man he had chosen to rob. A former slave who had bought his freedom back from his old master, he had gone on to make a fortune in the slave market. He was none other than the slave master who had sold Delia to Theo. The one who had bruised her so badly that she had been left with chronic headaches and a nearly broken spirit.

We sat in Father's tablinum with the doors sealed. In the old days, his tablinum had had no door, and stood separated from the atrium only by a decorated curtain. Later, he had added double doors. It was late autumn, and the weather had turned brisk. The closed doors provided privacy as well as warmth. I pulled the loose sleeves of my wool tunic over my chilled arms.

"Aniketos sells a variety of slaves, of course, but he specializes in children for the pleasure houses. He likes to teach them the rudiments of the trade himself. They say he has a genius for cruelty."

I curled my lip in revulsion. I had no admiration for slave traders. But a brutal beast like Aniketos deserved a different level of disdain. "Robbing him seems too insignificant a punishment. He sounds despicable. When shall we strike?"

"We will need to prepare carefully. His house is a fortress. He keeps new slaves there and holds the place as tightly sealed as one of Caesar's garrisons."

"How do we break in?"

"Every house has a weakness. Aniketos's security focuses on keeping people inside; he does not wish his slaves to run away. But he is not as strong in keeping intruders out."

"So we can get in. How do we get out?"

Father scratched his chest. "I have not resolved that problem yet."

I raised an eyebrow. "It seems like an important detail."

He shrugged. "I wrangled an invitation from his wife for an early supper tonight. We can see for ourselves what we are up against."

"How did you do that?"

He clasped his hands in his lap. "I steadied her when she staggered against a step and almost fell."

I looked at him suspiciously. "You tripped her, you mean."

"Well. That too. I told her about you. The famed beauty of Corinth. I should warn you, I suppose."

Something in his tone made me frown. "What?"

"She has an unmarried son." His eyes danced.

I blanched. "You are enjoying this too much." Clearly he meant to make me suffer for forcing his hand. I clenched my teeth and resolved to beat him at his own game.

Aniketos and his family lived halfway between the port of Cenchreae and the city of Corinth in one of the new villas that were sprouting around the busy metropolis and the seaport that fed it. It took us less than half an hour in our rented carriage to arrive at Aniketos's door. The villa was more grand than elegant, making up in ostentation what it lacked in style. It was clear that the man wished to impress. Too much carved marble, too many painted statues and busts—Roman replicas rather than Greek originals—dotted the landscape.

We were shown into the house by a pair of half-naked slave girls. Their identical features marked them as twins, a rare and expensive indulgence. I was taken aback when they showed us into the peristyle, the back garden of the house, with twelve columns on each side to support the partial roof. Half as many columns would have been elegant. Twelve blocked the sun and created an unwieldy space. A stunning table had been laid with gold plates and cups, surrounded by the usual three couches. The walls were decorated in deep vermilion. Colorful murals spread over every available surface. It must have cost Aniketos a fortune.

The garden smelled of rosemary and thyme, clumps of the late-blooming herbs growing in large pots. Pink and purple cyclamen and delicate white crocuses peeked through the landscape at the feet of garish statues of several gods.

Rarely had I seen so many expensive objects thrown together in one place. It hurt my eyes to observe this hodgepodge of opulence combined with such lack of taste. And why were we in the peristyle? It would have been an appropriate spot for an outdoor supper earlier in the fall when the mild weather made sitting outside a pleasant experience. But it was too cold to dine in the garden this time of year. Any hostess with the tiniest glimmer of sense would have known to serve supper in the triclinium, the indoor dining room.

And then I knew. We were here to be

impressed, not to be comfortable. The paintings and statuary, the columns and marble must have made this the richest space the villa had to offer. What mattered if we shivered so long as we were dazzled? Aniketos wanted his visitors to forget his humble beginnings, to remember only his spectacular success.

Our host and hostess arrived then. I studied Aniketos as he sauntered toward us. Reed thin and narrow featured, the man walked with the spare grace of a weasel. His eyes darted from Father to me. They rested on me with a calculating air that made my skin crawl. I had worn my blue tunic, the one that had catapulted me into acclaim, and his stare lingered too long on the wrong places. I was going to enjoy his misery, I decided.

Father made introductions, calling Aniketos's wife a vision of beauty. She was a vision of something. A wall of overpowering perfume hit me at her approach. I tried not to flinch, keeping a smile pasted on my face. Her makeup artist, if she had one, must have found her inspiration from an old Egyptian sarcophagus, for her cosmetics were thick and dramatic, black kohl outlining her eyes and extending to her temples. Her earrings were long enough to brush the tops of her shoulders. Fascinated, I tried not to stare at her lobes, which had extended so far that they looked like thin rolls of parchment.

A young man joined us. He had his father's

curly hair and roving eyes, with thick lips out of proportion with his tiny nose. I almost fell over when I realized he had bathed in the same perfume as his mother. The double dose of the powerful stench made me want to gag. Father gave a toothy smile. I could see my discomfort entertained him. Gritting my teeth, I smiled back. He would not find me so easy to discourage.

"This is my son, Dryops," Aniketos said. "Why don't you young people share a couch?"

I wondered how long I could hold my breath before losing consciousness. Was thirty minutes too long? Reclining on my left elbow as required by good manners, I tilted my head as far away from Dryops as I could without falling onto the table. According to Roman etiquette, Father and I had brought our own napkins from home, and I placed mine upon the table.

"Linen," Dryops said, examining the fabric. "The embroidery is middling." He handed me his. "This is what I consider fine."

I admired the napkin before returning it to the owner, forbearing to mention that it was stained. When the first course arrived, to my horror, I saw that it was roasted snails, covered in a revolting sauce. I hate snails.

"These were fed on goat milk, you know," said Aniketos's wife, whose name escaped me. "The greedy things fed so well, we could hardly extract them out of their shells." If there was one thing

I hated more than snails, it was talking about how they were prepared. I gazed balefully at my plate.

"Eat up, Ariadne," Father said cheerfully. "My daughter adores snails. How clever of you to have guessed."

"Why, you told me, Galenos." The lady of the house purred her words rather than spoke them. "Do you not recall? When I asked about your favorite dishes? You said anything I prepared would surely please you. But your daughter was inordinately fond of snails. I listened, as you see. Your celebrated daughter is the talk of Corinth. Anything to please her. I am sure my son agrees."

I needed a distraction. "Your paintings," I said, pointing to one fresco, "are so . . . vivid. And you have so many of them."

Aniketos preened. "You will not believe how much they cost."

"And the statues." I shook my head as though lost for words. Pointing to a random sculpture toward the back of the garden, I said, "Who is that?" My three hosts turned their heads in that direction. Two snails found their way under the couch.

"That is Psyche," Dryops said. "Cupid's beloved."

"Masterful depiction. I wish I could see your whole house. It must be a treasure trove of beautiful things."

"I will show you after supper, if you wish," Dryops said.

"Why wait? Food cannot compare with such loveliness."

Father cast a sharp look my way. "You need to forgive my daughter's impatience. The glory of her surroundings has bewitched her senses. We shall wait until after supper, of course. And we will go together."

"You are too wise, Father." I smiled shyly into my snails. The plates were cleared eventually, but not before I had forced three of those disgusting vermin down my throat.

Between courses, a young slave woman brought us warm water for the purpose of rinsing our fingers. She was of similar height and build to me, with long hair the same shade of chestnut as mine. Her pink tunic was too bright for fashion, but hard to miss. Her mistress called her Galatea.

Galatea kept her eyes lowered at all times and moved with silent grace as she cleared the table. Her hands trembled when she served Aniketos. I wondered what horrors the poor creature suffered in this household.

She did not know it yet, but she was going to help me commit my first crime. I smiled slowly at my father.

CHAPTER 16

—w—

AFTER TWO EXCRUCIATING HOURS, supper came to an end, and we began our tour. I found what I had been searching for in one of the bedchambers: a box of carved mahogany resting at the foot of a wide bed.

"Such delicate carving," I said, drawing an admiring hand over the chest.

"It's not so fine as the one in our chamber. My wife keeps the spare linen in this one."

Aniketos's wife must have been desperate for admiration, even from a couple of strangers, for she showed us every corner of that villa, including the coffer that held her jewels.

Father gave a long soliloquy on a pair of matching brooches. I thought them ugly myself, and wondered at his enthusiasm. Then I noticed that while speaking, he was not looking at the brooches, but a little lower, to the base of the coffer.

The lady of the house gave a simpering laugh, clearly delighted with my father's eager compliments. "My husband checks every single article at night before going to bed. He is a most careful man, as well as a generous one."

As we continued our tour, Aniketos pointed out his many safety measures. Guards were stationed at the doors day and night. No one was authorized to leave without permission, and strangers were not allowed entry without an invitation. The villa had no windows. Instead, it relied on two openings in the ceiling for light and fresh air. Both the main door and posticum, the side door used by servants, were sturdy and would require a host of soldiers to break down. The villa was situated on a modest plot of land with few trees, offering it a singular lack of privacy.

"You must host a banquet," I told Dryops as we came to the end of our tour. I did not have to manufacture false enthusiasm as I made the suggestion. "My friends need to see this stunning villa. There is nothing like it in Corinth, I assure you."

Father's eyes narrowed. "Let us not impose on the generous hospitality of Master Aniketos, Daughter."

"By no means!" Aniketos rubbed his hands together. "We should be honored. If you would provide me with a list of names, we would be happy to oblige."

"What were you thinking?" Father said when we were ensconced back at home. "Why did you encourage that man? Do you not realize how dangerous he is? And his son is cut from the same cloth."

"I have a plan."

"That much is obvious. It will not work."

"You don't even know what it is!"

"The house is a fortress, Ariadne. No way out. We can't do it. We will move on to another."

"Will you please listen?" I told him my idea.

His eyes bulged. "Have you gone mad? When I said you could join me, I meant as you did the other night. Waiting outside, sounding the alarm, creating a distraction in case of danger. I did not mean for you to take center stage."

"Well, this requires a woman. You can't do it."

He slashed his arm in the air like a dagger. "Neither can you. Absolutely not. And besides, it is pointless."

"What do you mean?"

"Most of that poor woman's jewelry is worthless." He held out his thumb. Under his nail I could detect a thin layer of pastelike substance. He scraped it into the palm of his hand, where it sat twinkling in the lamplight. Gold leaf. "The rest is of little value, semiprecious stones and hollow gold."

I heaved a puff of air, deflated. Father wiped his hands and leaned back, looking satisfied. Too satisfied. I frowned for a moment, thinking.

"You were staring at the base of that coffer." Father jerked his head back. Immediately he expunged all expression from his face, but I had seen enough, and pounced. "That's where he keeps the real valuables. Some secret compartment at the base. What is on show is merely a diversion."

"We don't know that for certain."

"Is there a second box under the coffer? Tell me that much."

He pursed his lips. "There is."

I leaned back, satisfied. Aniketos kept something of value there. I knew it in my gut, and by the look of him, so did Father. The feast was to take place at the end of the month. I had three weeks to prepare. And three weeks to change Father's mind.

We were expecting Theo back from Ephesus in four days. He planned to stay a week before taking another ship, this time for the port of Troas. He turned the household upside down by showing up early, Justus in tow.

"Can you feed two hungry men?" he said, his wide grin lighting up the house.

My heart almost burst at the sight of him, and I squeezed him like a mother bear might do its cub. "You rascal! Why didn't you tell me you were coming home early?"

He gave his characteristic shrug, one massive

shoulder moving with slow deliberation, clearly pleased by my show of welcome. "No time. Where is Delia?"

"I will fetch her for you." She would be pleased to know Theo had asked for her before even sitting down. I lingered a moment, hoping he would mention Father. He did not. I motioned to the dining room. "Come and sit, you two. I'll send a slave to wash your feet and bring you a plate of dried fruit and nuts."

Delia flew in the moment she heard the news, grabbing the bowl and towel from the slave who was washing Theo's dusty feet. "I will do it myself. How was your journey, master?"

"Long. It was long and arduous, Delia."

"My poor boy. You must be weary to the marrow."

"My bones creak like an old man's."

Delia massaged his feet and made comforting noises.

Justus caught my expression and we burst into laughter. Theo sniffed at our hilarity. Ignoring us, he presented Delia with a warm cloak, which she needed for the approaching winter. The woman, usually as tough as a legionary's hobnailed boots, burst into tears.

The next hour flew by as I arranged for Theo's favorite dishes to be served for dinner, changed into a pretty yellow tunic, and ran a comb through my loose, tangled hair. By the time I returned to the dining room, Father had joined Justus and Theo.

"It sounds as though you have entrusted Theodotus with greater responsibility, Justus," he was saying.

Justus plucked a handful of raisins and almonds from the silver plate on the table. "He is a credit to your house, Galenos. I have never known a man who learned as quickly."

Theo kept his head bent, wiping at a damp spot on his ankle. "Some jobs have to be done out of duty. Others, for pleasure. Fortunate is the man whose work overlaps both things. Thanks to Justus, I am such a man."

Father's face brightened. "This house is too quiet without you, Theo. But there is no greater joy than knowing you are happy."

Justus cleared his throat. "I have some news of Dionysius. The Council of the Areopagus has invited him to become a member."

Father's teeth snapped shut. Dionysius's talent came as no surprise to him. But this was different.

"How is that possible?" I asked. The Council of the Areopagus had started ruling Athens before it became a democracy nearly seven hundred years ago. They no longer had the power and prestige they once held, but they retained a mantle of honor, and were entrusted with directing the internal affairs of Athens, as well as maintaining responsibility for certain legal trials. Old men sat on the council, not young pups like my gifted brother, who was in his twenties.

"They made an exception for him," Justus said. "He has gained enormous respect and recognition for some of his writings in the past year."

I nodded. It was like an arrow to the heart, this good news. News that Dionysius himself had not bothered to share with us. We did not exist for him anymore. The good, the bad, the mundane of his existence was withheld from us. I rejoiced for him. Dionysius was meant to go far—achieve greatness.

For Father and me, I grieved. Henceforth, my brother's every success would be another reminder of what we had lost.

"My son, an Areopagite!" Father said. He wiped the moisture from his eyes. "A true man of Athens." He said the words without bitterness.

Before dinner arrived, Claudia the Younger was announced. "I beg your pardon," she said when she saw our gathering, her hands gesticulating wildly. Claudia liked to use her hands when she spoke. "I did not realize you had a feast, or I would not have intruded."

"Don't be silly," I said. "We are all family. Please join us for dinner."

"I don't wish to impose. Only, I have such news to share."

"You must stay and tell us," I insisted, curious.

Claudia and I reclined on the same couch, while Theo sat next to Justus, and Father was given the position of honor at the head. Dinner started with a green salad of crushed savory, mint, rue, coriander, and parsley.

"What is your news?" I said when we had been served.

"The most fortunate of events. I had lost hope that it would ever happen. But some deity in the heavens had mercy on our household. Claudia the Elder is getting married."

"No!" I dropped my napkin in astonishment. Claudia the Elder must be at least twenty-six now, a little long in the tooth for a Roman maiden.

"Congratulations!" Justus said.

"Thank you." Claudia threw Justus a censorious glance. "Although you gave no help in the matter."

"What did I do?"

"She was determined to have you for husband, and you would not oblige."

"There is no accounting for taste," I drawled.

Claudia ignored my interruption. "Not that I can blame you, mind. *I* wouldn't have her for wife if you gave me the grain of Egypt."

Justus smiled. "I'm glad we are in agreement."

"Who won her heart?" Father asked.

"She lacks that organ, sir. Her purse, however, will be filled by a man named Spurius Felonius, who recently moved here from Rome. He used to live in Corinth many years ago, and has returned to retire here." Claudia clasped her hands and looked into the heavens in an attitude of deep veneration. "I will forever be indebted to whichever god is responsible for that mercy. Father has forbidden me from buying a new tunic for the wedding." Claudia took a deep breath, looking tragic. "Weddings and dowries cost a fortune, and my parents have five of us to consider. As the youngest, I do not merit the expense of a new wardrobe. Once again, I shall have to be content with fading in the background. Not that it matters. I would wear sackcloth and ashes so long as I see my dear sister married off."

"Nonsense," I said. "You must borrow one of my tunics. Choose whichever pleases you. And Delia will help with your hair and cosmetics. She will make you ravishing, won't you, Delia?"

Delia, who was standing quietly in one corner, waiting to help with the next course, said, "Of course, mistress. Nothing to it."

Her subdued manner and soft voice caught my attention. "Do you have one of your headaches, Delia?"

Theo glanced up sharply. "To bed with you, now. You ought not to be serving when you are sick."

"I will take her." Putting a comforting hand around Delia's waist, I helped her out of the room, refuting her feeble objections. With each step I took, I had a strange sense that someone was watching me. Turning, I caught Justus staring with an odd expression. His face shuttered when he caught me looking at him. Frowning, I turned my attention back to Delia and walked with her to her cubicle.

"You are not to rise until tomorrow, Delia. Theo would be upset if you showed your face before lunch. You know how worried he gets for you when you are sick." I pulled the curtain that separated her cubicle from the atrium and returned to the dining room.

"How is she?" Theo said.

"She will be well by tomorrow. She suffers from blinding headaches," I explained to our guests. "They pound into her with such force, she is immobilized. A gift from the slave master who had her."

"I wish I could tear into that man with my bare hands. The stories Delia has told me about the way he treats his slaves would make your hair rise."

Theo, at least, would appreciate my plan. I hid a cold smile in my cup. Too bad I could not divulge it to him.

"How do you like the veal?" Father asked, no doubt eager to change the subject of our conversation.

"It's as good as I remembered."

We were now eating the main course, fried veal with raisins, cumin, and celery seeds, served with hot, aromatic wheat bread and vegetables.

"Ariadne had the cook make it especially for you, Theo."

"That reminds me," Theo said, setting down his spoon. "I have a gift for you, Ariadne."

Although our friendship was ruptured, genuine affection still bound us together. Sometimes I caught a longing in Theo's eyes when he looked at me, and I knew he felt as lonely for me as I did for him. But he could not bridge the gap, and I did not know how to bridge it for him. It was like him to think of me away on a trip, when at home he ignored me.

Pushing aside my napkin, I went over to his couch, careful not to knock over the tables and dishes in my path. He reached for my hand. With an almost shy flick, he placed a bracelet on my wrist and secured the clasp. It was an enchanting design made of gold, dotted with jasper and lapis lazuli beads. I gasped and brought my wrist closer to the light in order to see it better.

"This is beautiful, Theo! It's not even my birthday."

"I was thinking of you." His cheeks were flushed and his eyes overbright as he looked at me.

A peace offering. He was letting me know we could go back to the way we used to be, without the tensions of the last year coming between us. He wanted to repair our friendship. I sighed with relief.

Justus took a deep gulp of his wine before snapping his cup back on the table with a clatter. Claudia surged to her feet. "I . . . I forgot; I promised to be home for dinner. Father will skin me. Forgive me, Ariadne. I must go home before I . . . I am so sorry." She half stumbled, half ran out of the dining room.

I turned to Father, mouth open, wondering what I had missed. He had stopped eating and neglected to replace his spoon. It was suspended halfway between the table and his mouth, frozen.

Had everyone gone mad?

"Thank you, Theo," I said, twirling the bracelet around my wrist. "That was thoughtful. I fear I cannot return the favor. I can't afford to buy you another Delia or a chariot. You do not wear jewelry. So you will have to make do with a sponge cake and candied figs. And I might let you beat me at a sprint one day." I gave him a quick hug and bounded out of the room after Claudia. I caught up with her just as she was climbing into her litter.

"Will you come down a moment, please?"

"Well . . ."

"I would appreciate more haste. Before the men eat the dessert and leave nothing for us."

Claudia expelled a long breath and stepped out

of the frayed litter. Her father had used the same conveyance for over twenty years, and it looked its age.

"Claudia." I gave her a severe look. "You should not allow Theo to upset you. The boy is oblivious. He is my brother and I love him to distraction. But he is hopeless around women."

"Your brother?" Claudia shook her head. "I do not think that is how he sees himself, Ariadne."

"Of course he does. He is a little sensitive about the fact that it isn't official, with legal seals and such. That makes no difference to me. We grew up together, like twins. He was there from the day I was born. I know him inside out."

Claudia wrinkled her nose. "You may not know him as well as you think you do."

"Of course I do. Now, would you like some sponge cake?"

Her shoulders drooped. "I may as well. I am not going to get anything else." Sometimes she made no sense, that girl.

CHAPTER 17

—ɯ—

DELIA REMAINED IN BED the rest of that week, so wretched with headache and vomiting, Theo feared to leave her side. Father summoned a physician who dosed her with his potions. They made her sleep fitfully. When she awoke, she was still writhing in pain. I had never seen one of her headaches come on with such brutal force.

By the sixth day, we all loathed Aniketos. She would not tell us what he had done to her. But sometimes, she would wake up in the night screaming his name, her eyes haunted with anguish.

She improved enough to sit up in bed with a bowl of broth when Theo left for Troas. She kissed his cheeks, caressed his hair with the tenderness of a mother, and told him to comport himself as befit a famed charioteer.

"How is that?" Theo asked.

"Run faster than everyone else when you see trouble."

Delia's suffering achieved what I could not. It

convinced Father to consider my plan. "I will try to arrange things as we discussed. If the first part does not fall into place, we must abandon the idea."

"You will succeed," I said.

"We shall see."

The evening of Aniketos's banquet, I dressed with care in a loose forest-green long-sleeved tunic that had a tight row of buttons from the shoulders to the elbows. We had withheld our destination from Delia, saying only that we were attending a banquet. When she saw my tunic, she frowned. "Is that new? It makes you look shapeless."

"Thank you," I said. I had chosen to dress without her help and did not expect her to laud my efforts. She styled my hair simply as I requested and with her skilled, light touch, applied cosmetics to my face. Father gave the servants strict instructions to retire early and told them that we had no need of them upon our return.

A hired carriage came for us by midafternoon. Formal banquets started fashionably early in Corinth and went on late into the evening. The main meal lasted several hours, and light snacks and wine were provided throughout the evening.

Aniketos's wife greeted us at the door. She was wearing a blonde wig styled in intricate loops and folds, its hair no doubt plucked from the head of a poor captive from some faraway Germanic tribe. It made her look like a bruised pear with blonde hair. Having spent so much on her head, she barely covered it with a diaphanous veil, a nod to the modesty required of married women. She preened and cavorted from guest to guest. Many of them were strangers to her, my acquaintances and friends, there at my request. They had come motivated by curiosity more than out of loyalty to me, sensing the promise of entertainment. Some were aristocrats, others belonged to influential families, and most were wealthy. Their collective consequence had the desired effect on our hosts. They grew bloated with self-importance. Poor Dryops seemed a little lost in the exalted company. He told bad jokes and tried to ingratiate himself with an excessive eagerness that pushed the crowd away even more adroitly than his powerful perfume.

For dinner, Aniketos provided a spectacle calculated to impress. Roasted pig stuffed with sausages, and dormice, which were considered a delicacy. When a white hare decorated with swan's wings, arranged to resemble the fabled flying horse Pegasus, arrived on a large platter, the guests burst into applause. The sound did not quite cover their chortles. Like everything else, this exhibition was one step too far.

Two beautiful girls played the flute and lyre,

while a young man sang in a melodious voice. Between them, the musicians did not wear enough clothes to cover a toddler.

I coaxed my hosts to drink as heavily as their guests, so that by midnight, most of the company was far from sober. According to Roman custom, guests mixed their own wine and water, choosing the level of each. Father and I drank mostly water that night, pretending to pour wine into our silver chalices, while only splashing a dribble.

At midnight, we took our leave, showering our hosts with vapid compliments on their social success. Just before stepping outside, I slipped into a cubicle built as an annex to the vestibulum, where the guests had left their shoes and cloaks upon arrival.

Galatea waited within to help us with our shoes. I motioned for her to draw the curtains, providing the cubicle ample privacy. Father stood outside, chatting with anyone who might decide at that moment to retrieve their own sandals. We were finished in moments and pushed the curtain aside.

Father left Aniketos's house, and any observer would have seen me on his arm, my shawl wrapped firmly about my head, warding against the chilly night. Those inside the house saw Galatea emerging from the cubicle with a towel draped over one arm, head bowed, eyes on the floor as befit her station.

• • •

Dressed as Galatea, I worked for another hour before my duties concluded for the evening. On bare, silent feet, I snuck into the room with the carved mahogany box and pulled the partition curtain closed.

I lifted the lid of the box, thankful that someone had oiled the hinges. It was filled with linens of various sizes: napkins, bedspreads, towels. With haste, I grabbed an armful and shoved them under the bed. One more armful, and I was ready. Peeking outside, I ensured that there was no one in the corridor before swishing the curtains open again, leaving the chamber as I had found it. Swiftly, I crawled into the box and closed the lid behind me.

I could hear the boisterous commotion of the guests diminishing. People were taking leave and the house was growing empty of noise. Father and Galatea would be home by now.

All I needed was to wait. Wait two hours for the household to settle into deep sleep so that I could leave my hiding place undisturbed. Long enough for Aniketos to check on his treasure one final time as was his habit before crawling into bed.

I became aware, with a sudden itch of discomfort, of how dark it was in my box. How close. My breathing quickened. I could feel my heart racing uncomfortably.

I was going to suffocate.

My mind told me there was plenty of air for me to breathe. But my mind could not rule me. Heat like fire spread through my skin. My breaths turned into gasps. I was a caged bird, wild with the unreasoning need to burst out.

I could run faster than the greatest champions of the land, I could climb a tree, hang upside down from a branch, walk on my hands. But I could not lie still in a little box that enfolded its walls around me like a tomb.

I began to push at the lid. It opened, a crack at first, and then wider, enough that I could breathe again, when I heard the sound of footsteps. Hurriedly, I snapped the lid shut. The steps were heavy and slow. I felt them pass the box and heard the rustle of fabric. A man burped noisily.

Dryops.

My unexpected distress had caused me to forget all else but the need for open space. Of course, this was his chamber. I had no way out now but to wait.

Sweat drenched my body. I lay in a lake of my own making, shivering with unreasoning fear, one heartbeat away from screaming.

I tried to control my gasping breaths, to silence the whoosh of air that passed in and out of my tortured lungs. Blood pounded in my ears.

It was a matter of will. Willing myself to be still when every part of me shrieked to smash out of that benighted box and run. I ached for a taste of fresh, clean air.

I grew dizzy and lost track of time. Had it been only moments since I scrambled into the box? Had an hour passed? What if I fainted? Would this box turn into my sarcophagus, bearing my corpse with the household linen?

I could see a thin band of light through one of the joints in the box. Dryops had not blown out the lamp yet. Did that mean he was still awake? Or was he in the habit of leaving it lit all night?

A loud sound made me jump. I clamped down on a cry of surprise. Then the source of the clamor became apparent. Dryops snored. An earthquake had nothing on him. His nose was a military trumpet. It could awaken legions.

I started to laugh. Tears leaked from beneath my eyelashes. I loved that sound. It made me want to kiss Dryops. It was the proclamation of my freedom. That sound meant that soon, I could open this chest of horrors and escape.

I remained still for what felt like a whole century but must have been under an hour, before creeping out of my hiding place. By then, I hoped, his sleep would be deep, and not easily disturbed by my movements.

At the door, I hesitated. The corridor looked deserted, and holding my breath, I slipped into the darkness. The room where the jewels were kept was a diminutive annex, separated from

Aniketos's bedchamber by a diaphanous curtain. I could hear husband and wife snoring. A family trait, obviously. They had left a lamp burning in their chamber and weak light passed through the gauzy fabric of the curtain. It provided paltry illumination. But my eyes, after so long in that dark chest, had grown accustomed to the shadows and could distinguish objects in the gray light of the narrow room. I found the jewel box with ease.

My father had once seen a similar casket. The base, which looked like a squat, gilt column, was a hollow repository. I needed to find the hidden clasp that would open it. Find it in near darkness without awakening my hosts or drawing the attention of one of their multitude of guards.

I ran my hands along the column and found it smooth. No clasp. The casket that sat on top, posing as the true jewel box, also proved smooth on the edges. On our tour, I had seen Aniketos press the golden lion that perched at the edge of the box, springing the lid open. I pressed the lion and the box snapped open with a popping sound.

Aniketos moved restlessly in bed and stopped snoring. I froze. He sat up, running a hand over his face. I crouched low, trying to hide the bulk of my body behind the base of the column.

"What?" his wife croaked.

"Nothing, woman. Go back to sleep."

The man rose out of bed and stretched. My heart stopped. There was no good hiding place for me. He walked toward me. My stomach turned into a knot. Bile rose in my throat.

Just before passing through the curtain, he turned to the side and relieved himself in a chamber pot, noisily passing gas for good measure. Another military trumpet. Father and son could have led a host of armed forces between them. I dropped my head in relief.

I had to wait another hour to ensure Aniketos fell back into a deep sleep. At least this time, I was not suffocating in a coffin. When Aniketos's snores became thunderous, I returned to my task. I had unclasped the lid before my host awoke, and now it opened smoothly to reveal the same cheap jewelry as before. I felt the sides, the top, the bottom panel of the box, hoping to find a latch to the secret compartment, but discovered nothing.

I was running out of time.

The box had defeated me. Then my eyes fell on the lion again. Instead of pressing, this time I tried to push it to one side and another. It held firm. More out of frustration than intention, I pulled on that lion as if it were a lever, and to my giddy relief, the bottom panel opened. I bent low to peer inside.

It was filled with gold coins.

For a moment, I stood paralyzed. Then, one at a time, avoiding the noisy jingle of metal crashing against metal, I placed the coins in the cloth bag

I had brought. When the bag filled, I pressed the secret compartment and the jewelry box shut. I had stolen Aniketos's treasure.

All that remained was to get away. I said a prayer to the Unknown God, asking for his help.

CHAPTER 18

—⚏—

THERE ARE MANY USES for a chamber pot if only one has enough imagination. Struck by sudden inspiration, I placed the coins on the floor and pushed aside the curtains enough to creep into my hosts' bedchamber. Grabbing the pot, I returned to the annex.

A basin of feathery ferns adorned one corner of the room. I poured out the chamber pot's contents inside it, whispering a silent apology to the ferns, shoved my bag of coins into the emptied chamber pot, and arranged the fabric to look like a towel covering.

It was almost dawn. I was a familiar slave carrying my master's chamber pot. No one stopped me as I made my way to Galatea's tiny chamber, where she had told Father she slept.

At sunrise, one of the guards came to fetch me, as I had expected. "A man named Galenos says his daughter has a present for the master. Says he won't give it to anyone but you."

I rose from my pallet, head lowered, my hair a

long curtain around my face. Grabbing the basket Galatea had prepared for me, I whispered, "I know the gentleman. He left his cloak here last night. I will take it to him right away."

The guard shadowed my steps out of the side door, where Father's litter waited. The curtains on the litter were firmly shut. I approached and offered the basket to my father. "Your cloak, master. You left it behind last night."

A hand bid me to go inside the litter. I gave a quick look to my guard, seeking permission. Dawn's light was hazy, hiding my features in its shadows. The guard yawned and motioned with his hand that I could go. I climbed inside the litter. A moment later, Galatea alighted from within, wearing her familiar bright-pink tunic, her basket now bearing a note of thanks for my hosts, written and sealed by my hand, along with a glass platter of rare dried peaches all the way from Persia.

That morning, a letter from the Honorable Thief was discovered, posted in the public square. As always, it was written in impeccable Latin:

> Plato wrote: "When men speak ill of thee, live so as nobody may believe them." You have proven the opposite, Aniketos. For when any speak well of you, we only have to look at your life to disbelieve

them. Your coins, which you have made by causing the powerless to suffer, shall serve a better purpose in my hands than yours. Besides, I have far better taste in . . . well, everything.

Father and I went to visit Aniketos and his wife a week later. To commiserate.

"I am horrified by this violation," I said. "It happened on the night of the banquet!" I buried my face in my hands. "I insisted you should have that feast. It distresses me beyond words."

Aniketos's mouth turned down. "None of your party is responsible, you can be sure of that. I checked the coins myself after everyone had left. They were safe then."

"How did it happen?" Father asked.

"That is the worst part." Aniketos's wife wrung her hands. "We cannot fathom how he did it. Everyone had left the house. The doors were barred. We had guards at every window and door." She shook her head with a violence that made her wig move, tilting it askew onto her forehead. I itched to reach out and straighten it.

"I suspect the guards slipped some of the wine meant for our guests into their own cups and were asleep on the job." Aniketos spat on the floor. "That fiend of a thief must have crept in under their noses. I have dismissed the lot and hired fresh men."

Galatea brought us a plate of miniature sponge cakes, drizzled with honey. "She is a sweet girl," I said to Aniketos. "Did you train her yourself?"

"Yes. I take a hand in training all my slaves."

"So I had heard. Is she for sale? I need a personal slave, one with good manners, pleasing to look at, and obedient. It is so hard to find a trustworthy slave these days."

Aniketos, smelling profit, sat straighter. "Galatea is all those things and more. A jewel in my house. I would find it hard to part with her."

"But for the right incentive?" Father asked, biting into a cake.

Aniketos smacked his lips. "Perhaps." He named a price that would have ransomed a Caesar.

Father raised a brow and named a lower price.

Back and forth it went, until Father pretended to lose interest. Aniketos, aware that Father's final offer was still a fair bit higher than the girl would fetch elsewhere, gave in. "Only for you, Galenos. And your exquisite daughter."

We walked out of the house, Galatea in tow, the Honorable Thief's profits reduced by a substantial sum. Father stopped on the way and ordered Galatea's manumission documents on the spot. She wept, the poor girl, when we handed them to her and assured her that she was free.

She threw herself at Father's feet. "Please, my lord, may I work at your house? As a servant? I will do anything. Work in the kitchens. Help with the laundry. Clean, sew, weave."

We did not need another servant. If anything, we were trying to diminish the household. Cut expenses. But we suspected that for a girl like Galatea, who had been born into slavery, a life of sudden freedom without the protection of a virtuous master could lead to disaster.

Father sighed. "You can work for us, though your wages will be modest. I will keep you for as long as I can afford. I promise if a time comes that I cannot bear the expense, I will find you a worthy mistress amongst my own friends."

Galatea thanked us with tears. She would not have a hard life in our house. Her work would be light, and she would be treated with kindness. Nor did she need fear the unwelcome advances of any man, young or old.

She did not know our secret, of course. Father had told her that I was caught in a tragic romance, and that my lover and I were meeting for one final night to bid each other goodbye at Aniketos's feast. Father had solicited her help two weeks before the banquet and received the information we needed, as well as her cooperation with our plan. In exchange, Father had promised her freedom, if Aniketos proved willing, or money for her, if he could not. Even slaves found a pouch full of coins handy. Galatea had given her help willingly, though she could not have known for certain that my father would honor his word to her.

She had heard of the theft since then, no doubt. If she connected that event with my absent night, she never mentioned it. I suspect she would have cheered had she known. She despised her old master and would have welcomed the opportunity to give him a sharp kick on the way out.

I had committed my first intentional crime. When the excitement of it evaporated, I had a hard landing. My life would never be the same again. I could not recover my innocence.

Galatea settled into the routine of our household with ease. After two weeks, it was as if she had been with us for years. In the same way that Delia had grown attached to my foster brother, Galatea formed a special connection with my father. Her eyes followed him with adoration wherever he went. She had an almost-prescient sense of his needs, so that before he asked, she would serve him. If he thirsted, watered wine found its way to his fingers; if he hungered, food appeared on his table; if he grew cold, a blanket spread over his lap; if he felt hot, she showed up with a fan.

We heard from Theo that he planned to return home in a week. At first, I worried for Galatea. My foster brother, with his undeniable beauty, his newfound confidence, and his solicitous manners had grown nearly irresistible for young women. Galatea, though six years our senior, was still young enough to drown in Theo's charms.

I need not have worried. She barely seemed to take note of Theo's presence when he came. He told us he did not plan to travel for several months. With the onset of winter, the seas were impassible and the roads uncomfortable. He could work for Justus in Corinth until late spring.

Our house grew warm with his presence. The ice that had divided him from Father started to melt for the first time in two years. Those became some of the happiest months I had ever known. Months of hope. Months of healing. We shared suppers together, listened to Theo's stories, and told him about the latest gossip in Corinth. Sometimes Claudia would join us, and to my delight, Justus, too, became a frequent visitor.

Once only did I feel the jolt of an odd uneasiness, like the mild rumblings that sometimes come before an earthquake breaks a mountain in half.

Father arrived home one evening, carrying a mysterious bag. "Come and see the curiosity I have bought."

He sent Galatea to fetch towels and a large bowl of hot water, while Theo, Delia, and I gathered about him to investigate. Out of his bag, he pulled a round ball of a soft-looking substance. It was the color of cream and smelled faintly of fat.

"What is it?" I said.

"Soap."

"Well, that explains . . . nothing."

"I have heard of this," Theo said. "It's used for cleaning."

"Precisely." Father pulled the bowl Galatea had fetched to the middle of the table. "I thought we could test it for ourselves."

"What is it made of?" I asked, poking it with a finger.

"Tallow and ashes."

"Tallow?" I wrinkled my nose. "It sounds disgusting. What's wrong with using proper olive or grape-seed oil?"

"With soap, you do not need to scrape the body with a strigil, as you would with perfumed oil." Father threw a different ball to each of us, Galatea and Delia included. "Let us begin our assessment, shall we?"

The women brought more bowls of water as well as additional jugs for rinsing, so that Theo and I could share one, Delia and Galatea work with another, leaving Father with his own bowl.

Galatea began to wash a piece of Delia's hair, as Father had claimed that soap was supposed to be especially beneficial for that purpose. Father washed his hands, his feet, and a linen napkin. Theo and I engaged in a hilarious battle, more interested in soaking one another than cleanliness.

Father examined his hands as well as the linen,

seeming impressed by the results. "Although it is a German invention, it seems quite useful," he said. "The Gauls have it too, apparently, though theirs is reported to be inferior."

He tossed one of the balls into the air and caught it. "What do you think, Theo? Will there be a wider market for this? Would it be worth investing in soap?"

Theo picked up one of the balls and sniffed it. "The smell is not ideal. But it has possibilities for convenience if nothing else. I doubt Romans will willingly give up the use of a strigil. This cannot scrape up dead skin. It works faster, though, with less fuss."

"You could add perfume," I said. "A mix of myrtle, cypress, and lemongrass for men; roses for women. That would appeal to the fastidious Roman nose."

"I will say this much for it: this soap cleans hair much better than our oils," Delia said.

"If we add perfume as Ariadne suggests," Father said thoughtfully, "we could sell it as hair pomade. Nothing like it exists in the Roman world. Perhaps one day soap might grow quite popular."

"Mistress Ariadne, we should try washing your hair with this," Delia said, rinsing her hands.

"Let's do it now," Theo declared with a grin, and pounced. Before I knew it, he was trying to drown me in water. The man had earned a victory wreath for wrestling, and I proved no match for him. He wrapped a hand around my arm and pulled me toward him. I fell laughing against his chest, trying to push against him and wrest the jug of water out of his hand at the same time.

Abruptly, he dropped the jug on the table with a clatter. His laughter evaporated. For a moment he held me against him.

I felt a shift in his mood. In the air itself. Not understanding the change, I wriggled out of his arms. Something about his touch, his manner, the stillness in his gaze made me uncomfortable and I frowned.

To break the tension, I threw a ball of soap at his head. He did not even bother to catch it. It hit him on the head, near the silver streak in his hair, and fell to the ground unheeded. His face had turned stony.

I thought he was angry with me for throwing soap at him and apologized. He said nothing. Instead, he climbed on the back of one of the horses and left for a long ride. When he returned, smelling of sweat and horse and grass, he looked tired but restored to good humor.

Men, I thought. They had their own time of the month.

CHAPTER 19

―ww―

IN EARLY SPRING we attended the long-awaited wedding of Claudia the Elder to Spurius Felonius. The groom, a widower significantly older than the bride, had been a resident of Corinth for under a year. This explained the wedding. He did not know the bride well enough to run the other way.

That was the year Gallio was declared the proconsul of Achaia, and being a friend of the groom, he was in attendance at the wedding feast. Lucius Junius Gallio was a thin man with veiny legs who complained of the air in Corinth, which gave him a headache and hampered his digestion. He spoke of his health half the night, a trait he did not lose for the duration of his two-year term.

He may not have been a diverting wedding guest, but the presence of a proconsul, even a man who was hypervigilant of his health and spoke in an annoying nasal tone, added a deal of consequence to the festivities. We were rubbing elbows with the elite of the world, not merely the elite of Corinth.

For the occasion, I had loaned Claudia the Younger my best tunic, made from purple linen, embroidered with gold thread. Theo had bought it in Philippi for my birthday the previous year, at Father's request. He had found an establishment owned by a woman named Lydia who produced exquisite purple goods at a price we could afford. Although not made from true purple, a dye extracted from tiny sea snails and prohibitively expensive, it was by far the most luxurious garment I owned.

Delia had arranged Claudia's hair, twining fresh flowers into a coronet of braids, creating a clever arrangement that accentuated my friend's delicate features. I thought her lovelier by far than her eldest sister's famed voluptuous beauty, which had grown tired and petulant with the passing years.

Galatea had seen to my own cosmetics and hair. Although proficient, she had nowhere near the talent Delia possessed. I looked well enough in my yellow tunic. In the old days, I would have washed my face, combed my hair, used tooth powder, and called myself ready. Delia had changed me more than I liked to admit. I could distinguish an eyelid darkened with expert hands from one drawn by an uninspired attendant.

I cared little for how I looked. My happiness

came from Claudia's glowing joy. It was the first time she had outshone her feted sister; the first time she wore rich clothing instead of the second- and third-hand leavings of older sisters.

Justus approached me during the banquet. "I salute you," he said, lifting his cup to me.

"What have I done?"

"It is not every woman who places kindness before vanity. It was good of you to lend your best tunic to your friend."

Confused by this compliment, devoid as it was of his usual pinch of irony, I studied the floor. Coming to myself, I asked, "What news of Dionysius?"

Justus plucked a handful of almonds from a passing tray. I had the odd sensation that he was playing for time rather than satisfying an urge. "I have not seen him for some months."

"Has he not written you?"

"He has. Yes. He seems happy. Some new philosophy has all his attention. You know how he is consumed by knowledge."

I expelled my breath. "I hope they have women philosophers in Athens, or that man will never find himself a wife."

Justus laughed. "He is not so lost as all that."

I studied the bride and groom, seated in the place of honor. Spurius Felonius weaved slightly as he refilled his cup, omitting the water flagon. His new wife played with a necklace of pearls, a wedding present from her groom. She had not smiled, not once, in the whole time she had sat there.

"I suppose it could be worse," I said. "Dionysius could marry the wrong woman and spend the rest of his life unhappy." It occurred to me that I would never meet my brother's wife when he did choose to wed.

By mutual consent, Father and I had not discussed the possibility of another theft while Theo remained at home. We had gained enough gold from Aniketos to be safe from moneylenders for a season. Each theft required careful planning, research, preparation, and we did not wish to lose time to such things while we had Theo with us. He would resume traveling soon enough and be absent from us for months.

After seeing Claudia's happy transformation at her sister's wedding, I gave Theo a few coins and told him to set them aside. "Go back to the establishment of that woman. Lydia. Go back there and buy a tunic for Claudia the Younger. I wish to surprise her with a gift."

Theo gave me a hard look. "I hope this is not your misguided attempt at matchmaking. My affection for Claudia is that of a friend. It will never become anything else. Do you understand, Ariadne? Never. My heart . . . my heart is not hers."

So he was not as mystified by women as he pretended. "Of course not," I said. "I am not matchmaking. The gift is on my behalf. Not yours. We have nothing like Lydia's purple here in Corinth. And if we did, it would come at twice the price I can afford. Since you plan to travel to Philippi, I hoped you would not mind doing me this small service."

He took my money, his hand a fist around the coins. His lips were pursed, the well-formed lines thinned as if he wanted to blurt something but could not compose the words.

"What is it?" I asked, frustrated. For weeks now I had had the sense that he withheld some important knowledge from me. His unspoken words hung between us, irritating me like a thorn.

He rolled his eyes and left me standing in the middle of the courtyard. It occurred to me that I might not be the only one with secrets in this house. But at least mine did not turn me into a capricious and sulky child.

I thought the worst troubles in life came through unfulfilled desires. Came because our longings went unmet. I did not realize that the answers to our deepest pleas could be as painful as they were healing. I had not believed in miracles. Not until Dionysius walked into our home again.

I was hunkered on my knees before a pot of fragrant mint in the courtyard, pruning dead stalks and adding fresh soil, when I heard footsteps. Looking up, I saw the face I thought never to behold again. It had been over a year since I had seen him. I sat frozen on the cold mosaic of that courtyard, my hands full of dirt, eyes wide and unblinking as I wondered if I were dreaming. He fell to his knees before me. Without words, he clasped me in his arms.

A simple embrace can speak more eloquently than words. More than reams of letters. More than books.

He wept, shaking as he held me. I wept with him, tears and mucus and joy mingling in melting relief, in helpless gratitude, in elated wonder. Because I knew my brother had returned to me. By some incomprehensible spinning of their threads, the fates had brought him home.

"Forgive me, Ariadne," he said, wiping his eyes.

"There is nothing to forgive. Well, except that I wiped my nose a little on your tunic."

He laughed. The sound was slightly hysterical and utterly splendid. "I have missed you," he said.

Father rushed in, Galatea at his side. She must have fetched him when she realized who had walked into the house unannounced. A few steps away from us, he came to a crashing stop, frozen. His eyes devoured Dionysius. My heart contracted. I did not know if Dionysius had come only for me, or if he had enough mercy to stretch to Father.

My brother rose to his feet with a slow unfurling of long muscles. He ran—ran like a sprinter rather than an Areopagite—and enfolded Father in his arms.

There weren't enough tears in the world to throw at the feet of that moment. The long separation was washed away, cleansed in our thanksgiving. They had much to say to each other, those two men. Months of silence and hurt to bridge. But for those first few moments, embraces did the speaking.

When they finally disappeared into Father's tablinum, doors closed, voices a quiet murmur, I perched on a chair and gave thanks to the Unknown God who had brought my brother to us. If only I had known his name then, I might not have been so grateful.

Father and Dionysius spoke in private for long hours. We ate supper together that night, Theo joining us. The last time we had all gathered like this, I had been eight years old. I was now twenty-one. So many years lost.

That first supper became a feast for the senses. We had not found the equilibrium of being together yet. We wept and laughed randomly, shared memories, casual incidents that bound us, events no one else in the world could comprehend quite as we did. I don't think anyone ate. The platters of food returned untouched, congealing, to the kitchen.

I realized as I crawled exhausted into bed that in spite of the hours we had spent together, neither my father nor my brother had mentioned what had brought about Dionysius's change of heart.

Several days passed and a new pattern emerged in our household. In the mornings, Dionysius and Father would speak for hours in private, redeeming the stolen years, I supposed, spanning the thousands of events they had missed in each other's lives. In the afternoons, everyone came together for supper. We ate and talked, becoming a family again instead of strangers tied by blood and the accidents of fortune.

Some mornings, when my father and brother emerged from the tablinum, they seemed shrouded in a curious reticence, as though they were holding something back from the world. From me. They made veiled references to things I could not understand, spoke cryptic comments, smiled at odd moments.

Our home had become a house of secrets. Father and I hid our own mystery from everyone. Theo was hiding something that ate at him. And now Dionysius and Father were adding their own secrets to the growing pile.

My nerves grew stretched. The air itself seemed to sizzle with the unknown. I wondered where they would lead, so many dark threads of our lives weaving together. So many truths unrevealed.

On the eighth afternoon following Dionysius's arrival, Theo took him for an early supper at Justus's house. Men only. I was not invited, and Father declined to go. I did not begrudge them their young men's pastime. What hurt was watching my brother walk out the door, though in my head I knew he would return in a few hours. After all we had been through, even short partings strained my damaged heart.

I perched on my favorite couch in the courtyard. It was made of chipped marble with a large crack running through the middle that we hid with a variety of cushions. I used to conceal myself under the seat when I was a little girl, trying to evade my mother.

Father joined me. "Dionysius has invited a friend to supper tomorrow evening. Justus will join us too."

"Who is it?"

"A man named Paul. Of Tarsus. He is a Jew who has recently moved to Corinth. A Pharisee."

"What is that?"

"A learned man of their faith."

"Are they conducting business together?" It seemed the only plausible explanation for my brother inviting a stranger into our home at such a time. We had not even invited Justus to supper

251

yet, preferring to solidify our own relationships first, before opening the doors of our home to outsiders. Only those closest to us would be welcome in our midst so early after Dionysius's return.

"They are friends," Father said. "Dionysius has spoken much about this man to me. I look forward to meeting him. It is a happy coincidence that he lives in Corinth at the moment. He travels extensively, as I understand."

"Friends? Where did they meet?" I could not imagine Dionysius having anything in common with a religious Jew.

"In Athens. But I must let Dionysius tell you that story himself. I only wanted to warn you that you should expect company tomorrow."

Corinth was home to a large Jewish community. I had met several, though I did not know any of them on intimate terms. I remembered one pertinent fact, however. "Do they not eat a special diet, the Jews? What should I have the cook prepare for this man?"

"Dionysius assures me that he is not fastidious with his food."

"So he is not very religious, this . . . What did you call him? Pharisee?"

Father's smile was enigmatic. "He is a man of faith. But his faith does not burden him with troublesome religious rules."

CHAPTER 20

—⁓—

I STUDIED OUR GUEST as Dionysius welcomed him with obvious affection before introducing him to Father. Short and wiry, he had the legs of a man who walked long distances. His unruly hair had touches of gray. Large, dark eyes, wreathed in laugh lines, settled on me with sharp intelligence. It was not a shallow gaze. I felt stripped before that survey—not of my clothing, as I had at times experienced with other men, but of my defenses. You would not remain a stranger before that gaze for long. Instinctively, I lowered my lashes.

Father invited him into the peristyle, the roofed garden of our house, where I had arranged for supper to be served. He folded his body onto the couch with a singular economy of motion, as if he had no wish to draw attention to himself. Yet there was no doubt that he was the center of everyone's attention.

The man reminded me of a sheathed dagger, a storm held back. There was about him an air of power, wrapped up in silky kindness. *We have invited a hurricane under our roof,* I thought. *Any moment now, he will explode and wash away everything in his tide.*

"How did you meet Paul?" I asked my brother once the first course had been served.

"I heard him speaking in the public square in Athens a few months ago. For ten days, he stood in a corner of the marketplace and spoke to whoever happened to be there."

"I'm not bashful," Paul said.

Dionysius chuckled. "As I found to my detriment. I began to question him, for his ideas, while exotic and wild, had a cogency that intrigued me."

"He was not the only Stoic philosopher who questioned me." Paul set down his spoon. "There was a row of them waiting for me every morning when I showed up. And a different row made up of Epicureans. I don't know who they heckled more—me or each other."

Dionysius dipped his bread in fish sauce. "The Epicureans are a familiar target for our wit. You offered fresh pickings. Much more enjoyable."

The Epicureans believed that the principal aim of life was to find tranquility and happiness. Death simply marked the end of existence. They had no room for the gods or an afterlife.

My brother, by contrast, was a Stoic. He believed in the Logos, a force—a power within nature that sustained life and bestowed reason. Like the famed statesmen Cicero and Seneca, my brother believed in a universe permeated by reason, though some of his contemporaries called it God or Providence.

"After ten days of listening to him, I invited Paul to join us on Mars Hill," Dionysius said. "So he could speak to the Council of the Areopagus."

Paul wiped his mouth with a plain napkin. "I should note that Athenians seem to like nothing so much as talking. They spend untold hours discussing ideas. I have never heard so many words spoken in one place. If words could feed the belly, Athenians would be a stout people."

I guffawed. I could like this Jew.

"We do like the sound of our own voices," Dionysius admitted.

"What did Paul say to the high council?" I asked Dionysius.

"Do you remember the altar of the Unknown God? The one near the marketplace?"

At the mention of my favorite god, I stopped pretending to eat and sat up. "Yes. What about it?"

"Paul said he knew the identity of that god."

A shiver went through me. I stared at Paul and tried to quiet my stretched nerves. Anyone could claim to know a god. "And who is it?"

"He is the God who made the world and everything in it." Paul stretched his hand, like an invitation. "Can you imagine such a God—one with enough power to raise up a mountain as if it were an anthill, with majesty vast enough to create the skies, with beauty wild enough to birth the oceans—can you imagine such a God inhabiting a man-made temple? It is childish to think so."

"You sound like the Stoics," I said. "Out with the old divinities and their mercurial ways and pretty temples. Let us turn, instead, to the way of reason, to the force at work in the natural world."

"That is what I first thought." Dionysius sprang up from his reclining position. "But it is not so. For the Logos I believed in was not knowable. It was merely a power. A force at work."

I noticed my brother said *believed* rather than *believe.*

Paul pulled on his beard. "It would be sad, indeed, if the world were at the mercy of an impersonal force, a detached power without the ability to love. The God I speak of gives life and breath to everything. To this clump of mint, to you, to me. He knows the number of hairs on your head. He cares for the desires of your heart. Underneath the currents of your life, he stretches his everlasting arms. He has set his affections on you, though he knows your every weakness. The broken and the good in you. His love makes you whole. No man can give you this. Only God."

256

I laughed, but it was a forced thing, limping out of me. I yearned to be known and loved. To be made whole. I had longed for Justus to give me that. This Jew was claiming that somewhere in the world there was a god who could give me what I longed for.

"And how much will this god cost me?" I said, my teeth on edge.

Dionysius rubbed an eyelid. "I understand your skepticism. I felt the same. But Paul is not asking for your money."

"This is true. I am asking for a lot more."

Justus grinned. I glared at him. He held up a conciliatory hand. "What? He is amusing."

"What are you asking for?"

Paul did not seem discomfited by my unfriendly tone. I suppose he was accustomed to such treatment from strangers. "God's purpose was for every man and woman in every nation to seek after him. In the dark confusion of this life, he wanted us to feel our way toward him. To find him, though he is not far from any one of us. Wasn't it Epimenides who said, 'In him we live and move and have our being'? He is closer to you than your own heartbeat, Ariadne."

"What are you asking for?" I said again.

The brown eyes turned the full force of their power on me. There was an odd tenderness in that gaze, but also something unbendable and sharp. "I ask nothing. God . . . Well. He asks for everything. God wants you, Ariadne. Every part of you."

The rest of our dinner passed through a haze. I noticed Father and Justus and even Theo engaged in animated conversation with this odd man who said his god wanted everything. That claim alone should have caused them to turn their backs and run in the opposite direction. Instead they asked questions, probed deeper. The whole while, Dionysius supported Paul's claims, expanded on them with his own explanations.

I had seen Dionysius study philosophy all our lives. In his younger years, he swayed from one ideal to another, studying for hours, practicing rhetoric, until he threw his lot in with the Stoics. But this was different.

This wiry man with his mix of Roman and Hebrew education didn't offer a mere philosophy. He sought to change our lives. Under the layers of his gentle promises, he came with a volcanic eruption.

Late that evening, after our guests had departed and my brothers retired to bed, Father found me sitting in the atrium.

He perched on a stool in front of me. Without prelude he whispered, "Dionysius has asked me to give up stealing."

My head snapped up. "Wait. When—?"

"I have agreed." His voice was pitched low so

no one could hear us. In his quiet tones I sensed a firmness I had never heard before.

"What? *What?*"

"He is right, Ariadne. What I have been doing, what I have caused you to do . . ." He shook his head. "I have lived a life of misguided arrogance. Of selfishness. And I have tainted you with it. I want to start afresh. A new life."

"We have had this conversation before," I said, trying to calm him. My body started to feel icy cold. "Because of us, Galatea is free. How is that wrong?"

"If we wanted to free her, we should have paid for her with our own money."

"Which we don't have." I threw my hands in the air. "Be reasonable. All of Corinth loves you." I bent toward him. "Is this Paul's doing? This is what he means when he says that God wants all of you?" My lip curled. "This fresh start you long for is the dictate of some religion? We are going to lose our home and our land for the sake of a hokey God, raised up in who knows what crumbled corner of the empire?"

A touch of steel colored Father's voice. "Don't be disrespectful of what you do not understand. I am giving up the Honorable Thief. That is all you need to know."

I watched him leave in disbelief. He had never spoken to me like that, with that note of finality. With such unbending disapproval.

Dionysius found me in the early morning hours, still occupying the same spot on the cracked couch. Gingerly, he folded his long body next to me. "Father spoke to you."

"He said he is changing his life for you."

He adjusted the drape of his toga over his left shoulder. He had turned Roman in Corinth. In Athens, he wouldn't have touched a toga, though he had every right to it.

"You are angry with me."

"What right do you have to impose your precious beliefs on us? If Paul and his God are what you want, then go and extol your divinity. Laud and magnify him to your content. Why do you insist that Father should dedicate himself to your faith?"

"I insisted nothing, Ariadne. I did not impose my ideas on Father."

I crossed my arms and leaned away. "That poor man is so afraid of losing you again that he would go to any lengths merely to keep you. Is that not an imposition?"

"When I first knew I had to return to Father, I intended to give him an ultimatum: give up theft or lose me. Stealing is wrong. As a Stoic I believed it. When I became a follower of Christ and read the Holy Scriptures, I became even more convinced of its wrongness. I have memorized the books of the Jewish Law and they support my reasoning. I told Paul what I intended to do."

"I knew it," I cried. "That man is behind this."

"That man censured me for my harsh attitude. 'There is a world of difference between knowing the Word of God and knowing the God of the Word,' he said. The Lord offers us mercy, unearned and undeserved. That is the God I serve, Ariadne. Paul taught me that Father needs my forgiveness, not my judgment. I came to him in love. The decision to change was his, entirely."

There was bitterness in my voice now. "You are stripping him of everything he enjoys. You call that love?"

Dionysius came to his feet. "Perhaps he does not enjoy this life as much as you imagine."

Dionysius, trained as he was in rhetoric, would always have an answer to the objections I raised. He would win every argument. I was not Athenian; I was done with words.

I knew what I had to do. Dionysius expressed his love one way. I would love by another means. I would not allow my brother's new faith and moral convictions to rob Father of his home and lands. Of his dignity. We needed only two more robberies to pay off our debts and establish a secure future. Two more evil men punished.

We did not ruin lives, I told myself. We only took what was spurious, the crumbs of a corrupt man's luxuries. I would cause no harm. The opposite, in fact. I would bring about a touch of justice, and give my father the stability he deserved. I was not a thief.

I was not planning to make a life of thieving. My actions would be an aberration. An exception. Why, it was almost my duty.

Part 3
LOVE NEVER FAILS

—ɯ—

Love is patient, love is kind. It does not envy,
it does not boast, it is not proud. It does not
dishonor others, it is not self-seeking, it is not
easily angered, it keeps no record of wrongs.
Love does not delight in evil but rejoices with the
truth. It always protects, always trusts,
always hopes, always perseveres.
Love never fails.

1 Corinthians 13:4-8, NIV

CHAPTER 21

—ʍ—

IT TOOK SEVERAL WEEKS to decide who my next victim would be. Weeks to prepare, study the house and its fortifications. Weeks to devise a plan.

During that time, Paul was a regular visitor to our home. Sometimes he came alone. Sometimes he brought with him another Jew named Silas. He was a quieter man than Paul. When he spoke, his words were gentle, full of a soothing acceptance that made you feel the world was safe so long as this man was with you. A young half-Greek athlete called Timothy accompanied them occasionally. Theo liked Timothy and took to training with him at the gymnasium.

Justus seemed as drawn to Paul as Dionysius and my father. Even Theo delayed his travels to listen to him drone on about his precious Jesus.

When Paul spoke, he insisted on inviting every servant and slave in our household to join us if their duties allowed. He made no distinction between us, Roman or Greek, male or female, rich or poor. He seemed to think of us as equals, and even said so upon occasion. He could outrage you with claims like that, make you laugh the next instant, and befuddle you with convoluted doctrines before you had a chance to swallow your spit.

One night I joined them, sitting on the periphery, my arms crossed, my ankles crossed, my lips a flat line. Paul was speaking about love. His gaze swept the chamber, landing on different faces.

"The love of God is deeper than anything you have tasted," he said. "I will prove it to you. Close your eyes. Close them and think of a person you love with all your heart."

I kept my eyes firmly open. But everyone else obeyed the Pharisee.

"Now," he said, "let us put your love to God's test, for this is how *God* loves. Say to the one you are thinking of: *My love for you is patient. I have never been impatient with you. Not by word or deed have I ever shown you any impatience.*"

"Well, I'm done for already," Delia said. "I cannot say that without lying. I have no patience." Everyone laughed.

Paul smiled. "Now make this declaration if you can: *My love for you is kind. I have not spoken to you unkindly in all the years that I have known you. I have never harbored an unkind thought toward you.*"

A few people began to squirm on their seats. I was among them.

"It is a hard test, is it not?" Paul pulled on his beard. "But we have a long list to cover. Next, say this to your beloved: *I have never been envious of you. Never felt jealous of your abilities or possessions. I am not resentful or angry when you spend time with others or show them affection.*"

Justus snapped his eyes open and cleared his throat. I found this odd, for so far as I knew, the man had never tasted of jealousy in his life.

Paul moved about the room. *"I have never spoken rudely to you."*

By now, everyone had opened their eyes and was wincing a little. Who could make these claims with honesty?

He went quiet for a moment, then pivoted, locking his gaze with mine. *"My love for you does not make selfish demands. I have never insisted that I should have my own way."*

My heart began to pound. I felt for a moment as if he had burrowed into my thoughts and unearthed my secrets. Unearthed my insistence to have my way about the Honorable Thief. To keep stealing even though Father had forbidden me to do so and my brother thought it wrong.

He turned a fraction, and I could breathe again.

"My love is not easily angered," he said. "I have never held on to offenses you have com-

mitted against me. Indeed, I have wiped them from my heart and memory."

My brother's eyes welled with tears.

Still the man went on. *"My love for you has never given up, never lost faith, never stopped hoping for the best. I have not given in to despair or discouragement, no matter what we have faced. My love for you will endure through every circumstance."* He placed a hand on my father's shoulder. Father dropped his face into shaking fingers.

Paul now closed his own eyes as the rest of us watched him.

"My love for you never fails. Not even in the darkest hours."

Then, opening his eyes, he surveyed the room. "You see, my friends, true love is patient and kind. Godly love is not jealous or boastful or proud. It is not rude or irritable. It does not demand to have its own way. Love never gives up. Never loses faith. It is always hopeful. Love endures through every circumstance. That kind of love never fails."

If this was love's standard, then we had never loved. Not truly. The room sank under the weight of our failure.

Paul sat at the edge of a heavy pot bearing an olive tree. He studied us, eyes heavy-lidded with sympathy. *"We* fail. We fail because we have never tasted of such a love. We do not know how to receive it, how to give it. It requires a power beyond our own to live out this love. To experience it. That power can come only from God himself. From the Spirit of our Lord. How I pray that you will have the spiritual strength to comprehend how wide and long and high and deep is the love of Christ for you. And tasting of that love, learn to love as Jesus loves."

Paul waited in silence. Let his words sink in. Then he said, "My brothers and sisters, God is love. God is all that. And he asks us to live by the same measure. And when we fail even with his help, then he reaches out in mercy and covers our gaps."

Paul's speech was like a thunderbolt in a black sky, illuminating everything in sharp contrast. Those words made you see your own heart, the empty places you hid in the dark. They were words that made you hungry. Who wouldn't want to be loved like that? A love without boundaries, a love that endured and forgave all things. A love that never failed.

Those same words were a whip to the soul. I knew I had never loved anyone like that. Not Theo or Dionysius or Father. Not even Justus.

The man I targeted as my victim traded in antiquities. Velasio Grato had a fondness for helpless widows. While they were grieving and in shock, he would swoop down to charm, bully, and frighten them into selling valuable possessions for a fraction of their worth.

A woman of my acquaintance had lost two statues of inestimable value to Grato. Widowed young with two children still toddling, she had been frightened by his tales of doom and conned into hawking her fortune for a pittance. She could have had a comfortable life if those statues had fetched a fair price. Instead, she and her children lived in poverty. I brought them food each week and did what I could to help. From her, I heard other horror stories. Grato struck without mercy, leaving behind him a trail of misery, growing fat on the suffering of others.

His villa was situated two houses down from the residence of Spurius Felonius, Claudia the Elder's husband. I had been in the neighborhood for the wedding feast, which had been held in Felonius's home. Grato's villa, unlike Felonius's residence, did not offer tight security measures. It had no additional land attached to it. The villa's walls came up to the street, and other than the large central courtyard, there was no outdoor garden. Climbing its walls hardly offered a challenge.

I wrangled an invitation to Felonius's home through Claudia the Younger and met Grato there. From that meeting, it was only a matter of a few suggestive words to win an invitation for Claudia and me to attend a banquet at his house.

"Explain again why we are attending this boring party?" Claudia asked me on the night of the banquet. "Everyone will be twenty years our senior."

"At least his house will be filled with pretty works of art. Think of it as an education for your soul. Besides, you might meet an eligible bachelor. Your own sister is married to a man twenty years her senior."

"And look how that turned out," Claudia said. The elder Claudia had grown more sulky and vicious since her marriage.

"Yes. Well, perhaps that is not a good idea. But Grato is famous for the excellent desserts he serves."

Claudia, who in spite of her slender figure had a passionate love for sweets, grinned. "In that case, it would be rude not to go."

Grato was an unmarried man closer to sixty than fifty. We were greeted by his steward, an educated slave with the manners of a diplomat, who showed us into the dining room, where other guests had already gathered. Claudia's prediction had been astute. This group held no attractions for two young women.

"May we see your ravishing home?" I asked Grato. "It is said that none in Corinth can equal its sumptuous art." I had learned one thing from my misspent year among Corinth's rich and idle. Flattery opened many doors.

Grato obliged me with a winning humility that explained how he fooled so many. If I had not known the source of his collection, I would have enjoyed the tour. Most of what he showed us was too heavy to prove useful for my intent. In a side chamber, I finally saw what I wanted. He had a collection of small, jeweled boxes, delightfully constructed from gold, silver, and precious stones. Pulled apart and melted down, they would fetch a decent price. All that remained was for me to take them.

The following day, I walked over to the plot of land next door and settled on a smooth rock to think. Distracted by thoughts of Grato's house, I had forgotten to bring a shawl to ward off the chill in the air. I sat shivering in the wind, wishing Theo were with me. I longed to share my secret with him. To plan and plot with him. To enlist his help in swaying Father to my side or, failing that, enlist his assistance with robbing Grato's house. An impossible longing. Theo was as likely to expose me as he was to help me. I could not predict how he might respond to my plan. I expelled a long breath.

"That was a heavy sigh."

I started at the unexpected voice. "Justus!" The man had a way of always surprising me.

"Race you to the tree and back. For old times' sake."

The idea of beating him cheered me, and I nodded. Justus unpinned his cloak while I hiked up my tunic. I no longer had the speed I once enjoyed, but then neither did he. By the time I reached the tree, my breathing was jagged. I doubled back and pushed harder. Justus kept up step for step, but he did not pass me, and we arrived at the finish marker together.

I bent over, hands on knees, too winded to speak. To my satisfaction, Justus's breathing was no less labored. We caught each other's eyes and began to laugh.

"I fear I am growing old," he said. "It comes from too much work. Like Corinth's ancient king Sisyphus, rolling the same rock to the top of the hill only to have it roll back down, and I have to start again. Such is the labor of men."

"Do you not like your work?" I asked, concerned. The thought of Justus unhappy made my heart contract.

He sat on the stone I had occupied earlier. "I enjoy most things about it. Like all work, import and trade have their challenges. The unpredictability of the elements and the dangers of travel, the dishonesty of people, the endless problems that crop up when one least expects them." He shrugged. "Every good thing comes with a price. I have much to give thanks for."

A pair of golden finches flew into view. They danced together in the air, whirling one way, then another in a parallel arc before perching on the branches of a tree. Justus and I watched their graceful movements, entranced. "They are beautiful," I said.

"They remind me of you."

The breath hitched in my throat. "Me?"

"You and Theo."

"Me and *Theo!*"

"Can you still do it? That odd backward flip you used to do with him?"

"What?" I gazed at him, nonplussed. He was not supposed to know about that.

"The window in my tablinum opens this way. In the summer, a blanket of shrubs covers the view. But later in autumn, I can see the land clearly. I used to watch you and Theo train."

My eyes rounded. "That was private."

He laughed. "Then perhaps you should have removed yourselves to a more secret location."

"We were under the impression this was a secret location."

Justus held up his hands. "I have no quarrel with you. I merely wished to know if you could still do it."

Pride battled with irritation. It was not a long struggle. Pride won with ease. I stood still, knees touching, my feet aligned with my hips. Squatting, I stretched my arms behind me and swung them in a wide arc, gaining the impetus I needed as I jumped. Tucking my knees into my chest, I flipped backward and landed with perfect precision on my feet without staggering.

Justus's clap held a slow, mocking edge. "It's even more impressive up close. Theo told me about the man from Crete who inspired you."

"He told you?"

"Only after I shared my knowledge of your activities. I remember one time, I saw you climb a tree." He looked around and pointed to the gnarly sycamore. "That one. It took you a moment to scramble up. Then you hung from a branch, using your calves and knees, hands extended down. Theo grabbed your arms, and you pulled him up, that great lug of a boy, until he perched on the branch next to you. Can you still do that?"

Something about the intensity of his tone began to make me uncomfortable. "Why do you wish to know?"

He made a fluttering gesture with his fingers. The dark-green eyes shuttered. "Merely admiring your many talents, Ariadne."

"I might be able to," I said, opting for caution.

"It is an interesting skill, and surely not common. It put me to mind of a story I heard recently about a robbery at the house of a Roman official."

The blood drained from my face. "How odd," I said.

"I was traveling to Delphi. A short trip to resolve an unexpected problem with a shipment of goods. On the road, I ran into Brutus. Have you met him? The man whose house was almost robbed a couple of years ago. You must have heard about it. Corinth was in an uproar over the matter."

"I am not certain." My voice sounded strained to my own ears.

"Allow me to refresh your memory. I speak of the famous attempted robbery where the thief was almost captured in the garden. The man pursuing the thief thought he had vanished into thin air. But another guard reported seeing an accomplice who could climb trees with the dexterity of a dryad, hang from them upside down, and pull a grown man up with her bare arms."

Justus cracked his knuckles. "Brutus told me, while we shared a meal at a roadside tavern, that the man thought the accomplice was a woman. Her cloak had slipped from her head, and he had glimpsed a long braid down her back. Brutus thought this impossible, of course. But I knew better."

Justus leaned forward, his gaze sizzling into me. "Who was that, Ariadne?" His usually aloof manner had deserted him, the golden skin of his face turning an angry red.

I stared at him, my tongue paralyzed. With unbelievable speed, he was on his feet, standing in front of me. Before I could expel a breath, he pulled me hard against his chest. "More to the point, who was the thief who helped you?"

"What . . . What are you talking about?" I stammered.

His hands wrapped about my arms, holding me close. "I know it wasn't Theo. I have it on good authority that he was in Ephesus at the time. So you have roped someone else into this ridiculous ploy. Who is it, Ariadne? Who is the poor fool you have wrapped around your finger?"

Before I could think of a convincing lie, he bent his head and kissed me. It was as if his anger melted, soothed away by the simple touch of his lips on mine. His kiss, warm and soft at first, became deep and hungry, making me gasp. Strong hands slid up my back to the base of my neck, tangling in my hair. I shivered helplessly.

I hadn't had a chance to pull my tunic down when I had finished running, and my bare legs could feel the cold wind as it whipped against us. I burrowed deeper into him and moaned with longing. His kiss went wild, brimming with a raw edge of yearning that matched my own.

Happiness and confusion and fear were exploding through me like a cyclone. Justus wanted me! After years of neglect, he finally desired me. He thought I was a thief! He knew my secret.

I hardly felt the first pelting drops of rain as they lashed against us. Then the heavens opened as if to empty a lake over our heads. We were drenched in moments. Justus stepped away, looking dazed. Water ran down his cheeks. I ran tender fingers over his lips and down the grooves I had always admired.

He bent his head and gave me one more lingering kiss, as if in spite of the wind and the rain and our heated words, he could not help himself. Then he withdrew, arms folded against his chest. He studied me for a moment, gulped, and hastily turned his back.

"Take this," he said, offering his cloak over his shoulder, keeping his face averted. I looked down and choked. The rain had plastered my old linen tunic against my skin, soaked it so that it clung to my body, almost transparent.

"I will take you home," he said when I had covered myself in the soft folds of his cloak. His voice had turned as cold as the weather. I blinked, startled by the transformation in his face, which had gone from the melting features of a lover to the icy appearance of a magister. Then it dawned on me. The kiss was an aberration. He had not meant it to happen. Anger and disappointment had twisted into momentary passion. He was as surprised by his actions as I. There would be no more kisses.

This was time for sword and parry, for an interrogation that might change my fate.

I set my face into an apathetic mask, and we began to walk side by side, two strangers. The rain stopped before we reached my house. Justus hesitated.

"Was it a dare? A game gone too far with one of your old flighty friends? I cannot fathom what else would possess you to do such a thing."

"You've lost your mind."

"Where were you that night?"

He was going to press and press until I gave him irrefutable proof of my innocence. "I was with my father. You can ask him if you don't believe me."

"I didn't tell you what night."

Once again my tongue had landed me in trouble. "I knew what story you were talking about. I heard the rumors."

Justus did not reply. Instead, he motioned me toward the posticum, where we met with Delia.

"We are soaked through, as you see," he said. "Your mistress and I were caught in the downpour. You had best help her change into dry clothes before she catches a chill."

I noticed that he made no move to leave. "Shouldn't you return home to change as well, Justus?" I hinted. "Surely this damp threatens your health as much as it does mine."

He gave a tight smile. "I am practically dry." Water dripped onto his shoes from the edge of his tunic and ran in droplets from his plastered hair onto his exposed neck. "Delia, please fetch Galenos to me."

I realized at once what he meant to do. He wanted to test my alibi. To speak to Father before I could. It was a frightening thought. And yet I could do nothing about it without appearing guilty. I turned on my heels and climbed the stairs that led to my chamber. If the Isthmian Games had a competition for changing robes, I would have won that day. I raced down the stairs in time to see Father embrace Justus and invite him into the dining room.

Folding the cloak he had loaned me, I followed the men, using it as an excuse to join them uninvited. "I fear it is soaked." I handed the garment to Justus, and instead of leaving, leaned against the wall, pretending to be a fresco.

Father had someone fetch Justus towels and a fresh cloak. "And bring warm spiced wine with extra honey. That was quite a downpour," he said.

"Yes." Justus sank onto a marble couch.

Father gave him a quizzical look. He made a strange sight, dripping over our furniture when he could have returned to the comfort of his own home and changed into dry things.

"I have a question to ask you, Galenos. Will you tell me the truth?"

Father crossed his legs. Not even by one twinge did he betray the underlying offense of such a request. "Of course."

"The night Brutus's house was robbed—do you remember it?"

"I do. What is this about, Justus?"

"Please, Galenos. Answer my question. Was Ariadne with you that night?"

My father hesitated. He turned his face to look at me. "She was."

"Are you certain? It was quite some time ago."

"I have no doubt of it. We were awake together almost the whole night. I . . . needed help, and Ariadne remained with me into the morning. She took care of me. Hard to forget such an unusual evening."

A wave of relief washed over me as I realized how adroitly Father had averted a disaster. He had told the truth, but he had told it in a way that provided me with an alibi. Without telling a lie, he had implied that he had been unwell that night, and I had nursed him through ill health.

Justus seemed confused. "Ah . . . Forgive me for my impudence. Thank you, Galenos." He came to his feet. "I had better go home and change. These damp things are growing uncomfortable." He fumbled with the wet cloak. "Ariadne, perhaps you would be kind enough to accompany me to the door?"

I walked beside him in silence, my feelings a tangled mess as I considered the alarming accuracy of his intuition. He had come so near to discovering what I had done. I didn't even have words for his kisses. At the gate he turned to face me. "I apologize, Ariadne. Clearly I was wrong."

281

"Clearly," I said, my voice stony. In truth, I could not find it in myself to be angry. Frightened out of my wits and stupefied with love, yes. But I could not hold the truth against him.

"I . . . I could not think of another explanation."

"Of course not."

"And . . . I am truly sorry for taking advantage of . . . of the situation."

Now I was angry. "Indeed."

He rubbed the back of his neck. "I ought not to have kissed you."

I shoved the door closed in his face, and hoped with great sincerity that it had broken his stupid, crooked nose. What woman wanted to be kissed to distraction and then told it was a mistake?

CHAPTER 22

—⁓—

I STARED AT THE WOODEN BEAMS of the door, fuming. Something niggled at my mind. Justus's behavior did not make sense. He had erupted like a volcano, emotion leaking out of every word. That was not Justus. The Justus I knew had mastered a polished remoteness of manner that could chill you to the bone with one word. He was cool, even in anger. He did not blow up like lava.

Why had he pressed to know the identity of my partner with such vehemence? He had not jumped to the conclusion that my father was the thief, an error that had provided me with an alibi. Instead, he had referred to my accomplice as the man I had wrapped around my finger. The mere mention of my supposed partner had plunged him into fury.

Justus had not acted as a man investigating a crime with calculating logic. He had behaved like a man betrayed. He had acted like a jealous lover. I remembered with vivid intensity Justus's reaction when Paul told us that true love does not succumb to jealousy. At the time, I could not conceive of a situation in which Justus would have faced such an emotion.

My breath caught. He might not admit it, not even to himself, but Justus cared for me, not as the little sister of his dear friend, but as a woman. It was the only explanation that made sense.

I grew still, body and soul, everything coming to a stop. My heart swelled with hope.

With slow steps, I made my way to Father's tablinum, where I knew he would be waiting for me.

"What was that about?" Father demanded as soon as he saw me. "Why did Justus ask me about the night of Brutus's robbery?"

Sinking onto the stool facing him, I recounted what Justus had said. I left out the kiss, of course. He raked his hands through his hair. "That man is too sharp. He almost had you, Ariadne."

"One thing saved us. No one connected the attempted theft at Brutus's house with the Honorable Thief. You left no letter. Claimed no part in it. Everyone in Corinth assumed it to be the act of a common criminal. If the Honorable Thief had been known as the culprit, Justus might have realized you were my accomplice that night. As it was, he assumed I had partnered with a young man of my acquaintance. He suspected me guilty of youthful mischief that had gone too far."

Father laid his head on the back of the sofa. "Thank goodness we have stopped."

I knotted my hands in my lap.

For the length of a breath I toyed with the idea of complying with Father's wishes. Of stopping. If Justus had begun to love me, he would give us the financial help we needed. I could give up my plan to rob Grato. My father's heart would burst with shame if he had to accept money from Justus. He would rather be poor than receive charity, knowing he could never repay such a sum.

No. I would have to find my own way as I always did.

Father and I had cobbled together a patched-up peace between us. I did not speak of Paul or God, and he did not mention the Honorable Thief. To him, the subject was closed. Finished.

He spent his time with Dionysius and Paul and Paul's friends. When he was alone, he amused himself with a new hobby: German soap. He had become unusually enamored of the stuff and conducted his own experiments on its effectiveness. I thought he had grown a little too fond of cleanliness.

One afternoon, he brought home a fresh batch.

"Try this one," he said, offering me a light-green ball. I sniffed at it with caution. Thankfully, it had lost its unpleasant odor of animal fat and smelled instead of lemongrass and lavender.

"Smells better," I admitted.

"I had the man who makes them add perfumed oil to a batch, as you suggested. It makes them more expensive, of course. But I think it also adds to their desirability." He pressed several balls into my hands. "Try them on your hair."

"What for?" Being a man, he had no idea how long it took to wash and style hair as long and thick as mine.

"Because I wish to know if it works."

I expelled a heavy sigh, fisted my fingers around the soap, and walked off toward the baths. I saved the man from capture and death, robbed for him, planned and schemed for him; I even washed my hair for him. Did he appreciate me? Of course not! He preferred to pour his appreciations into the Jewish God with a dead Son who was, in fact, not dead. I wished someone would explain *that* puzzle to me.

I was whipping up a good storm of resentment when Theo stepped into my path.

"I am glad you are here," I said. "Smell this for me before I use it." I stuck the green ball under his nose. "It will probably make me bald."

He pushed it away. "I need to speak to you," he said in a wooden voice. He had turned the color of the soap.

"What is it?"

"In private." He took my hand and tugged. We did not speak as we walked to our favorite spot, where we used to race and train. One week before, Justus had kissed me here. Now he avoided me. I heaved a sigh, distracted. It took me a few moments to realize Theo had become like the pulled string of a bow, ready to snap. His jaw jutted and the veins on his neck stood out against his smooth skin.

Confusion turned me dumb. What ailed him now?

Finally we stood beneath the tree we had once climbed together. "Ariadne, Galenos told me about the Honorable Thief."

My eyes bulged out of my head. "He told you?"

"He said you helped him."

"I . . . might have. Are you angry?"

He shrugged. "I understand why he did it. And I am glad you saved his life. But to continue! Were you mad?" He shook his head. "Do you know what could have happened to you if they'd caught you at Aniketos's house?"

I smirked. "They didn't."

"Not that time. What concerns me is this: Have you truly given it up, Ariadne? It hasn't occurred to Galenos that you could be that headstrong. But I know you. Do you have some deranged plan to save him from his financial troubles? Another house to rob?"

My breath hitched. "I don't know what you mean."

"Ariadne, will you listen to reason?"

"I am the only reasonable person in this family!"

Theo kicked a rock, sending it flying into the distance. "Tell me one thing: How are you any different from Celandine?"

I felt like he had slapped me. He could not have paid me a greater insult. "Theo! I have nothing in common with that woman."

"You insist on having everything your own way, just as she did. You won't listen to your father or to Dionysius or to me. You think everyone is wrong but you. You endanger all of us, Ariadne. Worst of all, you endanger yourself. I want you to promise that you will not attempt another robbery."

I was still in the grip of his earlier accusation. Did he truly think me like my mother?

"Ariadne." His voice softened as he took my hand. He looked at his shoes, shifted from foot to foot. "I have something to ask you."

"I know. You want me to stop stealing." I was already forming an answer in my mind, coming up with the reasons I could not heed his request.

"No. I mean yes. That too. But I have something else to ask. It . . . I . . . It is very important."

What could be more important than the Honorable Thief? I was growing restless. Pulling my hand out of his, I planted it on my hip and tapped my foot.

"Ariadne. I must tell you something. A secret I have withheld from you."

Zeus's eyeballs. Was he a thief too? "What is it, Theo?"

"I . . . I love you."

I exhaled. "Is that all? I love you too. You know that. You must not allow the awkwardness of the past or this business with Aniketos to come between us."

"No. I mean . . ." He shoved a hand through his hair, making it stand on end, revealing the silver streak he tried to hide with careful combing and use of hair pomades. I reached a finger and caressed his hair softly back into place. I adored that silver mark. Although he thought it a flaw, an ugly defect, I always thought of it as a reminder of how special he was.

"Theo, you are my own dear brother. My twin. More my brother than Dionysius in some ways, for you know me better."

"No!" He screamed the word so loud, I jerked back.

"I am not your brother."

"Not that again."

"I was never your brother. I was your friend. Your companion. Yours in every way. But not in blood."

"What are you saying?" Even as the words

emerged from my mouth, I wanted to take them back. I did not wish to hear what Theo had to say.

"Ariadne, I love you. As a man loves a woman. We have never been brother and sister except in your mind. Not by blood. Not by law. Not in any way but in your imagination."

I staggered back, shaking my head. My stomach heaved. With those words Theo had sealed our pain. Our separation. I wanted to howl. I wanted to beg him to turn back time a few moments and undo what he had done.

Even sinking into a well of misery as I was, my mind worked on. Reason gave me understanding. Theo had never seen himself as part of our family, never felt that he belonged. To him, I had never been a sister. I had been his friend. His champion. The single stable ballast in his precarious life.

That his love for me had grown from the affections of a child into the love of a man was utterly natural, especially for a man as loyal as Theo.

Why had I never foreseen this? Why hadn't Father?

Theo's heart had led him to a road I could not travel. Unlike him, to me, he had ever been a true brother. My heart had claimed him so even if the law did not. There had not been a single day when in my eyes he had been less than my own twin. We had not shared the same womb, but I was as attached to him as if we had.

I could not cast a spell on myself and change what I held as true. I could not undo the weavings of my heart. I loved Theo. But I could never bind myself to him as anything other than a sister.

He saw it in my face. Saw the implacable rejection. Saw the impossibility of his desire. He turned. Without a word, he began to walk away. I did not call him back. I sank to the ground, under the tree that had witnessed so many of our conversations, so many skinned knees and scratched shins, so many tears, so much laughter, so much love. Under that tree, I watched him go and wept for his loss.

The following day, Theo vanished. None of us knew where he had gone, though he sent word to Justus of his safety. I told no one what had transpired between us. I felt ashamed of the pain I had caused him.

More importantly, his declaration was more his secret than mine. His to share with others if he chose. Theo would not want me to spill his confidences. I dared not add betrayal to the mountain of suffering I had already caused.

His loss ground me down; I became like dust at threshing. Theo was my anchor, and without him, I was adrift. I did not even have Justus to cling to. Since the day he had kissed me and called me a thief, he had avoided me.

I only had one goal I could hold on to. I wanted

to give my father the stability he would not forge for himself. It became like a lifeline, the one purpose to which I clung. In my mind, it was the only good thing left me.

CHAPTER 23

—៣៣—

A WEEK LATER, Claudia arrived at our doorstep, distraught and in tears. It took me a few moments to calm her. "He threw me out of the house!" she wailed.

"Your father?" I asked, shocked.

"Spurius Felonius."

"Your sister's husband? Why? Did you have a fight with her?"

"Ariadne, I cannot explain the matter. One moment, the man seemed rational. The next, he spewed the most awful accusations. He had me physically removed from the house. His brute of a freedman picked me up and dropped me in the street as if I were the day's leavings. I have never felt such humiliation."

"No!" I felt outraged on behalf of my friend. "Start from the beginning. What happened?"

"My sister had asked me to join them for dinner that evening. She enjoys showing off her riches to me, pointing out how important she has grown. I go because my father makes me. And the food is better than what we have at home."

I nodded my understanding. A street vendor had better food than what they served at Claudia's house. Her mother had transformed economizing in the kitchen to a new art form.

"We were eating supper, the three of us. Partway through the second course, Felonius received a message and left the table, promising to return promptly. We finished dessert, and still he had not made an appearance.

"After several hours in the company of Claudia the Elder I was eager to leave, as you can imagine."

"You should win a prize for tolerating one hour. Several would be beyond me."

Claudia attempted a watery smile and failed. "My sister insisted that I should take proper leave of her husband. It is her way of grinding my nose in Felonius's importance. I knew I would never hear the end of the matter if I left without a formal farewell. So I went in search of my brother-in-law, and came upon him in an alcove attached to his tablinum. You would never have known it existed, for usually it is hidden behind a tapestry. I would have missed it entirely, except that I heard the rustling of papyrus when I went to his room. I called out his name and stepped inside the alcove. 'I have come to take my leave,' I said.

"He began screaming at me, accusing me of

being a spy, a thief, a snoop." Claudia blew her nose in her handkerchief.

"Perhaps he was in his cups."

"He was as sober as ever I have seen him."

"What was he doing?"

"Nothing exciting. Riffling through scrolls in a large black-and-white box on his table. It's not as if I caught him canoodling with a slave girl."

"He threw you out for that?"

"And forbade me from ever stepping over his threshold again."

"Well, that's a mercy. Now you have an acceptable excuse for avoiding Claudia the Elder."

My friend sniffed. "Father isn't speaking to me. He says we cannot afford to offend Felonius. He called me a disaster walking on legs."

Families! Was there ever one that did not give you hives?

Part of me was outraged on behalf of my friend. How could her father lay the blame at her feet when Felonius was clearly in the wrong? A smaller part of me was perversely comforted to hear of Claudia's troubles. At least I was not the only one to bring grief to my family.

I waited until the dark of the new moon to strike Grato's house. I had a simple plan. Climb the perimeter wall. Grab seven diminutive boxes. Climb out.

I remembered the circuitous route Father

had taken the night he was almost caught on Brutus's property, and planned a similar trail to Grato's villa. This would make it hard for anyone to follow me home, should they chance to see me. In the light of day, I had traveled that route several times, learning it by heart so that in the cover of darkness I would not grow confused.

Following Father's example, I snuck out of the house through the side door. I was wearing men's garb, Theo's clothes, which lay abandoned in his chamber. Walking briskly, I came upon Grato's villa after an hour. I waited in the shadows to ensure no one was in the street to catch a glimpse of me.

The street near Grato's house boasted a few bulky bushes but no convenient trees that grew by the side of the perimeter wall. Smooth marble covered the facade of the villa, making it impossible to climb without rope or grappling hooks. I wished to avoid such tools. Grappling hooks were noisy and could slip. An untended length of rope could be discovered by a passing slave. They were not ideal for stealth in an occupied house. My success depended upon speed and silence.

Like most Roman architecture, the sidewalls of Grato's house, which were not in public view, were made of brick and stucco. Sensible and cheap. The stucco had disintegrated in places, causing cracks and chips. Enough to slip a finger or toe into if someone were agile enough.

I began to climb, lizard-like, and in moments I was lying stretched out on the top edge of the perimeter wall, my body a small hump, barely noticeable should someone happen to glance in my direction. They had left a lamp burning inside the courtyard. In its weak light, I could see the figure of a sleeping slave stretched out in the atrium in front of the main gate.

A voice in my mind whispered that it was not too late. That I could turn back. I swiped at it like a buzzing fly, ignoring its plaintive plea.

I lay still long enough to ensure that the slave was asleep. Then I began to creep. The interior wall was covered completely in marble. Slippery and long, it offered an intruder no help for climbing down into the courtyard.

It did not matter. I had no intention of going down. I aimed to climb up. The main body of the villa, where the bedchambers and Grato's tablinum were located, was two stories high, while the rest of the villa—its atrium, triclinium, and peristyle—were only one story.

The perimeter wall was so high that I only needed to ascend half a story to reach the roof with its overlapping clay tiles. Once I climbed onto the roof and crawled far enough, I would be able to hang down by my fingers and swing into Grato's tablinum.

I started to scale the second-story wall, again using the chips in the stucco and bricks for handholds. The roof posed a precarious challenge. Tiles were not always properly installed. They were slippery. If I caused one to fall on the ground below, it would make enough of a racket to raise the household. Or my foot could slip, causing me to fall over two stories.

I gripped the edge of the roof with one hand. I was now half on the wall, my toes tucked into a wide crack, my left hand wedged into a broad chip, and half hanging in the air, the fingers of my right hand clinging to the tiles of the roof. If the tiles shifted, I could easily fall backward.

They held. I brought my other hand up and pulled my whole weight until I could swing my legs onto the roof. I took a deep breath as the pressure eased off my arms and shoulders.

"Ariadne!" a voice whispered.

I jerked with shock and lost my hold. My body started to slip. Tucking my toes into the overlapping tiles, I managed to stop myself from sliding off.

"Ariadne, stop!"

I looked down in the direction of the sound. Father was climbing the perimeter wall. He had one leg on the edge and was pulling himself over. My blood ran cold. He did not have my skills. He was older and, in spite of his athleticism, weaker than I was. This was no place for him. There were no trees to sustain him. This kind of vertical climbing required a level of dexterity and power that was beyond him.

"Leave," I hissed at him.

"Not without you."

He pulled himself fully onto the edge and began to crawl toward me. When he came to the portion of the wall that sat under the second-story roof, he stretched up and began his ascent, one fingertip at a time.

"Stop. Stop! I will come down," I whispered, almost frozen with terror.

He gave me a brilliant smile and shifted so he could return to the perimeter wall. To my horror, his foot slipped. He caught himself, fingers gripping the crack into which he had wedged them. I was clambering as fast as I could, scrambling off the roof, off the fragile tiles, and down to reach him.

In the midst of my frenzied scrabbling I saw my father lose his hold and slip. Frantically, he flailed, hands grasping for a hold. They found purchase at the very edge of the wall. But only for a fleeting moment. The rolling force of his torso proved too great, and his fingers loosened.

He fell over the wall, into the darkness of the street. I heard the sickening crunch of his body as it hit the pavement, and a low sound of anguish, followed by silence.

My stomach heaved. I was mad with terror,

dizzy with it. My ears were ringing. How I managed to get off the roof, shinny down one wall, crawl over the ledge, and fling myself over the perimeter wall, I cannot say.

In the periphery of my vision, I saw the slave stir, sit up, and look about just as I heaved my body over the wall and began the climb down. I could hear the man calling out. Time had become my enemy.

I threw myself next to Father and saw to my relief that he was stirring. "My leg," he said with a groan.

Even in the darkness I could see the unnatural angle of his calf, twisted to one side. The bone had broken in two, though the skin remained intact. I turned aside and vomited. I could hear the slave within pulling on the bar, opening the front gate.

"God in heaven, help us!" Those words, brief as they were, were my first honest prayer to God, dragged out of my depths by desperation and horror.

Grabbing Father under the shoulders, I pulled him upright. The cry that came out of his lips made the hair at the back of my neck stand. It was the anguish of a wounded animal. I put his arm around my neck and began to walk toward the next villa. Grato's door was being pulled open as I half walked, half dragged my father. We were still in the open street, easily discovered.

Just as the slave stepped into the street, I pulled Father inside the doorway of the neighboring villa and hid behind the protruding edge of the postern. Father was barely conscious, his body slumped against me.

Grato's slave walked a few steps into the street, holding a burning lamp above his head. "Who is there?" he demanded.

He could not see Father and me, hidden as we were in the dark by the edge of the gatepost. Giving up, Grato's slave returned to the door. He placed the lamp inside a diminutive alcove built into the postern of the house for the purpose. The light was supposed to discourage intruders, though he need not have bothered. I had finished with my intrusion. The slave returned inside, and I heard the door being barred again.

"Can you walk?" I whispered to Father.

He answered with a low groan. I took that as affirmation and dragged him a few steps. He tried to hop along, tamping down his cries of pain.

I was covered in sweat within moments. My heart beat like a hollow drum. It dawned on me that dragging him this way was futile. Soon he would collapse from the agony I caused him. I stopped, bent my back, and drew my father over my shoulders, grunting as his weight settled on me. He murmured an objection. Ignoring him, I readjusted his body and staggered forward. Every few steps, I would stop and rest, shifting him. Sometimes I would sling his body over one shoulder and then back again.

"God, if you have any room in your heart for thieves, help us this night," I said. I felt hopeless. I knew I did not have the strength to carry Father all the way home. A few staggering steps were one thing. But a trail that had required one full hour of fast walking was beyond me.

I readjusted the route in my mind from the convoluted paths I had originally planned on, to the most direct road. It made the distance considerably shorter.

Still impossible.

At the rate I was stumbling along, it would take us two or three hours to get home. My body could not bear such a task.

Paul's words reverberated in my mind. *"Love never gives up. Never loses faith. It is always hopeful. Love endures through every circumstance."*

I hefted Father back over my shoulder and, bent over in half like a decrepit crone, lurched forward. This was love. Love that would not give up. Love that would not lose hope. Love that would endure even this impossible burden.

One step at a time, I forced my feet forward. My lips were cracked and bleeding after half an hour. My throat had grown parched. Pain shot through my back, and spasms of agony seized my shoulders, my neck, my stomach. There was no part of me that was not in anguish. But I clung to Paul's words.

"God of love, give me the strength," I whispered.

I was weeping with exhaustion and pain by the time I arrived at the villa. The sun would rise soon. I laid Father gently on the soft grass. Opening the side door, I carried him those last few steps and placed him on the tiled floor. He had lost consciousness long since.

"Dionysius." I tried to shout my brother's name. Only a croak emerged. Someone heard that pathetic whimper and fetched him.

"Lord be merciful!" he cried. "What has happened?"

"Fetch a physician," I said, then collapsed on the ground in a dead faint.

I woke to the sound of eerie shrieks. I jerked up and winced. My whole body was a mass of writhing pain. Muscles ached and locked. My head pounded. A gentle hand pushed me back into bed.

"Don't try to rise."

"Justus?" He was sitting on a chair to my right, which explained why I had missed him. My neck would not allow my head to rotate that far. The eerie shrieks beat against my skull again.

"What *is* that?"

Justus hesitated. Slowly, memory returned. "My father?"

303

"The physician is trying to set his bone. It's a bad break."

"I must go to him," I cried, and tried to get out of bed. Sinews and muscles mutinied against me, refusing to move the way I wanted. I stumbled and almost fell.

Justus caught me in his arms and gently laid me back on the mattress. "You are too weak to rise. He is not alone. Dionysius is with him."

I had started to shiver and could not stop. I felt like I would never be warm again. Justus poured hot spiced wine into a goblet and held it out to me. "Drink this."

My stomach rebelled. I shook my head. Justus moved to the edge of the bed. The mattress dipped under his weight as he sat next to my hip.

Through the thin sheet, I could feel the push and pull of long muscles as he moved, holding the cup to my mouth. "Drink. The physician added a tincture to the wine that will help you."

I took a sip to appease him. "More," he said, pushing the glass back against my lips. I turned my head.

"Always stubborn." He placed a hand under my head and lifted me a fraction. Even that small movement made me wince. "You need this. It will help the pain. Now drink."

I drank a few mouthfuls and grimaced. "Tastes like goat spit."

"Stop complaining and listen."

"What? I don't hear anything."

"Exactly. The screams have stopped."

I pushed the sheet off and again tried to rise. "I need to find out what has happened."

Justus put his hand on my shoulder and shoved. I fell back on the pillow. "You need to remain in bed. If I could trust you to be reasonable, I would go and find out news of your father's condition."

"Please!" I could not stop the flow of tears. They dripped down my cheeks and rolled off my chin, onto his hand. "Please take me with you, Justus."

His expression grew taut. For a moment, he stared at me. "Quit that!" he commanded. I cried harder. Swearing under his breath, he came to his feet. "I must have lost my mind." Bending, he lifted me against his chest. "Just for one moment. Then I am returning you to bed. And I don't want a single objection out of you. Do you understand?"

I nodded. In spite of his words and his exasperated tone, his touch was gentle. It still hurt. Every part of me protested at being moved. Not wanting him to revise his decision, I didn't even dare to wince.

"Why do you think he is quiet?" I asked, my voice quivering with dread.

"He is probably asleep. As you should be."

At Father's door, Justus paused to announce our presence to Dionysius, and only after my brother bid us enter did he heft my weight to push the door open. In the semidarkness of the chamber I saw Father, pale and unconscious, stretched out on his bed. His broken leg was bandaged thickly from the sole of the foot to the knee.

"Father," I whispered, my voice broken.

Dionysius vacated the only comfortable chair in the room. "Set her down here."

Justus placed me on the chair. Guilt gnawed at me as I gazed at Father's ashen face. Galatea was bathing his forehead and feet with rose water. Her fingers trembled as she smoothed the cloth over his skin. She seemed to have aged over the course of a few hours. I wondered what she had witnessed to put that dazed look on her face. I realized that my own unconsciousness over the past few hours may have been a mercy.

The room was shrouded in quiet, but Father's shrieks of pain still rang in my ears. I would never forget those screams, nor forgive myself as the cause of them.

The physician was clearing away the paraphernalia of his art, which he had spread on a square table near Father's bed. The fearsome bronze instruments seemed more adroit for torture than delicate surgery. A few pieces were red with blood. I swallowed hard, knowing if I were sick, Justus would carry me off before I had a chance to ascertain Father's condition for myself.

"How is he?" I asked, trying to sound steady. Trying to appear sane.

The physician turned in my direction. He had a thick shock of white hair and neatly trimmed brows. His fine tunic with its purple embellishments had become soiled with gore and blood.

Some physicians are sycophantic in their bed-side manner, desperate to make a good impression. Others are pleasant, even charming. Then there are those who care nothing for anyone's opinion save their own. Clearly this man belonged to the third category. "You should be in bed," he said shortly.

"That is what I said!" Justus agreed.

"I will return there at once, if you would answer my question."

He turned back to his instruments, cleaning them in a bowl of water and wine. "It is a dangerous break. The easiest fracture to treat is the one that occurs in the middle of the bone. A clean break, like so." He drew a line in the air to demonstrate. "Your father's bone has been broken close to the top, near the joint, which makes it at once more painful and harder to treat. Worse yet, the edges are fragmented." He drew a jagged line in the air. "We have stretched the muscles and sinew of the leg so that I could set the fragments in their right place. At best, the leg will be shorter. We will know in three days if the leg can be saved at all. With such a break, gangrene is likely to follow."

The room tilted. I felt the blood drain from my face. Leaning forward I pressed my hands against my thighs. "What happens if you can't save it?"

"I shall have to amputate, of course," he said, as if I were an imbecile for asking such an obvious question.

I felt like someone had punched me in the belly.

"That's enough," Justus barked. Without another word, he swung me back up into his arms and carried me out.

There are some burdens the mind is not equipped to carry. Father had howled with the pain of his crushed bone. I could not give voice to the wail of my soul. I had meant to help my father. Instead, I had destroyed him. Something inside me crumbled. Crumbled beyond repair.

Justus stood for a moment and gazed at me as I curled into a ball of misery. Then, without a single platitude, he gathered me in his arms and held me on the bed until the physician's tincture took effect and I fell into a restless sleep, too exhausted even for grief.

CHAPTER 24

—ɯ—

WHEN I AWOKE NEXT, I found Delia keeping vigil next to me. A hammer was pounding in my head.

"Delia," I croaked. Her chin jerked up. "How is my father?"

"The same as the last time you asked. Sleeping."

"His leg?"

"Too early to tell." She set her wool aside and came to stand by my bed. "I will fetch you hot vegetable soup and bread. First, drink this." She held a cup of spring water to my lips and I drank thirstily.

"Who is with Father?"

"Dionysius and Galatea never leave his side. Justus is with them now, though he was here most of the morning."

I pushed myself into a sitting position. As an athlete I was familiar with injury and pain. But I had outdone myself the night before, straining and pulling muscles I did not know I possessed.

309

Gritting my teeth, I swung my knees out and managed to sit at the edge of the bed. Before Delia could leave my chamber I called her name.

"Do you know where Theo is?" I asked, my voice expressionless.

She remained mute.

"I don't want you to violate his confidence. I merely ask that you tell him about Father. He should know. Whether he comes or not is up to him. But he would want to know how perilous my father's injury is."

Delia gave a jerky nod of her chin and left. My head had cleared substantially since the last time I had awakened with Justus as my nurse. Questions swirled in my mind. Why had no one inquired about the events of the previous evening? I had dragged home the grievously injured master of the house in the middle of the night and fainted at my brother's feet. Everyone must be bursting with curiosity. It seemed remarkable that no one had asked me what had taken place.

As hard as I tried, I could not explain away this mystery. I pushed myself to my feet. By holding on to a chair, I found that I could stand. Or at least stoop. I hobbled like an aged soldier who has been wounded in too many battles.

I was still wearing Theo's clothes. Removing them took an inordinately long time with muscles that went into spasms and seized upon the merest activity. Delia had left a pitcher of water on a stand. It must have been hot when she had fetched it, but had grown lukewarm since. Flinching, I performed a cursory wash and donned a fresh tunic. Shoving a tunic over my head was one thing. Bending over to tie the straps of a sandal was beyond my body. I walked barefoot to Father's chamber.

Justus and Dionysius were speaking in low tones. Galatea seemed glued to Father's side, wearing the same rumpled clothing and bruised look as the last time I had seen her. I limped over to the bed.

The men shot to their feet at the sight of me. I waved a soothing gesture, hoping they would not try to bundle me back to bed. I tried to look unshaken as I sniffed at Father's bandage. To my relief, it smelled clean. If his flesh turned putrid, there was nothing any surgeon could do. They would have to amputate the leg to save his life, and even that would not guarantee a full recovery. Father could spend the rest of his days as a cripple. He could suffer chronic pain without remedy. He could die.

Because of me.

I turned and faced the men. No sense in delaying the unavoidable. Best drink this poison quickly.

"This is my fault." My voice had turned wooden like the rest of me. "I did this to him."

"Of course it is not your fault," Dionysius

assured. "Father told us that you would say that."

"He spoke to you?" This was an unexpected twist. I rubbed my temples. "When?"

"After you fainted. Justus had already arrived. Father sent everyone else out and told the two of us what happened."

I was being enveloped in a whirlwind. My stomach heaved. "You seem very calm about it," I said.

My brother opened a hand in a philosophical gesture. Did they teach that in rhetoric classes—that calm, unperturbed air in the face of gravest betrayal? If so, I wished I could receive such instruction.

"He had given me his word, and I had hoped he would stand by it. But I suppose, under the circumstances, the pressure proved too great and he caved in."

"By Zeus's snarled beard, Dionysius, what are you prattling about?"

My brother stopped mid-explanation, dismissed Galatea, closed the window, and barred the door in Father's chamber before saying another word. I was left stewing in my welter of thoughts, trying to untangle Dionysius's words.

"I am disappointed, of course," my brother said, once he had ensured our privacy. "Disappointed and hurt that he would break his word to me."

"Break his word to you?"

"I wish you had called on me when you saw

him creeping out of the house, though I suppose you had no time. It is a wonder you managed to change your clothes so quickly and still keep up with him."

"Dionysius, either I have lost my mind, or you have the wrong story. In spite of the plentiful evidence for the former, I would wager my silver on the latter."

Justus came to his feet. "Ariadne, try to calm yourself. I know that Galenos is the Honorable Thief. He confessed it to me this morning. You need not fear that I will expose him. I will never betray him."

My legs gave beneath me, and I sat hard at the end of Father's bed. Justus knew!

"Galenos also said that you followed him last night, hoping to prevent him from another theft. No one blames you for what happened to him."

I rested my head in my hand. "Well, you should. And you have everything wrong."

"Father explained what happened," Dionysius said. "You called out to him, hoping to persuade him to return with you. It was an accident, Ariadne. Surprised by the sound of your voice, his foot slipped, and he fell. The responsibility rests with him, not you."

Justus drew near enough to take my hand in his. His hold was gentle, reverent. "Galenos said that you carried him for two hours." He shook his head in disbelief. "I can't fathom where you found the strength to manage such a feat. But I have never heard of a more courageous act."

I choked on a maniacal laugh. Father's story was superb, featuring enough hint of truth to make it plausible. Here was reprieve. Salvation. I could hide under Father's bushel of lies. I could hold on to Justus's growing admiration. Claim that reverent look in his eyes as my due.

I turned my head slowly, taking in the white figure on the bed. Love brimmed over my heart. Love and pain. He had sacrificed enough for me. He would not be reduced in Dionysius's eyes again for my sake. It was time I discharged my own debts.

Truth can be a sharp sword. A bitter companion. With this truth, I would cut the cord that bound Justus to me. He would hate me after this. I pulled my hand out of his and stood.

"Let me tell you a different tale. Father is the Honorable Thief. That much is true. I saved him from capture once, at Brutus's house." I turned to Justus and gave him a short nod. "You were right about that. It was me, that night, in the trees. After that, I helped Father rob another house."

"What are you saying?" Justus asked, his voice faint.

"I am saying that I, too, am a thief. We needed the money. When his ship sank, Father was left with a mountain of debt. Most of it is paid off now. But moneylenders are not interested in 'most.' They want everything they are owed."

The muscles of my back were quivering. I sank back on the bed. "We needed to rob two more houses, and we would be free. The Honorable Thief only robbed dishonest men. Why do you think Corinth adores him? He is more hero than criminal. I told myself we were doing more good than harm. Father wished to give up, even then. I was the one who pressed him to continue.

"Then you returned, Dionysius. You and Paul, and Father grew enchanted with your Christ. He walked away from that life. Walked away from it for good."

I held a shaking hand out to my brother, palm up. "He never broke his word to you. I was the one who left the house last night. He came in pursuit of *me*."

Justus had turned to stone. It was as if his mind, usually quick as a lightning strike, had frozen, incapable of comprehending my words. I twisted the hilt of the knife and pressed in the sharp edge of one more truth. "He climbed the wall after me, trying to persuade me to stop. The climb was too difficult for him. I turned back to help him. But I was too late. His foot slipped and he fell.

"This?" I pointed to the bandaged leg. "This is my doing. Father had asked me to stop. Theo, too. I would not admit they were right. I was convinced I knew better."

I would have knelt at my brother's feet if my

315

stiffening muscles had allowed. "Dionysius, Father did not break his word to you. I am the one responsible."

He took two long strides and came to stand before me. To my stupefaction, he extended his arms and gently, gently held me as if I had given him good news instead of confessing to being a liar and a thief. When he looked at me, his tearstained eyes were not brimming with judgment and anger as I expected. Instead, I found pity. Pity and an ocean of compassion.

"I forgive you," he said.

I finally began to understand what it was to be guilty, to run out of excuses. And what it was to be absolved. It dawned on me what Paul meant when he said, *"Love endures through every circumstance."* Dionysius's love had endured the burden of my culpability. It had washed away my debt to him. A giant boulder seemed to lift off my chest.

My brother could not free me from my self-condemnation, of course. I still bore the weight of my actions. Still, his forgiveness had lightened that weight. It had purchased a cup of hope for my future.

Justus, motionless until that moment, became a sudden flurry of activity. Without a word, he strode out of the chamber, his cloak flapping behind him like a whip. I had gained my brother back. But my heart was lost. The fragile, newborn feelings Justus had begun to nurture for me could not withstand the weight of my dishonesty.

"It is too much to ask for more than one miracle," I said, trying to sound strong. Inside, I felt mangled. Beyond repair. How do you live in a graveyard of dreams? How do you contend with the wreck you make with your own hands?

Dionysius returned to his chair. "The Lord is not stingy."

As if waiting for that name, there was a knock on the door. I had a glimpse of unruly hair as Paul's head appeared, his body hidden by the frame. "I have come to pray. May I enter?"

"Paul!" Dionysius cried. "Come! Come, and welcome. He is asleep, worn out from having the bone set. I am so grateful you have joined us."

Paul walked in, that restrained storm of a man, and immediately the feeling in the sickroom shifted. It was as if his mere presence expelled fear. I found myself awash in relief and an unreasoning hope.

Paul studied my father. "As the prophet Elisha once told an anxious king, 'This is an easy thing in the eyes of the Lord.'"

I sidled over. "The physician says it is a bad break. He fears it will go putrid."

"Bah," Paul said, waving a hand. "Physicians. They are only men, after all. What is to them an unsolvable case is to God a simple matter. We shall ask Jesus to touch your father." He gave me a lopsided smile full of mischief. I wanted to grin back, like a carefree child, as if I were not carrying a millstone around my neck.

CHAPTER 25

—m—

THE FOLLOWERS OF CHRIST prayed in a strange manner, for they offered no sacrifices. Not even a meager turtledove shed its blood for their petitions. Instead, Paul and Dionysius used the simple language of everyday men, their supplications more a conversation with an invisible being than a formal liturgy.

I began to understand what Dionysius had meant about the difference between their God and the impersonal force toward which the Stoics gravitated. They addressed their God as Father, and sometimes they even used a Hebrew endearment, *Abba*, which they said was the intimate term with which a Jewish child addressed a beloved father.

"We are his sons by adoption," Paul explained. It was as children that they prayed, lifting my father up to the care of one who had knit his bones together in his mother's womb. "Knit his bones together again, Lord," Paul said simply. "Restore them where they are shattered."

He anointed my father's forehead with a touch of oil, whispered a benediction, and stepped back.

Hours before, that chamber had been a place of torment, of unendurable pain, of bitter confessions and rejection. As Paul and Dionysius wove their prayers about my father, a strange peace settled around us. It was as if they had swept out the lingering effects of those hours, swept away the dark agitation and distress that had occupied the room like a noxious fume.

Paul turned to me. "I would like to remain, if I may, and to continue to pray for Galenos."

"Of course. You are most welcome." During my father's indisposition, Dionysius was the head of the household. Paul knew that he already had my brother's invitation to remain. I found his polite inquiry touching. A single woman could easily be overlooked in our world. By asking my permission, he had shown that he cared for my opinion.

My time at Father's bedside had reduced me to shivery exhaustion. I excused myself, thinking to rest for an hour.

Outside Father's chamber, I found Galatea crouching on the floor, knees clasped to her breast. I came to an abrupt halt. Why had I not perceived it before? Starved of goodness, Galatea had been won over by my father's daily kindness. She had been wooed by his generosity when he had set her free from that house of horrors for the sake of a promise few men would have kept. She had grown to love him because he had treated her like a human being rather than a slave.

"Galatea, you may go in." The poor creature slid past me and rushed into the room as if life itself waited for her within.

Back in my chamber, I tried to rest my body, even though my thoughts raced as fast as Theo's chariot. With surgical objectiveness, I pulled apart the open cuts in the flesh of my life. I examined my own actions, and for once, told the truth about the motives that drove them.

It seemed so clear now, my utter arrogance, my thoughtless disregard of others. I had insisted that I was serving my family, while in fact I had served my own desires.

I had wanted to be Father's savior. To be the one person in the family who stood by him. I had wanted to show I was better than the rest.

But when I examined my decisions of the past few months all the way to their knobby roots, I saw a simple truth: I wanted to do what *I* wanted to do.

Five years had passed since I had left my mother and grandfather behind, and I was still rebelling against their dictates. Still pushing against their boundaries. Defiance ruled my life, not love.

I never considered the cost to my father. The

anxiety I would cause him. The pain, were I to be caught. The utter disgrace my actions would win for our family. I had thought only of myself. Whitewashed my decisions with a handful of admirable excuses too thin to fool anyone but me.

In the court of my own mind, I dispassionately stood trial and judged myself guilty. I deserved the lofty price I paid. By insisting on having my own way, I had destroyed the budding affections of the only man I would ever love. And I had harmed the father who was the world to me.

I would have to live the rest of my days with these truths.

I pushed myself out of bed, intending to return to Father's chamber. On the way there, I spied Paul sitting on a marble bench in front of the diminutive pool in the courtyard, twirling a sprig of rosemary in his hands.

Without thinking, I walked toward him. "May I sit with you?" I asked, not wanting to offend his Jewish sensibilities.

"I was waiting for you," he said cryptically, sweeping his arm in invitation.

"Shall I order a meal? Some wine, perhaps?"

"I am content. It is your company I wish to share."

I perched next to him, perplexed by this revelation. The silence stretched between us. For a man who had wanted my company, he did not have much to say. It occurred to me that I could trust this man, trust him with my life. I had no proof of this wild conclusion. I barely even knew him. And yet some deep-rooted conviction compelled me to confide in him.

I had confessed my sins to Justus and Dionysius. My brother had forgiven me. Justus had not. Now I made a perilous decision. I chose to confess to this man. There was no rational reason for a stark confession, nothing to be gained by such an action. But my soul longed to do it, to disclose my offenses to a man who called God Father without being impertinent.

"I am a thief," I began. It grew easier after that.

I spoke as the shadow on the sundial in the middle of the courtyard lengthened. For a whole hour I confessed every sin I could think of, every vanity, every pride, every act of selfish rebellion. I laid it before him bare of excuses.

Finally, my story came to its conclusion. "Tell me, Paul, does your God have room in his heart for a thief?"

He gave me a lingering appraisal. "There were three crosses on Golgotha the day Jesus was crucified. He hung in the middle between two thieves. One of them, after acknowledging his guilt, said to him, 'Remember me when you come into your kingdom.'

"That was enough for Jesus. That drop of faith, that simple admission. He said to that thief,

'Truly I tell you, today you will be with me in paradise.' In paradise! That thief, who by his own admission was guilty and justly punished, is at this moment enjoying peace you and I can only imagine. He is swimming in joy, brimming with contentment. He keeps company with the Son of God and his angels. He shall live an eternity without tears or sickness or despair. One day, he will enjoy a new body that is eternal, imperishable, unbreakable.

"Yes, Ariadne. Our Lord has a tender place in his heart for thieves who repent. You have confessed your sins. This is an important step on the road to repentance." He gave a dazzling smile. "I told you once. God wants everything. Every part of you."

Now I understood what Paul had meant that day. This God did not move in half measures. He did not want to hold my hand; he wanted to have my soul. He wanted me. The broken and the good in me. And he wanted to love me whole. What I had always hungered for, he wanted to give me. But the price was my life. The end of defiance and self-rule. The end of arrogance and vanity. He wanted a child who would burrow her face in his neck and trust him with her broken future.

"It does not seem like he is getting a very good bargain," I said, thinking my life too tangled a mess to be worth much. "But I want what

Dionysius has. The power to forgive. The desire to love. I want God."

When I took my leave of Paul that day, I felt clean. Clean and right.

The following morning, I found to my amazement that Father was awake and cheerful for a lame man in danger of losing his leg.

As soon as he saw me, he asked everyone to leave the room so we could speak. "You need not concern yourself," I said. "I have already told Dionysius and Justus the truth. Paul, too."

His eyes widened in his wan face. "Ariadne, I wanted to protect you."

I fell on my knees by the bed. "You are the best father a woman could have. I do not deserve you. But it is time I bore the consequences of my actions. Dionysius has already forgiven me. God, also, Paul assures me, for I have asked his pardon. Now it is your turn. I ask your pardon, my precious father."

Tears clogged my throat. "I ask your pardon for my obstinate defiance, for my thoughtlessness, my selfish disregard of your wishes. I ask that you forgive me for causing you so much pain and costing you your health."

He was shedding his own tears. "I grant it, freely." He pulled me up from my knees and made me sit next to him. "You never met your grandfather—my father. He was a wonderful man. Died before you were born. Gone from me too soon.

"I have a memory of him teaching me to climb stairs. I must have been no more than a toddling babe. He had taken me by the hand and was helping me up. By the third step, I froze. I could not go up. I could not go down. *'No!'* I said with all the vehemence of a child.

"My father did not force me to go on. He tousled my hair and said, 'That's all right, Son. You did well to come this far.' He picked me up in his arms and carried me the rest of the way. Carried me safe. It never occurred to me that I had failed. I felt like a king who had conquered three steps by myself. That is what fathers do, Ariadne. They see how far you have come and cheer you, so you will learn to go the rest of the way.

"You have come so far, my girl. You will go the rest of this way as God gives you strength." He stopped. His cheeks turned a ruddy color. "And now, I ask *your* forgiveness."

"You have done nothing that requires my pardon."

"Ariadne, you have always blamed your mother for the divorce. For the rupture in our family. The lost, hard years. Yet I bore as much responsibility in the matter as she did. I knew how she would feel if she found out about my thieving. I chose to do it anyway. Like you, I did what I wished,

326

disregarding my own wife's needs. The blame is more mine than hers."

Before confessing to Paul, before asking God to take the reins of my life, I would have dismissed Father's confession. I liked looking at things through the prism of my own interpretations. But I had grown more aware of the perverse way I twisted truth to suit my own needs. I thought of my mother, a young woman from a proud family, discovering her husband's lawlessness. She had not been trained in the ways of grace. She would not have been able to cope with Father's betrayal.

I saw then that Father, too, was broken. If he had chosen a different path, he might have influenced my mother to become a softer woman. A more loving mother. His absence had changed all of us.

"I forgive you," I said, feeling the blood drain from my face. Forgiving him meant that I must forgive my mother, also. But that seemed an impossible task. She had hurt me too deeply. I realized I was no more equipped for grace than she. The bottled resentments of my childhood years presented an insurmountable block. How was I to get past them? I pushed the thought to the back of my mind. It was a good thing that God was patient. He would need to be if he wanted me as a daughter.

Father raised a hand. "I almost forgot. You said you told Justus the truth. What did he say?"

I pasted a smile on my face. "He walked out without a word. Hasn't returned since."

Father exhaled a long breath. "That is a pity. He may yet change his mind. Some men need time to navigate through their thoughts. If he rejects you, then he is not the man for you."

"Who said anything about him being the man for me?" I squeaked.

His mouth tilted up. "Come now. I have eyes. I know you care for him. But, Ariadne, as I have learned to my detriment, a happy marriage can only come between two people who, knowing each other's faults, continue to treasure one another. If he can know the worst about you and still love you, then he is right for you. If not, better for you that he should walk away."

The problem with wisdom is that it is devoid of comfort. It cannot mend an aching heart no matter how much sense it contains. The two men who could offer me the greatest consolation were both gone. "You have not asked after Theo since he left," I said.

Father closed his eyes for a moment. "I know why he left. And I know where he is."

"He told you?"

"He did not need to. I had known what was in his heart for weeks. He could not hide his feelings from me any more than you could." He pulled on the sheet, adjusting it. "This, too, is my doing."

"You take too much upon yourself."

"If I had adopted Theo as I ought to have done, then he would have seen himself as my son and your brother rather than a stranger. Instead, I created a world of uncertainty around him. Around all of us. In that uncertainty, you saw the world one way and he another."

"You know where he is?"

"He is staying with a couple named Priscilla and Aquila. They are Paul's friends."

"Paul's friends?"

"He needs a fresh start, Ariadne. A safe place to heal. And he needs God. Priscilla and Aquila will offer him those things."

"You've met them?"

"I have. They are exceptional people. I hope you will meet them one day."

I heard a commotion at the door and Galatea came in. "Forgive the intrusion, master. The physician is here."

Celsus strode in, his young slave in tow, carrying a pristine leather bag. Within moments, he had laid out his instruments. I noticed a deadly looking saw and gulped.

He began to unwrap the bandages around Father's leg. "These need to be changed every day," he explained. He seemed surprised by the lack of excessive swelling in the limb. Frowning, he poked the location of the fracture, making Father wince. "I confess, you have progressed far better than I would have expected, given the condition you were in when I first examined that leg. I can hardly account for it."

He made a motion to his slave, and the boy packed away the saw. I could have cried with relief. "If you continue to improve, I will splint the leg on the third day." He mixed a tincture of oil and wine and dipped a large wad of linen bandages into the liquid. Methodically, he wrapped the first piece from the sole of the foot in a spiral upward. The second bandage was wrapped in the opposite direction, covering the area of the fracture. He then spread a broader layer of lint over the bandages, and another bandage began with several spiral turns over the leg.

"I will return in the morning." He gave a narrow smile. "If you continue to mend at this rate, I shall claim myself a genius and raise my rates higher than they already are."

"Not very charming, is he?" I said when he had left.

"He does not need to be if he saves this leg."

"He had help. Paul and Dionysius prayed for you yesterday while you were sleeping."

"Paul?"

"For hours."

"You sound as if you approve."

"I do. He prayed with me, too."

Father laughed, and I found myself joining him.

• • •

Paul returned in the evening, accompanied by Silas. We prayed together, thanking God for the good work he had already begun in Father, and asking him to complete it.

I arranged for a simple meal to be served in Father's chamber, and we each found a spot to sit in the cramped quarters. Dionysius insisted that Paul should have the chair, while he sat on a stool. Silas and I settled on comfortable cushions, leaning against the wall. Galatea knelt at Father's bedside, feeding him one careful spoonful at a time. I noticed Father did not seem to mind being reduced to an invalid while Galatea lavished so much tender attention upon him. Delia joined us at my urging. She had grown pale since Theo's departure, and I worried for her.

When the door opened, I thought it might be one of the servants, bringing a fresh flagon of wine.

It was Theo.

Everything came to a crashing halt. Theo stood in the doorway, his eyes locked on Father. Unobserved, I could drink up the sight of that beloved face. Grief exploded in me. I felt as if someone had dug a crater into me. I could not approach him though he stood four steps away. I could not share my burdens with him, laugh with him, rejoice with him, hold his hand. He was forbidden to me now. My mere presence caused him pain.

Father lifted his arms in an invitation. Theo bounded to him and fell into his arms. Without waiting to be asked, we filed out, leaving them to talk in peace. This time, as I moved out of Father's room, I noticed Galatea perched on one side of the door and Delia on the other. For a brief moment, I flirted with the idea of joining them.

CHAPTER 26

—◇—

YEARS BEFORE, I had planted a border of flowers in our courtyard, and it had always been my duty to care for them. I had neglected them too much of late, and dead blooms covered the anemones, lavender, and rosebushes. It was late in the evening. Too late for gardening. My strained muscles were in no shape for the simple requirements of spring flowers. But my mind proved too restless for sleep, and I settled before the plants, pulling off battered leaves and dead flowers in the light of the burning lamps.

Low murmurs pulled me out of my reverie. I turned to find Justus walking toward me. Leaping to my feet, I grimaced as my back objected to the sudden move. He drew close, and for a long while studied me. Shadows danced over the golden skin and stained the green eyes. He looked weary and drawn. He looked wounded.

There was a tiny taste of shame under my tongue.

"Tell me why," he said. "Make me understand."

It was the kindest thing he could have asked. He wanted to bridge the gap between us. To walk in my shoes, to taste of my fears. He hadn't come in judgment or anger. He had come with a bid for understanding.

Once, I would have tried to leverage his good opinion on the fulcrum of my justifications. No more. Love is not self-seeking. So I told him about my mother, about the years in Athens and living apart from Father. I had attempted to fill the void of my mother's acceptance with every version of success I could carve out with my own hands. I had almost ruined myself with the effort. I did not excuse my actions. He had asked for understanding, and that is what I tried to give him.

We were sitting near the hedge of flowers, and the scent of roses and lavender and the burning oil from the lamp filled our nostrils. The sun had long since set, and through the opening in the roof we could see the faint glint of a thousand stars. I came to the end of my words. The end of my explanations.

I realized I was holding my breath, waiting. Waiting for Justus.

"What now?" he asked.

"That depends on God, and his plans for my life," I blurted. I was starting to sound like Dionysius and wondered what Justus would make of it.

"Paul has ensnared you in his net, I see." I was relieved that he was smiling.

"I jumped into it willingly."

He held up his hand as if in surrender. "I jumped into it before you."

"Truly?"

He did not answer. Instead, he leaned forward and kissed me, very softly, on the lips. "I love you," he said. I would have fallen over and cracked my head open on the rocks that lined the hedges if he had not pulled me into his arms. His mouth pressed against mine, a tender, searching touch. More than passion, that kiss bound us like a promise. A promise of belonging.

He unclasped me long enough to gasp, "And you are never stealing again."

I would have agreed to hand-stitch his undergarments for the next fifty years to have his love. Pledging something I had already promised to God and myself was easy.

"Don't you have something to tell me?" he asked, finally pulling away.

I recoiled, appalled. I had revealed every secret shame I could think of. What more could he need?

He laughed at my expression. "Let us try this again." He drew me into his arms once more. "I love you," he whispered against my lips. "Now you try it."

Relieved, I smirked. "I think I need another demonstration."

He pulled away. "I think you have had enough practice."

I caressed his cheek, his jaw, the dark-golden hair at his temple. "I love you, Justus. I have loved you for so many years."

He grinned. "This is an improvement. Now I will give you another demonstration."

We stayed up late into the night, speaking, sharing our hearts, laying our secrets bare. The walls between us began to crumble; with words, we hammered them down brick by brick.

"I knew your life in Athens had been hard," Justus said. "Dionysius hinted at it once. I did not understand how those hardships affected you."

"When families are shattered, pulled apart by the force of bitterness, by anger, by disappointment, something dark slithers into the hearts of all who survive that division. Each one of us carries the wounds of my parents' divorce."

Justus pressed a loose curl behind my ear. His touch was at once possessive and tender, as if he could not resist drawing close to me. "I wish I could undo that hurt."

"I am coming to trust that God is able to do so."

"Yes." The thick brows knotted for a moment. "My mother and father treasured each other. But it is no small thing to lose a mother so young. I was only six when my mother died. My memories of her are scant. I remember her smile, her perfume. I remember how safe she made me feel. For the most part, I have a vague feeling, an unassuaged longing when I think of her. It was all too long ago. Yet it still holds sway over me." He leaned against the stone ledge. "I suppose that is why I avoided you."

I gave him a puzzled look.

"I always found you beautiful. Effervescent, strong, full of a vivacity that was hard to resist. When you first returned to Corinth, I found myself in a quandary. You were not a child. But you were too young for me. The more you attracted me, the harder I tried to resist you. I had all manner of excuses. You needed time to mature. You were my friend's sister. Now I see that I was afraid."

I laughed. "Justus, I have seen you driving a chariot as if death were a myth. You are afraid of nothing, least of all me."

"I was not afraid of *you*. I was afraid of loving you. After my mother died, my father collapsed. With time, he tried to pull the pieces of his life together. But he was never the same man. Something of him died with my mother.

"Losing my heart to you meant that I would become vulnerable as my father had. I did not want to court that kind of pain."

"What made you change your mind?"

"It was no one thing. You wore me down, gradually." I slapped his arm and he grinned. "Dionysius once told me that the followers of

Christ believe there is no fear in love. Perfect love casts out fear. I suppose that is what began to happen in me. My love outgrew my fear." He shrugged. "First, I had to come against an impassable obstacle. Do you remember the night Theo gave you that bracelet?" He pointed to the gold circlet I still wore about my wrist.

"I remember."

"I knew that night that Theo was in love with you."

I drew a sharp breath. "You knew?"

Justus nodded. "Everyone in the room saw it but you. He leaked adoration when he looked at you. I had seen you flirt with dozens of men. None of them tempted you. You seemed immune to their ardor. But that night, I was shaken out of my security. The conceited assumption that if I should want you, I could have you. With Theo pursuing you, I could no longer be so certain. Theo is a rare man. I suspected that you saw him as a brother and only a brother. If I was wrong, though, I knew I would lose you. Perversely, that was the night I realized I wanted you. It was also the moment I decided to step back. I would never hurt Theo by trying to supplant your affections. Not if I thought he had a chance to win you."

Something within me twisted. To love Justus meant wounding Theo. *My* Theo. I squeezed my eyes shut. I could not bear the thought. He had borne too many hurts in his short life, borne them with dignity and courage. That mine should be the hand to deliver the deepest gash almost unraveled me.

Justus took my chin and turned my face toward him. "It's no fault of yours."

I tried to smile and failed. "I ache for him."

"God will help Theo endure, Ariadne. He has other plans for his life. We must accept that. If our lives are not mere happenstance, if there is a divine plan weaving our mundane existence into the glory of heaven, then you must believe that God has a different future for Theo. One that will satisfy his heart more fully than you ever could."

I had not thought of that. The possibility that Theo would find deeper fulfillment by being with another, as I had found with Justus.

Justus said, "You and I were not there when the physician set the bone in Galenos's leg, thank the Lord. Dionysius described the procedure to me. Because of the fracture, the tendons and muscles in the leg had shrunk. Before he could set the leg, the physician had to stretch it. It took three grown men to forcibly extend that fractured leg before Celsus could set it."

I winced, imagining the horror of it. No wonder Father had been shrieking.

"Galenos had to endure a deal of pain before the stretching of the sinews was complete. But after the procedure was finished, his agony subsided. The leg improved. I tell you this because it reminds me of what Theo is going through. The Lord is stretching him, heart and soul, to set what was broken in him. Broken by his parents who abandoned him, by Galenos and Celandine and your grandfather. In God's hands, the pain of your rejection can turn into an instrument of healing. His heart is being stretched to make room for the intercession of God. Those old fractures can be set rightly now."

We sank into silence. Could it be true, I wondered? Could God use what appeared to be broken dreams as a means of healing for Theo's shattered heart? Could he heal pain with pain?

"You are exhausted. Come," Justus said. "I will walk with you to your chamber."

I thought of a question I had meant to ask earlier. With an abrupt shift in mood I said, "Paul told *you* something as well."

He flushed. "I had hoped you missed that."

"Oh, I caught it. 'Love is not jealous.' I assumed he was wrong." I raised my eyebrows in question.

Justus rubbed his neck. "He was right. Jealousy is a bitter companion. At first, I was jealous of Theo. I envied your friendship with him and the exceptional closeness you shared. Then I heard the account of the robbery at Brutus's house and grew convinced that you had another man wrapped around your finger. I was consumed by jealousy. A new experience for me, and one I hope I shall never partake of again."

"I will not give you reason."

"I know," he said before kissing me one last time.

Later, hours after he had left, joy lapped at the edges of my mind as I lay in my bed, too radiant to sleep. Regret, too, nestled in my thoughts, sinking its sharp fangs into my new happiness. Joy and regret tangled in my soul, uneasy companions. Neither was strong enough to dispel the other.

Somehow mercy had won the battle. I had not received what I deserved. Paul would have called it grace. I just knew I was loved when I deserved to be spurned.

The next morning, Justus and I confessed our love to Father and received his exuberant blessing. For the sake of Theo, we kept our betrothal quiet, a secret pledge known only by my brother and father. In time, we would share our happiness with the world. Until then, we wanted to offer Theo an oasis, a chance to heal, to adjust.

That day, I received another undeserved gift. Celsus came to splint Father's leg. He unbound the bandages. Instead of proceeding, he sucked his lower lip and stared. Hauling a long string out of his bag, he measured the broken leg against the healthy one. "This leg has not shrunk."

"That is good, I think," Father said tentatively. Perspiration covered his brow. Unwrapping and rewrapping the bandages still caused him throbbing pain.

The physician extended a hand. "It is marvelous. I can't explain it." He sounded short of breath, as if he had run in the Olympics. "That injury should have caused a shortening of the leg. Should have caused a permanent limp."

The world came to an abrupt standstill around me. I covered my mouth with trembling fingers. God had done this. This miracle that left an arrogant physician gasping with wonder. I took a few unsteady steps and sagged on the bed next to Father.

"As the prophet Elisha once told an anxious king," I said, " 'This is an easy thing in the eyes of the Lord.' " When Paul had spoken those words, I had not been able to grasp them. Not the marvel nor the hope they held. It is an easy thing in the eyes of the Lord to leave physicians confounded and heal crippled men. I was young in my faith. But like Father's leg, I was growing into the right proportions.

Celsus raised a bushy gray brow. "Which lord is that?"

"The God of heaven and earth. The one who created you. He fixed my father's leg. And even if he had not, he would still be Lord."

Father flashed all his teeth. "Don't worry,

Celsus. I won't complain even though your medical predictions of doom proved faulty."

We were drawing close to July, the month named after Julius Caesar. Wearing the splint in the heat of summer would test Father's temper. The thought made me smile. Three days ago, I had feared he would be maimed, in excruciating pain for the rest of his life. Now I merely worried about the discomfort of a fat bandage and a splint in warm weather.

That was not entirely true. We still had our debts to consider. Added to our normal expenses were the exorbitant fees of the physician. These troubles, which a week ago had seemed crushing, now faded into the background of my mind. If we had to, we would sell our house. Our land. Move to a smaller home. None of it seemed too steep a price to pay for peace. For my father's health. For God's approval.

That afternoon, Father told me that Theo had left for Ephesus. It saddened me to realize he had not bothered to bid me farewell. I wondered how long it would be before he grew comfortable enough to come into my presence. How many farewells would I miss, how many greetings? I prayed God would mend his heart with the same precision he had used with Father's leg.

"Justus sent him?" I asked, frowning. He had not mentioned it.

"No. I did. For business."

"Business?"

Father rubbed his hands together. "I am going to become a soap merchant."

"There is no such thing as a soap merchant." I leaned over to examine his goblet of wine, which Celsus had medicated with his own tincture. "How much of this potion have you drunk?"

He ignored my jibe. "I have discussed it with Justus and Theo. They both agree my notion may succeed. We aim to sell it as hair pomade first. Rome has nothing like it. Efficient, convenient, fragrant." He counted off on his fingers. "It will become every woman's bosom friend. Theo and I have become partners. We have agreed to a modest beginning. Our hope is to expand by early next year."

"Well. You have invented a new trade." I wrapped a hank of hair around my wrist. "I had better start using the stuff if we are to be soap merchants."

Father intertwined his fingers and rested them on his belly. "Theo and I will give you a family discount. You have a lot of hair. You will probably require two balls of soap per wash. I hope you plan to marry a rich man."

"I shall do my best. Anything to afford your soap." Then, unable to swallow my mirth any longer, I burst into laughter. "God has washed our sins and cleansed us from our iniquities. I suppose it is right that we should help the world become clean, at least in body."

I thought life held no more surprises. We had gone through the worst, and by God's help, had emerged redeemed, more whole than before. I should have known God had not quite finished our restoration yet. I should have realized the God who used pain to heal pain would not flinch from allowing more hardship into our lives.

CHAPTER 27

—⁓—

THE FOLLOWING MORNING Dionysius and I were closeted together in Father's tablinum, poring over his accounts, trying to find a way to salvage our home. Father could not manage the stairs yet, and the physician warned him against immersing himself in regular activity too soon.

In three days, my brother would have to return to Athens. I had hoped he would consider moving to Corinth permanently. But Athens beckoned Dionysius the way Corinth called to me. He had delayed his affairs too long already and needed to attend to his duties as a member of the Areopagus.

There were too many leave-takings in my life. This would never change now that Dionysius had committed to making Athens his permanent home. At least this time his departure would be the parting between those whose affections were unbroken. Already we were considering plans for our next visit.

"Mistress?" I had not heard Galatea as she entered the tablinum, her bare feet silent from her years of strict training under Aniketos. She stood, twisting her hands, her face flushed.

"What is it, Galatea?"

"There is a man at the door who insists he must meet with you and my master. I explained that Master Galenos is sick and cannot be disturbed. He had the impudence to smirk at me. 'Broken bones, I expect,' he said."

I tried to read a column of numbers on a sheet. "By now, it is probably common knowledge that Father has broken his leg," I said. "You know how people talk, Galatea."

"Mistress, he refuses to leave. He is sitting in the vestibule, plucking roses from your pots. He insists on seeing you and Master Galenos together, and nothing else will do."

Offended by this abuse of my flowers, I set aside the scroll. "What is his name?" I asked.

"Aulus Papirius."

"Never heard that name," I said.

Dionysius came to his feet. "I will deal with him."

Curious, I followed my brother, wondering at the temerity of the unwanted visitor. A thin man with dark, curly hair and a prominent, bony nose had collected a handful of my roses by the time we arrived. He smiled when he saw me.

"The famous Ariadne of Corinth. You are

lovelier in the light of day than you are in the cover of night."

I stiffened at this presumption. "I have never met you, sir."

"Not formally. This is true."

Dionysius stepped forward. "I must ask you to leave our house, Papirius. You intrude upon us. Nor does your manner commend you to our welcome."

"I believe your sister and father will feel differently when they discover the nature of my . . . business."

"If this is a matter of business, you should return later. My father is unwell, as you have already been informed."

Papirius's overconfident air disturbed me. He seemed too sure of his welcome. It occurred to me that this might be the moneylender to whom Father still owed a considerable sum. But then why had he asked for me? And the loan was not due for another month. Still, it seemed the only thing that could explain his arrogance.

Papirius gave an unpleasant smile. "If you wish to discuss your private matters here where anyone can hear us, I have no objection."

A shiver went through me, like a warning. Best to find out what lay behind his innuendos rather than be left wondering. "Come," I said. "I will take you to my father. But my brother will join us."

"I hope you will not regret his presence. I aim to speak freely." He dropped my prized pink and white roses on the ground and rose to his feet.

"I keep no secrets from my brother." Exchanging an uneasy look with Dionysius, I led the way up the stairs toward Father's chamber. We found him awake, though clearly he was as ignorant of Papirius's identity as we were.

Papirius took the only chair without being invited to do so, folding his long limbs onto the thick cushions, making himself comfortable. "I have the advantage of you, for though we have not met, I had the opportunity of observing both of you for some time. A most entertaining evening, thanks to you, Galenos and Ariadne."

I felt like a mouse sitting between a cat's paws. He was playing with us. Playing as someone who had power. My stomach clenched.

"Speak clearly, man," Father barked.

"Allow me to share a diverting story with you." Everything about the man was thin, even his red tongue as it slithered out to wet narrow lips. "One cloudy night, I sat in the shadows of a street in upper Corinth, pondering a personal dilemma. To my bewilderment, I saw a figure slink into view, moving like a ghost. It seemed like one of the gods, for it could climb walls with its bare hands and feet. Up it went, until I lost sight of it."

Nausea clawed at my throat.

Papirius wet his fleshless lips again. "A few

moments later, another figure came into view. It, too, began to climb the wall until it reached the top. There seemed to be an exchange between the two, though I could not hear their words from where I sat. The second figure backtracked, trying to descend. It slipped, suspended in the air for a moment, before plummeting into the street below."

I knew where this story was headed. My mind ran ahead, trying to concoct a cover. Any excuse that would protect Father and me from Papirius's accusations.

The thin man leaned forward, his face glowing with perverse delight. He was enjoying playing with us, dragging us through this cruel suspense. "The first figure scaled down in pursuit. It was a wonder to behold, that climb, as if a vertical wall held no mystery to its hands and feet. By now, the household had been roused. The intruders barely had time to hide in a doorway. A servant emerged from the villa and looked about, seeking the source of the disturbance. He had a lamp, which he placed in the nook next to the door, and giving up his search, he returned within.

"That lamp." Papirius smiled his razor-thin smile. "That lamp was my friend. For now when the mysterious intruders returned to the street, I could see they were no gods, but human. An ordinary man and a woman who had disguised herself as a man. I did not recognize them, but I intended to remedy that deficiency.

"I followed them. It was not hard, for the woman had to carry the man, as he had clearly been injured by his fall. Slowly, they came here, to this very house. The home of Galenos and his daughter, Ariadne. Ariadne, who has won a garland of victory in the Isthmian Games." He pointed at me and Father. "The man and woman I saw that night, breaking into Grato's house."

I crossed my arms and stood like a beam. "What of it?"

"You are thieves. Not ordinary thieves, mind. You are the Honorable Thief. One of you or both of you together. I do not know. I do not care."

I could feel the blood drain from my face. "What mischief is this? I wished to play a trick on my friend Grato; that is all. Father thought it in poor taste and came to fetch me. The rest is nonsense you have made up in your own mind. You cannot prove it."

Papirius laughed. I had never thought the sound of laughter could be a thing of horror. A viper's bite, nipping at your heart. "In fact, I *can* prove it," he said, wiping his eyes. "You dropped a letter while you were helping your father. All that bending and shuffling and heaving and lifting. It must have come loose from wherever you had stuffed it. I saw it fall in your wake and collected it. So thoughtful of you to have left it behind."

My heart sank as fast and deep as the *Paralus*. In the excitement after Father's accident, I had utterly forgotten about the letter. The letter I had written, signed as the Honorable Thief. The letter I had meant to post at the *bema* once I finished robbing Grato.

I sagged against the wall. Unbidden, an image of Jesus, hung on a cross between two thieves, flashed before my mind. The thief Christ had forgiven was still crucified. He did not escape the consequences of his actions, though he received an eternal reward. What had made me think that I could elude payment for my crimes?

Papirius wagged a finger at me. "Take my advice, young woman. This is not the life for you. I do not question you have the courage, the impudence, the sheer physical stamina and grace for it. But you lack the complete ruthlessness it requires. You are too soft." He shook his head. "I, on the other hand, have more than enough ruthless resolve. Alas, my body will not comply."

"What do you want from us?" Father asked gruffly.

"I merely wish for your assistance. A simple exchange. I will give back your letter if you retrieve a box of documents for me."

"Retrieve them from where?" my brother said, his voice hard.

"From the house of a man named Spurius Felonius. His home is near Grato's villa."

I inhaled a sharp breath. Now I understood. "That is why you were there that night. You were trying to find your way into Felonius's villa."

Papirius shrugged. "I was merely looking. There is no law against that."

"It is impossible," I said, crossing my arms. "If you have studied the place, you know it is a fortress. I have been inside that villa several times. It backs into a rocky hill more vertical than a wall. No way to breach that rock. The front is guarded day and night. Felonius has not left a single crack in the defenses of his house. Do you take me for an eagle that I should descend inside his villa from the skies above?"

"You will find a way." Papirius smirked. "I am giving you excellent motivation to succeed."

The man set my teeth on edge. *"Love your enemies,"* Jesus commanded. Did God expect me to love this slimy insect? To be kind to him? Patient with him? I clearly had a long way to go in order to grow like Christ if that was his expectation.

"My father, as you see, is laid up with a shattered leg. He cannot even descend a flight of stairs, let alone scale a wall."

"I saw what you did at Grato's house. A girl as talented as you does not need her father's assistance. You can do this alone."

"Impossible," my father declared.

Papirius gave him a venomous look. "Then

prepare for the bliss of prison, you and your daughter."

I made a conciliatory gesture. "Where does he keep these documents?"

"I do not know."

I threw my hands in the air. "You must be mad. How am I to find them? Do you know how many documents any man of business keeps in his home? How do you expect me to recognize what it is you want? Even if miraculously I make my way inside, I need to know where to search."

Papirius thought for a moment. "He showed them to me once. They are kept in a distinctive box made of ivory and onyx. A ruby the size of a pigeon's egg decorates the top."

A vague memory stirred in the back of my mind. Where had I heard something about a box? It nagged at me, as if I were missing an important detail.

"Where is this box kept?" I asked, distracted.

"You shall have to discover that yourself."

I scraped my hands over my head. "You give me too much credit. I cannot see through walls."

"You are resourceful. I trust you will find a way."

I made him describe the box and its measurements more exactly, and shook my head. "It is too large for me to carry."

"I don't need the box. The scrolls and letters within are what I am after."

"What do these scrolls contain?" Dionysius asked. "Why do you want them?"

"That is my business," Papirius snapped. "Get them for me, or I will destroy you."

I could see from his manner that this was no empty threat. I gave him a sharp look. Under the layers of confidence and cold derision, I sensed a shivering apprehension. The man was not merely greedy. He was desperate.

That put a new face to my enemy. I wondered what documents Spurius Felonius held in his box that could bring a man like Papirius to his knees.

CHAPTER 28

—⁕—

"IT IS AN ODD REQUEST," Dionysius said. We had sent for Justus and told him about Papirius's threat. Now we had gathered in Father's bedchamber, the four of us trying to make sense of how to go forward.

"He does not ask for treasure or money. He does not even care if he receives a valuable chest containing a jewel that must be worth a fortune," Dionysius continued. "Papirius is after documents, which on their own could be worth nothing. Even if they are deeds, he cannot claim them. They will bear Felonius's name." He shook his head, puzzled. "What manner of man is Spurius Felonius? What does he do for a living?"

"He is wealthy," I said. "I do not know the source of his wealth. He drinks too much and has a temper. He threw my friend Claudia out of his house . . ." I stopped, arrested. "I remember!" I cried.

"What?" the three men said together.

"When Papirius described the box that contained the documents, I had a nagging feeling that I knew something pertinent, but could not recollect what. Just now, I remembered. My friend Claudia came upon Felonius riffling through the contents of that very chest. A black-and-white box, she said. That must be it! If he has not moved it, I know where to find that box." I came to my feet. "Whatever it contains, he guards it jealously. When Claudia saw him with it, he had her thrown out of the house."

Dionysius rubbed his temple. "Did she see the contents?"

"Not enough to read them. She said it was a chest filled with scrolls. Nothing out of the ordinary. But Felonius flew into a rage because she had seen them. He has not allowed her to return."

"Is she not his sister-in-law?" Justus asked. I nodded. "He threw out his wife's sister because she accidentally saw him with a box of documents? I grow more curious about these scrolls."

"Whatever they may be, Papirius is desperate to lay his hands on something within," I said.

"I have heard of this Papirius," Justus said. "He is a minor official in Cenchreae, but an important one. Everything that comes into the port goes through his office for tariff estimations."

"That office can be a gold mine for the right man." Father grimaced.

Justus nodded. "I have a friend called Stephanas

who owns several warehouses at the harbor of Cenchreae. He told me once that this Papirius has a shady reputation and warned me to be careful around him. No one has proved anything, but supposedly he has made a sizable fortune in bribes and illegal favors."

"Stephanas?" Father's brows rose. "I have met him at Priscilla and Aquila's house. He and his household were the first to follow Christ in Corinth. He is a sound man. I trust his judgment."

Justus twirled a stylus between restless fingers. "If someone had evidence of Papirius's dishonesty—if they had a document that proved he had accepted a bribe, say, or violated his position for personal gain—he would lose his post. That would be the end of a lucrative career. And the door to similar appointments would close permanently."

"You think Felonius has such a document? One that proves Papirius's shady dealings?" I asked.

Dionysius leaned forward, his eyes bright with excitement. "And if so, why has Felonius not brought such evidence to the right officials? Why keep it hidden?"

Father smacked his forehead with the flat of his hand. "Papirius is being blackmailed by Felonius. That would explain his eagerness to get his hands on the document. If that is the case, then we are caught in a battle between two corrupt men. Lord, help us."

I choked. "You mean we are being blackmailed by a man who is being blackmailed? Perhaps we can blackmail someone to rob this box for us." My voice wobbled with hysterical laughter.

"Or rob him ourselves, as Papirius demands." Father looked like he might be sick.

Dionysius held up a hand. "This is conjecture and hearsay. You cannot convict a man's character based on flimsy evidence. Even if Felonius is a blackmailer, it does not give you the right to rob him. 'You must not steal,' the Lord commands. He does not say, 'You must not steal from good people, but the evil are at your disposal.'"

I felt like I had swallowed a stone. It was very well to receive miracles from God, to accept his mercy and experience his undeserved grace. But there was a price when you belonged to him. You could not live your life on your own terms any longer. You could not explain away the wrong you did. Protect yourself with a web of placating lies. *"You must not steal."* To obey that command, Father and I would ourselves have to face imprisonment. A pall fell over the room. We could see no way out.

Dionysius took a sip of water and cleared his throat. "We think we have no choice but to give in to Papirius's demand. I say we should trust in the Lord. Commit our way to him, though we do not understand how he will save us. Ask him to open a way out of this predicament, one that is righteous."

Justus had turned the color of ash. He pulled me into his arms and held me as if afraid I might be snatched from him that very moment. No one spoke. No one could offer a solution. We had reached an impassable wall.

It seemed mad, but in the place of planning, we began to pray. My words were broken, my faith desultory at first. But as we pressed through the initial uncertainty, I found myself growing in strength.

I thought of Paul's urging that we do everything with love. This Jew and his God were going to kill me! Do everything with love? How was I to deal with a man like Papirius with any measure of love? Men like him only understood sharp weapons and forceful measures. How was love to solve anything?

Then I realized that I had already fallen short of Paul's charge. I had removed myself from the immediacy of God's presence by calling him Paul's God. The Jewish God. Had I so quickly forgotten that I was his daughter, and he my Father? I would not bow to such lies. I would bend my will to the outrageous truths of the Kingdom of God, rather than conform to the practical whispers of my own mind.

If that meant prison, poverty, public shame, then let it be.

I still had no solution. No scheme that would answer both Papirius's demands and God's commands. Other than a vague notion that I should get myself invited to Felonius's house, I could think of nothing after our earnest prayers. Even this ill-defined idea was an arrow shot blindly in the dark.

"We need Paul's help," I said after we finished praying.

"He is still lodging with Priscilla and Aquila." Dionysius gave me directions to their home and Justus accompanied me there.

Paul's friends lived in a two-story building near the agora. The ground floor housed a vaulted shop selling leather goods—tents, booths, awnings, cloaks. Inside, the shop was bright and orderly, with samples of leather stacked neatly on two marble shelves.

Absently, I fingered a square of dark-brown leather and found it surprisingly soft. The workshop was separated from the public store by a gray curtain edged with fine green and pink embroidery. Through a narrow opening in the fabric I could glimpse three men occupying benches, a large length of leather on their laps as they worked.

A woman approached us. "Welcome. I am Priscilla. How may I help you?"

She had dark-red hair piled on her head in a simple coronet of braids. A few tendrils escaped their severe captivity to curl about her face, glinting where the sun's rays hit them. Had I been a sculptor, I would have wanted to carve that face. Striking rather than pretty, it was a face with prominent bones, delicate lips, and skin that seemed too sheer to be real. She spoke with the elite accents of a highborn Roman but had the hands of a servant, calloused from working with a needle and awl. I remembered that Priscilla was the diminutive for Prisca, a noble name belonging to a well-known Roman family.

She was altogether a paradox. That bright hair and the blue eyes that accompanied it did not look Roman. The hands belonged to the lower classes, the accents to the higher.

I collected myself, remembering why we had come, and after cursory introductions, asked for Paul.

"You are Ariadne! Paul speaks highly of you."

I could not imagine why.

"He prays for you often."

That, I could understand.

"I am afraid Paul is not here. But if you come upstairs, I will give you a letter he left behind for you."

"For *me?*"

Priscilla nodded. "Before he left early this morning." She beckoned us to follow as she climbed the narrow steps to the second floor, which housed their private living quarters. She invited us to sit on a faded brown couch, offering us new wine and water, before going to fetch the letter.

I unrolled the letter and began to read.

> Greetings from Paul, servant of God, to Ariadne, my daughter in faith,
>
> Grace and peace from God the Father and Jesus our Lord.
>
> I am needed elsewhere for some days. But as I prepare to leave, I feel you heavy on my heart.

My shoulders slumped. I had hoped Paul would offer us a miracle. But he was gone. I forced my eyes back to the letter.

> I wish I could come to you, but circumstances prevent me. I do not know the nature of your need, only that you face danger. Whatever your circumstances, my child, do not grow weary in doing good. Be steadfast and immovable. Don't let life shake you! Remain watchful and stand firm in the faith. Be strong. Do everything in love. Remember that God will comfort you in all your afflictions. I will rejoin you as quickly as I can.

I closed my eyes, feeling a sting of despair.

Priscilla touched me softly on the arm, as though sensing my anguish. "I will pray for you."

I opened my eyes and found her watching me. It was not a paltry offer, I sensed, the prayers of this woman. I could only imagine the power unleashed when she prayed. I gave her a weak smile of thanks.

"There is a group of us who gather here in the evenings for fellowship. You are most welcome to join us. Come early and eat with us."

I thanked her and promised to return soon. For now, we had much to prepare. Should I survive the coming adventure and escape imprisonment or worse, I could think of no place where I would rather spend my time.

Papirius returned to our home the following day. Justus insisted on being present with me. "I will not leave you alone with that viper."

Our problem was eating into him. Under layers of burning rage lay a fear so deep he did not dare acknowledge it even to himself. I blamed myself for his pain. If I had not gone to Grato's house that night, if I had listened to my father and Theo, if I had trusted my future to God long before this . . . if . . . if . . . if. I was tormented by the ifs of my life. Tormented by the price Justus had to pay for them.

I knew it would be unwise to have him present in the same chamber as Papirius.

"Let him think me alone and friendless," I said. "You are well known in Corinth and have many connections that may yet prove useful to us. It is best that Papirius not discover our association. The more powerful he feels, the more likely he is to grow careless."

My proposition irked Justus. He had a charioteer's heart. Bold, brave, decisive in the face of danger. Hiding in the shadows went against his grain. But in the end, he saw the wisdom of my words. He concealed himself in a nearby alcove, ready to spring to my aid should I have need.

"What are your plans? When will you strike?" Papirius said as soon as I sat down.

"We need more time." My voice sounded strangely cool in my own ears. A calm sea in spite of gathering storms. "It is not a simple theft. I must find the location of the chest before I even attempt breaking into the house. This enterprise requires patience."

"How much time?"

I gave him a hard look. "As long as it takes. I need to befriend him. Or his wife. This is no easy matter."

I did not think it possible, but the thin lips grew thinner. "I want his box, not his heart."

"By the sound of it, his heart is in his box. The

closer I can draw to him, the better my chance of finding it."

Papirius exhaled a breath. He had the air of a caged animal, desperate to break free, wild with need. Leaning forward, I gentled my voice. "Tell me this. Is he attempting to extort money from you?"

Papirius's jaw slackened. The narrow eyes turned bleak. For a moment, I pitied him. He wiped his face clean of expression. "That is none of your affair," he spat. But I had seen what I needed.

I sent Claudia the Elder a complimentary basket filled with Father's best soaps and included a flowery letter overflowing with nauseating admiration for her superior taste. The basket contained perfume and oils that matched the scent of the soaps and was worth a small fortune. Three days later, she invited me for lunch.

"This soap you sent me for my hair—is it a new product from Rome?"

Although Corinth was the zenith of trade, Rome remained the capital of everything fashionable. "Romans imported the thing in the first place, of course," I said, forbearing to mention that it came from the barbarian Germans and Gauls. "With the addition of new perfumes, we hope it will grow in popularity throughout the empire. Since you are one of the foremost fashionable women of Corinth, I was interested in your opinion. Did you like it, Claudia?"

"It was not bad. The scent you used is a little coarse. Not fine enough for Rome." She shrugged a purple-clad shoulder. "I suppose it will do in the provinces."

"Yes, that is our hope. A small beginning. In time, Rome. Who knows? Perhaps even the imperial household."

Her eyes flashed interest. "You think the Augusta will wish to use this soap?"

I knew as much about Agrippina and her tastes as I did about the moon. "That is our hope. She is an exceptionally elegant woman."

"You can dream, I suppose."

"We are doing more than dreaming. Our first shipment will leave Corinth next month. We think men as well as women will want to use it. You may have noticed that it feels much cleaner than oil on the hair. Do you think Spurius Felonius might enjoy some? We have soaps that appeal to masculine tastes."

Claudia's expression shuttered. "Who knows what Felonius enjoys?"

"I brought a basket especially for him."

"He is not at home."

"May I leave the basket in his tablinum?"

"Gods, no! Felonius does not allow anyone near that place."

"How odd. My father leaves his door open to visitors all day long."

"Mine does the same. Felonius has different habits."

"Surely, as his wife, he would not mind you going inside? Just for a moment. Long enough to leave a basket. A surprise gift is always welcome from a bride."

Something flitted across the violet eyes. I had been watching Claudia carefully, or I would have missed it. Terror. An odd thing to find in the eyes of a woman newly married.

"You may leave it with me," she said, lowering her eyes. "I will see that he receives it. Don't pin your hopes on his good opinion. He is not interested in such things." The old superior manner replaced the momentary vulnerability. But now I knew it for what it was. A cover, a shield to hide behind. A shield I intended to crack. I pressed my advantage by poking her considerable pride.

"As his beloved wife, I am certain he would welcome your intrusion upon his sanctuary. After all, it is not as if you would be infringing upon his time. He is not even there. Why, even Claudius, Caesar though he may be, welcomes Agrippina into his august presence. How much more will Felonius be amenable to your sweet imposition?" I stood, grabbing my basket. "Let us go now, before his arrival."

The look of terror returned. Claudia snapped to her feet. "We should not go there! We should not."

What happened next, I cannot explain. It was like a breach, a tearing asunder in how I saw the world. Time slowed. I saw through the guile and artifice that covered us both. My manipulative attempts at forcing her to reveal her secrets seemed suddenly distasteful. I was ashamed of my own behavior. I remembered Paul's letter urging me to stand firm in the faith and to do everything in love. This was not the work of faith. It bore no resemblance to love.

I gazed at Claudia and what I saw was a woman in distress. A woman alone and fearful, hiding behind the tatters of her pride. Her riches were dust. I saw . . . more than mere eyes can see. I saw the truth.

"He blackmailed you into marrying him," I said. It was not a question. I knew it as surely as I knew my name. God himself had pressed that knowledge into my breast.

CHAPTER 29

—⟲—

I THOUGHT SHE WOULD DENY my assertion. Prevaricate. Grow angry. But I had underestimated her loneliness. God had known, of course. She began to weep. Not pretty, fetching tears, but gulping, messy wails that tore at your insides. She was no friend of mine. Until that moment. It is impossible to see suffering so deep and not feel compassion.

Love is kind. When the Love that established the universe starts moving within you, I suppose you lean toward kindness too. I held Claudia, awkwardly at first, and then with the comforting tenderness of a sister as the storm of grief swept through her.

Finally, she quieted and pulled out of my arms with a self-conscious jerk. "How did you know?" Her native shrewdness was starting to reassert itself. "Is he holding you under his thumb also?"

Trust is like a marriage vow. It should only be spoken in wisdom as well as love. I could not trust Claudia with my whole secret. "I am not indebted to your husband in any way. But I know a man who is. I would like to set him free. You also, if you will allow me to help you."

She sneered. "I have lived in the same house as that monster for months and I have not found where he keeps his treasure trove. What makes you think you can do better?"

"I think I know where he keeps his scrolls. I know what the box looks like, at least, and I know where he hides it."

She hesitated. I could sense hope and skepticism wrestling within her. "How could you possibly know that?"

"Let us say that Providence smiled upon me."

"Where is it?"

"In a secret alcove in his tablinum. No doubt that is why he forbids you to enter within."

Her face turned stony. "You can forget getting your hands on that box if it is in his tablinum. The place is always guarded."

"Let us suppose that we find a way inside. Will you be free of him if you find this box?"

"If I have the letter he holds against me . . . and another against my father. Yes. I could leave him then. There would be no impediment to a divorce. He would keep my dowry, of course. A price I am willing to pay if I can be rid of him."

That explained why Claudia's father had been furious with her when Felonius threw her out. He, too, was a victim of the man's extortion and feared the consequences of his anger. How many people had fallen into Felonius's clutches?

"Suppose I find the box. Will you give me the scroll belonging to the man I mentioned?"

Claudia waved a hand. "This is all a dream. You will never get the better of him. You do not understand how wily that man is."

I squeezed her arm. "Do not lose hope. I have a plan."

"A plan for what?" a voice said from the door. In the flesh, Felonius himself, smiling a hyena's smile, had appeared as if by magic. How had he come so silently that we had not heard the whisper of his feet on the marble floors? How much of our conversation had he overheard?

Claudia had turned into a pillar of rock, rigid and cold. If she did not gather herself together, Felonius would suspect her guilty of some plot. I sprang into action. Grabbing the basket, I jumped in front of Claudia, giving her time to collect herself.

"Felonius, the very man I hoped to see today. I have brought you a present from my honored father, Galenos. We are starting a new trade—in soap. My plan is to share it with the fashionable people of Corinth, like your beautiful wife and yourself, of course. If we win your honest praise, then our success is secure."

He sauntered in, his steps light and athletic for a man well in his middle years. I could smell wine on his breath as he drew closer. "A trade in what?"

I pulled out a ball scented with rosemary and sandalwood. "Soap. It cleanses hair." I studied the thinning fringe of gray that edged his forehead and quickly amended my explanation. "Hair and the body, without the use of a strigil. I hoped you would be willing to try it."

He sniffed at the ball and threw it on the table. Taking a seat on the couch, he invited me to join him. Claudia said, "I will call for wine," and left the room.

"I heard your father was left with an enormous debt after the sinking of his ship some years ago. The *Paralus*, was it?"

I almost admired him. He had swiped at me with his claw, drawing first blood without even batting an eyelash. He had struck fast, reminding me of a misfortune I had thought private. How had he found out about Father's debts? He must have unusual resources. But he did not know everything. It dawned on me that he meant to leave me unsteady. Easy prey for his prodding. I gave him a wide smile.

"At the time, it was a hard blow for our family." I twirled my palm with a careless gesture. "My father has many friends. With their help, we have recovered. Do you think you might enjoy using this new product?"

"Tallow and ash from Germania? Hardly."

It sank into my spinning mind that his initial ignorance had been a pretense. The man could leave you breathless. He played his game consummately. How could I match wits with him and win?

A wayward thought tiptoed into my mind. For all his shrewd insight, Felonius was no match for God. The knot in my belly started to loosen.

"In the right hands, even ashes can turn into a crown of beauty," I said, thinking of a verse Dionysius had once quoted from a prophet.

He gave me a quizzical look. "I should think the opposite more likely. Crowns are so easy to crush and destroy, leaving behind nothing but ashes."

No doubt he was speaking from experience. How many "crowns" had he destroyed, I wondered? How many people's victories and achievements had burned to ashes in his hands? "You are too wise for me," I said, forcing myself to sound deferential.

From the corner of my eye, I caught a cithara sitting prominently on a golden stand. "What a stunning instrument. Do you play?"

His gaze caressed the instrument like a lover. "That cithara is too beautiful for any but the most skillful musician to touch. The music of the heavens flows out of those seven strings." He turned over his shoulder. "What is keeping my wife?"

I rose to my feet. "I shall inconvenience you no longer." I collected the basket he had not wanted.

Claudia met with me at the front gate. "He knows nothing," I whispered in her ear as I bent to kiss her cheek. "Do not be fearful. Send for me when you are ready."

That night, Justus joined Father, Dionysius, and me for supper. As I described my conversation with Claudia, they gaped at me, forgetting their food.

"He blackmailed that young woman into marriage?" Father's jaw grew slack.

"All the scrolls in the box Claudia saw must contain incriminating information about different people." Justus's spoon clattered on his plate. "A blackmailer's fortune. Exchanging people's sins and errors for riches. If Papirius gets his hands on those scrolls, he will not be content to merely win his own freedom. He will slip into Felonius's shoes, using the documents to line his own pockets. Those poor wretches! They will go from one fire into another."

"We cannot give him that," I said. "We cannot dispossess Felonius only to empower Papirius. This evil must stop."

"You have a plan?" Dionysius said.

"I have a seedling of an idea. It rides on Claudia the Elder. What she is willing to risk."

"This is too perilous," Justus said, pushing his

plate away. "You cannot endanger yourself. That man is a snake. He will coil around you."

I lowered my head. "Danger coils about me whether I come against Felonius or not. This way, I may do some good for others."

Dionysius studied me, wide brown eyes pensive. "What if God has heard the cries of the many who are being pressed and trampled under Felonius's feet, and is using our predicament as a means of releasing them?" He did not say it, but we all knew that Father and I would likely emerge from this battle ruined.

"Does anyone know an expert cithara player? A female?" I pasted a reckless smile on my face.

"As it happens, I do," Father said. "Stephanas's eldest daughter is renowned for her skills with that instrument."

"She needs to be pretty."

"I think you will find her satisfactory. Chara turns heads in sackcloth and ashes."

"Do you know if she would lend us a hand?"

"I will ask Stephanas to pray on it."

I received another invitation to lunch with Claudia at her home. Felonius's disquieting intrusion into our initial conversation had demonstrated that their villa was not a safe place to plan. For all I knew, he had spies in the household listening to our every word.

I curtailed my conversation, sticking to the

latest gossip, the weather, our favorite market stalls, and a variety of incurable illnesses. Neither one of us mentioned a word about Felonius's infamous box.

"You have been generous with your hospitality," I said as I rose to leave. "Would you honor me with a visit at our house next time?" Extending this simple invitation had been the sole reason for sitting through three torturous hours.

"My husband would prefer that my friends visit me here."

So she was a prisoner in her home. Unless Felonius himself accompanied her to some event, showing her off like a new bauble, he was not willing that she leave her gilded cage.

"Of course," I said. "Your house is much larger and more comfortable than ours, in any case. Would he mind if we attend the public baths first? We can try my father's soap together."

The Roman custom of bathing had become an integral part of life in Corinth. No doubt Spurius Felonius's villa boasted its own private baths. In Corinth, ablutions were merely a small portion of the reason crowds attended the public baths, however. We socialized in the baths. Caught up on the news. Met with people we might not normally have the opportunity to converse with.

And we showed off. With our slaves in tow and our riches on display, we proclaimed our importance to the world. I hoped this might induce Felonius to allow his wife some freedom. He liked displaying Claudia's beauty and patrician heritage, hinting at his growing importance by association.

"I will ask," she said.

That evening, I received a message from her. *My husband is the most affable of men.* He must have been reading over her shoulder as she wrote it. *He has agreed that I may attend the baths with you. I shall meet you at the public baths near the temple of Poseidon tomorrow.* The city of Corinth enjoyed the services of several public baths. The most expensive of these, decorated with marble and semiprecious slabs of stone from Laconia, was the one she had selected.

I shall bring my slaves. I assume you will do likewise, she wrote. By which she meant she would be guarded by more than one spy. I sighed. Why was life never simple?

The following morning Delia and I climbed into the household litter and wended our way through the streets of Corinth toward the baths. The two slaves carrying us set the litter down gently and helped us alight. I spied Claudia waiting for us, two muscle-bound giants and a burly woman at her side.

"Hail, Claudia!" I cried with a jovial wave. "Are you ready for a glorious morning?"

"You are cheerful," she said, her tone sour. We

began to make our way into the public building. The two giants and her female slave followed us step for step. I raised a brow but said nothing.

At the entrance, we paid a fee to store our clothes before moving into the frigidarium, the chamber that contained a large pool of cold water. It had been a sweltering summer and the cool water felt delicious against our skin. Claudia's giants stood watch in one corner.

I had instructed Delia to keep Claudia's personal slave occupied if possible. I listened with half an ear to their conversation. Delia tried to speak of the latest hairstyles to the stocky woman and encountered no interest. She moved to clothing with the same results. Leather goods came next, but Felonius's strapping spy proved unresponsive.

Claudia and I sauntered to the tepidarium, the room that housed a warm pool. Our attendants followed behind, Delia chatting, the others watchful.

My companion discussed recipes and described meals served at recent banquets. I was beginning to grow desperate to shake our chaperones. How many ways can you cook a peacock? Heaven be merciful.

I suggested that we move on to the caldarium, the hot-water pool. The room was steaming. It had the desired effect on our guards. Within moments, they were sweating.

And then, finally, Delia struck gold. She introduced the topic of chariot races and, to my relief, found an eager audience. Felonius's spy was a fanatic for the races. When she discovered that Delia belonged to Theo and lived next door to Justus, she turned pink like a geranium. It was a beautiful sight. The two Herculean guards sauntered over and joined their conversation.

My Theo. He came to my rescue even in his absence. His very name was a guard over me.

As the torpor of heat and steam worked its magic, the four began to inch their way toward the exit, where a cooler breeze blew. Finally I could speak freely. Whispering, I told Claudia my plan.

She was shivering by the time I finished. In the vaporous warmth of the caldarium, she trembled, her arms crossed over her chest like bars. The mere thought of rising up against her husband reduced her to a quivering kitten.

She did not refuse to participate in my scheme. Nor did she agree. She needed time. Time to build up the courage for such a risk. Time I did not have.

"Why would you do this?" she asked. "Why risk your well-being for mine?"

"I told you. There is a document in that box that I need. I hope you will give it to me as a reward."

"Does Felonius hold some misdeed against your father?"

"Felonius has no power over my father or any member of my family." I bent my head. "But over this man, he holds sway. I cannot tell you more."

After we emerged from the heated pool, Delia and Claudia's servant scraped our bodies with bronze strigils and massaged us with scented oil. I wanted to pound at Claudia the way Delia was pounding into my muscles. I wanted her to agree to the only path that offered her any chance at freedom. Instead, I bit my lip and swallowed my carping and prayed. Paul was having an influence on me.

CHAPTER 30

—⟋⟍—

CLAUDIA ARRANGED for a small private banquet, inviting Dionysius and me. Father's leg, though improved, still hampered him, making it impossible for him to leave the house. My brother had delayed his return to Athens until such time as our dilemma could be solved. I felt safer for his presence, and grateful for the sacrifice of his time.

Of course, Claudia did not know of my betrothal to Justus. I did not think it wise to put her old jealousy to the test. We had no way of asking him to accompany us without revealing our close association. Where I was tested by what I must do, Justus was tested by the sting of inactivity.

I brought Stephanas's daughter Chara with me, offering her like a bouquet of flowers to our host. My father had not exaggerated her beauty. Her blonde hair flowed down her back like a stream of gold. Delia had woven a crown of fresh blossoms into that hair and dressed the girl in white linen. She looked like a glorious visitor from some ancient land. When she turned her amber-colored eyes on Felonius, he gave his hyena smile and stared, transfixed.

"I hope you will pardon my presumption in bringing dear Chara." I signaled Galatea, who had accompanied us, and she hefted over Chara's instrument. "She plays the cithara. I thought you might enjoy her music."

"She is most welcome." Felonius's tone indicated that he held no high expectation of the girl's musical talent. He probably believed he already knew every accomplished cithara player in the city.

Felonius was not the only one to knock an opponent sideways, however. I knew how to spring my own surprises. Chara did not perform for the general public, which meant that he would have had no way of hearing her.

After Felonius's slaves served us the third course, I asked Chara to play her instrument. Our host gave a tolerant nod, expecting a schoolgirl performance. Chara sat on a stool and settled the box-shaped body of the cithara on a slim thigh, inclining the instrument toward her torso. She did not tether the weight of it with a yoke to her wrist as many players I had seen. Rather, she held the instrument loosely, balancing it with her body.

Her bare arms lifted to the strings, and she began to pluck with one hand, using a flat plectrum. The sound wafted soft, a tender melody. Without warning, the fingers of her left hand joined in the music, dampening unwanted strings, and then, to our utter astonishment, producing harmonics that held us breathless.

Chara had seemed lovely before, a vision of old-fashioned grace. When she played the cithara, she became luminous. A spellbinding creature from another world. Her long neck inclined now forward, now back, a swan turned into human form. No one dared move lest we disturb the magic she wove about us.

When she came to the end of a movement, I nodded to my brother, signaling him to bring the performance to an end. So deeply had he been captivated by Chara's allure that he missed my gesture and I had to poke him in the ribs.

He cleared his throat and stood before Chara could start another piece. "We must take our leave of you now, Felonius. My thanks for a pleasant evening."

"What?" Felonius vaulted to his feet, upending a tray of figs in his haste. "You can't leave now! Chara has hardly started."

"I fear we must. I promised Chara's father that I would have her home early."

"There is yet time to play another song. I want her to play my own cithara." Felonius gestured to his prized instrument on its golden perch. "I insist you remain."

"You are too gracious," Dionysius said, dark eyes stern. "But I must keep my promise. You understand."

Felonius saw that my brother would not be moved. His face turned a dull red. "Indeed. If you must leave, then give me your word that you will return tomorrow." He directed his words to Chara. "Will you not honor me by coming here to play again, Chara? My cithara would be at your disposal."

Chara gave a slight nod. "If my father permits." She gave Dionysius a shy look. "And if Dionysius chooses to bring me again."

We had trained her well. My brother placed a hand about her shoulder in a protective manner. I did not think he had to playact very hard. "We cannot return tomorrow evening, Felonius, as we have another engagement. Perhaps next week?"

Felonius swallowed hard. "I shall anticipate it with delight." It had cost him something, that capitulation. He burned with anger at being denied.

I let out a long breath. He had swallowed my bait. Denying him had been part of my plan. Stewing with longing as he waited to see the girl again would serve to enlarge his craving.

Delia dressed Chara in a modest golden tunic and painted the girl's eyelids and cheeks with gold dust. She even brushed the shimmering dust into her hair, making the blonde curls spark like a living thing when the light touched them. A plain golden diadem sat at the crown of Chara's head. Majesty and modesty twined to make her appearance that of a heavenly being, as if God had sent one of his angels for a visitation.

In contrast, I wrapped myself in a severe tunic, dark blue and shapeless, making it easy to move and easier to blend into the night. Next to Chara's splendor, I faded like a crow standing near a swan.

She gasped when she saw herself in the mirror. Chara was shy, and I had turned her into the unmistakable center of attention.

"If you are uncomfortable, I will give you a different tunic to wear," I said. "Remember that you are meant to draw Felonius's eyes, and the eyes of his men, also. You are my distraction. My only protection tonight."

Chara smoothed the folds of her skirt. "I will keep this tunic." She smiled. "The Lord shall be my covering." Her gaze brimmed with reassurance. "And yours."

I had an overwhelming sense of grateful affection for the girl whom I hardly knew. I had found her sparing with words. Most people waste speech on useless matters. When Chara spoke, she accorded each word with significance, a quality I could not help but admire.

This time, Justus had managed to get himself invited, posing as Chara's escort, throwing off any suspicion that he may be connected to me. Dionysius and Justus acted like rivals for Chara's affections, adding misdirection to diversion, putting Felonius's eyes everywhere but on me. We hired a large enclosed carriage that afternoon, and the four of us along with Galatea wound our leisurely way back to Claudia's villa.

Felonius himself met us in the street, his manner distracted, greeting us with clipped words of welcome. Chara alighted last from the carriage. I had the sense that the man barely breathed until he saw her. The sun shone with steady afternoon light, making the gold of her tunic and the softer sparkles on her skin come to shimmering life when she emerged. Felonius could not hide a gasp.

Claudia's reception in the vestibulum, though proper, was far colder. She had arrayed herself in the robes of an empress, her hair, fingers, shoulders, neck, and wrists dripping with jewels. After the way her husband had ogled Chara when we had last come to their house, she no doubt wished to demonstrate her superiority. The girl might sparkle with youth, but Claudia shone with majesty.

Our hostess had arranged for the meal to be served in the outdoor dining room with its rectangular pool and fruit trees. She led us through a wide colonnade covered with a roof of red clay tiles.

Most visitors would be so entranced by the intricate design of the mosaics under our feet that they would miss the many doors leading to various chambers to our right and left. One of these was hidden behind a thick green curtain. A man whose muscles spoke of military training at some point in the past stood guard by that door. As Chara walked by him, his whole body swiveled, as if attached to her by strings. His distraction gave me a momentary chance to survey the curtain and the closed door behind it, which thanks to Claudia's tutelage, I knew led to Felonius's tablinum.

The table was set under a blue linen awning, protecting us from the afternoon sunlight. As we took our seats beneath its shade, I smelled roses. Felonius had splashed the awning with rosewater. He served us delectable food on expensive Roman glass platters. Wine from Pompeii filled our goblets. Nothing seemed too good for our Chara.

Just before the desserts were served, I placed a hand on my belly, wincing with pain. "I seem to have eaten something that disagreed with me."

Claudia gave me a haughty look. "At my house?"

I gave a convincing impression of a fish, my mouth opening and closing soundlessly. "Of course not."

The desserts arrived, an impressive array of sweet cakes with fruit compote and nuts. Instead of helping myself to a healthy selection, I eyed them with distaste. In spite of the heat, I began to shiver.

Chara came to sit near me. "Dear Ariadne, are you unwell? You are trembling."

"I feel chilled to the bone."

Chara looked from Dionysius to Justus. "Perhaps we should take her home."

Felonius sat up on his couch, his back ramrod straight. "No need for that."

Dionysius waved a hand. "She's had a sensitive constitution since childhood. These bouts are nothing to be concerned about."

"Perhaps you should have stayed home." Justus plunked a fig into his mouth.

"She is suffering, the poor thing," Chara said, her tone reproachful. "I can accompany her home and send the carriage back for you."

"No." I wiped my forehead with my napkin. "I would not dream of interrupting everyone's enjoyment. We have all been looking forward to hearing you play."

"Ariadne is right. There is no need for you to leave, Chara." Felonius turned to his wife. "Claudia, why don't you take Ariadne to a bed-chamber where she can lie down in comfort?"

Justus rubbed his hands together. "That is an excellent solution. Felonius, won't you fetch your cithara for our lovely musician? I, for one, cannot wait to hear her pluck those strings."

Felonius obeyed with alacrity while Claudia helped me to my feet. We could already hear the strumming of Chara's instrument as we began to walk down the length of the enclosed garden.

Claudia stopped outside the chamber that abutted Felonius's tablinum. The beefy guard watched our progress with intent eyes.

"The lady Ariadne is sick. She can lie down here until she feels better," Claudia explained as she led me within.

In the bedroom, she covered me with a cloak that sat neatly at the bottom of the bed. No sooner had I lain down than I grabbed my belly and doubled up. "Lavatory!" I cried loud enough for the guard and his maiden aunt in lower Corinth to hear.

Felonius's villa was a relatively new Roman construction, and like other prosperous modern houses, enjoyed an indoor toilet and piped water. Claudia helped me to my feet and we left the confines of the bedchamber once again. She rolled her eyes as we walked past the guard, who smirked openly at my discomfort. I clutched the cloak my hostess had given me and stared at my feet in embarrassment.

Claudia guided me to the room that housed the double stone receptacles, where one could enjoy seated comfort while going about one's business.

She stepped inside with me and closed the door behind us.

Galatea awaited us within. She had ensconced herself inside the small cubicle when we had first arrived. Felonius may have stationed spies everywhere in his house, but no one bothered to pay much attention to the lavatories. Even if they had, they would have merely found a servant, relieving herself. At most, she would have earned herself a reprimand for using a facility set aside for the master and mistress's use, not to be encroached upon by servants. Galatea had come equipped with a pitcher of water under her light cloak.

"Ready?" I asked. Both women nodded.

Growing up with boys meant that I had developed certain untapped skills. I might not be able to play the cithara, but I knew how to make a sound with my mouth that could fool a physician. As children, Theo and I had spent hours mimicking the sound of people who suffered from a surfeit of wind. It was an endless source of entertainment. I only prayed it would prove useful tonight.

I began my own private concert in the lavatory, the music of my lips interrupted by my convincing moans of pain. Galatea covered her mouth to stifle the sound of her giggles. I motioned for her to pour water into the stone receptacle. It splashed inside, the noise a plausible approximation of someone struck with painful dysentery.

I signaled Claudia to leave. Her fingers clutched at her chest, turning white. If she wished to turn back, to stop, now was the time. I held my breath and did not release it again until she walked out, her shoulders rigid. Through a crack in the wood of the door I could see her approach the guard. The lavatories were situated sufficiently close to the tablinum that I could hear Claudia's conversation.

"Cheap food from a street vendor, would you believe? The woman has the bowels of a cow. Disgusting." She looked toward the garden, where Chara was playing. "You can't see her very well from here. Can you?"

I missed the guard's response. Claudia said, "You may move closer. She plays like Minerva." Claudia waved a hand over her shoulder toward the lavatories. "You need not be trapped here, near that thunder."

On cue, I let loose a sound that would have startled a sleeping babe.

The guard said something about Master Felonius. Claudia shook her head. "If you stand behind that column over there, he will not see you. In any case, he is drunk with the music. Can't see anything but the alluring Chara. You are safe as long as she strums those seven strings."

The guard moved a few steps. Not enough. I vented a particularly loud series of sounds, followed by groans and more water splashing into the stone receptacle. He looked over his shoulder in my direction once, then walked ahead rapidly to hide behind the column Claudia had indicated. Within a moment, his attention was snared by the golden beauty who had started to sing with a sweet voice while playing.

I slipped out, telling Galatea to continue my work. She lacked my expertise but made up for it in enthusiasm. If anyone came searching for me, or the guard returned to his post, they could still hear sufficient evidence of my torment to make a hasty retreat without investigating further.

On bare feet I padded toward the curtained door and slithered inside like an eel.

CHAPTER 31

—ᨓ—

WITHIN THE TABLINUM the world was gray and still. Near the ceiling a row of narrow latticed openings allowed a faint ray of light into the room. Enough for me to see once my eyes adjusted. I had no time to dawdle. Everything depended on speed and silence. I turned and spotted a large tapestry hanging on a wall. With an impatient motion, I thrust it to one side. And found more wall.

My stomach dropped. Had Felonius bricked up the niche after Claudia the Younger witnessed its existence? Had he moved the box? Was this entire bruising exercise wasted? Spinning, I saw another tapestry, this one smaller, stitched in shades of red, blending into the vermilion-stained wall on which it hung. I rushed toward it. With more care than before, I tried to move it. It held fast.

I examined the bottom edge and found a hook. Undoing it, I was finally able to move the tapestry. A sigh of relief escaped me when I saw the opening I sought. I stepped over the edge and entered. The niche offered no light and I found myself blinded by the absolute darkness. I swept the tapestry aside again and spied a lamp. Felonius had thoughtfully left fire steel and flint next to it on a marble counter. As quickly as I dared, I struck the steel against the flint until the wick caught a spark. The room flooded with weak yellow light. I needed no more.

A big box. A small room. How hard could it be to find? Long, sweat-filled minutes passed and I could not unearth it. I looked into every spot I could think of, without success. My innards were twisting with pain.

I sank on top of Felonius's table. *Father in heaven, help me!* I looked to the ceiling instinctively as I cried out to him. And there, in the corner of the pale ceiling, I noticed a faint straight line. Too straight to be a haphazard crack. I lifted the lamp above my head and stared. The line, delicate as a spider's web, spanned into the shape of a rectangle.

A trapdoor in the ceiling! I never would have seen it if I had not cried out to God. Grabbing the chair from behind the table, I climbed on top with ease, worked out the mechanism of the door, and tugged it open.

Tucked inside a narrow space sat the black-and-white box with its ornate ruby sparkling in the light of my lamp. In moments, I had pulled the box down and set it on the table. I had instructed Claudia to line the cloak she had loaned me with a second layer of fabric from the edge to waist high, creating deep pockets. Into these, I wedged the scrolls, trying to spread them in such a way that would not look too lumpy.

When the last document had been shoved securely inside, I shut the lid of the chest, replaced it inside its hiding place, and closed the trapdoor quietly. Blowing out the lamp, I returned to the main tablinum and hooked the scarlet tapestry back into place.

I now faced the most vulnerable part of my plan. I had to leave the tablinum blind. Leave, trusting that the guard was still standing with his back to me, entranced by Chara's charm. I listened for the sound of rustling fabric, or an impatient shuffle of feet, any indication that he was back, and heard nothing. With agonizing caution, I cracked the door open.

The curtain diminished my scope of vision. As far as I could see, the guard was not present. I edged near the side and examined my surroundings. The guard had not moved from his discreet hiding place behind the column. I sprinted for the lavatories and signaled Galatea to leave. She would await us in the carriage.

Folding the cloak over one arm, I trudged forward, acting like I had just left the privy. As soon as Chara spotted me, she stopped playing.

"Ariadne!" she cried, setting the cithara aside.

I grimaced. "Forgive my intrusion. Truly I cannot remain. I need to return home."

"Of course," Chara said, coming to me. "You look very ill. We should have left sooner." She turned her gaze on Justus. "Do stay, if you wish." She spun toward Dionysius. "I am taking Ariadne home in the carriage. You can walk home if you like."

She was magnificent. She even had me convinced of her righteous outrage. Dionysius colored and sprang up. "Certainly, Chara. We will leave at once."

"I will fetch your shoes," Justus said.

Felonius looked like a child deprived of his favorite pet.

"Chara, why don't you and the gentlemen stay?" I said, my voice weak. "Finish your song. Perhaps Claudia can come with me so I do not have to go alone? We will send the carriage for you immediately after we arrive home."

"*I?*" Claudia said, sounding like she had drunk a cup full of sour milk.

Felonius leapt at the opportunity opened before him. "Absolutely. My wife shall accompany you home. Chara and the rest can return in my personal carriage. Claudia, you may come home then."

Time for retreat. I lifted the cloak I had folded over my arm. "I apologize, Claudia. I fear I may have soiled your cloak. I shall return it to you after it is cleaned."

Claudia sauntered toward me. "By the gods, keep the thing." She turned to her husband. "You wish me to leave with . . . with *that?*" Whether she pointed to the cloak or me, it was impossible to distinguish.

"Of course. Of course. Go now. Ariadne is in distress. We must not delay her any longer."

By the time we were in the carriage, Chara had picked up the cithara once more. "Farewell, beloved. I will see you no more," she sang in her rich voice.

In the carriage, I handed Claudia the cloak. "This belongs to you."

She shook as she took the garment. "I will not believe it until I hold those letters in my hand."

The carriage interior was too dark for reading. "Do you wish to go to your father's house? You are welcome in our home. Or if you prefer to read them in a place unknown to Felonius, I can take you to a safe place that belongs to a friend."

"Let us start with your home. If what I seek is not here, then I can return to him without his knowing that anything is amiss."

I gave directions to the driver. Like Claudia, I could not truly rest until we examined the documents I had smuggled out of Felonius's tablinum. For all I knew, we might have a mountain of scrolls declaring his ownership of his villa and slaves.

As soon as we arrived at our house, I dismissed the hired carriage and drew Claudia into Father's tablinum, barring the door. It took me a few moments to light several lamps. Claudia had spread the rolls of papyrus on Father's table and was going through them, her hands tearing into each with shaking urgency.

She had unrolled nine or ten documents and dropped them heedlessly at her feet when finally she found what she wanted. She sank to the floor, her legs powerless to hold her. The papyrus crumpled in her hands. She beat her chest with it, like she needed to feel its scratchy solidity against her skin to believe that it was not a figment of her imagination.

"The lamp," she demanded.

I brought it to her without comment. She held the letter to the fire and watched it burn. Watched it turn into black ashes.

"Now the other," she said, going back to the pile. She found the second letter more quickly and burned it with less emotion.

"You are free now?" I asked.

Her eyes glittered. "I am free of that vermin." To my relief, she remembered her promise and extended a hand toward the pile. "Come and fetch the letter you want."

I found Papirius's document after a few tries

and tucked it under a cushion on Father's chair. I had another battle yet to fight with that man. But my odds at winning had improved.

"Why did you not simply take what you wanted?" Claudia said. "Once you had the contents of that chest in your possession, you could have seized what you wished. You could have taken the whole box and I would not have been able to stop you."

"I am not a thief." The last time I made that claim, I had been deceiving myself. This time, I spoke truth. "As Felonius's wife, you have a right to those scrolls. You took what was yours, like the jewels you are wearing. They were yours to give. But not mine to take."

Claudia stared at her fingers, weighed down with precious stones and gold. She had known she would walk out of her house with nothing but the clothes on her back. Known that if our gambit proved successful, she could never return to Felonius's house to pack her belongings, nor would she be entitled to receive her dowry back from her husband, given that she was the one demanding a divorce.

The jewels were her future provision. Not enough to make her wealthy and give her the luxury to which she had grown accustomed, but enough to see her through the years with some measure of security. If she chose to marry again, she was free to do so. But she would not be pressed into marriage out of financial necessity.

She cast her eyes on the scrolls that now littered the table and floor. She picked one up at random. "These are mine?"

I saw the temptation that she faced. Those letters were valuable. They could make her wealthy. "Don't," I said, pressing her hand with mine. "These are the mistakes and tears of others like you. They are sleepless nights, terror-filled days. One day, when you face God to give an account of your life, you do not want this on your conscience."

She dropped the roll of papyrus on the table. "God? I did not know you were religious."

I laughed, self-conscious. It was one thing to speak about matters of faith with Paul or my brother and Justus. Claudia was another matter entirely. To her, my faith would seem at best quaint, at worst ignorant. "I believe in a God who does not take our sins lightly. Nor does he discount the sins that have been done to us. That God sent me to your rescue, Claudia. Now you have the power to set these others free."

"How?"

"I will return their letters as I did yours."

She took a scroll from the top of the pile on the floor and weighed it in her palm. Time slowed as she considered her future, and the future of the dozens of people that lay at her feet. "Take them," she said.

I rubbed my eyes with the heel of my hand. Relief exploded inside me. Not until that moment had I realized how badly I wanted to help the nameless, faceless men and women who had fallen prey to Felonius. "Thank you." We were silent for a time, recovering, pulling the edges of our relief-drugged thoughts back into some semblance of order.

"Where will you go, Claudia? Felonius will surely come looking for you. Will you be safe at your father's villa?"

"He can do nothing to me now."

"If you prefer, I know someone who will provide you with a safe hiding place for a few weeks. Felonius would never find you there. It will buy you time to settle your affairs without having to deal with your husband's unpleasant threats. I should warn you that although this is a comfortable dwelling, it offers none of the luxuries to which you have grown accustomed. It belongs to a husband and wife who work in leather goods. Tent making and such. Honorable work, but not glamorous."

She considered for a moment. "I would like that." The violet eyes settled on me. "You have been kind to me. Why?"

I struggled to capture what I felt without sounding patronizing. "I saw you. I saw *you*."

Her smile fluttered. "Will your friends be surprised to find me at their door?"

"No. I visited them earlier and spoke to them of my plan. They know you might choose to go to them, and they will do everything in their power to offer you a courteous welcome and a safe haven."

Claudia left me speechless when she embraced me. It was a warm embrace—a friend's clinging hold, drenched with affection and trust. Her months of living in Felonius's power had softened her. She was more human than ever she had been before suffering by his hand. God could use even this evil in the remaking of our hearts, it seemed.

The carriage bearing Chara and the men arrived shortly after Claudia's departure. The girl was wilting by the time she stepped into our courtyard. The hours of pressure had worn her thin.

I kissed her cheeks. "Bless you," I said. "You have helped save many. I am in your debt."

"You owe me nothing." She gave a ravishing smile. "I did it for my Lord, and it was little enough to pour at his feet."

"You found what you needed, beloved?" Justus asked.

"Everything is in good order. Claudia is on her way to Priscilla and Aquila's residence."

Dionysius cleared his throat. "I will accompany you home, Chara."

"Excellent idea," Justus said. "Take my chariot,

Dionysius." Dionysius's eyes brightened with enthusiasm. There was not a young man in all Graecia who could resist the offer of Justus's fast chariot.

When my brother escorted Chara out of the house, Justus and I returned to Father's tablinum to gather the scrolls I had left there. I turned to tidy the floor. Justus hauled me back against him. "Leave it for now," he said, his voice husky. He cradled my face. His fingers shook against my skin, shook with fear, not passion. Knowing the peril I would face in Felonius's house had rattled him.

He gave me a long, long kiss. "Don't do that to me again. Don't force me to sit through three hours of blind torture."

I wrapped both my arms around him and drew him close. In the aftermath of so much agitation and the dread of discovery, I was feeling light-headed and a bit out of control. I poured it all into the kiss: the fear, the relief, the excitement, the sheer exhilaration of besting Felonius, the delicious knowledge of having reached the successful culmination of our plans and hard work. It was an amalgam of passion and love and pent-up terror. He grasped me hard about my waist and kissed me back until we were unsteady.

"When will you marry me?" he said. "I am tired of waiting."

I smirked. "We have only been betrothed for one month."

"An eternity."

My face twisted as I remembered why we needed to wait. "Theo."

"Yes." Justus pulled a hand through his short hair. "Theo."

By tacit agreement, we stepped away from each other and spent our energies gathering the papyrus rolls Claudia had given me. We headed upstairs to my father's chamber. He was awake and, although Galatea had told him the news of our success, eager for more details. We had revealed part of our plans to Galatea so that she knew our desire to help Claudia, though she remained ignorant of our own need for Felonius's documents.

I described the events of the evening, telling how I had found the box hidden in the ceiling.

"How long before we can expect Felonius knocking on our door?" Father asked after I finished the tale.

"I give him an hour." Justus cracked his knuckles.

I waved the letter that Claudia had left behind for her husband. "I pray this will send him on his way."

"Shall we?" Father swept an arm over the pile of papyrus rolls on his bed.

I gave him the letter that proved Papirius's guilt

first. He whistled when he finished reading, then set it aside.

I settled myself next to him on the bed, careful not to nudge his broken leg. "You will notice an additional sheet rolled up with each letter, indicating dates and amounts. According to Papirius's sheet, he has paid Felonius a fortune in the last twelve months. No wonder he is desperate to retrieve the incriminating evidence."

We read the letters, not because we wanted to know these people's dirty secrets but because we needed to discover the identities of the owners in order that we might return their documents to them. And where merited, to expose them to the law. The accounts showed hundreds of thousands of sesterces being funneled into Felonius's pockets over long years. These people had been squeezed to the bone.

"How did he get his hands on such personal correspondence and documentation?" I said, stupefied.

Justus shrugged. "Disgruntled slaves and dishonest servants can be bribed. Even honest men and women can be pressured into doing what they loathe. We know this about Felonius: he is a bully and knows how to inspire dread."

Some were letters of an explicit nature from married women to their lovers. One document proved a man posing as a freedman was still a slave according to the law. There was a confession from a woman who had terminated her pregnancy because she did not wish to lose her figure, and lied about it to her husband. A will indicated that the ownership of a farm had fallen into the wrong hands. One letter by an official spoke vitriol against the emperor Claudius. Everyone vented against the emperor upon occasion. But if you were fool enough to record your complaints, you could be crucified for treason. There were many boring legal documents, which to the owners meant the difference between poverty and wealth.

Each of us went through different scrolls, noting down the name of the person concerned in a corner when we discovered it. Without warning, Father straightened against the pillows, gasped, and seemed to choke, unable to draw breath. My head snapped toward him. He had turned whiter than a senator's toga.

"What is it?" I said, wondering if he was ill. He shook his head. I reached for the scroll in his hand, intending to set it aside and help him lie down. He shook my hand away.

"No!" He made a visible effort to calm himself. "No. I need to think on this."

"What have you read?"

Before Father could answer, we heard loud banging below stairs. Felonius, as always, had rotten timing. I grabbed a blanket and threw it over the pile of documents that covered Father's bed, in case our visitor took it into his head to examine every room in person. As I darted down the stairs, Justus followed behind me, his reassuring bulk like a shield at my back.

CHAPTER 32

—∽—

FELONIUS CAME IN bellowing. "Where is my wife?"

"You will not like what I have to say," I told him calmly. "Your wife has left you. She is seeking a divorce." I handed him Claudia's letter.

"Leave me? I will crush her with one word!"

"That is between the two of you," I said.

"Where is she?" he screamed again, and strode forward. Quietly, Justus moved in front of him, muscles cording in his neck and shoulders. Justus could be very intimidating when he smiled like that, I realized, fascinated.

"Your wife is not here, Felonius." Justus took half a step closer. Felonius took a hasty step back.

"You are welcome to look," I added, my tone conciliatory. "You will not find her here under my roof, I assure you. She left our house not long after she arrived, charging me to give you that letter."

Felonius must have seen the truth in my face. "Where did she go?"

I shrugged. "Read her letter."

His mouth curled. With jerky motions, he broke the seal of the letter and unrolled the papyrus. His face turned puce as he came to the end. With a choked sound, he whirled about and ran out into the street. I motioned the slave to bar the door behind him.

"What did she write?" Justus asked.

"That she had his scrolls, and that she intended to return them to their owners."

"He will come back here," Justus said. "Once he finds his box is empty."

I nodded. "He will return a serpent defanged, with no power to harm us. If he makes himself too much of a nuisance, we shall call the magistrate. But I suspect he will want to leave Corinth soon. All those people he has pushed about for years will now be free of him. Free and enraged, looking for revenge. He will not find this a pleasant place to remain. I suspect that is why he left Rome. He must have outlived his welcome there as well."

Justus grinned. "You are a cold, cold woman, and I love you."

I pivoted toward the stairs. "We have unfinished business."

Father had managed to push himself out of the bed and was sitting in his chair, staring blindly out the window. He still looked pale, clutching at the scroll that had had such a devastating effect on him.

"What is it? What have you read?"

"Shall I leave you to speak privately?" Justus asked.

"No." Father looked into his lap. "This concerns you most of all." He made a vague gesture toward his bed and Justus and I sat side by side, stiff with alarm and burning with curiosity.

"I considered destroying this. To spare you, Justus," Father said. "But it is impossible. You must know, hard as the knowledge will be for you to bear. Justus, this letter concerns your mother. Your mother and your father. And . . . and one other. That is why you must read it."

We looked at the sheet listing Felonius's account first. The payments had started twenty-one years ago and continued with regularity for nineteen years. Two years ago, they came to an abrupt halt. Whatever the case concerned, it was now over.

The parchment was blotchy with age. Justus unfurled the letter. We began to read, our heads bent together, touching.

Parmys, your adoring and ever-faithful wife, to my beloved husband and master, Servius.

Justus took in a gulping breath. The letter was from his mother. We read on.

> Not a day has gone by that I have not thanked Ahura Mazda for bringing you to me. Your love has been my home, my country, my happiness. You and Justus have brought me more joy than I thought possible.

"Who is Ahura Mazda?" I asked.

"Persian god." Father twirled his wrist. "Read on."

I flinched when I saw the next paragraph.

> When that brute violated me, my world shattered. But your love remained unshaken. You gave me hope to go on, go on for you and for my son. I may have survived that single atrocity if it had not been for the child. I hoped, how desperately I hoped as I carried that babe, that it would be yours.

I choked, reading those words. How she must have suffered! Hand covering my mouth, I read the rest of her letter.

> One look at him, and I knew that he was not, for he carried the mark of his father.

412

Looking at him was an arrow to my heart. A constant reminder of the horror I had borne. But I loved the child, Servius! He was bone of my bone, flesh of my flesh. My own son as much as Justus ever was.

I do not blame you, you understand? I could never blame you for what you did. You meant to protect me from the pain. You saw my tears and worried that I would break, trying to raise him. I know why you abandoned him, and I forgive you.

Now you must forgive me. I cannot bear this sorrow. Having him and losing him, both daggers in my heart.

For when I love Justus, I am overcome with guilt, knowing my younger son is abandoned somewhere, with nothing but a soft blanket and his lion rattle to keep him safe. No mother to care for my boy, who must be dead by now.

I cannot bear the burden, my love. You would not have taken him if I had been stronger. His loss is my own fault. I am taking the coward's road. Fare thee well. Love our son twice—once for me, and once for you.

My mind was in a whirl as I grappled with the ramifications of her words. Justus clutched the

413

parchment, a glazed look on his face, trying to come to terms with his mother's agony, with the knowledge that her death had come at her own hand.

My heart ached for him, for the horror he must feel at the brutal assault on the woman he adored. I reached out to touch his arm. Shaking his head as if to awaken himself from a nightmare, he scrabbled about on the bed, looking for the accounting sheet that had come with the letter.

"He extorted money from my father!" he cried when he had found it. "As if he had not suffered enough. All those years, Felonius squeezed my father, getting rich on his guilt and pain," he spat, his eyes wild. "I will kill that man with my bare hands!"

"Sit down!" My father's voice was hard, compelling.

Justus sat down.

"I cannot imagine your pain, Justus. But I told you that letter concerned one other. It is of him we must think. This is no time for revenge." He tried to rise, forgetting the splints on his leg, and collapsed back on the chair with a faint cry. "Blast this shattered leg!" he roared. "Ariadne, inside the wooden cabinet by the window you will find a carved silver chest. Bring it to me if you please."

For once I asked no questions but sprang to action, my mind reacting to the undercurrent of urgency that ran through Father's command. I placed the chest on his lap. He moistened dry lips and opened the silver lid. From inside, he pulled out an exquisitely woven blanket and a golden rattle. It looked like a lion.

I felt dazed, as if I had smashed my head against a mountain. I had seen those things years before when I was a little girl. Standing in this very room. With Theo. *"These are yours,"* Father had said to Theo. *"I found you wrapped in this blanket, with this rattle tucked inside."*

"Lord God in heaven!" I said, trembling. "Theo. Theo!"

Justus leaned forward and took the blanket and rattle out of Father's hands. His eyes filled, overflowed. In a strangled voice, he whispered, "Theo?"

Sometimes silence booms like thunder, carrying too many revelations for the mind to absorb. Shock had rendered us immobile.

Father recovered first. He had had twenty-one years to think on this puzzle, after all. "Your mother gave birth a week or so before Ariadne was born. Everyone was told that the child died, and your mother, too, of childbirth fever. This timing is important, as you shall see.

"You may have noticed that Theo has a silver streak in his hair, though he tries to hide it. He has had that streak since I found him. It is hereditary, I am told. Having seen it, Parmys would have recognized it, if his father had had the same mark. It would be how she would have known that the child did not belong to Servius.

"All this and the blanket and lion rattle point to one undeniable fact. Theo is your half brother, Justus."

Justus scrubbed his face with his hands. "I . . . I have a brother!" His voice broke. His frame shook as tears dribbled down his cheeks.

"You have a brother," Father confirmed. He placed a bracing hand on Justus's shoulder. "And he needs you."

"Theodotus!" Justus cried gruffly. "You named him Theodotus. 'Given of God'! Surely God himself led you to find him, Galenos. To raise him so close to his own blood brother. I loved him as a friend. Always. But now, he is so much more. He is the son of my mother. The only family left to me!"

"Do we tell him?" I asked. Nausea rose up like a storm in my belly. I was catching up with Father's thinking, catching up with why he had considered destroying this letter before Justus and I ever saw it.

"What do you mean? Of course we will tell him," Justus said, too caught up in his own emotions to understand. "He has a brother who loves him. He will want to know that."

"Think, Justus! Think of your mother's words.

Of the man who fathered him. The manner of his conception."

Justus froze. "Ah."

"His father raped his mother. She took her own life, partly because she could not face him. Your father abandoned him like a sack of refuse. And now, you, his own brother, are marrying the woman he loves."

Speaking the stark reality out loud shook me. I bowed my head and wept, my voice strangled. It was too much, the pain Theo would have to endure. Surely it would splinter him.

Justus stared at me through bruised eyes. "To protect him from those hard realities, we would have to rob him of the best things in his life, Ariadne. Rob him of a brother who cherishes him. Rob him of a mother who loved him, loved him in spite of the circumstances of his conception. She called him bone of her bone."

We were startled when Dionysius came in. "Why the glum faces?" he asked cheerfully.

We told him. Theo was his brother too. "This is a matter for prayer," Dionysius said gravely when we finished. "You would never have seen that letter, or discovered the mystery of Theo's parentage, if God had not aligned a hundred different things. He has led you to uncover this old secret. Uncover it for his own divine purpose. Now we must ask him for wisdom that we may complete the good work he has begun in us, and in Theo."

I prayed that night as I had never prayed before, because my supplications were not for me. They were poured out on behalf of one whose heart was already bruised. Merciful heavens, but how it hurt to love so much!

We did not sleep or eat, but stayed up through the watches of the night, asking God for strength to do right. At dawn, Paul joined us. "The Lord told me to come," he said simply. And when he heard our tale, he added his supplications to ours.

I sent for Papirius the following day. My body was weak for hunger and lack of sleep, but my soul had grown stout from the hours of prayer. This time, Justus joined me. Papirius's nasty smile slipped a little when he saw Justus next to me.

"I have your letter," I said.

"Letters, I think you mean."

I shook my head. "You can have yours in exchange for mine. That is all."

Papirius stood, putting a hand to his hip. "You grow fond of jail, I see."

I leaned into his face. "You can have your freedom, or you can have my incarceration. But you cannot have both. In either case, you shall never see the other documents. Now choose. I have no time to waste."

He fetched my letter in under an hour. When we had made our exchange, Justus grabbed the front of his tunic and hauled him up until Papirius's body stood on tiptoes. "You know me?" he asked.

Papirius nodded.

"Then you know this is no empty threat. I have spies watching you. Cheat again, and you will go to prison. Speak a whisper against my future wife or father-in-law, and you will find yourself crushed. Do we understand one another?"

Papirius nodded. Without the Honorable Thief's letter he had nothing but his loose tongue. If Justus had not been on our side, he might have been tempted to wag it, for the sake of revenge if nothing else. Justus posed too great a threat to his well-being, however. He had many powerful connections at the harbor. Either Papirius went straight in his dealings, or he better find a new post at a different port.

"Papirius!" I called as he reached the door. He turned and waited.

"I am praying for you." It was no empty promise. I had finally determined how to love such a man. He was not safe to befriend. He would twist honest compassion into his own ends and try to take advantage of it. But I could intercede for him with God. Bless him even. One day, that prayer might melt his heart enough to make him approachable.

He flinched. Spitting on the ground, he looked at me to make sure I knew what he thought of my offer and stormed off. Some men had no appreciation for love.

CHAPTER 33

—ᴍ—

JUSTUS INVITED MY FAMILY to his house for dinner. Theo, who had returned from his trip two days before, came with Paul, even though he knew I would be there. Paul had told him that we had important news to share with him.

He looked thinner, his longish face all angles and cheekbones, the silver streak in his hair well hidden. He would have reason to loathe that streak even more by the time the evening was done. I sat to one side, where he would not have to look at me.

When the first course was cleared, Justus dismissed the servants and told them not to return. He looked feverish, his color high, his hands shaking. "Theo," he said, "Paul has told you that I have news for you?"

"He has."

"Theo. I . . . I am your brother," Justus blurted.

"I appreciate that. I feel the same."

Justus slashed the air with his hand. "No.

421

I mean—Theo, listen. My mother was your mother. We are half brothers."

Theo went still. "Your *mother?*"

"She . . . Our fathers are different. But we were born to the same mother. I never knew, until yesterday."

Theo pulled a hand through his hair, making it stand on end, revealing the silver mark. "I don't understand."

Justus leaned toward him, hand extended, like a plea. "Before I tell you more, I want you to hear me. Until yesterday, I thought I had no family. Now, I have discovered that I have a brother. It's like being given the world. You are a treasure to me, Theo."

"You are my brother?" Theo stood up and abruptly sat down again. "If this is true, I am the most blessed man in the world."

"It is true."

"How do you know? How did you suddenly come by this knowledge?"

To pave the way for the hard news, Justus and Dionysius took turns telling him about Felonius and Papirius. As they explained how I had stolen the box of letters, Theo's eyes sought mine for a brief moment and slid away again.

"Among those scrolls we found a letter from our mother," Justus said. "In it, she spoke of you. She loved you, Theo. My father abandoned you at the *bema* without her knowledge."

He shook his head, confused. "Why? Did your mother have a lover? Am I the result of her infidelity?"

"*Our* mother. And no. Not . . . exactly," Justus said, and gulped. We had agonized over this part, wondering if we should tell him the truth or soften the blow by telling him a gentler version of his conception. Paul had warned us that God was not the father of lies, not even well-intentioned ones.

We knew, in any case, that Theo would insist on seeing the letter. He would not lightly let go of that one evidence that shone a light on his parentage.

"Theo, we don't know who your father is. We probably shall never find out. Our mother's letter does not give a name. What it intimates is that your father forced himself on her. We don't know the circumstances."

Theo had grown rigid. "He *raped* her?"

"It makes no difference, Theo. What happened is no fault of yours. I could not love you more if we shared the same father."

Theo tried to stand, and collapsed. "Are you mad?" His words slurred with emotion. "Of course it makes a difference. I am worse than a by-blow. I am the result of violence and violation. God in heaven! I am a monster!"

Paul came to his feet. "Be still, Theo. Listen to me. What happened to your mother was an unspeakable horror. But God reached into that brutal moment and planted one good thing. That was you, Theo.

"You have come to know the Lord Jesus. You know that he died to call you his own. To claim you. To restore you. Would he pour such a sacrifice at the feet of a monster? No, Theo. You are his prize, his treasure.

"The man who fathered you sinned gravely against your mother. One day, he will stand before God and answer for his crime. But you are not responsible for his shame. The Lord has set his affections on you, Theo, and that imparts more value to you than all the stars in the heavens."

Justus stepped forward. Without a word, he pulled Theo into his arms. "Please, Theo. Please. Now that I have found you, I cannot bear to lose you." Theo stood rigid, a wooden beam, an iron post in Justus's embrace. His eyes were wide, unseeing.

It pierced Justus, that resistance. He broke. His tears didn't come silently, with dignity. They burst out of him like a crack born out of an earthquake; they came with heaving and wails. We all wept, witnessing this thunder-cloud of sorrow. My chest ached, my head ached, my throat burned. My heart was about to split in two.

Theo's mouth softened. Justus's desolation

pierced the fog of horror that had choked him. He pressed a hand on Justus's back and swallowed convulsively. Swallowed again, and melted. The two men came together like one statue carved out of the same piece of marble. They fused together with tears and sorrow and love.

When the storm passed, they sank onto a couch, next to each other. If they had been women, they would have held hands. Men are not so blessed. Their shoulders touched. That seemed enough.

We all needed a bit of silence, a slice of peace to recover. When some time had passed, Theo said, "Can I see this letter?"

Justus retrieved his mother's scroll. Theo had lost every scrap of color by the time he finished reading it. Then it was Father's turn to fill the gaps. He had brought his silver box. "These are yours," he said, handing him the blanket and rattle.

When Theo leaned to take them, my father captured his wrist, drawing his attention. "I have ever been proud to have you for a son. Will you let me adopt you as my own? A little late, I own. But no less heartfelt in spite of it."

Theo's eyes filled with tears again. "I will think on it."

"That is all I ask."

As Theo resumed his seat, I stared at the two brothers, trying to find traces of the mother they shared. There was a vague resemblance about the shape of the eyes, the curve of their chins, the way they smiled. Easy to miss unless you knew to look for it.

Two men who possessed my heart in such different ways. My eyes rested on Theo for a moment, lingering on that achingly familiar face, so far from me now. They moved to Justus, who had captivated my heart. Love and grief welled up in me. We had all lost so much to our parents' disasters.

I felt the weight of his stare. Theo had been watching me as I gazed at his brother. And he had seen. Known how I felt about Justus. As always, he had read me without words. We looked at each other for a moment. A moment of farewell, of regret, of ending. Theo came to his feet. "I had better go."

Justus rose. "Will you return?"

"Give me time . . . Brother. I feel like I am swallowing a whale."

"Take all the time you need. I will always be here for you."

Father sold most of his land save for a small orchard of apple trees and paid off his debts. He had enough left to invest in a sizable cargo of soap. Theo had thrown his own savings into the pile, and between them they had managed to create a respectable partnership. Father handled the business in Corinth, taking care of production, while Theo traveled, promoting and selling their hair pomade, as they called it.

Who knew soap would prove so popular? Their first cargo made enough money for Father to keep the house. He freed his slaves as a means of economizing. Most asked to remain and work as servants. He could not refuse them, of course. So much for economy. Money would always stretch tight in his hands.

The stern physician finally unwrapped the bandages from Father's leg, threw out the splints, and pronounced him cured. He had no hint of a limp. I never ceased to thank God for that miracle.

Eight months later, I married Justus. The week before the wedding, Paul brought a package to our home. "I asked my friend Lydia to send this for you. A wedding present."

"Lydia of Philippi? The seller of purple?"

"The same."

"You know her?"

"I baptized her. Will you open your package or shall I return it?"

"Don't you dare!" Inside, I found the most exquisite purple tunic and lavender *palla* I had ever seen. Squealing like an adolescent, I touched the soft silk. My heart sank. "Paul, dear Paul. I cannot accept this. It is too costly."

He shrugged. "Your brothers paid for it. I was merely the instrument of purchase. And the means to a friendly discount."

"My brothers? Plural?"

"Dionysius and Theo."

I buried my face in the luxurious fabric, my eyes hot with tears. Theo had been spending more time with Justus in recent months. But he still avoided me. Justus had foisted a large piece of prime property and a sizable amount of cash on him, saying it was his inheritance. Father said Theo intended to build his own house there.

Dionysius arrived from Athens on that same day. Before he had a chance to greet us properly, he sped off to Stephanas's house. He had been corresponding with Chara for months. A blind man could see Father would have another wedding on his hands soon.

On my wedding day, I had more dear friends attending me than I could once have dreamed of. Delia applied my makeup and put my hair up as befit a proper married lady. For the first time, I donned the veil of marriage, taking on the mantle of traditional modesty. Galatea, who had helped Delia with my preparations, pronounced me beautiful and blessed me in the name of the Lord Jesus, in whom she had placed her trust.

I had three Claudias attending me: Younger, Fourth, and Elder. Felonius had thankfully vanished as I had suspected he would, leaving Claudia the Elder and her father in peace. The violet eyes examined my wedding finery with approval. "It would have looked perfect if you could have filled up the top a little more," she said. "But you are so charming, no one will notice the lack." And that was quite a compliment coming from Elder.

"I am so happy for you!" Younger cried. "You are ravishing. Justus's eyes will pop out of his head with admiration when he sees you." It was hard to believe the two women were related.

Fourth and Junia adjusted the folds of my veil, kissed the air above my cheeks, and quoted Ovid. All this fuss over the girl who once could not boast of one true friend outside of Theo. I could have burst with thankfulness for all that God had done.

Dressed in Lydia's purple, white blossoms in my soap-washed hair, I walked into Justus's arms and knew myself known, the good and the bad in me, and loved whole.

I had not expected him to come, but Theo surprised me. He embraced Justus first. "I wish you all the happiness this world can offer, Brother." Then he took my hand in his. His smile had a tinge of pain. "May God bless you, Ariadne. My sister."

I squeezed his hand. He had been through so many valleys. Even his conception had been an unconquerable canyon, his birth a cavern of despair. But God was a higher rock. Slowly, Theo was climbing out of the depths and conquering the old ruined places. "May God restore to you the years the locusts have eaten," I said, my heart in the blessing. And I knew it would come to pass.

A month after our wedding I received a letter from my mother, her first in six years. My fingers shook as I broke the seal. The roiling bitterness of years rose to the surface of my mind. What poison did her letter contain? What fresh accusations did she have for me after so long a separation?

There was no greeting. No farewell. I read three words, all that the scroll contained, and allowed the parchment to slip from my nerveless fingers. Justus, who had stood by my side, quiet and sure like an immovable mountain, bent to pick it up.

He gasped when he read the words: *I am dying.*

Dionysius had forwarded the scroll and included one of his own, assuring me that this was no ruse. Our mother had been fading over the past months. The physicians thought that she would not last the winter. *Come quickly, Ariadne,* he wrote. *It is time for farewells.*

Unforgiveness is a marauder. A bigger thief than my father ever was. It robs the heart of peace.

I had not vanquished this old enemy; the bitterness against my mother still exerted its power over me. In these final days of her life, I could wield the sharp edge of revenge against her. I

430

could withhold my presence. Not go to Athens. Let my absence speak the last word.

But I knew that I would regret such a choice, because it was a choice against God as much as it was against my mother. The Jesus who had welcomed a thief into paradise, the one who had extended forgiveness to *me,* now waited silently for my decision.

I had to go.

It took Justus several days to arrange for our trip to Athens. I spent those days thinking of all the words I wanted to say to my mother. The long list of wrongs she had committed against me. As true as they were, they left a bitter taste in my mouth. I realized that I would find no satisfaction in finally expressing them. On the night before our departure, I lay sleepless, striving for some measure of peace.

"Father, help me," I implored. I remembered with sudden clarity the many prophets God had sent his people over the years. They had gone to reason with his children. To speak truth to them. Show them the error of their ways. Tally their wrongs. Help them to repentance so that there could be reconciliation. It had rarely worked! In the end, God had not won the hearts of his people by reasoning with them. By explaining their wrongs. He had won those who were willing through . . . love. A love so deep it was willing to die.

That was what my mother needed. Perversely, it was also what *I* needed.

Not my vengeance and condemnation. Not words that would vindicate me and prove her insufficiency. The only healing I could receive was through the balm of love. Undeserving love. Sacrificial love.

A love crucified.

I was not at all sure I had such a measure of love in me when I boarded that ship, my husband by my side. Dionysius met us at the harbor when we disembarked. I sensed a calm in him in spite of the hollows that sorrow had carved in his cheeks. His peace was not of this world, I knew.

I had dressed carefully for this meeting, donning a plain tunic of white linen, my artfully arranged hair covered under a modest *palla*. I presented the picture of Greek femininity so admired by Mother and Grandfather. It was not one final bid to win her approval. I was cured of that. I merely wanted to give her the only gift I could.

Before entering through the gates of my grandfather's house, I took a gulping breath, and placing my ice-cold fingers into Justus's hand for strength, I pressed forward.

Dionysius ushered us into my mother's room. It looked the same as I remembered. Nothing had changed, as if time itself had ground to a halt in this airless chamber. The same alabaster jar of perfumed oil, the same ivory-topped table, the same mirror of polished silver, the same windowless walls, whitewashed to cover the grime of generations. I remembered the words of a psalm Paul had taught me:

> For a thousand years in your sight
>   are but as yesterday when it is past,
>   or as a watch in the night.

I thought how to God the years that had separated us had been no more than a whisper, a sigh, while our lives had burned like a lamp wick. And now, hers was coming to an end.

Grandfather sat by her bed. It shook me to see him. Had he always been that small, that frail? He had seemed so imposing in my mind. Now he seemed a shrunken old man with red-rimmed eyes. Powerless to hurt anyone.

Powerless to save his daughter.

My mother lay huddled under too many covers, a skeletal creature made of skin and brittle bones. Her eyes bored into me like fire. I moved forward on legs that wobbled and sank next to her on a stool, facing Grandfather.

Her arm lifted with a flutter and her fingers touched my hand. "Beautiful," she murmured.

It took me a moment to realize she meant me. She meant that I was beautiful. Something in me broke. "I am sorry," I said. Sorry that she

433

suffered. Sorry that she was dying. Sorry that I had resented her, hated her, even. Sorry that I had not wanted to see her for six years. Sorry that we had wasted so much time and now it was too late.

She squeezed my fingers. "And I." She fell asleep after that.

"She had a rough day," Grandfather said, his voice gruff. "In the morning she will be stronger. She will speak more then."

"May I sit with her through the night?"

"She would like nothing better."

Dionysius took Justus for a quick meal and a hot bath. I expected Grandfather to leave with them. I never imagined him the man to wait patiently in a sickroom. But he did not budge. We sat in silence.

"It's good you didn't marry Draco," he said without preamble. "The boy ran to drink. Became a disgrace to his family. Dionysius speaks glowingly of your Justus." He studied my middle with narrowed eyes. "Could you be with child, do you think? I won't live forever. I would like to hold a great-grandchild in my arms before I'm done."

I sputtered. "I've only been married a month."

"It only takes one night. Don't you know anything?"

My mother groaned in her sleep. I gripped her hand. "Can we do something to comfort her? Give her a tincture? Some wine?"

Grandfather shook his head. "She has stopped eating and drinking." He rubbed his eyes. "A man shouldn't live to see his child die. His only child."

He loved her, I realized. He had heart enough for that. Her death was cutting him to pieces. I felt the stirrings of compassion. Gingerly, I reached my free hand and took his. He jumped, then grew still. His hand shifted, turned up until it grasped mine tightly. The three of us sat like that for a long time, with me holding on to both, the man and woman who had once been my nemeses.

I dozed on and off through the night. Justus brought pillows for my back and hot broth that I could drink from a cup without releasing my hold on Mother.

Late morning, Mother began to stir.

"Still here?" she asked.

"Still here."

She took a rattling breath. "It's not fair, you know." Her voice, though weak, was coherent.

"What isn't?" Dionysius asked. He had joined us at dawn and sat next to me on the floor.

"Your father broke all the rules. But he always received the lion's share of my children's love."

I had never thought of it from her perspective. She had been the good one. The one who had obeyed the law, followed the rules. She couldn't see that in the process of *being* right, she had forgotten to love right. "I am sorry," I said again, helplessly.

She gulped painfully. "I am proud of you. I should have said. I am proud of you, my daughter." She paused, then asked, "Dionysius, will your God have me?"

"Gladly, Mother."

"Then I wish to go to his home."

She fell into a fitful doze after that and awoke only briefly over the next few days. I rarely left the room. That airless, windowless chamber that I had once hated became a hallowed place. A place of mending what had broken, a place of farewells, a place of release. It became a place of love, and the love endured all things, even our twisted past. In the end, it even conquered the raging of death and covered our gaps.

A NOTE FROM THE AUTHOR

—∿—

OVER THE PAST YEAR, fans have been asking me for a book they could share with friends who are not practicing Christians. I wrote *Thief of Corinth* mostly for them. I wrote it, also, because I wanted to tell a lighthearted story that still managed to grapple with a few important issues.

If you are a student of the Bible, then you know there is no Ariadne there. She is my own invention. Her brother, Dionysius, however, appears in Acts 17. I was intrigued by this man of learning and influence, who, unlike most of his contemporaries, chose to follow Christ. According to church tradition, Dionysius went on to become the first bishop of Athens.

Some of the minor characters in the book are also historical. Lucius the Butcher really did have a shop in Corinth. And Iuventius Proclus actually was president of one of the Isthmian Games in the first century. According to an inscription from Delphi, that year a man named Hermesianax entered his daughters into the Games for athletic events, including running (Jerome Murphy-O'Connor, *St. Paul's Corinth*).

The treatment of Galenos's broken leg is based on *De Medicina*, a first-century medical treatise by Celsus. For my research, I used W. G. Spencer's translation of *De Medicina* (book VIII, chapter 10). Having now written a number of scenes set in ancient times in which medical treatment is necessary, I found Celsus's almost-modern approach to setting bones fascinating (and a relief!).

The name *Whirring Wings* is derived from Isaiah 18:1. Some biblical translators understand this to be a reference to ships.

The land we now know as Greece was called Hellas by its original inhabitants. I thought that term might be confusing to readers. However, *Greece* is a relatively modern term. So I settled for *Graecia*, the term used by the Romans.

While the butterfly bush is considered a weed in modern Britain, I have no idea if that was the case in the first century.

When Dionysius quotes Paul as saying, "There is a world of difference between knowing the Word of God and knowing the God of the Word," he is actually quoting Leonard Ravenhill in *Why Revival Tarries*.

One final note about Theo: I love him too much to leave him like that. That's all I will say for now!

The Bible provides profound inspiration for novels like this. However, the best way to study the Scriptures is not through a work of fiction, especially one this flawed, but simply by reading the original. This story can in no way replace the transformative power that the reader will encounter in the Scriptures. For Dionysius's story and the account of Paul's first visit to Corinth, please read Acts 17:16–18:21. You will find Paul's thesis on love in 1 Corinthians 13:1-8.

ACKNOWLEDGMENTS

—〰—

I STARTED TO WORK on *Thief of Corinth* while in the midst of a protracted move, and it only became more complicated after that. So first, thank you to my husband, who bore the burden of so much while I was writing. You are a gift. Thank you also for all the engineering and architectural help (a fact I forgot to mention in *Bread of Angels*), and the idea of hiding Felonius's box where we did.

I am grateful for my agent, Wendy Lawton, who read the book when she didn't have time, told me she loved it when I needed to hear those words, and held my hand while I freaked out.

Thanks to the team at Tyndale who worked on *Thief of Corinth* from cover design to plotline and beyond: Stephanie Broene, Kathy Olson, Karen Watson, Jan Stob. I appreciate every one of you: your unique gifting and the extra time and gracious effort you poured into this book. I know how hard you worked, and I am deeply thankful knowing how much better this book is because of you.

I would like to thank the amazing professionals who surround the books once they have been written and help to place them in readers' hands: Cheryl Kerwin (who works long after she is supposed to), Maggie Rowe, Emily Bonga, Sharon Leavitt (thanks for those special prayers!). I am honored to work with you. My special thanks to the sales force who help spread these books all over the world. Do you ever have a hard job! I love you for holding on and pushing through.

I am deeply indebted to Dr. Christopher Gornold Smith, who graciously wrote me detailed e-mails in answer to my copious questions about Corinth and directed me to the right books. Advice like his is gold for writers of historical fiction.

I am more than grateful to my best friend, Rebecca, who conducted a compelling edit of the first fourteen chapters of *Thief of Corinth* while dealing with a deadline of her own. Friends like this are rare. I am keeping her.

Thanks to Lauren Yarger for her help with the prologue, and I know you don't even like prologues. I appreciate Dr. Joy Hong's medical advice regarding Ariadne's injuries.

Most of all, to my readers, who willingly explore this mysterious and ancient world of the

Bible and allow me to create these characters, my most heartfelt thanks. Without you, there would be no books. I can't tell you how much your prayers, notes, and photos mean to me. It is an incredible privilege to write for you.

DISCUSSION QUESTIONS

—m—

1. This type of novel is called "biblical fiction," a genre that sets stories during the time of the Old or New Testament and incorporates people we know of from the Bible (in this case, Paul, Dionysius, Priscilla, and Aquila). Do you enjoy reading biblical fiction? What are its benefits for contemporary readers? What are its drawbacks?

2. Did you enjoy the historical information about the city of Corinth and its customs? In what ways does it add to or detract from the story?

3. How well were you able to identify with Ariadne? Have you personally experienced any of her struggles—family relationships, desire for popularity, wanting to help her father?

4. Ariadne hopes to win approval through her athletic ability. How does that work out for her? Do you have gifts or talents that people value? How can we be sure that we are using our special abilities appropriately?

5. Ariadne's family is torn apart by divorce, something that is all too common in our day. In what ways do we see God working through even this painful situation to draw the characters to himself? Have you or someone you love been affected by divorce? Have you seen God's work in the midst of such pain and brokenness?

6. Theo confesses his love for Ariadne, but she feels only sisterly affection for him. How does this alter their relationship? Have you ever had a friendship that was marred by differing expectations or desires between the two of you?

7. Claudia the Elder goes from being Ariadne's adversary to being a friend and confidante. Did you find this transition believable? How can painful experiences sometimes change a person for the better?

8. Theo receives quite a shock at the end of the book. How do you think it will affect him?

Has anything ever reshaped your understanding of your identity or your place in the world?

9. Ariadne forgives her mother just before her mother dies. Did this seem realistic? Are there family members you've had a hard time forgiving? How might the issues or feelings change if the person dies before you are able to reconcile?

10. Were you challenged by Paul's definition of love (drawn from 1 Corinthians 13)? Do you, like Ariadne, feel that you fail to live up to the biblical expectations of love? How can we reconcile that failure with the grace we find in God through Christ?

ABOUT THE AUTHOR

—⚹—

TESSA AFSHAR is the award-winning author of *Bread of Angels*, *Land of Silence*, and several other historical novels. Her novel *Land of Silence* received an Inspy Award in the general fiction category and was voted by *Library Journal* as one of the top five Christian fiction titles of 2016. *Harvest of Gold* won the prestigious 2014 Christy Award in the historical romance category. *Harvest of Rubies* was a finalist for the 2013 ECPA Book Award in the fiction category. In 2011, after publishing her first novel, *Pearl in the Sand*, Tessa was named New Author of the Year in the FamilyFiction–sponsored Reader's Choice Awards.

Tessa was born in Iran and lived there for the first fourteen years of her life. She then moved to England, where she survived boarding school for girls and fell in love with Jane Austen and Charlotte Brontë, before moving to the United States. Her conversion to Christianity in her twenties changed the course of her life. Tessa holds an MDiv from Yale Divinity School, where she served as cochair of the Evangelical Fellowship. In addition to writing, she now serves on the staff of one of the oldest churches in America. But that has not cured her from being exceptionally fond of chocolate. Visit her online at www.tessaafshar.com.

Books are
produced in the
United States
using U.S.-based
materials

Books are printed
using a revolutionary
new process called
THINKtech™ that
lowers energy usage
by 70% and increases
overall quality

Books are
durable and
flexible
because of
Smyth-sewing

Paper is
sourced using
environmentally
responsible
foresting methods
and the
paper is acid-free

Center Point Large Print
600 Brooks Road / PO Box 1
Thorndike, ME 04986-0001 USA

(207) 568-3717

US & Canada:
1 800 929-9108
www.centerpointlargeprint.com